CAST OF CHARACTERS

MICE

Wraith Mice (magical mice that can become invisible)

Crispisin	Dikiner's novice
Colobi	an archer, who loves to gossip
Dejuday	an inept scout, Sibyna's younger brother
Hokadra	King of the Wraith Mice; father of Johajar, Zuryzel, and Mokimshim; mate to Demeda
Johajar	Zuryzel's twin brother
Mokimshim	oldest child of King Hokadra and Queen Demeda; brother to Johajar and Zuryzel
Orgorad	Sibyna's mate
Sibyna	a messenger, friend of Zuryzel, older sister to Dejuday, mate of Orgorad
Zuryzel	(zur-EYE-zel) second child and only daughter of King Hokadra and Queen Demeda, twin of Johajar, sister of Mokimshim

Rangers (mice who patrol the northern half of the earth)

Cinder	Lady Raven's second-in-command ("Hetmuss")
Crow	Lady Raven's daughter; future leader of the Rangers ("Herttua")
Rainbow	Ordinary Ranger ("Orlysk"); she transports Lady Raven's secret messages
Lady Raven	Leader of the Rangers; long-time friend and ally of Queen Demeda

Graystone Mice

Opal	one of Feldspar's oldest friends
Chite	one of Feldspar's oldest friends
Feldspar	mouse from the south, looking for adventure in the north

Cliff Mice

Glor'a	Ran'ta's friend; takes refuge in Pasadagavra
Ol'ver	orphan, friend of Feldspar, long-time friend to and in love with Ran'ta
Ran'ta	Ol'ver's sweetheart and long-time friend

SQUIRRELS
(live in tribes, easily identified by tattoo on cheek)

Bow Tribe

Biddah	maiden and good friend of Zuryzel
Karrum	warrior
Sharmmuh	Tribequeen, leader of the Bow Tribe

Coast Tribe

Verrah	warrior

River Tribe

Tiyuh	female elder

Sling Tribe

Deggum	Tribeprince, Wazzah's brother
Fraeggah	Tribeprincess, Wazzah's sister
Wazzah	Warriorqueen, leader of the Sling Tribe, sister of Deggum and Fraeggah

Stone Tribe

Fuddum	Tribeking, leader of the Stone Tribe, father of Jaccah
Jaccah	Tribeprincess, Fuddum's daughter
Rhonndan	Jaccah's young son
Shjeddah	friend of Jaccah

DARKWOODS FOXES

Blood	Oracle, Fawn's mentor
Fang	Oracle, recorder of the Oracles
Fawn	Oracle's apprentice to Blood, descendant of old kings
Hemlock	senior Oracle
Ice	Oracle, a slow-thinking young vixen
Knife	second most senior Oracle, apprenticed at a higher age than her contemporaries
Rosemary	daughter of Sage
Sage	runaway Oracle's apprentice, mother of Rosemary
Scythe	former senior Oracle, against the war waged by her colleagues

DARKWOODS

Marta K. Stahlfeld

Book Publishers Network

Book Publishers Network
P.O. Box 2256
Bothell • WA • 98041
PH • 425-483-3040
www.bookpublishersnetwork.com

10 9 8 7 6 5 4 3 2 1

Printed in the United States of America

LCCN 2011903267
ISBN10 1-935359-77-0
ISBN13 978-1-935359-77-7

Cover designer: Laura Zugzda
Typographer: Stephanie Martindale

DEDICATION

This book is dedicated to all the "tweens" and teens that enjoy exploring other worlds and reading epic stories as much as I do – particularly my brother, Karl, with whom I have shared many such stories.

I hope you enjoy reading this tale as much as I enjoyed writing it.

Contents

Acknowledgements

There are many people who have encouraged me as a writer and am grateful to all of them.

A special thank you to Barbie Kinney for all her help with the initial editing of this book and for her constant encouragement of me as an author. Likewise, many thanks to Cheryl Knight and Susan Sieg for their early and enthusiastic encouragement.

I would also like to thank Selah Elmquist, Lindsay Wood, and Becky Schmidt for their belief in my dreams of being an author. They are fabulous friends to have!

Most of all, I thank God for His many blessings in my life.

OTTERS

River Otters

Anamay	younger sister of Danaray, in love with Mollusk
Danaray	eldest child of Mudriver
Orionyap	served King Hokadra in the past
Shinar	princess in service of King Hokadra
Shorefish	future chief, vowed revenge against the sea otters
Sky	aunt of Shorefish, killed in a skirmish
Streamcourse	aunt of Shorefish, occasional helper of the Wraith Mice

Sea Otters

Brine	Mollusk's sister
Anemone	member of Mollusk's clan
Crustacean	chief of Mollusk's clan
Current	sea otter chief
Kiskap	chief of otters in the far north
Mollusk	in love with Anamay
Northstar	allegedly a sea otter chief; Kiskap's sister
Palm	ineffective sea otter chief
Pine	member of Palm's clan
Ripple	member of Northstar's clan
Saline	Anemone's daughter

THE STORY BEGINS ...

I, Muryda, have a story to tell you.

The story must not die out. It begins with the fatal illness of Oracle Scythe of the Darkwoods foxes. For many seasons, the Darkwoods foxes had been followers of the Serpent and under the influence of the Blight. But so far, they had not engaged in a battle of any size, thanks to Oracle Scythe, who, with her superiority and, I grudgingly admit, her great wisdom, kept the others from leaving the boundary of Darkwoods.

But as Scythe fell ill, fellow Oracles seized the opportunity to put different plans in play. In their quest for power, they chose war on all the earth, for they believed this would bring them great power. Scythe was too ill to stop them from waging war in the west, a story for another time. This story concerns the war in the east.

Many heroes arose in the east. Princess Zuryzel of the Wraith Mice, only daughter of King Hokadra; her twin brother, Prince Johajar; Tribeprincess Jaccah of the squirrel Stone Tribe; and, in a small way, Warriorqueen Wazzah of the squirrel Sling Tribe. And I must include the two river otter sisters Anamay and Danaray, who did not fight in the battles but worked as scouts for the armies.

Now I begin my story. The Wraith Mice, as well as other tribes and armies, had gathered at the home of the squirrel Bow Tribe, just east of Darkwoods....

1

THE NEW ORACLE

Oracle Scythe was dying.

The entire castle knew it. The foxes in Darkwoods were running around jittery with excitement. The death of the vixen meant a new Oracle, and the change of power promised new plans of conquest, which Scythe had firmly and resolutely opposed. Scythe's impending death now promised more victories in their war and maybe even rule over all the earth.

Only Ice seemed removed from the excitement. She would replace Scythe as Oracle, not in the senior position but as a member of the ruling five, and it looked as if she didn't feel very good about it.

Ice sat alone, gazing over the ramparts to where a few rays still lingered from the setting sun. She did not wear her usual extensive array of shawls and scarves and other frivolous clothes; she was clad only in a simple blue tunic. Her red eyes gazed relentlessly westward, as though longing to be where the sun set, where it drowned in the sea, away from where she would soon have to take the position of Oracle alongside four other greedy and power-hungry foxes.

She was not the only fox thinking about Scythe's impending death. Oracle Blood sat on a bench in the corridor outside the room where Scythe was slowly dying, feeling pensive, even a little regretful. The Blight, the control exerted by the evil Serpent, might have possessed Oracle Scythe as it did all Oracles, but in his apprenticeship, she had always taught him with only patience and wisdom. He would miss her, and he wished now he had sought her advice on what to do after she was gone.

He caught movement out of the corner of his eye. Careful not to attract the attention of the others in the vicinity, he sidled to the end of the bench. When he was sure none could hear him, he murmured, "It's dangerous for you to be here, Fawn."

The voice of Fawn, his apprentice, whispered a reply from under the bench. "I know, but I had to make sure the rumors about Scythe were true. Ever since Sage left things have been so uncertain, so unsettled."

"Fawn," Blood warned, "grief is not a reason for recklessness. I know Sage was your best friend, and I know you miss her, but your grief does not give you an excuse." He reflected on the dispositions of his colleagues. "In fact, it would most likely get you into *more* trouble."

"Maybe so, but I wanted to make certain. Ice seems so … reluctant."

"She is close to Scythe, remember. She probably thought of Scythe as a bit like her mother."

"I suppose. She had no one else to guide her, and Scythe was willing. She needed someone."

"She did, but she is ready for her new responsibilities."

"I guess I can understand her reluctance. Right now, the idea of being an Oracle doesn't appeal to me, especially not since Knife and Fang and Hemlock still live. It must be horrible to be an Oracle when the terrible three are right there all the time, no?"

"It is," Blood replied fervently. "But you get used to it, and besides, by the time you are made an Oracle, Hemlock will probably be dead."

"Knife worries me more."

"That is wise."

The dark shape of the healer-vixen Cutthroat emerged from Scythe's room. Blood held his breath, and it sounded as if Fawn did too.

Cutthroat curtly said, "Scythe is dead."

To Blood, it seemed as though two creatures left Scythe's room, Cutthroat and Scythe herself as her spirit journeyed to the Serpent's Land. But there he was wrong. A third creature left the room as well. Unbeknownst to all within the castle, a Wraith Mouse had snuck in, entered Scythe's room, and was now invisibly making her way out of the castle.

As a Wraith Mouse, Zuryzel had magic in her blood. She could vanish in the darkness, which gave her freedom to go anywhere at night. But the magic also limited her – she could not disobey an order from a superior or break a promise or oath, even if she wanted to.

She slid unnoticed between the foxes. All the way down to the ground level of the castle, she mulled over what she had just heard. Scythe was dead. The one-time most feared warrior of the whole earth was dead.

At first, she thought the news bore good promise for her kingdom, her friends, and her allies—very, very good promise. Age had plainly caught up with the ancient Oracle, and now they were rid of her.

But then a new thought entered her mind. Scythe had posed a danger, true, but many Wraith Mice believed Scythe was often all that had restrained Hemlock, Fang, and particularly Knife.

Oracles as well, Hemlock and Fang were vicious, ruthless conquerors, already intent on ruling the earth, yet Knife, the vixen Oracle, was different. Just as evil, she had more cunning and a dark slyness about her. Few completely trusted her. Though Hemlock, as the oldest, would take on the senior Oracle position and officially have charge of the foxes, everyone knew that Knife would hold true leadership. Only Scythe, aged though she had been, could control Knife. Now, Knife was free of the restraint.

With no one constraining Knife, Zuryzel realized, the Wraith Mice could not help but fear far more terrible times were to come.

Zuryzel made her way through the woods surrounding the castle, Darkwoods, as they were known. No patrols operated here—no guards, gatherers, or even stray thinkers. Just the trees. The Wraith Mouse glided up to a particularly thick hornbeam and leaned against it to rest. The magic of invisibility came in handy, but using her magic tired her.

"You can come out, Dejuday. No one's here."

Another Wraith Mouse materialized right alongside her, and she flinched.

"How do you know?" Dejuday hissed, his black eyes darting to and fro.

"Scythe is dead," she said shortly.

Dejuday's eyes drifted toward her, but instead of continuing back and forth, they lingered on her face. "Really? I don't know if that's good news or bad news."

The other shook her head. "I don't know either."

They stood in silence for a while, Dejuday watching his companion, and she gazing out into the woods, lost in thought.

"Zuryzel?" said Dejuday finally.

"What?" Zuryzel's eyes found Dejuday's, and she tipped her head to one side, showing she was ready to listen.

"What are we going to tell your ... I mean ..."

Zuryzel was startled. "*Cerecinthia!*" she exclaimed, switching her long, thin tail in agitation. "I hadn't thought of that! What will we tell my father? ... What do you think?"

"Tell him that Scythe is dead and no more? The bit about Sage can't possibly be any use."

"I guess so. Right. Let's go."

Without another word, the Wraith Mice vanished back into the moonless night to begin the long journey back to the camp.

A week after the death of Oracle Scythe, a dark moon hung over the nightly hornbeam forest. The shadowed woods held no semblance of peace or harmony and evoked only sadness with their patches of brambles so woefully neglected and barren of fruit. Nor did any other plant within appear to provide edibles. Yet the evil foxes that lived in the castle in the center of the woods somehow managed to satisfy their hunger.

The young mouse that strode through the trees was beginning to wish that he had stayed on the moors, even though that route would have taken longer than penetrating the forest. At the sudden sound of voices, he dropped for cover in a patch of black-leaved brambles, the inch-long thorns piercing through his tunic and light golden fur to his tender skin. Ignoring the pain, he held his bright brown eyes shut to avoid detection.

Two foxes strode hurriedly through the woods toward his vicinity. Abruptly, one of them, a blood-red male in a long cloak and a golden colored tunic, stopped dead still and listened for a moment. Then he turned to his companion, a beige vixen, and whispered to her, and she closed her eyes.

The mouse studied her through half-open eyes. She wore a gorgeous green tunic, edged with a hem of golden leaves, trees, brooks, and nuts. About her neck, draped a necklace of red beads edged with gold, and in her paw, she carried a beautifully carved short spear, a close-combat spear with a long blade.

After a long while, she reopened her eyes and nodded several times. Then both foxes began searching the surrounding shrubbery. Before long, they were literally treading on the mouse's whiskers. The vixen dragged him roughly out of the brambles and showed him to her companion. He nodded approvingly and produced something from his flowing robe, and then the mouse felt rough cords binding his paws.

The next thing he knew, the two foxes were dragging him over every root and twig in their path. Despite the cruel treatment, he didn't dare squeak out loud. He knew the punishment from the foxes for talking in their presence, even if he had had the courage to speak up. Instead, he chose to suffer silently as they dragged him along.

Sometimes, though, an especially sharp stick would poke him and cause him to cry out involuntarily, and the vixen would turn and glare at him with her red eyes for such impudence. But the male never bothered;

instead, his expressionless eyes remained fixed on the way ahead. Throughout the journey, the mouse felt an evil sort of whispering enveloping him, as if from the trees, but he could never make out any words. The two continued to drag the mouse through the darkness for a long time, until, he guessed, sunhigh.

Suddenly, a very fine mist enshrouded them. Gazing at the young vixen, the mouse could have sworn her eyes' redness lessened a little. The mist seemed to soothe the mouse, too, as though it were giving him strength to bear the ordeal. The mouse liked the swirling gray marble veil; it offered such a pleasant break from the black and dead-looking plants.

The foxes dragged him through the mist into a castle with blood-red doors and along a passage down to some cells. Guards opened one door and threw him in.

"You in there, fix the new one's bonds. Share bread. No more will be brought till tomorrow," the guard shouted in.

"Oi," an insolent voice called out from the cell. "Since when are you our boss?"

The fox did not reply. Instead, he swept up the passage and vanished.

"Gone to report you, pal, if I know that one." A new voice, much more friendly than the foxes spoke up. "Well, the first thing you got to do is to get to know us. I'm Ol'ver, and Sir Insolent is Dejuday. What's your name?"

"I'm Feldspar," the mouse replied. "Look, I don't mean to be rude, but could you get me out of these bonds?"

"No beast is going to think you're rude for wanting to get out of those cords," responded Ol'ver.

Both Ol'ver and Dejuday moved forward out of the shadows to reveal themselves as mice like Feldspar. Or at least, Ol'ver was. Dejuday's black fur and white face clearly gave him away as a Wraith Mouse. And both of them had friendly smiles.

Ol'ver addressed Dejuday as if continuing a conversation.

"So what were you saying about the battle? But remember to keep your voice down."

Dejuday immediately picked up the conversation. "I said, King Hokadra— yowch!" He reeled back, as though struck by a stone.

"Haven't you worn your tongue out yet, Wraith Mouse?" snarled a voice from the top of the cell where Feldspar thought he had seen a window.

Ol'ver sighed. "Oh, sorry; forgot to tell you. We aren't the only ones in here. Jaccah, come out here. Lend a paw, will you?"

"That depends on what you want me to do." The new voice, clearly a maiden's, sounded tired and irritated.

"Help me cut the ropes. Come on. You're the only one who still has a knife. I can't undo these knots. What would your father say if he saw you refusing hospitality and courtesy?"

"I'll thank you to leave my father out of this." Despite her angry retort, Jaccah tossed Ol'ver a sheathed knife. Ol'ver worked quickly, cutting the thick ropes with a few strokes. Once freed, Feldspar took out his water pouch and poured a little water on his chaffed paws.

Ol'ver shook his head, sighing as they heard Jaccah curling up again as she prepared to sleep. Grinning, Dejuday called out to her. "Hey, Tribe-princess, come out here, will you? Come meet Feldspar."

Jaccah didn't move.

"Oh fine, just come out so we don't feel as if we're talking to shadows and listening to echoes."

Jaccah grunted and then shifted forward. Light from the narrow window showed her large dark eyes, long bushy tail, and squirrel tribal tattoo on her cheek. She gave Dejuday a spiteful look, apparently too tired to glare properly, then turned to Feldspar and Ol'ver.

"Well, apparently they *forgot* to tell you who I am, so … I'm Jaccah Tonnah, Tribeprincess of Pasadagavra and daughter of King Fuddum of the Stone Tribe. And heiress to the position of leader of the Stone Tribe, at that, but that's not one of my official titles. So … who are you?"

Ol'ver's eyes soared skyward. "You'll have to forgive Jaccah," he apologized. "She's not usually this short-tempered and rude."

"He's right. I'm not, except when someone disturbs my sleep," she said, shooting a nasty glance at Dejuday.

Dejuday blinked. "Don't blame me. I didn't know you were up there until right about now!"

Ol'ver rolled his eyes as Jaccah retorted in a hot voice. They could feel the slight breeze from her angrily twitching tail, but they ignored her as best they could. "She's just angry with herself for letting herself get captured," he explained to Feldspar in a low voice. "Don't mind her."

Feldspar shrugged. Not yet satisfied, Jaccah said something in a language Feldspar couldn't understand that obviously offended Dejuday. He muttered to himself in the same language and left off the argument.

"Just where am I?" Feldspar asked.

"In the dungeons in the Darkwoods Castle," Dejuday answered grimly.

"I don't understand," Feldspar protested.

"The Darkwoods surround the castle. You couldn't have gotten here without going through them. The foxes live in them—and here in the castle. They used to keep to themselves, but now they've become conquerors."

Ol'ver made an irritated noise and nervously pulled at a whisker. "This is where they keep prisoners."

Dejuday snorted contemptuously. "Conquerors, my paw. They're just greedy fighters that have gotten lucky enough to get a little more territory than they used to have, about a cycle march from the castle."

"Cycles?"

"How we measure days here in the north," Ol'ver supplied. "I guess you measure time differently where you come from?"

"I come from the south, from Graystone," Feldspar responded, stifling a yawn, "and we measure in months."

"Same thing," Dejuday explained, "mostly. Hey, you look pretty worn out. Maybe you should get some sleep."

"Oooh … uh … mmm," Feldspar said with a drawn-out yawn. Exhausted from his unexpected adventure in the Darkwoods, Feldspar lay down and immediately curled into a warm ball, too tired even to think about food. "Thanks … for … mmm …," and sleep overtook the mouse before he could get all the words out.

2

THE PRINCESS

The Wraith Mouse Princess Zuryzel strode into the squirrel Bow Tribe camp, separated by a moor from Darkwoods. Even in her simple walk, Zuryzel carried a special aura about her that few creatures failed to notice. She held her head high; not in a nasty superior way but just because she had so much confidence about her. And always, she seemed to clench her paws, as if determined to have her way—or else. Her black eyes she kept focused forward, never showing the nervous darting from side to side of the other mice but still taking in everything about her.

Many creatures respected Zuryzel, despite her young age of only twelve seasons, thirteen at the end of winter. The river otters, who sometimes served with the Wraith Mice in their army, called her "One who was born to lead."

Zuryzel sat down opposite her mother, Wraith Mouse Queen Demeda. After sipping at a wooden mug of tea, she made her report.

"I slid into the woods completely unnoticed. The only enemy movement to report is that they captured Dejuday ... again."

"What was he doing to get captured this time?" her mother queried, sounding as tired as Zuryzel felt.

"Oh, daydreaming, for a change." She made no attempt to hide the sarcasm in her tone, for the only time Dejuday hadn't been captured on a scout mission was when he was with the princess—though, admittedly, he hadn't been given many chances.

"Are you serious?"

"Not quite, but he wasn't paying attention."

"And where was this?"

"Just outside that gully where the stream used to flow."

"When?"

"About a day ago, now."

"Well, you'll have to get him out."

"Why me? Why must I always get him out? Why can't Johajar do it for once?"

Queen Demeda shook her head in despair. "I was wondering when you'd ask that."

Zuryzel rolled her eyes bitterly, knowing full well why her mother would not ask her twin brother to help. "How does this sound? We leave him in there for a while. Then after, say, twelve days, I get him out. How's that?"

Queen Demeda tilted her head to the side, stroking her whiskers in thought. Then she said, "You know, that's a good idea. All right, twelve days. Just do me one favor and don't tell your father about this."

"Sounds good! Now is there any food left? I'm famished!"

Queen Demeda smiled. "Go ahead and ask Biddah. I think she saved you some bread."

Zuryzel hurried off to find her squirrel friend. Before long, she spotted her sitting on a low hanging oak branch. Gathering her tunic about her, Zuryzel pulled herself gracelessly up onto the branch. Smiling, Biddah shoved a plate toward her with the delicious squirrel nutbread smeared with honey. Biddah questioned her about her scouting mission while she ate.

"Did you find any enemy bases?"

"No."

"What did you see?"

"I saw Dejuday getting himself captured." Zuryzel flicked her paw and twirled her long, narrow tail in irritation.

"How did he get captured this time?"

"Several foxes found him and roped him up."

"No, I mean, why didn't he run away before they caught him? He must have seen them if they carried rope."

"He was doing the usual."

"Skylarking?"

"Yes."

"And talking to himself?"

"Of course," Zuryzel scoffed disdainfully.

"About Colobi?" giggled Biddah.

"Did somebody call me?" Colobi, a pretty Wraith Mouse maiden, called from where she was sitting on a stone.

Both Zuryzel and Biddah replied at once, "No." When Colobi continued to look skeptical, Zuryzel continued, "No, we were talking about your Dejuday, actually. He managed to get caught. Again."

"So, when are you getting him out?" Colobi asked

"In twelve days."

"Why so long?"

"To teach him not to skylark when in enemy territory. Hopefully, it will keep him from getting captured again."

"Since when did you care about him getting captured?" Colobi teased.

Zuryzel snorted. "Since I've had to get him out every time he gets captured."

"Well, no one is asking you to."

"You're right. No one asks me; they force me."

"Well, maybe, if you didn't have to be forced …," Colobi suggested, almost teasingly.

Zuryzel knew exactly what she meant. She was about to make one of her favorite stinging remarks when she became aware of blue eyes watching her; apparently, Colobi did too.

"Darn her ears," Colobi muttered for Zuryzel's ears alone.

Zuryzel leapt down and stalked over to the fire where Lady Raven sat. Lady Raven the Swift—her full title—cut an interesting figure. Small for a Ranger Mouse, especially a leader, she had solid black fur and pale blue eyes the color of the western sky at sunrise. But her demeanor, vast experience, and as her title suggested, speed made up for her size.

"What's so funny?" Zuryzel inquired as she sat down next to her.

Lady Raven turned her laughing eyes on the Wraith Mouse princess. "You know, I wouldn't be surprised at all if Dejuday … mm … changes in your esteem before you're much older," she grinned.

Zuryzel knew Lady Raven well enough to understand she meant the same thing Colobi had meant. "No chance of that," she replied flatly.

Lady Raven became serious now. "Oh, I don't know. When I first met *my* mate, he taunted me for being small and weird." She blinked back a tear to think of him. "Creatures change a lot, Zuryzel. I hated Shale at first because he was so mean. But he changed, and I changed." Her blue eyes began to laugh again. "It is not as if Dejuday has ever been cruel to you."

Zuryzel glared at Lady Raven. "If you *must* say things like that, at least keep your voice down." She looked around at the other fires, but no one had heard.

Lady Raven glanced around too and kindly changed the subject. "You know, this is a very strategically located place to have a war camp."

She had spoken true. The squirrel Bow Tribe had once called the area home and had made good use of the nuts from its extensive woodland. East of the moors that surrounded Darkwoods, it lay a safe distance from the castle—or had until the foxes began stirring up trouble. Many creatures had left their homelands to fight the continuing invasion of the foxes and had gathered here, spending their time now training for war, alongside the Wraith Mice armies.

Save for Lady Raven's tribe. Officially Rangers of the Northern Earth, they more often went simply by the name Rangers. Their realm covered perilous terrain with extreme weather conditions and seemed constantly at war. But the harshness only produced great warriors. All could fight quite well, and their deadly archers used arrows with potent poison.

Zuryzel sighed. "Maybe, but it isn't what I'm used to," she explained. "I'm used to having a *fortress* for better defense."

Lady Raven shook her head. "If you say so. The Rangers could never manage to fight in a fortress."

"Why not?"

"Well," Lady Raven began, "in our home, we have much territory to defend and not as many to defend it. We can't afford to have fortresses that we can occupy only every now and again since we must constantly patrol our borders. Should some enemy get inside, we could never get them out." Lady Raven shrugged. "Besides, we'd feel trapped, having all our territory and not using it, not living in it."

Zuryzel thought how she would feel more intimidated by such a large territory and safer inside a fortress. The halls of Arashna, the main city of the Wraith Mice, were made of dark obsidian and mostly closed in. The city had rich tapestries and silver ornaments. The clearing Lady Raven spoke of, without so much as a roof, was strange to Zuryzel. However, she reflected, it was much harder to find than Arashna, which stood on an island in the mouth of a river. The Sling Tribe home would be a safe place for a while, until the foxes found it.

Raven seemed to guess Zuryzel's train of thought. "Don't overestimate it, though," she warned. "No place is impenetrable." She smiled and changed the subject. "Don't be too hard on Dejuday. We all have different talents; some just don't have a skill for scouting."

Zuryzel rolled her eyes. "But Dejuday gets captured almost every scouting trip. That's just *stupidity*!"

Lady Raven shook her head. "No, it's inexperience. Don't worry, Zuryzel. He won't always be like that."

Zuryzel shook her head. "Worried is the last thing I am."

Lady Raven frowned at her. "You should be."

Zuryzel didn't understand. "*Why?* He's not exactly—I mean—it's just not worth the time!"

Lady Raven sighed. "Do not dislike him, Zuryzel, for his few mistakes." Her eyes filled with sorrow, and she continued. "I knew one warrior, just as inexperienced, who did not have half his courage. Because of arrogance and certainty, many, many suffered, though that young warrior suffered the worst. Dejuday has courage, if not talent. His biggest problem is failing to think. But he has courage."

Zuryzel sighed and glanced at Lady Raven's paws, where chains had once rubbed them terribly. A few scars still showed through the black fur.

3

Jaccah's Flute

A young river otter maiden slipped into the water without a single ripple. She knew her destination well and knew the danger involved—at least to her reputation. It couldn't endanger *her* any more than that. She worried more about whom she was meeting, but that concern could not prevent her going. Determination carried her on; she couldn't live without this. Still, chaotic feelings filled her head, and it felt as if her paws were swimming in wind.

A sudden noise told her to slip under a blackthorn bush. Silently she watched the fox patrol wander out onto the riverbanks. To her alarm, they slipped into the stream and swam almost as well as otters, though they were struggling against the current a lot and making large ripples, and their large bushy tails dragged them more than her sleek one ever would. The patrol crossed the river and worked its way onto the bank where she lay hidden. Silently, she listened to the snippets of conversation that reached her ears.

"Any beast here?"

"No. Never is."

"But still, Oracle Hemlock said there would be."

"Remind me why we are looking for any thing."

"You'd know if you listened to the Oracles, dimwit. The Serpent is unsatisfied. He needs blood. We need to get him that. You know he likes the otters best. If we don't get otters, we'll have to do with three mice and a squirrel for all five fox clans. Fancy being the one to tell the Oracles that?"

"I see your point, friend."

"Well, let's try downstream, shall we? We spent nearly two cycles trying to get here, let's not waste them."

Oh no! They could not be allowed to go downstream!

Silently, she lifted a stone and threw it upstream with all her might. Sure enough, it worked. The foxes scrambled upstream, looking for the source of the noise.

She cautiously emerged and found the whole bank deserted. Silently sliding into the water, she swam downstream until the river forked and then slipped onto the bank where she waited for the sea otter she was meeting to arrive.

He didn't keep her long. She saw him swimming against the current of the river with a little more difficulty than she had, but swimming well all the same. He emerged on the bank, dripping wet. Giving himself a shake, he ran up to meet her. Smiling, he clasped her paws, and murmured a greeting to her.

"Good to see you again, Anamay."

"Good to see you too, Mollusk."

She had been meeting Mollusk for nearly a month now. They had had to meet secretly, of course, because his sea otter clan didn't think much of river otter rogues. But Mollusk didn't let that get in the way of their friendship.

"Mollusk, listen," Anamay began urgently. "A patrol of foxes came this way earlier, intending to come downstream. They've gone upstream for now, but I don't know how far or for how long, so we can't stay here but a moment. Also, a new rogue of a river otter has entered the area here. His name is Nighthawk, and he is a thief if ever there was one. He has a daughter, too, still young, called Shorefish. And—"

Further words were cut off by a furious groan from upstream.

Mollusk looked at the bank and whispered quietly, "Go!" Not waiting to see the source of the sound, Anamay slipped off into the water, having no desire in meeting any other sea otters, let alone foxes on patrol, today.

"At last, they remembered that there are more than three down here!"

Six days had passed since Feldspar had been thrown in the prison, and their captors had forgotten until now that they numbered four captives instead of three.

Dejuday stretched blearily as the door shut, though Ol'ver looked as if he had not slept at all. Feldspar had managed to get only a few hours of sleep.

Yawning, Jaccah stretched in the morning light, having woken up at the harsh sound of the door closing, and smiled, the first time that Feldspar had seen such an expression on the squirrel's face. Climbing down from the large rock shelf where she slept, she fell hungrily on the bread. Feldspar was amazed. She had slept for only a few minutes, but she seemed thoroughly refreshed. Also, she ate the bread with amazing hunger. Usually, squirrels ate only berries, nuts, and nutbread. Her first sleep for days was clearly good for her. She yawned again, stretched again, and opened the bag that the foxes had let her keep. After a little rummaging, she pulled out a soft dogwood bark bag. She opened it and pulled out a flute made of dark pinkish stone. Smilingly, Jaccah put it to her lips and began to play.

She played an ancient tune, and she played it so well that when Feldspar closed his eyes the notes created the story in his mind. He saw a forest glade with a stream running along the ground. Beside the stream sat an enormous brown bear—*the Bear King!*—the ruler and creator of the world.

The picture dissolved as Jaccah finished playing, and smiling proudly, she put her flute away. Grinning, Ol'ver addressed her.

"Hey, Jaccah, won't you play another one? You're pretty good at it. Come on!"

Jaccah needed no more persuasion. She took the flute out again and put it to her lips. But before she could sound a note, Dejuday cried out.

"What stone is that made of? It is not like any stone I've ever seen."

"Alabaster," Jaccah replied.

Dejuday whistled. "What an expensive stone! Oh, but of course, you are the princess of the Stone Tribe."

Jaccah and Ol'ver burst out laughing. "Dejuday," Jaccah laughed, "Pasadagavra is *made* of alabaster!"

"I know that!" Dejuday argued.

"What is made of alabaster?" Feldspar asked. Jaccah ignored him.

"Pasadagavra has no shortage of rare stones," she continued. "I understand Wraith Mice would think it rich, but—"

"Arashna, Dobar, and Dombre are made out of obsidian," Dejuday snapped indignantly. "You can't tell me that obsidian is less rare than any other of your precious stones. Mirquis and Kardas, I might add, are made from basalt from an island in the sea!"

Jaccah hurriedly put the flute to her lips to cover her surprise.

"What are they talking about?" Feldspar asked Ol'ver.

Ol'ver shrugged and said, "Tell you later," as Jaccah began to play again.

🐾

Zuryzel returned from her scouting trip and slumped down glumly across from Lady Raven the Swift, leader of the Rangers. She helped herself to a bit of nutbread and answered Lady Raven's questions.

"Why so glum?"

"Well, you know the plan that my mother and I worked out? About rescuing Dejuday?"

"Yeah." Lady Raven seemed a little disapproving.

"I'm going to have to go back tomorrow to get him out."

"But you just went today to find the cell. I thought you had six more days."

"Well, I'll explain it at council."

Lady Raven shook her head sadly. "Do not be too hard on Dejuday. He tries. But some have talent for scouting, and Dejuday clearly does not. It is not his fault. Perhaps he just has very bad luck."

We've been through this before, Zuryzel thought irritably. "Bad luck wouldn't want to have anything to do with him," she grinned. "He's too unlucky already."

Lady Raven's blue eyes sparkled with compassion. "So it would seem."

Zuryzel nodded thoughtfully. Then she gave herself a shake all the way to the tip of her long tail. "You seen Biddah anywhere?"

Lady Raven nodded and gestured to a small maple. Zuryzel hurried off to find Biddah.

Biddah was sitting alone on the tree, waiting for her. Smiling, she helped Zuryzel up onto a limb and then passed her a plate of nuts and berries and a mug of hot mint tea. Still smiling, she sat in silence and watched a group of squirrel youths eating their meal and talking and laughing about the news of the day.

Zuryzel smiled craftily at her squirrel friend. "Why so starry eyed?"

"What do you mean?" Biddah queried.

"Only that you usually talk to me at dinner. Usually, you ask me about scouting or my brothers or something else. But today, you're staring starry eyed over at the same bunch of warriors. What's going on?" When Biddah hesitated, she added, "Oh, come on. You can trust me. I'm as silent as a grave."

"Well … it's just … well," Biddah stammered, "that Karrum … well … he is …"

"Handsome? Great? Wonderful? *What?*"

"All of those, I guess. He's a good warrior, too. Have you seen him with the bow? He's great with it!" Biddah's face looked embarrassed, but her eyes were gleaming with pride and happiness.

Zuryzel smiled. Opening her mouth to make an encouraging comment, she snapped it shut when she heard Lady Raven calling for the council of war. With a sigh, she slipped down from the tree. As princess of the Wraith Mice, she was entitled—if not expected—to attend every council of war. She seated herself next to her mother and was about to make her report when her elder brother, Mokimshim, panting hard, charged into the clearing that served as the home for the squirrels of the Bow Tribe. *Why back so early?* Zuryzel wondered.

Before he even sipped the tea that Queen Demeda offered him, he broke the news from his scouting mission.

"The hares have fallen! Their fortress is destroyed, up in flames, and every one of them is dead. Every one of them! Yes, the babes, too! Now the foxes who conquered them are marching straight towards Pasadagavra!"

Stunned silence met the news.

Then Lady Raven commented in an offpaw manner, "That place has some great warriors and plenty of defenders in it. I can't see them passing Pasadagavra." But there was just a *hint* of uncertainty in her eyes, as if she didn't believe her own words. *Why wouldn't she?* thought Zuryzel. Pasadagavra lay in the valley of an otherwise impassible mountain range. No army the size of the foxes could possibly hope to reach the lands beyond the mountains and have the resources to fight if it traveled over the treacherous range. They would have to go through that valley, and they would have to conquer Pasadagavra if the foxes wanted the rest of the earth. And they were too far into the war to back out now.

Then Zuryzel spoke her piece of news. "When I went to find Dejuday's cell, I found that he was not alone. Two mice that I had never seen before were in there, but they looked as if they were rather enjoying themselves, listening to his … chattering. Also in there with him was Jaccah. You know, Tribeprincess of the Stone Tribe? She had been caught going through Darkwoods. I talked to her through the window, and she looked tired. She told me that she hadn't slept for days due to Dejuday's *chattering*, and she looked pretty skinny, too. With the news of the foxes marching to her home, I suggest we get her out of there as soon as possible."

Sharmmuh, Tribequeen of the Bow Tribe, spoke up this time. "I remember Jaccah. She was never wary of discussing anything with anyone, but she always was rather solitary. I can't imagine her being too pleased being stuck in a cell with others."

"And," added Queen Demeda, "we need to get her out of that prison as fast as possible. I'll tell you what. Zuryzel, you sneak into that castle disguised as a fox and slip your way down to the cell. Get Jaccah out and leave the others there. That really should teach Dejuday a lesson. Make it obvious only to him who you are. Call yourself Jewel. You know what else to do. Be careful."

"Me? Why me? I just got back from finding out where he is!"

"Because you are the only one who knows where he is. Go. Now."

Zuryzel trudged off a few paces.

"Hurry."

"I'm tired!" Despite her complaint, her mother's order sent Zuryzel's feet moving faster. Her mother smiled ruefully; the Wraith Mice magic had certain advantages for the superior issuing the orders.

Feldspar shuddered in the hands of two fox guards. They had come by that noon and taken him for questioning by an Oracle, and he dreaded the Oracles.

The guards knocked ceremoniously on the frame outside a curtained door.

"Come in," called a voice from within.

Abruptly and without concern for their charge, they dragged Feldspar in and threw him onto the ground.

The beige vixen glared at the guards. "Go," she snarled.

They obeyed.

The vixen turned and looked at the mouse, pushing a plate of pastries toward him.

"Eat," she said curtly.

Feldspar didn't touch the food.

"Come, eat; starving will do you no good," snapped the vixen, keeping her eyes solidly on Feldspar.

He lifted a small pastry. It had a light, flaky crust and was filled with a sweetened mixture of blackberries and raspberries.

"Here," added the vixen. "Drink." She pushed a carved pottery pitcher filled with sweet, dark elderberry wine across to Feldspar. He took a few sips.

"That's better," nodded the vixen. For a moment, her eyes took in Feldspar. "Now tell me, what is your name?"

"Why would I tell you?" demanded Feldspar.

The vixen shrugged. "If you want it that way. Have some more food."

Feldspar was wary, but so many days without anything but stale bread finally wore on him. He took another pastry.

"Where do you come from, warrior?"

"South," replied Feldspar automatically. The vixen looked away.

"Well, I see. Where were you going?"

"I didn't know. I was just wandering."

"Why were you wandering?"

"What difference does it make?"

The vixen turned her eyes to the mouse. He realized that the red color was slowly draining, fading into dark pink. "It makes no difference to me if it makes no difference to you. What do they call you?"

Feldspar let out a sigh of resignation. "Feldspar," he replied.

"I see," replied the strange vixen. "My name is Fawn."

Fawn … what a strange name, he thought.

"Did you have any reason for leaving your home, Feldspar?" asked Fawn.

"Well, yes, several, but I'm not sure exactly which one was strongest."

"Where did you think your trail was heading?" she asked.

"Wilderness."

"Hardly," replied Fawn. "It leads to Pasadagavra, the greatest fortress and city on this earth. Were you going there?"

"No."

"Which god do you worship?"

The question caught Feldspar by surprise. "The Bear King. Why?"

"Would you tell me about him?"

"Well, he … he is kind and loving and merciful. He protects and cares for everyone."

"Even for foxes?" chuckled Fawn mirthlessly.

"Yes."

"I see …" Fawn looked pensive for a long moment, pacing up and down. Feldspar thought she might ask some more questions, but she didn't. "Guards," she finally called through the curtain.

The guards came and dragged Feldspar through many passages, past foxes that Feldspar could not name, back to his cell. He decided not to tell the others about Fawn. It was easier decided than done, however, when Jaccah virtually attacked him with questions.

"What happened?"

"They questioned me," he replied dully.

"*Who?*"

"A young vixen."

"What was her name?"

Feldspar glared at Jaccah, but she seemed desperate.

"Fawn," he relented.

A sigh of relief escaped Jaccah's body. "Well, you got lucky. *I* got interrogated by Knife. She tortured me—look!"

She held out her forepaw. Four red lines against her auburn fur stood out where claws had slashed her.

Feldspar turned his head from the sight and shuddered.

4

RESCUE

Zuryzel hurried through the dark forest, running lightly over trails that she knew well. She skirted the brambles whenever possible and avoided running through the streams. Before long, she came in contact with other creatures.

"Who are you?" demanded a fox that she had almost run in to.

"My name is Jewel," Zuryzel replied harshly, exactly mimicking a vixen and adding to her disguise. The invisibility magic of the Wraith Mice gave her the power to use the night to appear as any creature she wanted. Her father said it was because it was hard to tell the difference between one creature and another in the night, especially when they were much the same size.

The guard evidently remembered "Jewel." "Carry on," he snarled bad-temperedly.

Zuryzel hastened past him; not long after, she ducked behind a tree to avoid a loping figure. She didn't want to meet more foxes than necessary.

"Oh," it muttered bitterly. "I ain't cut out for this. This is ridiculous. What would my ma say if'n she could see me? Ugh! Stupid thorns! If only I was back where I belongs, then I'd be better off. Aye, and I wouldn' have any o' this herb bilge water!"

As the figure drew nearer, Zuryzel recognized Ice the Oracle. Her fur had been dyed, but she didn't seem to be wearing as much jewelry as usual. As the Oracle bumbled on, Zuryzel noticed that she had a strange stride. She recognized it as familiar, but she couldn't put her paw on where she had seen it before. Zuryzel shrugged, turned back to her trail, and shuddered as the castle gates wove into view.

Jaccah pulled the flute from her lips for the fifth time that night. She had just played a long piece about a great river, but she was hardly panting, and she was smiling. Feldspar shook his head in admiration.

"I still don't know how that thing shows pictures," Ol'ver commented for the fifth time. Jaccah's smile brightened.

"Like to see more? Close your eyes and be prepared to be astonished."

Jaccah put her flute to her lips once more and began to play.

This time she played of a beautiful building, almost like a fort, made out of the same stone as her flute. To Feldspar, it looked like some sort of hollow shell, made in layers. Ornate carvings decorated the first layer on all sides. In the shape of a chevron, it connected to a second, bigger chevron-shaped layer above it. The second layer, likewise, attached to the third layer, and so on for nine layers. It had a beautiful ornate gate made of stone, with a little postern set into it. In the very center of the layers, a great dome rose majestically up, up, up, connected to the last layer with clear stone, brilliant diamond. The whole place had an air of unsurpassable beauty that took Feldspar's breath away.

The song stopped abruptly. "Sorry, but I just wanted to show you Pasadagavra. I don't think you would like to see all of the guard towers. They can get rather eye blurring."

Zuryzel slipped unchallenged into the fox castle and down to the cellars. She had been here before, many times. She knew it better than the back of her paw. Her flowing cloak hid the definite shape that would have pointed out to anyone that she was a mouse, not a fox. She paused at the top of the stairwell down to the prisons and then said to the fox that guarded the stairwell in her best vixen voice, "Oracle Hemlock told me to take your place guarding the prisoners. He also said to collect everyone you meet on your way and bring them to him. The five lower floors are closed off to any beast but me, as the guard. You are to gather silently outside his room until he calls you. Orders, you know."

Instantly, the guard slid off. Zuryzel waited until he had gone and then opened the door silently. She slipped down, stopping at the cell where the captives were. She listened to the notes describing Pasadagavra and heard them cut off abruptly, followed by Jaccah's remarks. Then she heard Ol'ver question her about other music.

"Surely you can play something other than squirrel tunes," he pleaded. "I really like the tune called 'Rolling Green Meadows and Mountains.' Surely you know that one. I was there when you learned it."

"No! No!" Dejuday's sharp plea rose up to where Zuryzel was listening. "No! Anything but that!" As expected, Dejuday's plea went unheard by the Tribeprincess She instantly began to play the monotonous tune, repeating the same phrase over and over again. Dejuday hated the boring repetition, but Zuryzel liked it.

Knowing it was a long song, Zuryzel decided to intervene. She made a loud sound with a rock, then slipped down with all the litheness of a Wraith Mouse, and approached the cell.

"Hision! Hision!" Zuryzel hissed the word for silence in her native tongue, Simalan. With any luck, only Dejuday would recognize it.

It worked. Dejuday stood, and she knew his eyes could see right through her disguise. She also noticed that he was trying to say something but could only mouth the words, due to her order. She smirked at him. Then she noticed Jaccah looking at Dejuday, puzzled. Silently she slid her dagger into the keyhole and pushed some lever or other, which lifted the bar holding the door closed. It was so complex she wondered how the Darkwoods foxes had found brains enough to make the lock. Upon opening the door, she beckoned to Jaccah. "Come. The Oracles want to see you. No, not you. *Ki doe meir.*" Under her hood, she smirked with satisfaction. "Talk if you wish," she added to Dejuday, "but not to say my name. Do not talk to the others until I am gone." And then beckoning to Jaccah, she said, "Come."

Jaccah slipped past her and up the corridor a little ways. Zuryzel was about to follow her when Dejuday muttered, *"Princess?"*

"What?" Zuryzel hissed.

Dejuday switched his speech to the Western Tongue. "Is there some reason you're getting her out and no one else?"

"Kyani," Zuryzel grinned. "Yes. I was ordered to leave you here."

"What about Ol'ver and Feldspar?" Dejuday argued, still whispering.

"I will get them out in due course, but speed is of the essence, and they would slow us down," Zuryzel answered.

"And what about me?" Dejuday demanded.

"Queen Demeda thought it would be a good idea for you to stew in your own juice, as they say," Zuryzel smirked. "Maybe that will teach you to pay attention."

"I *do* pay attention," Dejuday argued vehemently. "I don't *like* getting captured, and if you think I could get scatterbrained in dangerous territory, you're an idiot."

"Well it's not my decision," Zuryzel retorted. "Get yourself out if you're so worried."

"I can't," Dejuday snarled. "Your blessed father ordered me not to. I have no choice but to wait for someone else to get me out!"

"Not my problem," Zuryzel almost squeaked with delight.

"How long am I going to be in here?" Dejuday demanded.

"Probably until you can get yourself out," Zuryzel shrugged.

"So you're going to leave me here for the rest of my life?" Dejuday demanded incredulously.

"Probably." Zuryzel's voice was exultant.

Wounded disbelief filled Dejuday's eyes as Zuryzel closed the prison door. He didn't move, and his expression didn't change as his princess turned and led Jaccah out of the castle.

Once they were out the gates and into the woods, Zuryzel lifted her disguise. Jaccah jumped with disbelief. "Princess Zuryzel! Thank you! But why did you leave the others?"

"They'd slow us down," Zuryzel answered half-truthfully. Though that was her reason for leaving two of the mice, she was strangely reluctant to share her reasons about leaving Dejuday in the cells. The betrayal on his face made her feel just a little guilty, even though she knew perfectly well he deserved it.

"Why do we need to run so fast?" Jaccah demanded.

"Not now. Later. I'm taking you to Sharmmuh's camp. You should stay there until you are strong enough to travel. I promise you, you'll be safe," Zuryzel said. Secretly, she hoped that Sharmmuh would tell Jaccah about the hares being destroyed and their conquerors marching toward Jaccah's home. Once she learned the news, she would want to get to Pasadagavra with all speed, but she would have to regain her strength first, to eat, and to rest at the closest and safest camp. Zuryzel had to convince Jaccah to get to the Bow Tribe camp. She cautiously extended her magic just enough to give Jaccah the disguise of a fox as well. Using magic that much was exhausting, but it would have to serve.

After passing through Darkwoods, they dashed across the moorland so fast that Zuryzel began to doubt her instinct about getting Jaccah to the camp because she needed food and rest, but soon Jaccah slowed off. When they reached the woods, Jaccah stopped and sat down to regain her breath.

Zuryzel was about to insist that they hurry because that was her order until a face broke out from the woodlands and hailed them cheerily.

"Hey, Zuryzel, you really aren't hurrying."

"Hey yourself, Johajar. Hurrying is going as fast as possible, and I can't go much faster. Not with having been mostly on the run for four days, and being disguised," Zuryzel replied cheerfully to her twin brother.

Johajar had a charming smile and a handsome face that made him attractive in a way that neither Mokimshim nor Zuryzel could claim.

Heavily, Jaccah got to her feet. "I can make it to the camp now. I just needed a breath. Let's go." She struggled a few paces forward and then broke into a run with Zuryzel and Johajar.

Zuryzel had appreciated the break as much as Jaccah and now forced herself to keep going. She kept thinking of beds and blankets and her warm room at Mirquis or her quarters at Dombre or her glorious apartments at Arashna or Dobar. Even her little room made out of wood at Kardas with its homely smell she would have welcomed.

As soon as they entered the clearing, Queen Demeda and Shinar, one of the river otters who served under Wraith Mouse King Hokadra, greeted them. Both of them smiled with relief.

"Well, I see that you got back early, Zuryzel. No don't reply. Just go get some sleep. Jaccah, Sharmmuh would like to see you. She wants news about Pasadagavra. Then you can sleep, too."

Zuryzel tapped her mother's shoulder nervously. "I need to talk to you," she whispered.

"All right," Queen Demeda answered, drawing Zuryzel aside.

"When I was in the prison, Dejuday asked me how long it would be until he got out," Zuryzel explained. "I told him he could get himself out. He said that father told him not to. What was with that?"

Queen Demeda sighed. "Do you remember when the border patrol at the moor was taken captive?"

"I don't know what you mean."

Queen Demeda shrugged. "I guess not. You were in Pasadagavra when it happened. Well, there were ten of them, and six of them, including Dejuday, were captured. It wasn't their fault, mind. Anyway, they tried to escape, and it … didn't go so well. Your father ordered all of them not to try to escape until someone came and got them. The same order applies to almost all the scouts."

Zuryzel felt a weight of guilt in her chest. Her mention of escaping by himself must have stung Dejuday pretty badly.

Queen Demeda patted her daughter's shoulder. "Don't worry about it right now," she said. "Just go rest.

Zuryzel nodded and trudged off to the tree where she and Biddah ate their meals. But when she realized that she would have to climb the tree to get to the bed that had been made for her below Biddah's, she felt faint.

She was just about to give up when she saw Biddah's head appear through the foliage. Smiling, she put a paw down and helped Zuryzel up to one branch, murmuring encouragement. Branch after branch, she continued until Zuryzel reached her bed. Just before sleep claimed her, Zuryzel saw Karrum smile up at Biddah and Biddah return the smile.

"Well! She could have said something encouraging. 'We'll get you out soon, too,' or 'Don't worry.' Something!" Dejuday complained—once he found his voice. He had been silent for a long while.

"Who?" Feldspar demanded.

"Or," Ol'ver added, "she could have said something encouraging about a particular maiden." Feldspar knew Ol'ver had made that up on the spot. Dejuday had no love of his own.

"I," declared Dejuday, bad-tempered for once, "am going to sleep. Please don't bother me." He threw himself down on the hard stone of the cell. Feldspar thought that must have hurt him.

"Hey, Dejuday," Ol'ver called out cheerfully, "you seem to know that fox!"

Dejuday raised his head and glared at Ol'ver. "For your information, she isn't a fox."

"Oh, really?" sniggered Feldspar, catching onto Ol'ver's joke. "Who was she then?"

Dejuday ignored this, save for a glare, lay down his head, and was silent again.

Feldspar lay down not far away and drifted off to a dreamless sleep himself.

When he woke up, Feldspar noticed Ol'ver staring off into space, a faraway look in his eyes. "What is it?" he queried.

"It's just … well … I'm finding myself missing… mm … Ran'ta."

"Who?"

"Ran'ta. She's … I guess you could say she's my betrothed." He looked at Feldspar's expression and laughed. "You see, when I was a babe, my parents abandoned me. I don't know why. But the Coast Tribe squirrels found me. They looked far and wide for some mouse family to take care of me and finally found one that lived not far from where I think I was born. They had no children, so they agreed to adopt me. They named me Ol'ver. I never knew my birth name, but I think I was born in Harboday, a city on the coast. Anyway, the wife had a sister, who had been married and widowed, twice, I think. She has two sons and a daughter, Ran'ta. She was the only creature my age in the village, so we played together all the time growing up. Naturally, we became great friends. One day we found out that we probably will be married, but both of us treat the situation as if it doesn't exist. We're both happy as friends. Still, I really can't help but miss her a lot. I think about her every day. And every day I spend in here, I find myself realizing how much she means to me. Now I'm feeling pretty overwhelmed with her not with me."

"Where is she now?"

"Pasadagavra. Lots of cliff mice went there when the foxes advanced too near to their homes. I went there with them. King Fuddum sent Jaccah and me out looking for a mouse babe, and that's how we got captured. Every time I think about never getting out of here, I feel awful about never getting to say good-bye to Ran'ta. And every day, I worry about how she is doing."

"Was Pasadagavra that fort that Jaccah played about?"

"Yes."

"Then I'll bet she is in good paws—and more. I don't think you have to worry."

Ol'ver nodded, and then closed his eyes. "I can see that place now. What a wonder. Beautiful, well built, good location. Four squirrel tribes live there, plus the Stone Tribe. If you ever get there ... you'll hear ... about its history ... foundation ..." And Ol'ver's voice trailed off to sleep.

Clink. Clink.

"Whoever is in there, get this. And wake Dejuday up." A bundle came through the window and fell onto the floor. "And tell him that he better be grateful, because he's making his escape six days early."

Feldspar scrambled up to the ledge where Jaccah used to sleep and peered out the small window. He could see nothing but shifting shadows. Scrambling down to the earth, he picked up the bundle. It contained a fancy dagger and some twine and other tools he could not identify.

Frowning, he shook Dejuday, none too happy to be woken up. But once he caught sight of the bundle, he brightened. He picked up the materials and scrambled over to the door. For a little while, nothing happened. Then Dejuday hailed him.

"Get Ol'ver and let's hurry. The passage is clear."

Feldspar shook Ol'ver, waking him in no time at all, and told him the situation. Dejuday glanced at the two and then thrust door open. He slipped into the passage, almost vanishing in the few heartbeats Feldspar and Ol'ver watched. Then the two followed, both of them as silent as a graveyard. All three of them stalked out the main gate and into the woods.

"Well, it's good enough to be out again," Ol'ver commented once they were in the woods. "Now, the first place *I'm* going is Pasadagavra. You coming with me, Feldspar?"

"No, the first place you are going is the Bow Tribe Camp," a harsh voice sounded out of the night. Both Feldspar and Ol'ver jumped with fright, but Dejuday seemed unbothered.

"Hello, Sibyna. Who gave you the right to say where they are going? I am sure that they will be pleased to oblige you, but I might ask why you are so insistent. And I might ask … oh, never mind. Why do you get to say where we are going?"

"Orders." And out stepped a Wraith Mouse maiden from the underbrush. Feldspar couldn't help but notice that not a leaf rustled at her appearance, even when Sibyna passed the shrubs. Instantly he felt chilled. He couldn't help but notice that she had the skills of a much better warrior than Dejuday. And she seemed to be taking their situation far more seriously.

She took one glance at Feldspar and Ol'ver and then turned back to Dejuday. "Come. Keep up."

Instantly, Sibyna set off through the woods. The three former captives followed her. Dejuday began to melt more and more into the night, and Sibyna was often at the point where she was barely visible. It didn't help that they went on a varying course, weaving through the trees instead of simply going in a straight line. The branches and undergrowth never swayed when they slipped by. Feldspar could have sworn that Sibyna's feet even went right through a patch of bracken as if it wasn't there.

As they journeyed, Feldspar could hear Sibyna and Dejuday arguing. "You're impossible," Sibyna snapped at her brother so quietly Feldspar barely heard it and Ol'ver clearly did not. "You can't seem to stop getting yourself captured. Do you know what she—?"

"Who?" Dejuday demanded in a whisper.

"I'm not blind, and I'm not an idiot, Dejuday," Sibyna retorted, keeping her voice low. "We both know who I'm talking about."

Dejuday's replied furiously, struggling to maintain a whisper. "Why don't you keep your paw on your own problems instead of worrying about mine? I know *you* have plenty to worry about."

Sibyna drew in her breath sharply. Feldspar, glancing at his friend's face, realized he wished he had not said that. "Sorry," Dejuday murmured.

Finally, at the edge of the moor, she stopped. By this time, the sun had risen, though Darkwoods had too much cover to tell that. Feldspar had never run so far in his life, and apparently, neither had Ol'ver. However, the two Wraith Mice weren't even breathing hard.

"The sun is well up," Sibyna commented. "We should reach the camp before midnight. Get your strength together; we'll be going through a bit of moorland with no shade. Are you ready?" Without waiting for an answer, Sibyna went ahead. For a while, they continued struggling through the thick moor grass. After nearly two hours had gone by, even Dejuday looked hot, not yet adjusted from his confinement in subterranean temperatures and shade.

At moonrise, they reached the forest, and the going was even more difficult, having to go around trees and over roots. After what seemed like an eternity, Sibyna slowed her pace. Not long afterward, they reached the camp. Sibyna did not wait for them, or even acknowledge them, but stalked off toward Zuryzel with Dejuday in her wake.

Afternoon sunlight glittered through the trees as Feldspar woke up. He was aching all over; the long run compounded by a small bed that seemed little improvement over his cell's hard mat had given his body little rest. But he was ready to get to Pasadagavra. Lying in his bed for a few minutes, he waited for Ol'ver to wake up. Ol'ver was just stirring when Feldspar heard a cry coming up from outside. After shaking Ol'ver a bit, Feldspar slipped outside the bushes.

He noticed an older Wraith Mouse sitting on one of the logs by a fire. He looked tired, but not weak.

"Who is he?" Feldspar murmured.

"King Hokadra," a Wraith Mouse standing next to him. Though Feldspar didn't know it, this was Prince Mokimshim. "He has been on a scouting trip with others. I don't think his news is good. Did you hear the hares have fallen?"

"The hares? The ones who had that fortress by the prairie?"

"Yes."

"How?"

"The foxes burned the grassland. The heat of such a fire caused the wall to collapse."

"Are many dead?"

"All are dead."

"Who?" asked Ol'ver, who was struggling out of the thicket.

But Mokimshim was moving away toward the fire to sit with his father. Feldspar watched King Hokadra clap a paw around his son's shoulders. In the blink of an eye, both Johajar and Zuryzel hurried across to greet him, too. All the king's family listened—and Ol'ver and Feldspar eavesdropped—as he broke the news.

"The Coast Tribe and the Mountain Tribe have both set out for Pasadagavra, and so far as I know, there is no trouble there about feeding all the inhabitants. I met Jaccah when she was heading toward Pasadagavra, and she told me that the hares have fallen. Is she correct?"

"I'm afraid so," Queen Demeda replied gravely. "The foxes are becoming more and more powerful, and I've also seen plumes of smoke coming from the direction of the hedgehogs' fort. It could be nothing, but I don't like it."

Ol'ver tugged at the sleeve on Feldspar's tunic. "Come on, we need to set out soon if we're going to reach Pasadagavra before the foxes do. Let's find Sharmmuh and get some food. We should get going before nightfall."

Both mice searched for Sharmmuh. Before long, they found her leaning against a tree, deep in conversation with a solid black mouse. Feldspar had never seen a creature like her. She had the most beautiful of blue eyes and wore the oddest of clothing—a short tunic and a pair of trousers, shoes constructed of some sort of glossy material, and armor made out of toughened bark cloth. She carried the most dangerous looking bow that Feldspar had ever seen. Taller than he, it had a bowstring made out of material similar to that which made up the mouse's shoes. Over her shoulder, she carried a quiver of jay-feathered arrows. However, she did not have many scars on her, which Feldspar guessed meant that she had not fought in many battles. He was willing to guess that the mouse was thirteen or fourteen cycles old.

She sighted both of the mice over Sharmmuh's shoulder and beckoned them join with a jerk of her black head.

"So," she commented, smiling slightly, when they approached, "you're finally awake. You slept most of the day away."

"Indeed you did," agreed Sharmmuh. "And I would suspect that you are rather anxious to get to Pasadagavra. Whenever you are ready, there are packs of food for you, enough to last seven days if you pace yourself. Go due nor'east, and you should reach Pasadagavra by noon in seven days. Look out for foxes or rogues, and don't hurry. You have plenty of time. May the Bear King go with you."

Ol'ver said a lot of formal things, but Feldspar was only half listening. They were going to Pasadagavra! Who knew what wonders he would discover in that place?

Both mice picked up their packs and set out northeast from the camp. But before they got thirty paces, Dejuday hailed them.

"Hey, thought you were going off without saying good-bye, did you?"

Both of them turned around to face their friend as he kept talking.

"I would have liked to have you meet some of my friends, but you slept through the day."

"Yeah, well Sibyna set a tough pace; we had difficulty keeping up with her," Ol'ver explained.

Then Dejuday became unusually serious. "Don't take it out too much on Sibyna. She's my sister, to begin with, and I don't tolerate others talking about her too harshly. And to end with, she's not going through the easiest of times right now. Trust me; she used to be scarcely serious. Listen pals; do me one favor, and say a prayer for her to the Bear King. She needs all the help she can get. I don't doubt her endurance, but still, she is having some challenging times right now."

"Hey, Dejuday," said Ol'ver suddenly, tactfully drawing the situation away from Sibyna, "who was that mouse talking to Sharmmuh?"

"That," replied Dejuday, "was Herttua Crow Blue Arrows."

Ol'ver's eyes widened, but Feldspar didn't have a clue as to who Herttua Crow Blue Arrows was. "Who?"

Ol'ver's eyes glittered incredulously. "Lady Raven's daughter! The best archer in the whole world! One day, she's going to rule half of the earth! She's been in more battles than half of the Wraith Mice put together! How do you not know about Herttua Crow Blue Arrows?"

"Well, I come from down south. I never even heard of squirrels before I came up north."

Dejuday sighed wistfully. "It must be peaceful down south if you never heard of Herttua Crow Blue Arrows or squirrels."

Feldspar nodded. "It is."

Dejuday shook himself. "Well, you're sure in for a different time up here. Watch out on your journey. I'll see you at Pasadagavra in a cycle or two."

Both mice nodded. Dejuday gave the two a farewell nod and then hurried back into the camp.

The two mice walked until nightfall, and then took shelter in a natural cavern beneath the roots of a rowan. Night birds called, owls hooted, and a few late-out crickets chirruped.

How can there be a war on, Feldspar wondered, *when all is so peaceful?*

🐀

A few days later, Biddah was enjoying talking to Karrum while she ate dinner. The squirrel warrior was wonderful company and seemed especially attentive and friendly to her. True, she still felt a twinge of guilt when she happened to glance over at Zuryzel and remember she wasn't spending time with her friend, but still, Zuryzel hadn't seemed too bothered when she had come in, weary and hungry from her scouting, and seen Biddah talking to Karrum.

The Wraith Mouse Sibyna hurried into camp. She made her report to Hokadra, watched carefully by Zuryzel and Mokimshim, and then started toward one of the campfires. She stopped abruptly when she saw her mate, Orgorad, chatting away animatedly to another maiden. She stood still for several moments and then flung herself down next to Johajar, her black eyes blazing.

Mokimshim shook his head pityingly. "Things don't seem to be going very well for Sibyna and Orgorad," he commented. "Do you think he doesn't like Sibyna much anymore?"

"I would hope he does," his sister replied. "Personally, I think his problem is that he isn't noticing he's upsetting Sibyna when he doesn't spend time with her."

Mokimshim nodded, and both siblings sat down at the fire where Sibyna sat.

Karrum was just about to make a comment to Biddah when Sharmmuh called him for the evening patrol. "See you later, Biddah," he smiled. He gave her paw a gentle squeeze and hurried off.

Out of the corner of her eye, Zuryzel saw him go. She wanted to get up and talk to Biddah, but Sibyna was still in a towering rage. There was no way she was going to leave Sibyna alone. She was beginning to develop a respect and friendship for Sibyna as she watched Sibyna struggle against her mate becoming far too friendly with other maidens.

Before long, Herttua Crow Blue Arrows and her friend, Storm, hurried across to the fire and helped themselves to some food. The two mice instantly began to talk about bows and arrows with Sibyna, a topic all of them enjoyed. Storm took out one of his arrows that he had fitted with owl feathers and showed it to Sibyna and told her of the time he had found the owl. The minute Sibyna was distracted, Zuryzel slipped away from the group and paced over to join Biddah.

The squirrel was looking cheerful, and Zuryzel was glad to see that. She had been quieter than usual lately as she had become more and more drawn to Karrum. Now, after the warrior had come over and actually talked to her for more than just a few moments, she seemed much happier. She, too, fell into criticizing Orgorad.

"Sibyna still loves him; that is rather plain to see," Biddah said. "Is he blind or something?"

"Aren't most males blind?" Zuryzel joked. "But we don't need to gossip about it."

Biddah obligingly changed the subject, and they talked until the evening patrol returned. Before Karrum could see her talking to Biddah, Zuryzel jumped down from the tree branch where they sat and hurried over to join Sibyna and Herttua Crow Blue Arrows.

The patrol made its report to Sharmmuh and Lady Raven. To Zuryzel's surprise, Lady Raven called her daughter and gave her orders in their native tongue, one that Zuryzel didn't understand. Herttua Crow nodded once and signaled to her archers. As her force collected quivers of arrows (three quivers apiece), Lady Raven spoke quietly to her daughter. Crow seemed to be listening closely, and whatever her mother said seemed to make her angry. Zuryzel saw her breathing faster and shallower after a while. Finally, the herttua nodded stiffly and turned on her heel and selected three of her own quivers.

"Well," she said, striding over to the fire Zuryzel sat at, "I had a three-day scouting trip, hardly had time to rest, and now I've got a long mission, Zuryzel."

Zuryzel stood up. "When will you be back?"

Herttua Crow shrugged. "Who knows? But Zuryzel," she added, swiftly lowering her voice, "would you do me a favor?"

"What is it?"

The Ranger yanked something from her neck. "Keep this safe for me. It's a treasure that my mother entrusted to me. Where I am going is not the place for it. Keep it safe, won't you?"

Zuryzel nodded. "Of course. What is it?"

Herttua Crow pressed the small object on the chain into Zuryzel's paw. "It is like a key. I'll tell you the rest later. Until then, stay safe. Bear King protect you."

"And go with you."

Herttua Crow managed a smile before swinging her quivers onto her shoulder and picking up her bow. Flicking her bushy tail in anticipation of the coming mission, she gave a single shout and then gathered her archers together.

Lady Raven watched as the small force of crack-shot archers slipped off into the gathering night. Then, with a weary sigh and drooping head, she retired to her bed in a small thicket. Mokimshim and Johajar both stood up and struggled into the lower branches of an elm where their beds were. Zuryzel was left sitting alone with Sibyna. The latter stared into the fire while the former stared into the night. Both sat in silence for a while. Surprisingly enough, it was Sibyna who broke the silence.

"I feel so alone, Zuryzel."

Zuryzel squeezed her friend's paw encouragingly. "You're not alone, Sibyna. Orgorad still loves you."

"I hope you're right, but still, I can't help but have my doubts. I talked to him last night. He didn't even listen to me." Here, Sibyna's eyes filled with tears.

Zuryzel was at a loss for what to say. She knew her mother sometimes got mad at her father when he didn't pay much attention to what Demeda had to say. Was that Orgorad's problem? She had the utmost respect for Sibyna, a deadly archer and a fierce warrior. And she had tried to be a loyal mate to Orgorad although she didn't make that look easy.

For about an hour, both Wraith Mice sat in silence, listening to the gentle breeze blowing through the trees. Then Sibyna stood up and slipped silently over toward her bed and melted into the shadows.

Zuryzel stayed by the fire, her heart aching for her friend. She thought how, before, Sibyna had smiled and laughed and talked with ease and animation all the time. Now Zuryzel could hardly remember when she had last seen Sibyna smiling, let alone laughing. Instead, Sibyna remained quiet and withdrawn on her better days. Other times—and more frequently of late—she wore a stiff face with eyes that usually sparked with annoyance or blazed with anger. But through it all, she had never shed one tear—at least, not that Zuryzel had seen.

She was just about to let sleep claim her when a shape moved near the edge of the camp. Peering cautiously in that direction, she saw the shape of a mouse working its way lithely toward the exit of the camp. Silent as a shadow, Zuryzel got down from her bed and followed.

She passed though the woods completely unnoticed but was having a difficult time following her quarry. Only the sound of shifting plants or branches on the windless air gave her a clue to of the path to follow. Then her quarry passed through a shaft of bright moonlight, and she recognized the scarred face immediately.

Orgorad! What was *he* doing out here?

Orgorad slipped into the shadow of the trees and was lost to sight and sound. Zuryzel decided to go home now and tell her father what she had seen, but no one else.

Especially she would not tell Sibyna.

5

PROMISE

"Wake up, sleepy tail!"

Feldspar's eyes flew open to see Ol'ver sitting beside him, nudging him gently with his paws.

"Come on," Ol'ver continued impatiently. "We need to get to Pasadagavra, remember? Here, have a slice of nutbread and let's go. It looks as if it's going to rain today, so wrap your blankets up in a piece of bark cloth. That way they'll keep dry. Hurry up!"

Smiling, Feldspar struggled to his paws and wrapped his blankets up in a piece of waterproof bark cloth. He threw his pack on his back and picked up a piece of the squirrel delicacy, preparing to eat it on the way. Wrapping himself up in a cloak, he set out after Ol'ver.

By sunhigh, the clouds had rolled east, toward the Unsettled Lands, so they now covered the whole sky. Enough of a threat from rain still remained to keep the trekkers in their cloaks. Now, wanting nothing more than to reach their destination, the two mice engaged in very little conversation.

Darkness had just begun to descend, and rain was clearly coming. Both mice began to discuss where a good place would be to sleep when a maiden's voice hailed them from the shadows.

"There is a good place just this way."

They jumped with fright as two lithe figures slipped gracefully from the shadow of an ash tree. The two Wraith Mice grinned and introduced themselves.

"I'm Karena," explained the maid who had hailed them.

"And I'm Dikiner," continued her companion, a sturdy looking male. "We're brother and sister, you see, and we've been on patrol. There's a nice cave up that way, completely dry. Just perfect, considering, too, the fact that it's near the river. I'd advise you go for it. It's not far."

"We'll show you," offered Karena. "It's only a little out of our way. Anyway, we'd be interested in hearing some news from the camp. I can tell you've been there. Follow us; we'll show you."

Both Wraith Mice slipped into the brush. Feldspar and Ol'ver, both of whom had noticed the clouds growing over the moon, closely followed them. A little way along, but not far from the trail, they came to a gurgling river, which Feldspar guessed was the Bakkarra River. Following it for a short distance, both Wraith Mice soon disappeared into a shadow. Feldspar followed them and found himself in a roomy cave, dry and clearly perfect in which to sleep out the storm.

It took no time at all to get a proper fire started. The Wraith Mice listened to the reports of the fallen hares and the danger the hedgehogs were in and, most particularly, to the bit about the foxes marching to Pasadagavra. Then both of them broke their news.

"Well, we just came from Pasadagavra," explained Dikiner. "The place has plenty of food and a solid defense. We didn't see Jaccah in our travels, but then, we didn't come the fastest or most direct way here. We swung away east, needing to patrol the area. If Jaccah were traveling the quickest way, our paths never would have crossed. I'll bet she's there now. It's only four days to Pasadagavra from here, and I doubt Jaccah would have rested. I mean she probably wants to get home to her family. Oh, by the way, Feldspar," he continued, "since you are going to Pasadagavra, you might want to know that a fox is in the city."

"What? You mean Sage is still alive?" Ol'ver interrupted. "I thought she was dying when they found her."

"She was still alive when we left," Karena replied. "But her daughter, Rosemary, she's still there. Oh Great Cerecinthia, we need to go!" she exclaimed when she saw the high moon. "We need to be back to camp in seven days, and we still need to check out the river ford. Well, good-bye. Bear King go with you." With that, both Wraith Mice slipped out of the cave and into the gathering night.

"Tell Dejuday we said hello!" Ol'ver called after them. Dikiner raised his paw in acknowledgement before both Wraith Mice were lost to sight in the darkness just as the rain began.

"Ol'ver, tell me about Rosemary and Sage, please," Feldspar begged.

Ol'ver sighed. "About a cycle ago, when I first arrived at Pasadagavra, Jaccah, her mate Argoss, and another young squirrel called Shjeddah found a fox mother and child wandering. They brought them back to Pasadagavra and somehow kept them unnoticed until King Fuddum could decide what to do with them. Shjeddah suggested that he let them live in Pasadagavra. Both Argoss and Jaccah wanted to send them back to the foxes. But when he heard the story about why the foxes were wandering, King Fuddum let them stay. He announced it publicly. Shjeddah took upon the responsibility for raising Rosemary, the daughter, because Sage, her mother, is too weak. Jaccah doesn't like the foxes living among them, and I can tell that she doesn't like or trust Rosemary. But she hides her feelings well, partly because her son is a really good friend of Rosemary's. So she plays with Rosemary; she's kind to her. The problem is Shjeddah keeps telling her a few lies, which will only hurt everyone in the end."

"Jaccah has a son?" Feldspar couldn't help interrupting.

"Oh yes. He's a nice little fellow. Jaccah raises him well. He could be a pawful in the wrong paws. But he respects Jaccah and his father and most adults. He's a devoted friend to Rosemary, and he's kind to most. He'll make a great tribeking one day. His name is Rhonndan, named after his great-grandfather. Everyone adores him. He likes to learn, and he likes to help, and he loves his parents and his grandfather."

"Does Rosemary respect Shjeddah as a mother?"

"Well, that's a hard question to answer. She doesn't know that Shjeddah isn't her mother because Jaccah refuses to interfere with Shjeddah's raising the fox; she doesn't even know that she's a fox. Jaccah found them when Rosemary was only a few weeks old. And now her pelt is dappled a little, but it's red, like all the squirrels she knows, so it's not as if there's nothing to back up her belief. She respects Shjeddah, but I don't think she loves her the way she would one she believes is her own mother. She honors Jaccah a whole lot more than she does Shjeddah. She's sensible enough to know that Jaccah doesn't really like her that much, but she still seems to prefer Jaccah, I guess, because she realizes that Jaccah is trying to do the best for her. And Jaccah really is.

"It's kind of odd, actually. Rosemary loves to learn, but you sometimes get the feeling that you need to learn from her."

🐁

Anamay slipped into the river without a single ripple. She was eager to get to her meeting with Mollusk today more than ever, for three reasons. First, Mollusk had promised that he would bring his sister, Brine, about whom she had heard so much. Second, she had witnessed the fall of the hedgehogs, and she needed to tell him that. And third, it would be the last time she would see him until next autumn. She was going north to try to rendezvous with Herttua Crow and would not be back down here until summer. The three sea otter clans went to a great fortress by the sea for late spring and summer and even early autumn. The fortress had once belonged to the Wraith Mice, but it had fallen in battle. Now it belonged to the four sea otter clans as it had for nearly twenty-one cycles.

As she drew near to the island where they always met, she heard voices.

"Ooh, Mollusk, I don't like this; I really don't."

"Look, Brine, there's no reason to get all panicky. You'll like her, I promise."

"That's not what I'm afraid of. Are we safe? You said she's Mudriver's daughter. Can we trust her?"

"Of course we can. The only one who I don't think I entirely trust is you. Remember, you're not to say a word about this."

"I know, but I still don't like this."

"If you say 'I don't like this' one more time, I'm going to push you into the river and cover you with mud. Then *you'll* be Mudriver."

Anamay rounded the bend to see Mollusk sitting on the island, enjoying the sun's warmth, and a female sitting beside him. She was rocking nervously back and forth, but she swiftly stood as Mollusk stood up and called to Anamay.

"Anamay, over here."

Anamay climbed onto the bank and shook herself off before greeting Mollusk. As she sat down across from Mollusk and Brine, she saw the reeds behind them sway against the wind, and she could have sworn that she saw a flash of brook-colored fur. But the next second, it was gone and she turned her attention to Mollusk and Brine. She listened to what they had to tell and enjoyed getting acquainted with Brine. Then she broke her news.

"Well, the hedgehogs have fallen. The foxes again. Those foxes are marching to Pasadagavra. Herttua Crow Blue Arrows—you know, daughter of Lady Raven—took her archers to the battle, but not quickly enough. So far as I know, they're trying to catch up with a party of foxes that left. They don't know where they are going, but they need to kill or capture them before the foxes reach their destination. We—my sister and I—have been trying to find them, but no luck."

Suddenly, a great gust of wind rattled the trees and sighed through the reeds. This time, Anamay was certain of it—she'd seen a brook-brown otter hidden in the reeds. The otter swiftly slipped behind a log, but not quite silently. Both sea otters looked around at the sound of the gentle rustling.

"What was that?"

A thrush's call sounded from the log, and the bird flew up into the open. Both sea otters relaxed. Anamay relaxed with them, both because they did and, mostly, because she had recognized the eavesdropper.

"Well, we had better be going. I'll see you later, Anamay." Anamay tried not to be wounded by his carefree farewell. She hadn't told him that she wasn't coming back until next autumn. He was still a sea otter, and it was always better if he didn't know all the movements of her own kin.

Mollusk got up and brushed himself off. Then, followed by Brine, he slipped into the water and swam away.

Anamay got up and made as if to swim away herself. Getting in the water, she silently and almost invisibly swam around to an inlet behind the log. With a great *whoosh* she pounced on the otter crouching behind the log.

Both of them rolled. Anamay could feel tense muscles in the other otter's body, muscles that soon relaxed when the otter caught sight of her.

"Anamay, what are you doing here?"

Anamay grinned at her older sister, Danaray. "I might ask you the same question, Dana. I thought you were supposed to be out scouting for Herttua Crow. Not shirking our duties, are we?"

Danaray drew herself up indignantly. "You're supposed to be looking for her yourself, Ana. If anyone is shirking her duties, you are. You said you were going off to find something to eat, but instead, you're meeting a *sea otter*. How long have you been meeting him?"

"Who, Mollusk? Oh, about a month now. Don't even think about telling me that I shouldn't be meeting him or start saying that you don't like it. Because if you do, you'll find that you're not the only one who's stubborn. Remember that!"

"Maybe not, but I'll tell you one thing," Danaray growled. "Father is going to hear about this."

This took all the bravado out of Anamay.

"Dana," pleaded Anamay. "Please don't tell Father. I just don't see how this could be dangerous."

"I'll tell you how," Danaray snarled. "He's a *sea otter!* Have you *never* listened to the stories we hear? Kyka told us about how they slaughtered his family when he was a babe, just to get at Zurez! Streamcourse told us about how her crew was thrown from their home when she was a babe, and the sea otters hardly even live there! Do I need to tell you about Doomspear, Moonpath, Lukkall, Sky, Wave, Rain, Yular, Kway-han, Orionyap, Arpaha,

Kiskap, and all the others? They each have a story in them about the sea otters' selfishness! And you're *meeting one!*"

"What would I have to do in order to make you not tell Father?" murmured Anamay with tears in her eyes.

"Promise me you'll never meet him again—*and keep your promise!*" growled Danaray.

For a while, Anamay was torn between indecision. Then she sighed. "I promise, Dana," she sighed.

Dana hugged her sister. "Ana, you have to make better decisions in the future! I don't trust the sea otters—most of them, disregarding Mollusk, are selfish brutes! They weren't always like that, but they are now. I don't want to see you in trouble because of them! I'm sorry, Ana. I couldn't see anything wrong with Mollusk, but you could get tangled up in the others all too easily from this one. I'm just thinking of your safety and thousands of others' safety."

Anamay nodded miserably. "I know."

🐁

The darkness of evening shrouded Darkwoods; even in the daytime, the dense grove of trees prevented any light whatsoever from filtering through, almost as if some kind of magic had cast a spell on the forest. As night deepened, heavy rain clouds formed and made it almost as dark on the moors. Soon rain fell so heavy that it penetrated even the tree cover.

Johajar flitted through a patch of ivy as he crouched down beside his sister. "Why can't he be a little quieter?" his sister grumbled.

"Give him a break, Zuryzel," Johajar breathed back. "Dejuday's a lot bigger than you. It's easy to be silent when you're small as a novice."

"You're not so tall yourself!" Zuryzel snapped back at her twin. In fact, both of them had the sinewy build that made good scouts. Dejuday did not. A whole gully away and Zuryzel could still hear him shifting in the undergrowth.

"I never said I was," Johajar retorted. "I only said Dejuday was."

The three mice were engaged in a scout patrol. Six or seven trios of spies checked out various places on the Darkwoods perimeter or about six miles in, while a major patrol, usually consisting of a hundred or so warriors, waited on the edge of the moor, about an hour's easy walk away. This patrol, however, was taking longer than expected to cover their ground—a whole day longer.

Zuryzel sighed. "Why can't night get here so we can vanish?" she muttered.

"The days are getting shorter," Johajar reminded his sister. "Winter is coming."

Zuryzel rolled her eyes at her brother. "Stay here," she ordered irritably.

Noiseless even without her magic, she slipped down the gully and up the other side to where Dejuday crouched. "Can't you hold still?" she snarled.

"Yes, Your Highness," Dejuday retorted. "You told me to get to the tree and wait." He nodded at a particularly gnarled trunk.

Zuryzel blinked. "You're a scout. Can't you do it *quietly*?"

Dejuday kept his voice low. "Just when are we returning?" he asked. He still sounded slightly angry. All three of them were frustrated after two days of slinking under the bushes in this awful forest and in the rain, but, remembering Johajar's comments, Zuryzel guessed Dejuday was having the worst time of it. Why *was* he a scout? He would have been better with a sword.

"As soon as it gets to be night," she replied. "Really night, not just cloudy. We can't vanish until the sun has actually set." *Maybe the rain will stop then, too*, she thought.

Dejuday cocked his head. "Do you hear that?" he asked anxiously.

Zuryzel dropped down and listened carefully. Closer to the earth, she could feel the *thud-thud-thud* of many paws. *An attack!* she thought in alarm.

Rising just slightly she made a couple of frantic gestures to her brother. Johajar slipped down the gully side and scrambled back up. "Do you hear that?" Zuryzel breathed.

Johajar pressed his ear against the wet ground and nodded silently. Zuryzel slowly rose to her paws, looking this way and that and sniffing the air with for a telltale scent. The army was nowhere near; she could see no dull glint of iron, hear no squeaking of armor. The attack force was quite a ways off and quite large if they could hear the thudding in the ground this far away.

"Where are they, do you think?" Zuryzel asked Johajar, who had the sharpest ears.

Johajar thought about it. "I couldn't hear them where I was," he mused quietly, "So they must be somewhere in that direction." He nodded toward the Darkwoods castle.

Zuryzel didn't like the way this was going. "In other words, heading right toward the Bow Tribe camp," she hissed.

"You don't know that. They could be heading west," Johajar pointed out.

A thrill of alarm sprang into Zuryzel's mind. There were virtually no defenses in the west—all the strength lay in the north and east, at Pasadagavra and Miamur. The first conquests of the foxes involved a several-cycles-long march that had brought the foxes just north of the settlement of Graystone. From Graystone, where they had not lingered, they had gone on to Arashna and Dobar. Tiny Kardas, a small Wraith Mouse farming community, had fallen within two hours, but Dobar, the fortress that protected Arashna, was still under siege. King Hokadra's three most trusted generals were withholding the sea of foxes in the west, with the help of some sea-faring mercenaries. It was generally assumed that the foxes already in the west would march east and rendezvous with the main army in the east, thus subduing the wilder lands in between and flanking Pasadagavra. If the bulk of the Darkwoods army started marching west instead of towards Pasadagavra, however, it could pose some serious problems.

Zuryzel made a gesture with her head in the direction of the castle. The three scouts worked their way carefully through the darkness. Zuryzel strained her eyes for any sight of other creatures, and Johajar kept his ears pricked. But the pouring rain made use of all their senses more difficult. As far as they could tell, the marching had stopped, and several minutes passed before they saw the army.

But it was not one army. There were two, and of far differing sizes.

One plainly stood out—the Darkwoods foxes. Arranged orderly in rows and clad in mail, they numbered perhaps fifteen hundred. The other remained hidden in the trees. Some they spotted in the branches and others in the undergrowth. There were more, so spread out and well hidden that they knew they could not count them all. It consisted of a few river otters, but mostly squirrels

"River Tribe!" Dejuday breathed in alarm.

The River Tribe was an aggressive squirrel tribe that had split in two during the recent wars. Most of the warriors and tribe members were willing to wait for the best conditions to attack the foxes whereas the smaller half longed to attack as soon as possible. At some point in the past several cycles, the squirrels who wanted to attack split from the rest of the tribe. Zuryzel knew there had been very few reports about them, but she also knew they had been gathering rogues and mercenaries to swell their ranks into an army. It appeared that they were preparing to attack now. Zuryzel could see the squirrels with their cheeks still tattooed with the telltale tribal brand—a few wavy lines for the River Tribe. She could make out random river otter rogues and even one or two rogue foxes.

"*Dejuday!*" Zuryzel hissed in desperate alarm. "Run back and tell King Hokadra fast! Ask him to send the patrol here to help!"

Dejuday vanished in a heartbeat. "Do you think Father could stop this insanity?" Johajar asked, surveying the horribly outmatched renegade army.

"I can only hope so," Zuryzel breathed back. "There can't be more than three hundred in the River Tribe army—and at least five times that many foxes!"

"They have the advantage of surprise, though!" Johajar pointed out hopefully.

After a few minutes, the army of foxes began to march again—toward the east. *At least they aren't going west*, Zuryzel thought gloomily. Then a thought occurred to her. She and her twin were perched on a hill that towered above the castle. Eastward from the castle there were gullies that made easy pathways around the forest. They *also* made excellent ambush opportunities for River Tribe guerillas. Now looking more carefully, Zuryzel could see the squirrels perched in trees along these gullies and the river otters hidden just behind the tree trunks. *They're planning an ambush!* Zuryzel decided. Well, that would give them an advantage, too.

"Should we help them?" Johajar breathed.

Zuryzel gave her twin a severe look. "What good could we possibly do?"

"I meant talk them out of it," Johajar explained.

Zuryzel hesitated, which she instantly regretted. "Too late now," she observed as the fox army began to move into the ravine.

The ravine was very narrow, and if the River Tribe had planned this well and would execute it well, then the Darkwoods foxes could be in for a rough time. If only the River Tribe would start the attack before the foxes could run back into the safety of open ground ...

They did. It seemed to Zuryzel to be a masterful plan. She saw the foxes on the outsides fall, pierced by arrows. If Dejuday could only get to the main patrol in time, just maybe they would win this fight.

The foxes hastily tried to climb the edges of the ravine, but the soaked ground made ascent difficult, and the squirrels were pretty good at keeping them down. Zuryzel began to hope. They had a chance for victory!

Or not.

Just above the pelting rain, Johajar's keen ears picked up another sound. He gestured desperately to his sister and pointed. Zuryzel turned and gasped. Another group was sneaking through the underbrush, these obviously not squirrels. As far as Zuryzel could tell, they were foxes all from Darkwoods. *Darkwoods! How many do they really have?* Zuryzel wondered. As Zuryzel watched, the foxes raised their bows, aiming at the squirrels and their mercenaries.

Zuryzel put her paws to her mouth and blew a shrieking noise that sounded passably like an eagle.

One of the attacking squirrels looked round and just saw the ambush in time to shout a warning; he didn't last much longer. To make it worse, these new ambushers held the higher ground. The River Tribe guerillas had to turn from attacking the foxes in the ravine and fire at the foxes behind them—which meant that the foxes in the ravine were no longer penned in. If Dejuday didn't hurry, the River Tribe guerillas would die right here, caught between the two fox armies. Even if Dejuday hurried, they might still die.

Zuryzel immediately saw that the River Tribe guerillas had no plan for retreat if it became necessary, and it was now necessary. They were outnumbered by at least thirteen hundred, but they still fought on.

Hurry, *Dejuday!* Zuryzel thought desperately.

An older warrior, probably the age of Zuryzel's father, faltered and fell from his tree. A javelin, hurled from a tree, missed its target. Two younger otters slipped on some slick rock, slid down the sides of the gully, and were fallen upon by the foxes. Zuryzel's ears rang with their screams of agony as the foxes tore them apart in a frenzy. She felt her muscles tensing up, longing to help those who were falling, but she didn't dare. It would be suicidal. She could do nothing.

The rain began to let up, but it was getting darker. Zuryzel let herself slip into the night and Johajar followed her example. The squirrels and otters had no such advantage. Barely a few moments after that, however, a familiar war cry sounded, and yet another band of attackers broke from the trees.

Zuryzel half hoped this was more squirrels and part of a backup plan, but the leader of the new attackers on one side of the gully was her mother Queen Demeda, and on the other side, it was Lady Raven. Zuryzel scanned the patrol for Dejuday but couldn't see him. She made a silent gesture to Johajar, and the twins eased their way past the still-dripping branches toward their army.

There was still enough fighting to do. Zuryzel cautiously loosed her sword and pointed at a couple of fox archers about a hundred feet apart, well hidden in the deep foliage. Johajar nodded eagerly in return.

Sneaking up from behind, Zuryzel and Johajar fanned out to different sides. Zuryzel carefully measured up her target before she moved. The first thing she did when she got close enough in the foliage was to send her sword flying through the bow; then she stabbed the enemy in the neck. Johajar approached almost carelessly.

"Shouldn't you be a little more careful?" Zuryzel asked.

"I don't think the foxes want to deal with Lady Raven or Mother just yet," Johajar explained. "They turned back into their fortress pretty fast."

"They had the upper paw, even after Mother and Lady Raven arrived. There were so many of them!" Zuryzel observed.

"Zuryzel," Johajar said patiently, "when you plan a war, you plan every detail carefully, especially with that many soldiers. But you still can't plan for everything, and when something unexpected comes up, you fall back. You regroup. They don't consider us a threat in the long run, but they weren't prepared to deal with an ambush *and* another group attacking led by Lady Raven. They may be some day, but not today."

Zuryzel nodded. "Okay. We should go find Mother."

Queen Demeda had not gone to the trouble of pursuing the foxes back to their castle; the main patrol was already too close. She was grimly surveying the dead in the valley. Raven was examining those on the hills.

"I recognize some of these otters," she was saying to a Bow Tribe squirrel as her children approached. "What they were doing mixed up in this suicide is beyond me."

"Mother," Zuryzel said in a small voice.

Queen Demeda turned weary eyes to her daughter. "Zuryzel," she sighed in relief. "What kept you in Darkwoods these past two days?"

"Patrols," Zuryzel explained. "They were much more thorough than usual. We were stuck."

"This army must have been here for a while," Queen Demeda murmured, looking around at the carnage. "The Oracles must have wanted them trapped here." She laughed a short, bitter laugh. "It was a waste of time on their part. These squirrels weren't going anywhere."

"How can you tell?" Johajar asked curiously.

A sudden, furious shriek shot out from the top of the hill Queen Demeda had been on. The rest of the patrol jumped, startled, and the six or seven Rangers immediately began talking amongst themselves. "I think Raven just found out," Queen Demeda sighed. "Come on."

At the top of the rise, Raven was standing over the body of a young squirrel. She was cursing savagely. "Blast!" she hissed. "*Look* at that!"

The knife sticking out of the squirrel was a squirrel's knife.

"Did one of his comrades turn on him?" Johajar asked, sounding sick.

"No, Johajar," Queen Demeda sighed. "He saw that his army was doomed, and he killed himself. He was so dedicated to this attack that when it failed he felt he had nothing left to live for. I've seen nearly a dozen like him, and I can almost guarantee there are more."

"The phrase," Raven scowled, "is 'zealot.'" She cursed again. "I *despise* zealots."

"Zuryzel? Johajar?"

Zuryzel turned and saw her brother, anxiously searching the valley. "Mokimshim," she called.

Her elder brother looked up, and smiled with relief. "Did Dejuday find you?" Zuryzel asked her mother.

Queen Demeda nodded. "I made him stay back," she explained. "He was exhausted. Your father took part of this patrol to the north of Darkwoods because we haven't heard from the scouts in that area yet either."

Zuryzel nodded as Mokimshim puffed his way up the hill.

"Did you see them when you were scouting here?" he asked, indicating the slaughtered soldiers.

Zuryzel shook her head mildly, but Johajar snapped, "If we had we would have sent word!"

"Johajar," Queen Demeda interceded swiftly, giving him a slightly stern glance. She then looked around at the various segments of the patrol. "If we don't get out of here soon, the foxes will close off the border, and we'll have to fight our way out. We'd better get back."

"And the dead?" Raven murmured, indicating a Bow Tribe squirrel that had been killed.

Queen Demeda turned to her older son. "How many are there?"

Mokimshim spread his paws. "I counted two hundred thirty-seven squirrels and otters," he replied, "but I'm sure there are more. Three were killed from our own patrol ... I only saw about two hundred dead foxes. There should have been more, given the ambush, but ..."

"It would take days to bury them all," Queen Demeda decided. "We have to go *now*."

She shouted some orders, and the patrol gathered more or less in a circle. At night and in Darkwoods, marching in straight lines was a dangerous waste of time.

Zuryzel and Johajar stayed to the back. Johajar intended to listen for cries of wounded soldiers they could not have heard over the noise of the rest of the patrol. Zuryzel had another reason for hanging back, although she waited until they had almost reached the border before she began speaking quietly to her twin.

"Do you think we should have helped them?" Zuryzel asked.

Johajar shook his head. "The two of us alone? No. It would have been suicide. It's those squirrel zealots' fault they got killed. They chose a good site for the ambush, but they should have had a plan to get out if it went bad, as it did."

"I know, but ..." *Two hundred thirty-seven.*

"Zuryzel," Johajar reminded his sister, "if we had joined the fighting before Mother and Lady Raven arrived, it would have made no difference except that there would have been two more dead – us. You know that. And think about this: you gave them some warning of the counterattack, and that helped them." When his sister didn't respond, he added, "This war won't last forever, and when it's over, you and I will have different instructors—ones who will teach us what we really have to know, like politics or literature, and everything a prince and princess should know. This ... this sword fighting is temporary, but we have to stay alive to keep it temporary."

"That's Mokimshim's job," Zuryzel murmured. Johajar's words to the contrary, guilt continued to dominate her thoughts.

"Zuryzel," Johajar continued, "our duty is to fight for our kingdom, not throw our lives away in zealots' battles." His tone was so firm that it pierced Zuryzel's descending melancholy. She met her brother's eyes.

"You're right," she agreed. "Besides, Mokimshim will need all the help he can get." She tried to smile at Johajar, but she couldn't stop a couple of tears for the fallen leaking out the corners of her eyes.

Johajar grinned, and then blinked fiercely as he glanced one last time at the gully where the battle had been disastrously lost. For a few moments, Zuryzel thought he was crying, too. Then she realized that the rain had started again.

WARRIORQUEEN

Feldspar and Ol'ver had both had a sleepless night, kept awake by the sound of the rain pounding outside the cave. Dawn had just broken, and they now trekked wearily through the woods. Soon they came to a stretch of plain that practically separated the woods in two.

"Hurry up, there," Ol'ver murmured urgently. "You don't want to be caught walking this neck of the earth. Come on. Don't talk. Just hurry."

Both mice hurried across the open area before the sun had risen fully. As soon as they had crossed it and entered the woodlands, Ol'ver blew a sigh of relief, which quickly turned to a shout of alarm as a squirrel landed on top of him.

Feldspar found himself equally attacked. He was flat on his nose before he even knew it. Out of the corner of his eye, he could see Ol'ver struggling under a female squirrel with a sling tattooed on her cheek and a pair of wooden studs set in her ears.

"What are you doing on our territory?" the squirrel demanded harshly.

Ol'ver was clearly not in a mood to be intimidated. "To begin with, this isn't your territory; this is the Stone Tribe's. And also, we are just passing through, not spying, not stealing, just traveling. You've got absolutely no right to attack us!"

"Oh, yes?" the squirrel who was holding Feldspar down retorted. "Remind me what right you have to decide which rights are whose. You are on our territory. And talk so disrespectfully to Warriorqueen Wazzah like that again, and I'll slay you!"

"You first, Sharvas!" a completely new voice broke in, making both the captors start with fright. "And you especially, Wazzah!" Instantly, a whirring noise whizzed over the downed mice, and Ol'ver's captor rolled off him, a nasty wound slicing across her back. Taking to their feet, both squirrels fled, pursued by a spear.

The two mice stumbled to their feet, relieved one moment, wary the next. Three more squirrels dropped gracefully from the branches. Two of them had a graceful imitation of a wave on their cheeks. The third had an unidentifiable shape etched on his.

Ol'ver relaxed visibly when he caught sight of the tattoos. "Well, you came along with good timing, there. I can't stand idle threats. They really get infuriating."

"None of the threats you heard were idle, Ol'ver," replied the squirrel that seemed to be leader, the one with the odd shape on his cheek. "Both Wazzah and Sharvas would have slain you for speaking that way to Wazzah, the warriorqueen of the Sling Tribe. Not that our threats were idle either," he added, with a smile of satisfaction. "The only thing that saved Wazzah's life was her swiftness. Come, you two look tired and hungry. Come have a meal with us and get some sleep."

The three squirrels led them to a watchtower carved completely out of onyx, carved all around with the same symbol as on the leader-squirrel's cheek. On the sturdy oaken door was painted what looked like the head of a huge cat. Golden rays flowed out from its golden head. And those eyes! Feldspar had never before imagined eyes shining with such unlimited strength, as if they continuously drew power from the strength of stone and the heat of fire and the might of the river. The cat looked capable of swimming the sea!

Inside the watchtower, the pair found comfort and warmth and, soon, satisfaction for their hungry stomachs. The three squirrels brought out refreshments for their guests—delicious nutbread made from almonds and hazelnuts, juice of apples and cranberries mixed with water, some sweetened blackberry-and-raspberry jam, and a plate full of crystallized lilac buds. Feldspar was very partial to lilac buds.

All three squirrels listened with interest to the two mice's news. All of them had seen plumes of smoke from the direction of both the hares' fortress and the hedgehogs'. They also had some interesting news of their own.

"I don't suppose you know of the rogue Mudriver," commented Verrah, the only squirrel maiden in company. "He normally lives in the east, in the Unsettled Lands. Well anyway, for reasons best known to himself, he brought his crew to a place not far away. He's very old, so I just don't know why he left his home, but he has two daughters. I don't know what the younger one's name is, but the older one is called Danaray."

"Sea otters are the ones who need to be warned about it, not us," Ol'ver flicked his tail dismissively.

Verrah didn't seem convinced. "You know, Zuryzel was up here about a month ago. We told her the news about Mudriver. She seemed to think that it was important that he was here, almost as if she could tell he would be needed or something. Zuryzel always seems to know when something is or will be important."

"But that doesn't necessarily mean important to us," Feldspar pointed out.

All the squirrels, even Verrah, seemed satisfied with this. The two mice finished up their meal, and then they were shown to pinewood bunks. Both mice collapsed onto a different bed and almost instantly drifted off. Just before sleep claimed him, Feldspar heard Ol'ver murmuring, "I'll see you tomorrow, Ran'ta. I really have missed you. I'll tell you all about the adventures I've had, and …"

Here Ol'ver gazed over at Feldspar, as if making sure he was asleep. Feldspar had swiftly closed his eyes and then heard Ol'ver continue.

"I know a mouse that just might like Glor'a. Who knows, she might like him, too!"

🐀

Zuryzel hated being where she was. She had offered to go with Sibyna to the brook that day, although she was regretting it. Sibyna loved the feeling of cold water flowing through the fur on her foot paws and the "singing" of the current. But Zuryzel was a different story completely. For her, the singing took on more of a babbling tone. And she so hated listening to anything's ceaseless, senseless jabbering. She also hated going to the creek amid all the mosquitoes.

Silently, she sighed with relief when she saw Sibyna standing up and drying off her foot paws. Swiftly putting all the stones she had collected into her small bag, Sibyna led the way back to the tribe camp.

Both Wraith Mice gladly accepted the food that was served at midday. Going to the river always made both of them hungry.

The meal had just begun when Dikiner and Karena scurried into camp. Karena hurried over to join her friends while Dikiner sat down across from Mokimshim and Zuryzel.

"I thought you were supposed to be back *five* days later. You're very early," Sibyna teased her old friend. "What's the cause this time?"

Before Dikiner could reply, Karena flounced down next to her brother. Dikiner chided her as gently as he could.

"What's the matter, Karena? What happened? Don't say it's nothing; it would have to be something to get you so worked up. What is it?"

Karena muttered something (it sounded suspiciously like "I'll tell you later, when we're alone") and swiftly took a sip of mint tea.

Zuryzel glanced casually in the direction Karena had come and saw Mokimshim glance her way a few times. Zuryzel sighed, wondering if her brother had said something tactless.

Suddenly a shout came from one of the lookout trees. Warriors reached for their weapons. Zuryzel began to draw her sword but stopped abruptly when she recognized who it was coming through the trees.

Her two oldest friends, Kiarna and Asherad, princess and prince of the Kingdom of Miamur, along with a small escort, were being ushered into the camp. Without much of a thought, Zuryzel hurried over to greet them. Kiarna's white coat was as neatly groomed as ever, and her blue eyes sparkled with all her usual friendliness. Her brother, Asherad, was smiling pleasantly, his gray fur equally clean and neat and his own blue eyes gleaming. Zuryzel liked them both a lot, attracted as much to their friendly and, even, naïve demeanor as to their unassuming skills as powerful warriors.

All of the newcomers were seated around fires and served food. Zuryzel vaguely heard Mokimshim and Johajar talking to Asherad. But all her interest centered on Kiarna. Zuryzel practically pestered Kiarna for answers to her questions.

"How is your mother?"

"She's fine. Mother is always happy when business in the city is doing well."

"And how are your siblings?"

"Sick and tired of being left at home while we're out scouting and fighting."

"Any trouble with the foxes?"

"No. We're having so much trouble with rogues, though, that if we had to, we couldn't fight the foxes as well. That's actually the main reason we came, to tell you we can't help."

"Pity. The foxes are marching to Pasadagavra. I'd like to see them break into *there*."

"Well, I've never been there, so I couldn't tell you how safe it is." The Miamuran princess gave the Wraith Mouse princess a scrutinizing look. "My turn to ask questions. How are *your* brothers?"

"Haven't changed."

"Good. Zuryzel, …"

"What?"

Kiarna looked around casually. "Has your father been contacting my oldest brother without going through my mother first?"

Zuryzel shrugged. "Possibly."

"It really doesn't bother me, but he just seems to know things he has no reason to know," Kiarna explained. "And my mother is … loath to admit he's old enough to rule on his own. Being a regent gives her power, you see."

Zuryzel's family was a strange ruling family in that it was an actual *family*. Kiarna's was a little more archetypical: too many children, an ambitious regent, and no real love or trust between its members.

Before Zuryzel could reply, Lady Raven approached. Her blue eyes were a little darker than Zuryzel was used to, but not too far out of the ordinary.

"Kiarna, King Hokadra wants to see you. Hurry up; it shouldn't take long."

As Kiarna hastened off with a last look at Zuryzel, Lady Raven glanced at the younger warrior.

"Zuryzel, come with me. There is someone I want you to meet."

Zuryzel stood up warily. Lady Raven looked more serious than normal, not to mention worried. What was going on? Zuryzel couldn't quite put her paw on it although she tried. But above all, Lady Raven almost looked furtive. Why? Where were they going? Who were they meeting?

Once out of the camp, Lady Raven picked up speed until her strides were somewhere between a jog and swift walk. Zuryzel had little difficulty keeping up. Something was definitely bothering Lady Raven, no doubt about it.

"Lady Raven?"

"Call me Raven, Zuryzel. Lady is only for strangers."

"Well, Raven, where are we going?"

"To the river," Raven replied, shrugging carelessly.

"Why so secret?"

"Oh, nothing to do with where we're going. I don't want the wrong creatures to follow us."

"Who would?"

"I don't know. I just don't want anyone following us."

"Why?"

"You'll find out."

Now Zuryzel was utterly bewildered. If Lady Raven was showing her wherever they were going, why not anyone else?

But the Ranger lady obviously knew what she was doing. Her paws made no noise, and her blue eyes flitted back and forth. Then Zuryzel noticed with a silent gasp that she kept her right paw upon her rapier hilt. Zuryzel began to feel a little frightened. What was happening?

Suddenly, she understood. Lady Raven dropped to the ground, dragging Zuryzel with her. Raven's eyes focused on something not far away. Zuryzel looked and saw the trees waving. The deciduous woods were not something Lady Raven was used to, though Zuryzel could tell she knew what was happening. Her black fur began to bristle, and the blue eyes began to darken with anger. Silently, she slid a little to the right and vanished completely.

Zuryzel was shocked. Wraith Mice could vanish at night, but this was high noon, when the sun was brightest, and Lady Raven had just disappeared! She must have been really good at camouflage.

Suddenly she heard a cry. Zuryzel saw two black shapes erupt from the trees before one of them fled. Zuryzel was confused—a black fox?

"Are you all right?" Raven called.

Zuryzel nodded. "What was that?"

Raven shrugged. "I don't know. But come on. We've wasted enough time."

Wasted? So this was important. All the same, the darkness in Raven's eyes and the bristling of her fur had subsided, so she no longer feared pursuit.

Zuryzel's confusion continued stronger than ever. Why did the Rangers favor secrets so? What was going on?

Before long, the sound of water reached her black ears. Not the faint babbling of the brook she had been to earlier that morning, but the sound of rushing water, a powerful torrent speeding toward the sea. This was the Okirraray River, a fast, strong, wild stretch of rapids that Zuryzel had never dared go near. What did Lady Raven want here?

EEEEEEeeeeeeeeerrrrrrrr! Zuryzel heard Lady Raven give her eagle cry, one she used when she wanted to signal unobtrusively. To Zuryzel's surprise, a kingfisher's call echoed back through the woodlands, barely audible over the river's rage.

Raven glided forward through the dense undergrowth, keeping her head below the higher-growing blackberries. Nervously, Zuryzel followed suit. Before they had gone long, a squirrel dropped out of the tree right in front of Lady Raven. Zuryzel expected the Ranger lady to jump, but she hardly reacted.

Turning, she spoke to the squirrel, "Old friend, it's good to see you again!"

The squirrel was not from the Bow Tribe. He had a cocky, fearless aura, hard muscles showing on his paws, and scars tracing over his face. Zuryzel could just make out the tattoo: a line that went up and down twice. River Tribe. *What?* Sharmmuh always refused to have anything to do with them. Why did Lady Raven trust them?

The squirrel bowed. "Lady Raven, my friend," he said formally. He turned to Zuryzel. "Princess of Arashna, welcome."

That was flattery for sure. The prince – or princess – of Arashna was the one destined to rule after the reigning monarch died. That was Mokimshim, not Zuryzel.

"As usual, Raven, you're a little late," he added.

Raven shrugged off the friendly insult. "We had a run-in with something. Nothing to worry about." She tipped her head to the left. "I suppose Tiyuh is still all right?"

The squirrel blinked. "Of course. Come with me."

"Who?" Zuryzel breathed as they set off after the squirrel. Raven glanced at her.

"Tiyuh is one of my oldest friends. She is an elder of the River Tribe, and immensely wise. She requested to see you—I do not know why—and so I told her I'd bring you."

"Without my parents knowing?"

Raven smiled lightly. "Not at all. I asked your mother first, of course."

"What about my father?"

Raven shrugged. "Of course he knows, though I doubt he thinks I have any paw in it."

"Why?"

Raven shrugged. "We—your father and I—have never been on good terms. We disagree on reasons of war and on actions against war. We can discuss, or argue, those issues. But you must understand, events—in the past, mostly—some can never forgive. In Hokadra's case, that is more important than a disagreement on battle tactics."

"And to you?"

Raven's blue eyes, normally gentle and renewing, flashed furious. "I do not think I am much at fault. But that is not important now."

"And who is this we are following?"

"Warriorking of the River Tribe."

"How do you know him?"

Raven's reply was forestalled by the warriorking turning back to Zuryzel. "Careful not to slip."

Scarce had the words left his mouth when Zuryzel felt her paws slide. It took all her balance to not fall. Raven, to her surprise, hardly seemed to notice the slickness. The solid sandy earth had given way to water-slicked rocks. Trembling with sudden fright, Zuryzel realized the Warriorking was leading them right to a set of rapids on the Okirraray.

At first Zuryzel thought there was a cave behind the rapids, leading to some kind of camp. Instead, the Warriorking veered off and plunged back into the undergrowth just after entering the rapids. Soon after, he vanished into the foliage.

"Wait here," said Raven, leaning coolly against a tree.

"Raven?"

"Mmm?"

"Are you angry at my father because he blames you for … for … whatever … or for some other reason?"

Raven blinked. "You are very observant, Zuryzel, but I hold no anger for your father. I was wronged by an unforgivable accusation. That is all. Your father, if your mother kept her promise, does not even know about it."

"Of course mother kept her—how does she know?"

Raven looked at Zuryzel strangely. "You'll find out."

"When Tiyuh talks to me?"

"When you have proven yourself worthy."

"What happened?"

Raven sighed. "I was accused of being a coward. For a Ranger, that is the most terrible accusation there is. A severe penalty is always in store for someone who acts like a coward—and that includes lying, cheating, and leaving fellow Rangers in battle. I have seen that last one only twice. Only once was the guilty punished."

"Why not the second time?"

"I could not carry out the punishment."

"Why not?"

"Out of sheer softness. Or perhaps blindness. I do not know. But as I said, it matters not."

Indeed. The only reason you won't continue is because it matters greatly, thought Zuryzel. Lady Raven was *so* fond of secrets!

From a rustling in the foliage, an old squirrel, half gray with long cycles, emerged. Too old to leap from tree to tree like the fitter squirrels Zuryzel knew, she merely waddled out and greeted them.

"Zuryzel," said the elder, "I am honored to meet you."

Honored? Zuryzel had received various greetings in her short life, but never one such as this.

"I have been trying to speak to you for some time now," the old one continued. "I am Tiyuh, elder of the River Tribe."

Zuryzel smiled as calmly as she could. "I am honored to meet you as well, Tiyuh."

Tiyuh sat down. Zuryzel knelt down, but did not really sit out of respect for the elder.

Suddenly, Zuryzel realized both Lady Raven and the warriorking had left them. Zuryzel did not fear the elder, but she did fear being alone not too far from Darkwoods with one hardly able to climb.

As if Tiyuh sensed her feelings, she said, "Don't be afraid. The foxes are nowhere near. All I wanted to say is this. Beware the foxes, utterly evil, greedy, and not afraid to kill. Their terrible record speaks for itself, a history of wickedness beyond conception. An ancient story holds that, once, one of the clans was a tribe, ruled by a king and then corrupted by the Serpent. He can work his evil anywhere, but the Bear King can work his good anywhere. There may yet be foxes that survived, descendants of the ancient kings, who still cling to the Bear King. When the castle is conquered, search in the dungeons, everywhere, for those left from the line of Bronze, the first king. It is not impossible to fake the Blight. There may be none left; I do not know. But if you find even one, do not kill him—or her. It would be a terrible fate for the line of the kings to die out."

"I do not think I'll have much paw in it," said Zuryzel humbly.

"I sense what you think," said Tiyuh. "But ponder this: the Bear King gives qualities to those born. Why did he give your brother the talents for following and you the talents for leading?"

FIRST SIGHT

Midday was not far off. Feldspar's paws were twitching with agitation. Midday was supposed to be the time that they saw Pasadagavra. Both of them had eaten their fill, bathed in the stream, and collected plenty of small nuts and fruits. "After all," Ol'ver had said, "we should bring back something of value."

Without warning, the dense woods gave way to a stretch of peaceful field. At the end of the field, a chain of mountains rose up like a village of anthills. And in the valley of two of the greatest slopes, the fortress-city of Pasadagavra stood, its top almost dwarfing the mountains.

Ol'ver must have noticed the look of awe on Feldspar's face. "Big, isn't it, mate? Wait till you see it up close. It's huge. Huh, if Dejuday saw how much alabaster is used, he'd go crazy. More than a mountain's amount of alabaster."

Feldspar nodded dumbly. What did Ol'ver mean by "up close?" It looked as if it was no more than a few minutes' walk away. "H-how far away is it?" he stammered. How far could it be? How much *bigger* could it be?

"Oh, about two hours' walk. Huh, the foxes are going to be in for a real surprise when they see how big the field is. I can tell you, it's a real eye-opener, and that's no exaggeration or sarcasm. Hmm, if anything, it's an understatement. Trust me, there isn't a safer place on earth!"

Oracle Hemlock sat in his rough, black, lava stone throne. He had just called a meeting with the other Oracles of the fox clans. When they attacked Pasadagavra, everything would have to be properly organized.

His door opened, and the vixen Ice walked in. Anyone other than a fox Oracle would have laughed at the sight she made. Each ear had eighteen piercings from which strings of seashells and dried berries hung. She had dyed her red fur white and blue and wore clothing to match—lots of white, gray, blue, and black shawls and her tunic splotched with the same colors. On her wrists she wore bracelets from which every kind of seashell and stone dangled.

Without a word (but with much clanking), she swept into a chair opposite Hemlock. She nodded her head in greeting but stayed silent until Hemlock spoke.

"Where are the others, Ice?"

She answered in a voice that sounded like ice breaking. "They are coming, O Oldest Oracle. They must get ready. They did not foresee this meeting, but I did."

"Say that again, Ice, I dare you!" The curtain ruffled, and the male fox Fang entered, followed by the vixen Knife. Both of them claimed their seats, on either side of Ice. Knife wore as many shawls as Ice, and Fang wore the male Oracle's cloak, like Hemlock.

A few minutes passed. Fang began tapping his claws impatiently on his chair arms, and Knife twisted her shawls into ropes and untwisted them again. Even Ice's long patience was growing short.

"Blood is late," snapped Knife impatiently, "again. He always is. I say we start this meeting without him!"

"I am afraid you will have to, Knife, and end it without him, too." The curtains rustled softly, as if a touch of good had entered the evil room. Fawn, the apprentice Oracle to Blood, strode into the room. Clad only in a sky blue tunic and a sea-blue shawl, she wore a necklace of red stone beads trimmed around the edge with gold that Oracle Blood had had made for her. Even apart from her attire, she hardly looked like an Oracle, let alone a typical fox. The Serpent's Blight often took and controlled foxes, showing itself in their red eyes. But Fawn's eyes no longer flared deep red. They had softened to a dark pink with no savagery burning or bloodlust dancing. The Blight had seized her but did not control her. She alone, of all Darkwoods foxes, secretly began questioning the worship of the Serpent. Fortunately, the darkness in the castle rooms kept any from noticing the color change and suspecting her inner doubting.

She spoke respectfully to Hemlock. "Blood—may the serpent look with favor on him—is too ill to attend this meeting. I am representing him. May the Serpent honor you, Hemlock!"

Fawn stepped lightly over to stand beside Knife. Knife could just hear her muttering, "Indeed, I think the Serpent does look with favor on Hemlock, for he certainly deserves it." Knife caught the distaste in her voice and knew that her words were far from complimentary.

"May attending this meeting do you good, Fawn," Ice said approvingly. "I am sure it will add to your already admirable amount of good sense and knowledge."

"Enough! We've already wasted too much time," Hemlock broke in before the other Oracles could greet Fawn formally. "We have an important battle to discuss. First, our scouts report that many tribes have gathered at Pasadagavra. Even so, they are not outnumbering us—yet. I think that we should attack now!"

Several nods around the room showed agreement with his words, but Fawn's head did not move with the others. Everyone could tell that she had something on her mind, but she did not speak up. Fang urged her to speak her mind.

"Come now, Fawn; I can tell you are troubled by something. Speak up! We want to know what you are thinking."

Fawn hesitated for a while, but her instincts told her to speak. "The way is long and hard, and our troops are tired. They cannot possibly hope to fight and win against the squirrels—most of whom are fresh warriors— after a long trek. Also, the Wraith Mice have provisioned and upgraded the fortresses Mirquis and Dombre. T'would be foolish to go up against such a fortress as Mirquis, and I would not think that, even if we defeated Mirquis, we could afterwards go up against Dombre. Nor can we merely pass them on our way to Pasadagavra. I think we should lie low and study them both from every angle and decide whether or not to attack only once we find some weakness in both of them. We would definitely need reinforcements if we attacked Pasadagavra after taking both of those fortresses, anyway."

A stunned silence greeted these words. Fawn was still young, and no one had imagined her capable of such intelligent thought. In a breathing space, everyone reflected that, for a while, she had been one of the best warriors before becoming an apprentice to Blood.

Hemlock, however, was smiling. "Your words make sense, Fawn. However, I think that only the troops' fatigue gives us reason enough to delay. We will give them a cycle to recuperate. Then we will march. You see, reinforcements we have, easily. Also, we have a spy who has told us all the weaknesses of the fortresses. He knows the secrets of Mirquis and Dombre." Hemlock's eyes glittered both cruelly and cleverly. "We will destroy them easily, with the proper sacrifices, of course. This meeting is at an end, I think."

Fawn followed the rest of the Oracles out, completely baffled. Silently, she slipped along to her own chamber and looked in her mirror that hung just opposite her bed.

Her eyes were scarcely even pink anymore, she realized. To her surprise, she felt glad about that. She couldn't explain why, but she had hated being seized by the Blight. The other foxes called it assistance from the Serpent, and so had she, for a while. She had been as ruthless and evil as any other fox. But then she had found that her prayers to the Serpent remained unanswered, and her weeping and wailing and sacrificing to him got her nowhere. She had tried harder to win his favor by becoming the Oracle's apprentice, but even that resulted in nothing from the Serpent.

Then, chance prisoners had revealed another possibility to her. The capture of the mouse and squirrel three weeks earlier had sent her scurrying down to their cells in curiosity, having never seen a squirrel up close before. Approaching it, she had overheard them speaking of the Bear King, a creature of whom she had never heard, and then questioning of the captive mouse had given her more, but still limited, insight of this god of theirs.

Until recently, she had welcomed the Blight as a means to share in the Serpent's will, one she thought gave her great power. But in time, she began to feel that, instead, the Blight was enslaving her to his will, giving her no choice but to wreck havoc and spread terror, grief, and death in an evil destruction of others. Within, she fought this enslavement, wishing to be free of the grip of the Blight. She had asked the Serpent to remove it from her body, but needless to say, he had ignored her request. Then about two weeks ago, she had tried asking the Bear King for cleansing from it. To her surprise, she had seen the redness leaving her eyes.

For a few weeks. Then it had returned again, though her dreams did not stop.

Her dreams had been ... odd, to say the least. She hadn't actually *seen* anything in her dreams—unless swirling mist counted as something. She couldn't see past the fog, but she could hear—oh, yes, she could hear—beyond it. And what she heard pierced her very heart—cries of pain, shouts for help, and screams of wounded creatures. And, although she seemed to hear the voices for but a few minutes, she discovered the dreams had lasted the whole night. Waking, she felt the pain as if she suffered with those hidden bodies without ever having received the whip or sword or knife. Worst of all, she recognized some of the voices in her dreams as the cries of those she had killed in war.

Fawn decided that it would be a good idea to go down to the cellars and prison stalls and speak to the prisoners.

She was on the fifth floor when she heard the commotion. She rolled her eyes. "Not the Wraith Mouse *again!*"

She raced down the stairs just in time to see two squirrels. "Okay," she muttered. "not the Wraith Mouse this time."

Guards took the two captives back down to the cells, and Fawn lost sight of them. She waited for the entry hall to clear and the guard to take his position at the top of the stairs. Then she hurried past him unchallenged. After all, she was an Oracle's apprentice. Down the stairs she rushed silently, once around a turn, and checked every cell for the squirrels. She heard the sound of soft murmuring in the air, and tried to use it to find the captives, but the sound echoed, and her desperate search for them proved fruitless. Finally, she stopped dead still.

"Oh, Great Bear King," she murmured, "help me find them. If you are real." She did feel a little foolish, but she wasn't going to ask the Serpent for help. Even if she did ask him, she highly doubted he would help her.

Once again, she began to search for them, this time listening to the murmurs that reached her ears.

"Karrum, what do you think they will do to us?"

"I don't know, Biddah. Dejuday isn't with us, so no one will probably think to look here for us for a while. You and I will have to get out ourselves. The Bear King will help us."

There, they said it, again she heard his name—the Bear King.

"Do you think that we could find or use Dejuday's tools?"

"That's assuming that he was in the same cell. There are a lot of cells down here. Hang on to the tree branch, though! Here's his flute! He must have been in here!"

The Wraith Mouse—he had been thrown in the same cell as the other mouse and that other squirrel! Now Fawn knew where the squirrels were. She hurried over to the third cell on the right, coming from the direction of the stairs. She tapped on the door.

The squirrels jumped, and Fawn didn't blame them. Nervously, she pushed the door open. The female squirrel shrank back nervously; Fawn felt a rush of savage contempt that she knew came from the Blight. She thrust it away quickly as she faced the male squirrel, which stood to face her.

"Hello. Don't worry; I will not harm you. My name is Fawn. What are your names?"

The male squirrel held her gaze whilst he held on tightly to the female's forepaws. After a brief hesitation, he spoke. "I'm Karrum, and this is Biddah. If you'll excuse me for saying so, you don't strike me as the normal type of fox."

Fawn shrugged. "Not important." She glanced at Biddah, still cowering in the shadow.

They are scared of me, she realized and had to force away another stab of pleasure.

She made her decision in an instant. "I will help you get out," she declared. "It is nearly dark: I should be able to draw away the guard so you can run by. Here." She brushed calmly past the door, and from inside a pocket of her tunic, she drew a few biscuits stuffed with berries. "Eat these. They will give you strength. I have no water with me, but I will go get some if you need it." She inwardly winced at how harsh her voice sounded.

"Fawn," Karrum questioned warily, "how can you remove the guard? How can you be sure that he will heed you? And why would you help us escape?"

Fawn hesitated. Both squirrels would have heard about the bloodthirsty Oracles who led the fox clans. Supposing they did not trust her? But common sense told her that the truth would be wisest here. Taking a deep breath, she summoned up every scrap of courage.

"I am an Oracle's apprentice. But I disagree with the others. I am to be Oracle if something happens to any of the others, but I do not wish to be. Thus I would welcome an opportunity to injure Hemlock in any way he will remember." She had spoken the truth but not the whole truth. Fawn kept her main reason for helping them to herself, not yet ready to voice it, even to herself.

Karrum and Biddah looked at each other nervously. Fawn had to thrust away a bolt of pure delight when she realized they did not trust her. *Calm down. You've had your share of treachery. Time to pay the price.* Her thoughts appealed to the Blight in her.

"Does anyone know where you are?" Fawn asked them.

This time, the squirrels hesitated. Finally Biddah replied. "We were supposed to be taking lunch by a stream near the moor. Tribequeen Sharmmuh and my friends Zuryzel and Sibyna knew where we were, but no one else."

"Right. It must be pretty dark now. Follow me, and stay behind me. I'll get rid of the guard, and lead you to the darkest part of the woods. If you know your way across the moor, then I'll leave you at the border. If not, I'll go with you to your land."

"Thank you," replied Karrum. "I think we should be able to get across the moor. But we don't know our way through the woods. And," he added, "we won't tell anyone who rescued us so you don't get in trouble."

Fawn shrugged. "I'll get in trouble regardless. The guard will remember I am the only one who came down here, and the other Oracles will find out about that sooner or later. But for now, let's get you out of here. Follow me, keep quiet, and you'll be okay. Ready?"

Both squirrels nodded. Judging by the way their fur was prickling and their tails were twitching, they were very tense. Fawn felt the same, but she had to have courage. Courage and confidence would get them out of this. She had to believe that.

She rose to her paws and slipped silently out of the cell, followed by the two squirrels. They stayed right behind her, taking care not to be too obvious. With a deep breath, she boldly faced the guard.

"The Serpent has told me that the two prisoners behind me will answer questions I have about Pasadagavra. I will take them out to the forest. If the Serpent tells me to bring them back, I will. But do not expect them back." With that, she swept out, followed by the two squirrels.

They hastened out the main gate and into the woods. Fawn shivered as they passed the red gate of the outer barrier. With the squirrels right behind her, she hurried on. She heard them struggling over roots in the darkness of the hornbeam forest and slowed her pace. When she heard them panting, she stopped by a stream. All three creatures gulped down water thirstily. Fawn *still* felt savage rushes of pleasure when she heard sounds of struggling, and she was fighting a raging fire in her mind now, resisting the urge to leave the squirrels in the woods utterly lost.

After nearly half the night had gone by, the three drew near to the edge of the forest. Tipping her head to one side, Fawn could hear shouts and hollers coming from the moor. She turned to the two squirrels.

"Here," she whispered. "Here I must leave you so that I may say that I never saw you crossing the border. But before you go, two things I have heard. One, the foxes have a spy. I do not know whom, but be wary of everyone and tell your leaders. Also, the foxes have reinforcements with which they plan to take on Pasadagavra. I do not know what, but still, I should think they are pretty vile. Look out for strange creatures and especially rogues. Good-bye."

Karrum hesitated. Then he grasped Fawn's paw. "May the Bear King light your path and protect you," he said softly.

Fawn didn't know how to respond to that. She merely took an awkward step backward and murmured, "You too."

Biddah clasped Fawn's free paw. "We owe you so much, Fawn. Thank you. We will repay you someday. Good bye."

Without another word, the two squirrels scurried off out of the woods. Fawn realized, with a stab of disappointment that she quickly flung aside, that their gratitude had banished their fear. "Oh, come off it," she snapped to herself. "Time to head home." And then she added, "For however much longer it is my home."

THE WARHAWKS

"Are you certain she was a fox, Karrum?"

The two squirrels had made it safely to their home, and now both were being questioned about their adventure and escape. Zuryzel simply couldn't believe that a fox would help squirrels out of prison. She wasn't the only one, either.

"Yes, Lady Raven, I'm certain she was a fox. No other creature has such a tail, bushy with a white tip. And she knew her way around the castle, all right."

"Foxes aren't the only ones to know their way around that castle," Johajar spoke at once. Both he and Zuryzel had been sent on multiple scouting missions in that castle and knew it well.

"And," Hokadra mused, "you say she said the foxes have a spy. I wonder whom." His eyes flashed briefly toward something over Zuryzel's shoulder. She did not need to turn to know that he was looking at Orgorad, remembering the night that Zuryzel had mentioned Orgorad sneaking out of camp.

Sharmmuh seemed agitated in hearing about Fawn. "If those foxes ever find out that the Blight is leaving her," she fretted, "she'll be killed for sure. Poor thing. I wish we could help her."

Raven rolled her eyes. "Sharmmuh! You're too soft. This whole thing could be a trick. What if, just think for a moment, the foxes didn't have a spy and *wanted to plant one* in our camp!"

Hokadra inclined his head. "She has a point. There were reports from Kardas that some foxes had figured out a way to hide the Blight."

"Yes, I've heard the same," Raven said and then, turning to Biddah and Karrum, she added, "Dismissed, both of you."

As soon as the squirrels were gone, Raven rounded on Sharmmuh. "You want to go drag out some fox whose name you hardly know, who's actually an Oracle's apprentice! You're crazy, or foolish!"

"Raven," Sharmmuh protested indignantly, "we usually aren't on a war campaign."

Queen Demeda took Raven's side of the argument. "Then what *do* you usually do?"

Sharmmuh didn't answer.

"Supposing it isn't a trap, though," Johajar burst out.

Queen Demeda looked at her son with a hint of pride. Johajar always saw the good in creatures. It was a quality that ... he hadn't gotten from his family.

Until this discussion, Zuryzel had not recognized that Fawn's rescue of the squirrels had put herself in danger, but now she understood. She was hardly surprised when Queen Demeda spoke her thoughts. "Suppose one of us went over to ... help, for want of a better word, get her out. Then we have either an ally or a prisoner; either way, we win. If she hasn't lost the Blight, then ... think what we have for a prisoner." Her gaze swiveled around the fire and landed on Zuryzel.

"Good thought," Raven agreed.

Zuryzel wasn't sure if she meant Queen Demeda's plan or using Zuryzel to carry it out.

Zuryzel didn't need any orders or persuading. She immediately volunteered. Queen Demeda and Hokadra both gave their assent and some food for Zuryzel to take with her.

She walked to the edge of the woods and then set off at a run across the moor. She knew the way so well by now that she could have easily run it in her sleep and not gotten lost. The late afternoon and early evening wind ruffled her fur and bent the grass, wrapping it around her foot paws. She took off her shoes as she used to when she was younger, and she began to feel absolutely part of the earth. She ran on and on until moonrise, at which point she reached the foxes' woods. She put her shoes back on, all feeling of peace gone.

It was nearly moonlow by the time she reached the foxes' castle. Following a group of soldiers entering the castle, she melted into the darkness, hurrying along up the stairs of the castle.

🐭

Fawn hurried to the castle, and as she crossed the threshold, a young, ginger fox rushed up to her.

"Oracle Blood is dying. He wants to see you in his room."

Fawn nodded.

She forced herself to change her train of thought and concentrate on Oracle Blood. She needed to see him right away—after all, she owed him so much.

The Oracle's room was filled with healers and guards. Yet when Fawn entered, Oracle Blood lifted his head wearily. "Leave us," he commanded.

The healers, guards, and others went. Fawn sat down by the Oracle's bed, kneeling in respect. The Oracle reached out a paw and touched Fawn's face; his gentle claws traced over her brown eyes. Fawn looked deep into his and realized that he must be dying. The Blight was wearing off, and his eyes had returned to their natural pure blue, though dimmed in the shadow of death. Fawn wanted to cry. Oracle Blood had taught her so much, had shared so much wisdom, had given her so much more than teaching. So often in her training, Fawn had come close to calling him father. Now he was dying.

Tears must have clouded the look in Fawn's eyes; Oracle Blood reached up and wiped them away. His voice rasped, but was steady.

"Fawn, you must not weep. Death is not the end of everything; it is the beginning of anything. And I know I can tell you now. In my last moments, I have felt the love of the Bear King. Am I right to assume you have too?" He saw the agreement in her eyes and continued. "I feel better now, knowing that I will not leave you without some help.

"Fawn, you have more wits than Knife; her evil craftiness smothers what little she has. Use yours well. The Bear King has already given you good judgment; wisdom he will add to it.

"Yet I must give you some last advice. The world was never a sure place, but it is getting worse and worse. Fawn, more often than not, the world will be opposite than it seems. I was not always without the Blight; and Blight or no Blight, I can still read omens.

There will be one, kin of a friend
Who cannot be trusted.
He knows no evil, yet at his end
Only will the earth be bested.

"Remember that, Fawn. I saw it written in the earth and in the rain many days ago. And promise me one thing."

Fawn would not try to hold back. "Anything, sire."

"Sire is not for me," rasped Blood. "It is for the righteous kings of old. But no matter. Promise me that you'll do everything in your power to defeat Knife and Fang and Hemlock, and all the rest. Yet hold sympathy for Ice; use your wits on how much you use, however."

Fawn nodded earnestly. "I will, I promise. But, well, I mean …"

"What is it, child?"

Cutthroat, the oldest healer, bustled into the room. Oracle Blood raised a paw.

"Go then, child. Remember what I said, Fawn."

Fawn returned to her room, her head bent; earnest that no one should see her tears. Tears were not the way of an Oracle's apprentice and especially not a warrior. For that matter, any Darkwoods fox abstained from tears.

Once in her room, she sank down onto her small bed and stared at her reflection in the mirror. In the light of the many candles and lamps, her coat reflected her name. And complementing the fawn color, her eyes no longer glowed pink with savagery but shone a beautiful medium brown.

Fawn began to feel tired. She did not want to stop looking at her soft eyes, so free from the Blight, but sleep overtook her.

Fawn expected to see the dream of the mist—she could remember it now. But none appeared. Instead … water. And it tasted strange. Kind of sweet. But how could she even taste it? Her mouth was closed! Nothing made sense.

Then the dream changed. The Bear King stood before Fawn, his own brown eyes burning with love. When he spoke, his voice was deep and calming, like a soft summer sea.

"Fawn, you are now my follower. Once you were dead to the Blight, but you are alive now. Once you were the Serpent's slave, but now you are my slave; you belong to me. Do not misunderstand me. You are not your own; you were bought at a price."

Fawn could hardly believe it, but she spoke to him. "I still have the Blight."

"If you did, you would not have the dreams you have been having."

"What do you want me to do?"

"I will ask no great slaughter; no major service, no killing for my sake. I ask that you worship me only, do not take my name or me for granted or use my name for witchcraft. I ask that you treat your fellow beings as you would treat yourself."

"Basically, be what the other foxes are not."

"Very good, child. Be an example. But if you are attacked, yes, by all means, defend yourself, your friends, and your family. Defend what you will defend, but do not start war for no reason. And do not be afraid to run when you are attacked for my sake."

"When?"

"Yes, child, when, for it will happen, and you must be ready."

"I will do my best."

The dream dissolved. Fawn felt tears of happiness coursing down her face. She knew that sometime in the future she would have to be brave; but right now, she let herself rest in the calm of the moment.

Her peace did not last long. Shouts came up to her from the lower levels. She immediately began to feel tense. Something was not right.

"Blood!"

"He's dead!"

"Someone, get Fawn!"

"Blood is dead!"

"Find Oracle Hemlock!"

Fawn had just enough time to pull on a veil when her door ripped open. Cutthroat and Claw, one of the soldier's from Knife's clan, came hurrying in.

"Fawn, come quickly. Blood is dead!"

Fawn could hardly retain her patience. Claw had a flair for pointing out the obvious. "Yes, Claw, I heard. Why do you think I am wearing a veil?" How could she have *not* heard?

"Well, you should come to pay your respects to him. Also," he continued, "Oracle Hemlock called a meeting to take place in one hour to lament Blood as well as formally welcome you."

Fawn dismissed him with a wave of her paw. She was just about to close the door when she heard a voice whispering her name. She stood at the doorway. No one was in the passage.

"Who's there?" she challenged.

Zuryzel materialized from the shadows, disguised as a fox. She held up a shrouded paw to tell Fawn that she would answer questions later. "Please let me in, Fawn," she begged. "I'm not a fox. Please let me in."

Fawn beckoned her into her room. She lowered the curtain that served as her door and then led Zuryzel to sit in a sheltered chair. Anyone looking in from the doorway would not see the chair.

Zuryzel threw off her hood to show that she was a Wraith Mouse. "My name is Zuryzel. I'm the daughter of King Hokadra and Queen Demeda. They sent me here."

"What for?" Fawn took off her veil and handed Zuryzel a drink. Her eyes were glowing soft brown.

Zuryzel had taken an immediate liking to Fawn. She did not hold back the message for a moment. "I am to tell you that if you have need of it, you are very welcome in the Bow Tribe camp—that's where we are sheltering. I also offer you my assistance in any way possible if you want to leave now or need help."

"Thank you, friend Zuryzel. I certainly could do with the help. But first, follow me."

Fawn pushed hard on the wall opposite her bed. It groaned slightly, and then swung inward to reveal a hidden room. Fawn took one of her lanterns and beckoned for Zuryzel to follow her. Both creatures hurried into the room, and Fawn closed the door. She hung up the lantern, opened the air vent, and started a fire in the fireplace.

Zuryzel sat down on a bench at a table, and Fawn joined her.

"Now, Fawn, tell me everything you know," she said quietly.

"I just know that this spy, whoever he is, knows the secrets about Mirquis and Dombre. I know that they won't be attacked for about a cycle. Although, if I get found out, the foxes will definitely change their mind and attack as soon as possible. Also, they somehow got reinforcements. I don't know who—"

The rest of Fawn's words were drowned out by a loud screech. Both creatures hurried to the air vent to look out.

A huge bird, roughly twice the size of the room they were in, was flying around the towers and terraces of the castle. It had solid black feathers and the blood red eyes of the Blight.

"Warhawk," Zuryzel murmured. For indeed it was, the fearsome, powerful, evil bird that was the terror of all who ventured to sail the Saltwater Lake.

Wheeling and plummeting, the Warhawk soared down to a large courtyard that was raised off the ground. It spread its wings, and then spoke in a voice that was harsher than a fox.

"I am Chiraage, she-leader of the Warhawks. I will fight with you, Oracle Hemlock, and my birds will obey your commands during the war. You have my solemn oath, so long as you help me remove the Wraith Mice from the earth."

With that, the huge bird took off. With her ascent, her wing feathers brushed the air vent where Fawn and Zuryzel had been watching. Fawn was trembling, but Zuryzel felt only wave after wave of anger.

A loud, harsh bell sounded. Fawn roused herself. "Come on. Oracle Hemlock is summoning all the other Oracles. I would rather not go, but I have to."

"I'll come with you, Fawn."

Fawn doused the fire and lantern. "Ready?" she asked Zuryzel.

Zuryzel nodded. She followed Fawn to the door, stopping as Fawn stopped.

"Here," murmured the vixen. "I'm not leaving unarmed."

From behind a tapestry, the vixen drew a shortspear, a difficult-to-use weapon that was both throwing spear and stabbing spear at the same time. She hefted it.

"Like it, Zuryzel?" she smiled. "Oracle Blood made it for me. He may have been evil, but his paw was very skilled. Well, let's go."

Zuryzel followed Fawn into the main room, past the curtain, and down the passageway, concentrating fiercely on blending in with the night. Fawn in her light blue tunic and black veil was easy to follow, but no one would easily see Zuryzel. Indeed, Zuryzel was at the point where no one but a Wraith Mouse would feel her. That was part of the magic in her blood. She was practically part of the air now, like a wraith, a mere apparition.

Fawn hurried down to the courtyard where Chiraage had perched, Zuryzel right behind. Oracles Hemlock and Fang were waiting for her.

"Ah, good, Fawn," commented Fang. "You, at least, show up on time, something that Blood never managed to do. You are already doing better than he did."

"Indeed you are, Fawn," Hemlock agreed. "And the first thing you will need is a new name."

Knife and Ice entered just as Fawn replied, "Why do I need a new name? I like mine just as it is."

"Well," Knife pointed out, "a fawn is soft and defenseless."

"But it grows into a powerful stag or doe, neither of which is defenseless," Fawn protested lightly but beginning to feel defenseless herself. Ice had not said anything, and that was rather unusual. Glancing at Ice, she saw that Ice's eyes had glazed over. Fawn shuddered. Ice was speaking to the Serpent. Now she would be revealed for sure.

Fawn wasn't wrong. Ice's eyes cleared of the glaze, and she pointed an accusing paw at Fawn.

"Why do you wear the veil, Fawn?"

Fawn was finding it very difficult to control her nerves. She was just about to give up and run for it when she felt strength coursing through her. In a flash she remembered that the Bear King was with her. She met Ice's eyes through her veil.

"Oracle Blood has just died. It would be disrespectful to show my eyes so soon after he has died."

Ice seemed convinced, but Knife just laughed harshly. "You never respected or honored Blood. Well, maybe you did once but not of late. Take that veil off." Swiftly, her paws shot out and shredded the Fawn's veil.

Every single creature there saw her eyes.

Rage coursed through Knife. "Traitor! *Traitor!*" she shrieked and flung herself at Fawn. Her claws ripped into Fawn's fur, slicing her skin. Fawn ducked away from Knife, but Knife was fast and lowered herself down so she was even with Fawn. Her claws scored another row of wounds not far from Fawn's throat. Her other paw ripped near Fawn's eyes and across her ear. Her first paw clawed again, this time at Fawn's paws.

Zuryzel took in the scene. All the light in the courtyard came from candles on a cloth covering a single shelf. Clouds covered the moon and the stars. With a swift motion, she sprang from her hiding place and jerked on the cloth. Every last candle fell off the shelf, and the whole courtyard became like one solid black block to the foxes.

But not to Zuryzel. She could see perfectly in the solid darkness. After all, she was part of the night. She saw the outline of Knife, still crouched over Fawn. Zuryzel shoved her whole weight into Knife, sending the Oracle completely off balance. She then grabbed Fawn's paw and raced out of the courtyard with Fawn in tow.

The two creatures raced along a passageway, out the main gate, and into the woods. Once in the darkness of the forest, both creatures stopped to catch their breath. Fawn's face tightened with pain with each breath she drew.

"Knife was named … Knife … because of her claws," she gasped. "Small wonder … They are … as sharp … as a knife."

Fawn and Zuryzel worked their way along through the woods, going rather slowly as Fawn's foot paws and legs pained her and continued to bleed. Zuryzel wished that she knew a remedy to stop bleeding, but she knew none and had to resort to tearing up the fox's cloak that she had brought along and fold it a little and bind it to Fawn's wounds. That slowed the bleeding pretty well, but it didn't stop it, especially as they kept moving.

They weren't too far from the border when sounds of pursuit reached their ears. Crouching down a little, she could just make out about five foxes racing through the trees.

Zuryzel knew that she could fight five foxes, but not here. She couldn't fight them, win, and keep Fawn safe. Swiftly putting Fawn's paw around her shoulder, Zuryzel picked up her pace. Fawn matched Zuryzel step for step, grimacing at the pain. The two creatures broke out onto open moorland

and began making their way through the grasses. But when Fawn stepped in a rabbit hole, she fell flat upon the ground and had not the strength to get up or go on. She merely sat and waited …

The five foxes raced out of the woodlands. Immediately, they spotted Zuryzel with Fawn sitting at her feet and charged for the Wraith Mouse, all of them shouting.

Zuryzel let them come. When they were a few pawsteps away, she drew her sword, and soon the singing of steel upon steel sounded out. The foxes paused for a moment and then carried on charging. Zuryzel didn't charge at them; instead, she stood her ground, shielding Fawn.

The lead fox was just about to attack her when a throwing knife seemed to grow out of his neck. A similar thing happened to the one right behind him. Zuryzel's beautiful sword took care of the rest.

Glancing around, she saw the river otters Danaray and Anamay racing down the slope. Both of them dipped their heads politely and introduced themselves. Zuryzel greeted them formally, and thanked them for slaying the first two foxes. Danaray spoke for them both.

"It was a pleasure, Zuryzel. The foxes are our enemy as well. Just say the word, and we, as well as our crew, will be happy to help fight them."

"Thank you, but, unfortunately, that is not my decision to make. However, I will tell King Hokadra of your offer. By the way, I don't suppose you've seen a black female archer mouse named Herttua Crow Blue Arrows at the head of about two score?"

"No, but we've been looking for her. We came back south this way to see if we could pick up the foxes' trail, hoping it would show they'd gone back to their own territory, but no such luck."

"What foxes?"

"A small party of foxes was ordered to detach from the main body and head southeast to the small settlement of Graystone," Fawn explained, having caught her breath. "I think they should be about at the Keron River by now."

Both river otters' eyes lit up with delight. "That makes it much easier," Anamay commented. "We should be able to get on their trail right away. That is," she added, "if you don't need our help."

Fawn shook her head. "I'll be all right."

"We're not going very far," Zuryzel added. "But why are you searching for Herttua Crow?"

Danaray shrugged. "A fellow chief sent her crew after those foxes, and I got word from her. We were trying to find her to tell her that."

Zuryzel nodded. "Very well. I'll tell Lady Raven this too."

Both river otters nodded in return. Danaray beckoned to Anamay with a swish of her tail, and they set off south towards the Keron River.

"Farewell!" she called over her shoulder.

Zuryzel got Fawn to her paws. "Come on. We don't want to run into any more patrols. Let's go."

For several hours, the mouse and the fox staggered across the moor. Nearly a whole day had passed when they came into hailing distance of the trees.

"Zuryzel! Zuryzel!" the shout rang out from the trees. Kiarna and Asherad bounded forward onto the moor, words pouring from their mouths.

"Zuryzel, what happened?"

"What did you see?"

"Is this Fawn?"

"Why are you back so early?"

Zuryzel held up a paw to tell them to be quiet. "I'll explain later. Fawn, these are my friends, Kiarna and Asherad. Here, you two, help me get her to the camp."

Without a word, Kiarna took Fawn's paw. Fawn leaned on her and struggled through the woods, over roots, under branches. Zuryzel walked behind, supporting Fawn. Asherad whispered his questions to her.

"What happened to her?"

"She was clawed by another fox."

"How did you ever get her out of that place if they knew that she was no longer possessed by the Blight?"

"Made a mad dash for it. That was about all I could do."

"You didn't get hurt?"

Zuryzel glanced at Asherad's blue eyes. They expressed a concern for her that she had never seen before. "No," she replied. "No, I didn't get hurt.

Asherad glanced at her, and their eyes met. For a moment, Zuryzel felt as if she would drown in Asherad's blue gaze, and the skin under her fur began tingling with a feeling she had never felt before.

Zuryzel was jerked back to her senses when Fawn stumbled. Zuryzel moved up to her side, catching the fox before she fell. But part of her mind still held onto Asherad's gaze.

Shinar coming out of the camp was the first to see them approaching. She gave a cry of surprise, and instantly, a young soldier called Elvinene from Kiarna and Asherad's escort hurried over to join her, followed by Johajar. Sharmmuh leapt down from the tree she had been sitting in and swiftly snatched Fawn's paws. "Great Cerecinthia," she murmured sympathetically. "Here, come."

She led Fawn to a log, which she sat her down on. Passing her a bowl of water, Sharmmuh bade her drink. Fawn drank a little before lowering it. Sharmmuh whispered urgently to a young squirrel. He bounded off and came back with Marruh, the healer. Marruh gave no reaction to the injuries Fawn had sustained. Instead, she just sat down and began examining the wounds before she questioned Fawn about how she had come by them. Marruh pulled out a few herbs and ordered Fawn to suck on them. Fawn hesitatingly obeyed. Then Marruh set about fixing Fawn's injuries. First she pulled off the makeshift bandages Zuryzel had made. Then she carefully selected a few leaves that Zuryzel didn't recognize. These she wet in a bowl of warm water and crushed them between her paws. She put the poultice onto a wound on Fawn's left fore paw. Then she drew some clean bandages out of her bag and wrapped them around the wound. She repeated this process until she had taken care of every wound.

"There," she commented, satisfied, when she had finished. "You'll be right as rain after a few days and—"she looked pointedly at Sharmmuh, "a bit of sleep."

Sharmmuh nodded, picking up the hint. "Go get sleep now, Fawn. You look exhausted," she urged kindly.

Zuryzel glanced behind Sharmmuh. Raven stood there, looking torn between mistrust and pity. And with her stood Zuryzel's mother.

Fawn didn't argue. She stood up slowly and, leaning on Marruh, staggered off.

Queen Demeda fixed Zuryzel with her gimlet gaze. "Now, Zuryzel," she urged her daughter, "what happened? I need you to tell me every thing."

Zuryzel began. "We didn't find out about the spy. But we did find out who is reinforcing the foxes." Here, she hesitated.

"Go on," murmured Lady Raven.

"You won't like it," she continued. "Warhawks."

9

PASADAGAVRA

Feldspar woke up feeling comfortable—much more than he had for a long time. He was now lying on soft and springy ground under a small willow by a creek that twisted its way through Pasadagavra. Early morning sun glinted off the stream.

Beside him, Ol'ver stirred. He had slept well, once he had fallen asleep. But he hadn't seen Ran'ta yesterday despite spending the whole day with Feldspar touring the fortress part of Pasadagavra. He'd seen not even a whisker of her.

Today, Ol'ver had promised to show Feldspar the city part of the Stone Tribe's home. He said there was nowhere else on earth like it, and he had promised to show him everything that made the squirrels proud of their city-fortress—the Large Fire, the Growing Fields, the Fountains …

Hmm, what is a fountain? Feldspar had wondered.

Ol'ver yawned and blinked. "Well, mate," he said drowsily, "ready to see the city?"

Feldspar nodded, ready to experience the wonders he had only heard about.

Ol'ver heaved himself up. "Right, then," he yawned. "Follow me. Let's go see if we can't find some food. I'm famished!"

They had scarcely vacated the willow branch when they heard someone calling Ol'ver. Turning, they saw a young female squirrel with a wave tattooed on her cheek racing through the lower branches of a maple tree. She somersaulted neatly out of the tree and bounded up to them.

Ol'ver clearly knew her. "Hey, Rimmah! Good to see you again!" he called.

Rimmah dipped her head politely. "I see you made it back. Huh, so did that mouse babe you were out after."

Ol'ver introduced Feldspar. Rimmah greeted him civilly, her voice always cheerful. "Pleasure to meet you, I'm sure. There are a lot of mice here, and I've met most of them, but there is no one here from the south." Her voice was only mildly curious, but still Feldspar felt uncomfortable.

Ol'ver quickly changed the subject. "Hey, Rimmah, I don't suppose there's a chance of getting any food for us? We've been living on berries for some time now."

Rimmah vaulted off and came back carefully carrying a stack of hot almond nutbread topped with honey and crystallized pear slices. "Here, how's this? Oh, by the way, you might want to know, the maples are being sugared today. You know where they are?"

Ol'ver was clearly excited. "You bet I do, Rimmah! Thanks for the tip! You want to come along?"

Rimmah declined the offer. "No thank you. I've got enough to do, supervising some young ones. They'd only get in the way at the sugaring. I'll see you later!"

Ol'ver hurried off through a wide-open gateway—past the chevrons of the fortress into the dome of the city. Feldspar figured that if the enemy ever got past the fortress, these gates would hold them off for a while. Once past the gates, the two mice hurried up a grass-covered slope flanked by stone walls. Up on the slope, they found themselves on the lowest level of the dome that sheltered the city. Bounding up one of many earthen hills, they faced a clear diamond wall. Beyond that, on a terrace, several leafless maples were being sugared, their sap drawn into buckets and then poured into a huge kettle over a huge fire.

The two mice watched the sugaring for a while. Then they went to see the Large Fire. Inside a huge fireplace, the biggest fire Feldspar had ever seen was burning. Ol'ver explained that it was kept burning to provide enough heat that the plants would always grow and Pasadagavra would always have food. The air was continually warm in the city, and the smoke could escape through narrow funnels that were too small to let any cold air in.

Next, they went to the Growing Fields. So many types of crops were growing in Pasadagavra that the fields used up a whole floor. Sunlight streamed through the clear diamond walls, adding warmth to the heat from the Large Fire, and multiple streams watered the crops. As they surveyed the scene, workers busily harvested a row of strawberries. Feldspar's nose twitched in pleasure as he smelled the fruit mixed with the rich, moist earth.

Next, Ol'ver beckoned Feldspar towards a flight of pink stairs. They rounded a turn in the stairs, and they became white marble instead of pink alabaster. A whitish, fresh light streamed down the staircase. A sound like rain pattering on a lake was issuing from the chamber above. The two mice climbed the last few stairs and met with a sight that took Feldspar's breath away.

A room with diamond ceiling and walls enclosed a huge, white marble dome in the middle. Out of small gold circles on the surface of the dome, water shot many feet high, which pooled down in a large puddle around the dip of the room, making it feel as if the mice were standing on the edge of a basin. The water level was never rising, and Feldspar guessed where all the streams of water had come from.

Ol'ver nudged Feldspar. "There. That's what Jaccah is normally like. She's not usually short tempered and irritated Look."

Feldspar followed his gaze. There indeed was Jaccah, tribeprincess of the Stone Tribe. Her dark eyes were bright and merry, and she was laughing in the strange, squirrel's laugh.

"And," added Ol'ver, pointing, "there're Rhonndan and Rosemary. Look at them, they're wet as fish!"

Sure enough, he was right. The squirrel babe and the fox babe came splashing around the dome, their fur and smocks saturated. Both of them were so concentrated on their game of splashing each other that neither noticed Jaccah sneaking up on them. Wading into the water a little ways, Jaccah splashed both of them soundly. Both babes whirled on her, only to get a face-full of water apiece. When Jaccah stopped splashing them, they were both giggling so hard that they could scarcely breathe. As soon as they recovered, they both soaked Jaccah, tunic, fur, and all. Jaccah immediately fled the puddle, racing over to the diamond walls.

Instantly, her face became serious. She concentrated hard on something coming from the northern moorland. She stared for a moment and then hurried down towards the puddle. She shared a quick conversation with another female squirrel before hurrying out of the fountain room.

Both mice hurried over to see what had caught her attention. They saw tall grass waving and what looked like many creatures, both young and old, making their way laboriously toward Pasadagavra.

"Tribe," Ol'ver murmured. "I'd guess it's the Wind Tribe. They're friends of the Stone Tribe. Come on. We should see this."

Both mice were about to hurry out of the fountain room when the sound of a maiden laughing caught their ears. Ol'ver stopped dead and turned about. Feldspar saw his gaze soften and looked where Ol'ver was looking.

Two mice, one a field mouse, the other a harvest mouse, were talking together. The field mouse said something, and the harvest mouse laughed again. Glancing at Ol'ver, Feldspar guessed that the harvest mouse was Ran'ta.

The harvest mouse caught sight of Feldspar and Ol'ver and gaily called out to Ol'ver. Catching sight of the two over her friend's shoulder, the field mouse showed less enthusiasm. Her face fell slightly, as if she wasn't glad to see Ol'ver back, but then her eyes fell on Feldspar, and the expression on her face turned to curiosity.

The harvest mouse hurried over to greet Ol'ver. The field mouse followed more slowly, resentment burning in her eyes as she glared at Ol'ver. Feldspar stayed behind Ol'ver, where he could not really hear what his friend was saying, but it didn't matter. His brain had suddenly clogged, and all he could concentrate on was the field mouse. Her fur was pale tan and her eyes sparkling dark brown. She wore a yellow tunic but nothing on her paws.

"It's good to see you again, Ran'ta," Ol'ver greeted the harvest mouse cheerfully. He glanced swiftly behind him as if making sure that Feldspar was right behind him. "This is my friend, Feldspar," he added.

Feldspar nodded at Ran'ta. "Pleased to meet you," he greeted her civilly.

"Pleasure's all mine," Ran'ta replied cordially, her whiskers twitching. This time, she glanced over *her* shoulder, as if making sure the field mouse was behind her. And, by this time, she was. "This is my friend Glor'a."

Glor'a nodded, not curtly, but by no means in the friendliest way. Her eyes still were filled with resentment as she glared at Ol'ver.

Ran'ta and Ol'ver began talking, mostly of things Feldspar barely understood. Both he and Glor'a stood politely to one side, although Feldspar could tell that she was getting impatient. Finally, after a while, she tapped Ran'ta's shoulder. "Ran'ta," she murmured politely, "didn't you want to see …" her voice trailed off with a tilt of her head.

"Go on without me. Go ahead. I'll be there soon," Ran'ta promised.

Glor'a heaved a sigh of resignation. She made for the stairs, and then she paused. "Do you want to come with me, Feldspar?" she murmured politely.

"Where?" Feldspar asked.

"The gate. You really should see its opening."

Feldspar hesitated. Then he relented. "All right," he replied, equally quiet. He tapped Ol'ver's shoulder. "I'm going with Glor'a," he murmured. Ol'ver nodded, and then went back into his discussion with Ran'ta.

He descended the stairs with Glor'a. He couldn't help but like the field mouse, even though he'd known her for only a few moments. She made friendly conversation, though she seemed not to talk too much.

"So, Feldspar," she said now, "where did you meet Ol'ver?"

"Foxes' jail," Feldspar replied bitterly.

"If you'll pardon me for asking, how did you get caught?"

"Fox Oracle figured it out. They're really annoying."

"I've heard of them. Do they really wail when they go into a trance?"

"Oh, yes …Where are you from, Glor'a?"

"I'm from a city, over to the west. It's a pretty small place, but it's got a fort to defend itself."

"What's it called?"

"Diray. In the Common Speech, it means small town, or small earth."

"Do you have any family there?"

"Yes. Although my mother disappeared before I ever got to know her, my father and brothers are still there, defending it. I was sent here, because this is supposedly the safest place on earth."

"It certainly looks like it is to me."

"I'll say. Just off the main fountain room, a small terrace has lots of wheat and barley growing, along with some nut trees. It's huge, big enough to feed everyone who's here for at least a month, and it still has food to mature. And on top of all that, they have an emergency storehouse in a cave in the mountain just behind us with an escape tunnel. It's got so much food and water we'll never be starved out."

"Mm, hmm. I'd like to see the foxes break through the walls, as well."

"Oh, indeed. The walls have never been breached, you know."

They continued in this vein for nearly an hour until they reached the main gate. They were just in time to hear a sentry call out from the ledge inside the wall. Apparently one of the arrow shutters was open, for the pair could hear a voice shouting from the outside. Feldspar couldn't help but notice Jaccah, her fur now dry, standing beside an old-looking squirrel.

"Do you come here in peace, Tribeking Darag?" the sentry called out.

"I and my tribe come to Pasadagavra in peace," a voice, cracked slightly with age replied. "We are searching for shelter."

"Then come in and welcome," the old squirrel standing by Jaccah answered.

Jaccah shouted this time, her voice rising commandingly toward the ceiling. "Open the gate!"

The great diamond-backed oak gates creaked open. Unbelievably huge, they required squirrels at the top to shove them open along a track.

As soon as the gates had opened wide enough, the tribe marched in. Tattooed on their cheeks was a three-pronged swirl. Feldspar thought he could guess who they were.

"Wind Tribe," Glor'a confirmed. "They come from the moors to the north. They share the moors with the Moor Tribe."

The old squirrel strode forward to meet the slightly younger squirrel leading the Wind Tribe. They spoke some greetings that Feldspar didn't really hear.

Jaccah shouted up to the gate-squirrels. With a loud groan, the gates swung closed. Glor'a beckoned for Feldspar to follow her. "The place is going to be chaotic for a while. We might as well go somewhere else and not be in the way."

"But Ol'ver and Ran'ta won't know where we are," Feldspar protested. "How will they find us?"

Glor'a didn't seem concerned. "They'll find us sooner or later. They always say that they'll be right there, but they never are. Every time Ran'ta sees Ol'ver, she completely forgets what she's doing. She'll tell me to hurry along and she'll be right behind, but she never is." Here, Glor'a heaved a sigh of resignation before continuing. "She'll always find me sometime later by the lake. Have you seen the lake yet?"

"No," Feldspar replied. "I've only seen the garrison and the city. Not really anything else."

"Well, then," Glor'a smiled, "I take it that you haven't seen the Spider Streams or the fishing hole or the Stream Source or the Little Village, the armory, the herb fields, the Harvest Woods, the River Gardens, or the carpenter's shop?"

"No," Feldspar again replied. "I didn't think any place could be so big, either."

"No, neither did I until I saw this," Glor'a agreed, still smiling. "Follow me."

She paced off towards the place where the willows grew. "I've been here," Feldspar said swiftly.

Glor'a nodded. "I know. This is the Willow Brook. It flows into the lake."

She followed the Willow Brook into another chamber. Sunlight streamed into this one, and a few bees buzzed in the air, making it very pleasant. It had a huge jungle gym on which young mice, squirrels, and even a few river otters were running, jumping, climbing, hiding, searching, and sliding all over. "This," Glor'a smiled, "is the Little Village. It's a playground for young ones, a place where parents can easily keep track of their whereabouts and not worry about dangers. Look there," she added, indicating a rock slab with a sheer face and spurs jutting out from it. "I can climb to the top of that. I'll show you some time, if you like."

They wandered on. Glor'a paused at the door to a small room. "The armory here looks small from the outside, but it's really huge. Come in and see." She opened the oak door.

Inside, it was dark but not unpleasant. A long shelf ran the long wall with what looked like arrows lying in bundles on it. A few simple bows hung on the wall just above these. On the opposite wall, double-ended spears, favored by the Stone Tribe, were hanging, all with strange carvings on them. Feldspar identified other equipment, like armor and knives, but he couldn't put a name to some of the strange contraptions hanging on the wall.

After the armory, the two mice followed a small granite pathway until the walls on either side of them widened. Sunlight streamed through the diamond ceiling, and large shutters were opened, letting the midday's warm fresh air flow through. Above, beautiful birds fluttered and sang about in the treetops and bushes. Below, streams and waterways of all sizes gurgled about, watering the flowers of exotic types that grew everywhere. Indeed, in one of the warmer sections of the room, Feldspar was sure he saw an orchid. Lots of the little brooks were filled with black, smooth pebbles that looked for the entire world like little spiders.

Glor'a was smiling. "This is the River Gardens. The little streams with the black pebbles are the Spider Streams. The windows here are thrown open each day for a few minutes in the winter. In the summer, they stay wide open for hours at a time. Look, they're closing the windows now."

Wandering on, they came to a part of the gardens where some workers were pruning off large branches. A few carried axes and saws for cutting larger parts of the trees. Glor'a was still smiling as she listened to the worker's songs. "These are the Harvest Woods. They supply all the fuel needed to keep the Large Fire burning, as well as the carpenter's fire."

Feldspar saw the workers cutting rowan, beech, birch, and pine, and even apple and cherry trees. When he asked Glora why they didn't save the fruit trees for harvesting, she replied, "They have orchards elsewhere, and these trees are mostly too old to have fruit."

He also noticed great oak trees, greater than any he had seen before. "Why aren't they taking any oak wood?" he asked Glor'a.

Glor'a willingly explained. "The squirrels consider the oak tree special. They use oak only for building and repairing, never for burning. King Fuddum's chamber is in a huge oak, one so big they think that it was planted as a seedling when Pasadagavra was built."

"Wow," Feldspar whispered.

The two mice continued wandering. Before too long, they came to a small pond where squirrels and a few mice sat around with fishing poles. As they watched, a squirrel's line gave a jerk. Pulling and reeling skillfully, the squirrel landed his catch, a beautiful, pink-skinned fish. Feldspar had never seen such a one before. "Do you know what kind of fish that is?" he asked Glor'a.

Glor'a licked her lips longingly. "Salmon. It's really good if you bake it with thyme, lemon juice, and a few onions. Eat that with a bit of corn dripping with butter and a cup of cold mint tea or raspberry cider, and you have a meal fit for the Bear King!"

Feldspar grinned. He knew by now that Glor'a was not given to exaggeration.

Wandering on, the two mice came to large rocks, out of which gushed water that flowed into many streams. Oak bridges crossed over these waterways, making for a very peaceful and refreshing pathway. Glor'a tapped the largest rock.

"This is the Stream Source," she explained. "Most of the water this side of the city gates comes from this rock."

They continued their pleasant meandering and eventually passed a row of oak doors. Glor'a paused outside one of them. Murmuring a quick "Wait here a bit," she hastened off and returned with a heaping pawful of the small nuts. "The carpenter loves these nuts. I know a special tree, somewhat hidden, that has these even now in the winter. He'll trade you one of his figurines for a few of them, since they're hard to get this time of year. Come on."

She shoved on the door they were standing by, and as the door opened, a bell rang. Feldspar followed her in, curious to see what the shop looked like.

Similar in size to the armory, it had more light pouring in, enough to see well by, and a pleasant mixture of the scents of oak, ash, pine, maple, and many other wood shavings. An old squirrel was sitting at a table and looked up at the sound of the bell ringing. His face lit up with pleasure at the sight of Glor'a.

"Well, Glor'a, my friend, come in. Who have you brought with you?"

Glor'a smiled charmingly as she introduced Feldspar. The carpenter, Onair, seated them both on maple stools. He had a friendly face, a cheerful smile, and a pleasant tone of voice.

The carpenter's shop was just as pleasant. Shelves of figurines lined one wall, and hooks holding carved signs hung from another. From wooden rafters hung stools and benches, tables and chairs. At a third wall sat the carpenter's worktable and workbench. On the farthest wall hung tools used to make toys, like baby rattles.

The carpenter conversed with the two mice as he went back to his work. "So, what brings you two here on this sunny day?"

Glor'a replied for them both. "I'm showing Feldspar around. He just got here."

Onair looked up. "Where do you come from, Feldspar?"

Feldspar replied readily enough. "I come from the south, from a plot of land near the city of Graystone on the Bakkarra River."

Onair smiled knowingly. Rummaging through a box, he pulled out a beech wood figure. "Does it look anything like this?"

Feldspar could scarcely keep his mouth from falling open with shock. "Yes! Graystone looks just like that. How did you know what it looks like?" After all, Feldspar had never even heard of Pasadagavra before he had been thrown in the foxes' prison.

Onair continued smiling. "My friend, Streamcourse the river otter crew leader, brought me back a picture of Graystone from when she went there several cycles ago. I used it and carved this. Here, you keep it. Consider it a welcoming gift," he added when he saw Glor'a reaching for some hazelnuts.

Glor'a took out a few hazelnuts anyway. "How many hazelnuts would you like for that hummingbird?" she queried.

"Four, I think," replied Onair. He wrapped both figures up in soft cloths and passed them to the mice.

When they had taken leave of Onair, they wandered the street, stopping to look at a few shops containing clothing and tools and one store with many carefully whittled flutes.

Without warning, the walls opened up again into a room with diamond walls and ceiling. Sunlight streamed down into the huge chamber and sparkled on a lake that lay in the very center with brooks and streams bubbling down into it Great fields of herbal plants surrounded the lake. Feldspar breathed in the air, savoring the scent of thyme, basil, rosemary, sage, lavender, and many others that reached his nose. A few bees buzzed in the air, sparrows and chickadees called to one another, and kingfishers hummed and fished over the lake.

"How beautiful!" he breathed to Glor'a.

Glor'a nodded. "One of the largest rooms of Pasadagavra. The herb fields and the lake. You know, I think they have five different types of thyme around here."

"Five different types. Exotic, aren't they?"

"Mm, hmm. I like the smell of lemon thyme best. What about you?"

"The heather. My mother used to grow heather. I don't know why, but she always used it when she cleaned. She thought that the heather made you stay healthier."

"I never got to know my mother," Glor'a sighed wistfully. "My father took another wife when mother disappeared. She's okay, I guess, but she's very *patronizing*. Bit annoying, actually.

Both mice heard a shout from the lakeshore. Turning, they saw several squirrel babes, two mouse babes, and a young female otter racing after a moorland bunny. The little creature hopped and skipped from tussock to tussock, the babes racing after it.

Feldspar and Glor'a laughed so hard that tears rolled down their cheeks. It was the funniest thing Feldspar had seen for a while and the hardest he had laughed for an even longer while. For just a few moments, he felt as if all his grief and cares and sorrows had vanished, as if they had never happened.

"Come on, now," called one of the squirrel mothers when the rabbit had disappeared. "Time for dinner."

"You know, Shjeddah has a point," Glor'a commented. "I'm pretty hungry. Let's go find some food."

"Good idea," Feldspar agreed. The two mice wandered along the lakeshore to the other side where a few stands displayed various enticing foods, all with a low price. The two picked out some cheese studded with hazelnuts, a flask of raspberry and lemon cordial, a loaf of warm barley bread, and a few slices of dried dace, and Glor'a left some coins. Carrying their food, they selected a spot to eat, not too far from the entrance to the gardens. It didn't take long for the cheese and bread to disappear. Sipping the cordial and slowly chewing the dried fish, they watched the sun sink below the horizon, spreading its last rays of red to mix with blue and purple. Before too terribly long, the light died, and the stars and moon showed their faces. Comets blazed across the sky in temporary streaks of unearthly glory. The brooks seemed to sing a song, which the stars, reflecting on the lake, seemed to dance to, shimmering and swelling.

After a while, Glor'a stood up and brushed herself off, saying, "I'm pretty tired. I think I'll go to bed. See that brook over there?" She indicated a stream with a willow twig floating in it. "That's the Willow Brook. Follow it back and you'll probably see Ol'ver looking for you. The fountain has been turned off by now, so Ol'ver and Ran'ta will realize they've been up there for a very long time, nearly four hours. You see, you can't tell time by the light in that room. When darkness comes outside, they light the fountain room. Well, see you later." She strode off into the gathering night.

Feldspar stayed where he was for a while. He felt no resentment whatsoever towards Ol'ver for taking the whole afternoon with Ran'ta. Instead, he felt a sense of calming peace falling over him.

When Ol'ver finally got back from the fountain room, his face was the picture of guilt. "I'm sorry," he apologized. "I didn't realize I had been up there so long. I didn't mean to stay there, really. I'm sorry. I just lost track of the time. And I kind of *had* to talk to her, if you know what I mean. I'm sorry."

"Don't be," Feldspar urged. "You haven't seen her for a long time. I've had you all to myself for a long time. Anyway, it's not that I didn't enjoy myself. You never told me about the herb fields and the lake!"

Ol'ver grinned painfully. "I wanted to show them to you before you'd heard about them. That's what Rhonndan did to us."

"Us?"

"Ran'ta and me," Ol'ver explained. "He and Rosemary showed us around when we first got here with the rest of our village." He sighed a little. "I'm tired," he stated at last. He slipped under the branches of the willow.

Feldspar didn't follow him right away. He couldn't help but think that Ol'ver *had* meant to leave him alone with Glor'a. After all, he had heard Ol'ver saying to himself that he thought Feldspar might like Glor'a.

10

THE ATTACK

Zuryzel and Sibyna had grown to like Fawn. Now that the Blight no longer possessed her, she showed genuine consideration for others and a quiet grace. She also had a very optimistic attitude.

Which was more than could be said about Lady Raven. Zuryzel was rather puzzled about the way that Lady Raven was worrying more and more about what was going to happen to Fawn. Fawn wouldn't be fit to go into battle for at least another cycle, and they couldn't afford to have her here if she couldn't defend herself. All the squirrel babes and the younger ones' mothers had been sent to Pasadagavra. But would that work so well for Fawn?

Tribequeen Sharmmuh had thought it would. "Why don't we take her to Pasadagavra?" Sharmmuh had naïvely suggested as they discussed Fawn, but Queen Demeda was worried.

"The thing is," Queen Demeda had pointed out, "Fawn is probably in more danger than the rest of us. Zuryzel heard Knife—she called Fawn a traitor. If the foxes do break into Pasadagavra—it's not exactly likely, but if they *do*—then Fawn will probably be clawed to death, and it would go much worse for all of us because we had her with us. She should go some-place where the foxes aren't likely to go."

It was Lady Raven who had come up with the solution. "There are foxes down south of here, aren't there?" she had asked. "Without the Blight, yes?"

Queen Demeda nodded. "Yes. Down by Graystone."

"Supposing," Raven suggested, "you sent Fawn down to make contact with some of them. It would be helpful for us to have a connection with them. You told me yourself there was some renegade from there who has joined Darkwoods." She stood and began pacing.

Zuryzel and Johajar silently shifted behind the bush they were listening from. Mokimshim had been invited to this meeting, but Zuryzel and Johajar hadn't. But no one ever said they couldn't listen in.

Lady Raven continued. "If Fawn could convince them to fight for us, it would be a plus. On the other paw, if she is a spy, there's not a whole lot of damage she can do." She turned to look right at the bush where Zuryzel and Johajar were hiding. They ducked, but Zuryzel figured they weren't fast enough.

"She could convince the other foxes to fight for Darkwoods," Mokimshim warned.

"They'd have done so before now if there's some renegade that joined them," Lady Raven pointed out. "They'd know about the other foxes, at any rate, and it's still better than sending her to Pasadagavra."

Hokadra agreed. "That makes sense to me. Raven, could you tell her, please?"

"I'm sure Zuryzel and Johajar could do that," Raven suggested, a little smirk on her face. "Fawn trusts them more than she trusts me."

Mokimshim muttered something that sounded like, "Not without reason," but Raven ignored it.

Hokadra continued. "Mokimshim, go scout out the paths between Mirquis and here. If you meet with any rogues or foxes, even a lone scout that you slay, I want to know about it. When you get to Mirquis, tell Lurena to scout out the paths between Mirquis and Dombre. Stay at Mirquis until she has reported back to you. Tell her also to send someone to scout out the paths from Dombre to Pasadagavra and report back to her, and that she is to report back to you; then you report back to me."

Mokimshim nodded before racing out of the camp in the direction of Mirquis.

Sharmmuh dismissed the meeting. Only Raven didn't move. She kept looking at the bush where the twins were.

"Good spot to listen," she teased. "But you shouldn't make so much noise when you duck."

Both of them stood up. Caught!

Raven smiled at them. "You could have simply asked to attend!"

"We figured we'd hear more this way," Johajar confessed.

Raven tipped her head thoughtfully to one side. "You probably did," she agreed, still smiling. She turned. "I'd go tell Fawn if I were you!" she added over her shoulder as she glided toward one of the sentries.

Zuryzel and Johajar exchanged relieved looks, pleased not to get into any trouble. Then they started toward the glade where Fawn was staying, although "being kept" better described it in Zuryzel's mind. Fawn had no visible guard, but she also didn't have complete freedom; she had to stay there.

The twins were nearly at the glade when it happened—a shout from a lookout tree. Next second, they heard the sound of many creatures charging through the underbrush. Both Zuryzel and Johajar spun around and raced over to the camp entrance, along with the entire army.

Stopped just outside the entrance to the squirrel's camp stood Knife the Oracle. Armed with a terrifying-looking battle-axe, she brandished it about, her teeth bared, and then spoke in a deadly low voice.

"Squirrel, you have a traitor fox sheltering within your home. You will give her over to me to be dealt with."

Sharmmuh bared her own teeth and did not back down from the line of snarling foxes behind Knife. "I am Tribequeen Sharmmuh. You do not order me around, fox! You are guilty of too much blood for that. You nearly mortally wounded Fawn and later attacked Zuryzel. Your eyes are still red, and I do not deal with the Serpent. Four hundred of my archers are positioned in trees, ready to shoot you or any Warhawks you send at us."

Zuryzel felt pride thrilling through her veins. She could sense Knife's surprise that Sharmmuh knew about Warhawks.

Suddenly, Zuryzel noticed Kiarna signaling to Asherad. Quiet as could be, those two gathered up the Miamuran patrol and slipped with them silently out of the camp the back way. Zuryzel focused her attention on Knife again.

Hokadra challenged the Oracle. "What right do you have to come marching in and make demands of us all?" he demanded.

Knife didn't rush to defend herself. Instead, she gave Hokadra and Queen Demeda a long look. Finally she spoke. "You are bold, King Hokadra. Why indeed, you and Oracle Hemlock are very similar. We could have peace. We could rule the earth together, the foxes and the Wraith Mice. The Oracles would welcome you. You would have power to share with us. Join us, and let us be friends. You, your kind, and your families would live."

Rage filled Zuryzel. Furious, she shouted out in a great voice, the voice of a leader, of someone born to rule, of a future queen.

"You lie, fox," she shouted, her voice carrying through the trees. "You lie! I heard for myself the words of Chiraage. She said she and her warhawks would fight on your side if you helped them to slay all the Wraith Mice. All liars are found out, fox. You have my solemn promise as a Wraith Mouse princess!"

As Zuryzel spoke, Knife's eyes filled with fear. For a moment, the fox was speechless with terror, but she soon recovered herself. She pointed a condemning paw at Zuryzel. "You have a big mouth, mouse. You are all mouth, however, and no sword. You couldn't even begin to fight a real battle."

She was just about to give the order to attack when a cry rang up from behind the column of foxes. Queen Sharmmuh wasted no time. Drawing back her bowstring with the arrow notched to it, she took aim and fired.

The arrow embedded itself deeply in Knife's shoulder, and Raven rolled her eyes at Sharmmuh's miss. Shrieking in agonized pain, Knife drew her axe and faced her attacker.

Sharmmuh scowled at the fox. "I did not kill you, fox. I only wounded you. Just to teach you what it felt like for Fawn, having to stagger all the way here with your claw wounds too terrible to imagine. Fire!"

From the surrounding trees, a hiss of vicious arrows cut the air. Zuryzel barely had time to marvel that none of the archers missed a mark before she heard her father shouting the order to charge.

She whipped out her sword and flung herself into the fray. Her steel sword was carving a passage of death and destruction, and she felt numerous foxes fall to her sword. She was furious for Fawn. She was furious for Karrum and Biddah, who had been imprisoned. She was angry for the hares, the hedgehogs, and for every other beast that had been killed by the foxes.

Before she knew it, Knife, in desperation, was shouting for the foxes to retreat back to the moor. Zuryzel paused for a moment. Then she heard the sound of the retreating foxes soon followed by the shouts of victory from the squirrels and mice. She heard her father calling out orders to the Wraith Mice in the Northern tongue. But she heard all this only for a little while.

She heard it all until she realized that she had been fighting side by side with Asherad. All sound fell to the background as she turned to him with a triumphant smile but said nothing after seeing him gaze at her with relief. Relief? Had he truly thought the whole army would lose a battle against a small patrol? Or did he have another reason for fear turned around? Dared she think …?

Once again she felt as if she would drown in his gaze.

She gave herself a shake. She had to prove that she was a worthy commander and a worthy daughter of King Hokadra.

"Johajar!" King Hokadra shouted. "Take your command and charge them head on. Zuryzel, take your command and swing around from the south to hit them on the flank. Go!"

Zuryzel waved her sword to summon her command. They all gathered behind her and followed her without question. She slipped quietly along on the moorland, following the direction the foxes had taken, but continually moving more to the south, so she would swing around and attack the foxes from the side and behind. With any luck, Johajar's force should cut them off from making a move toward the woods. The rest of the warriors would back him up, circling the foxes behind them.

Zuryzel swiftly caught sight of the foxes; they looked as if they were in hearing range, but Zuryzel knew better. The almost flat moor gave a deceptive perspective and objects looked closer than they actually were.

"Fan out and circle around behind them," she called quietly to her warriors. They obeyed her command without question. Zuryzel worked her way stealthily forward a few pawsteps to a small mound of earth where she could command a good view of both the foxes and the positions of her own warriors. She gazed around where her warriors were circling. One of them stopped a short way behind the foxes, waiting for the order to attack, her eyes fixed on Zuryzel. Zuryzel motioned for her to keep circling the foxes and to spread out more. Her warriors obeyed willingly.

Gazing around, Zuryzel spotted Johajar and his command sneaking up on the foxes themselves, spreading out. Johajar's gaze met Zuryzel's, and she knew that he was waiting for her signal to attack.

After all, Zuryzel had been born first.

She scanned the grass tussocks the warriors had hidden behind. All waited at the ready. Slithering from the grass mound, she crouched down, waiting also—for her father to arrive with the others.

He didn't keep her long. With a nod at Zuryzel, he ordered the rest of the Wraith Mice, Lady Raven's warriors, and Sharmmuh's archers to surround the foxes.

Zuryzel leapt to her paws and shouted the order to attack at the same time. All her warriors charged, as well as Johajar and his warriors. The foxes looked up in dumb surprise and hastily grabbed their weapons, but it was too late.

Sharmmuh's archers fired into the foxes' ranks, followed by a terrific spear salvo from Raven's warriors. The rest of the warriors charged.

Not a single fox was given the chance to escape—all were slain, all but … Zuryzel scanned the scene and noticed that Knife was missing: she had abandoned her troops to their deaths.

Raven marked the absence of the so-called leader, as well, and her eyes blazed in fury. "Coward!" she exclaimed angrily. "She said that Zuryzel was all mouth, and she won't even stand and fight! *Coward!*"

Queen Demeda's eyes widened in shock at Raven's tirade.

Raven stayed angry all the way back to the camp, nor was she the only one. Zuryzel could scarcely contain her disgust. She had seen for herself the savage fury of the fox and her viciousness when attacking the unarmed Fawn. But she couldn't face real warriors, even with an army around her!

Fawn and Marruh were waiting for the small army to return. Fawn was gnawing worriedly at her lip, and Marruh had her healing bag at the ready.

Zuryzel, Sibyna, and Kiarna flung themselves down on the log that Fawn was sitting on. All three of them were upset that they hadn't managed to get at Knife. Fawn, however, wasn't surprised.

"You see," she explained, "most of the Oracles received training as warriors before they became Oracles. But Knife is a different story. Her parents had to give her up to the Oracles in order to be forgiven by the Serpent for something they did. I never heard the full account; that's all I know. But she never got to be a warrior, and she never learned how to fight. Knife isn't a coward; she was doing the only sensible thing. She probably figured that her best chance was to race back and get reinforcements, with orders for her patrol to retreat into the woods if they were attacked."

Zuryzel sighed. Admittedly that was the sensible thing to do, but how hard could it be to fight with the axe Knife had?

She shrugged and stood to wander off—she wasn't interested in having her minor scratches fussed over by Marruh. She slipped away from the main crowd only to feel a paw on her shoulder. She jumped, surprised, but it was only Johajar.

"Zuryzel, I have to talk to you!" he whispered. "No one else is listening to me, not even father!"

"What?" Zuryzel asked in a low voice.

"Look, I know what you said about Fawn and all that, but what if—just think for a moment—what if everything that happened was a trick? Supposing Fawn is still on their side? Supposing she led them here to destroy us?"

"They didn't have nearly enough soldiers to destroy us," Zuryzel pointed out. "But I don't get what you're worried about. How could Fawn possibly 'lead them here' when she was already here?"

"Suppose they found some way to track her?" Johajar breathed.

"Johajar, no one followed us."

"Except for those five soldiers at the border of the forest!" Johajar was really worked up.

Zuryzel looked around. They were too close to the main body of soldiers. "Come with me," she ordered.

Johajar followed her into the woods. They sat down on a fallen log, and Zuryzel faced her brother again. "You think that they didn't know where the camp was before Fawn came here?"

Johajar hesitated. Finally he whispered, "I don't know. I just don't trust Fawn. You saw her—she was the one who captured Dejuday, remember? She was leading that patrol."

"That doesn't say anything," Zuryzel pointed out. "He'd been captured so many different times before."

"Zuryzel, what if the Oracles watched her through their … arts?"

"What arts?" Zuryzel scoffed. "I saw Ice in her trance when she was supposedly speaking to the Serpent. I also saw her swallow something before. She took some herb or medicine that made her eyes fog over."

"Why would she do that?"

"Who knows?" Zuryzel shrugged. "Bluffing? Trying to show off?"

"But … Knife? How did she know something was wrong?"

"That would've taken common sense to—wait a minute!" Zuryzel stopped. "That doesn't make sense anymore. We know the Oracles are fakes. They don't talk to the Serpent, but … I just realized, Fawn's eyes were still pink. There was no way Knife—or any of them—could have told anything by her eyes. It was too dark, anyway. She could've had white eyes, and they wouldn't have been able to tell there—or anywhere in the dark castle, for that matter. Someone *told* Knife that Fawn was deserting the Blight. Someone who knew."

"And someone told Ice," Johajar added.

"This is either a very, *very* clever ruse, or there really is a spy. This wasn't a lucky break, and this wasn't showing off." Zuryzel began to feel fear pulsing in her ears. "We do have a spy."

"But, wait," Johajar interrupted. "Wouldn't Hemlock have known? Wouldn't the spy have reported to him?"

"Yes, unless …," Zuryzel mused. Suddenly her fogged mind cleared. She snapped her eyes to her brother's face, her mind made up. "But this makes some sense. Knife and Ice aren't on friendly terms. Knife must have her *own* spy. And someone *else* told Ice—she wouldn't have heard it from the other Oracles; she's too new. Hemlock's spy must not be in the commanders; they're the only ones who knew about Fawn. Maybe Hemlock was bluffing when he said his spy knew about the secrets of Mirquis and Dombre. Something is up. They may, at this rate, end up fighting a battle amongst themselves!"

"But who would have spied for Ice?" Johajar asked slowly. "If they were on the side of the foxes, wouldn't they spy for the commander, like Hemlock? Or wouldn't they spy for the cleverest, like Knife?"

"What are you saying?" Zuryzel asked. "You think Ice may be a rebel?"

"Knife and Fang hold that position." Johajar shrugged. "I saw them debating some plans once."

"I remember that," she snapped. "But why can't there be another rebel?"

"No one's luck could be that bad, not even Hemlock's," Johajar snorted. "And our luck cannot possibly be that good."

"I don't dispute that," Zuryzel agreed. "Could Ice be on Knife's side?"

"Would you trust Ice to be your comrade?" Johajar scoffed. "Especially in some secret cabal?"

"I ... guess not." Zuryzel shrugged. "And father wouldn't listen to you?"

"He and mother were arguing."

"What about?"

"Pretty much the same thing I'm talking to you about," Johajar smiled. "Only mother thinks Fawn may have been tracked and still be innocent. Father still thinks she either is the spy or has had a fast change of heart, and he wants her sent away."

"That's funny," Zuryzel groaned.

"I'm serious!" Johajar insisted.

"No, I know," Zuryzel explained. "It's just, Mother's is such a nicer theory, but in any event they would never send Fawn away."

"Why?"

"Can you imagine what Sharmmuh would say," Zuryzel laughed, "if we sent some innocent fox out to fend for herself?"

"Yeah, pretty easily. But even though Father's is a lot more negative, it's much easier to carry out."

"What does Lady Raven say about this?" Zuryzel asked.

Johajar shrugged. "Nothing. I half thought she'd take Father's side because she agreed with him, and I half thought she'd take Mother's side because they're friends, but all she said was something like, 'They didn't intend to destroy us. They wanted something else.' Then she turned on Sharmmuh and demanded why she had attempted to give Knife a moral lesson when she could have killed her. Sharmmuh's defense was something like, 'I know what you think, Raven, but I'm not an idiot.' Raven looked really appalled, and she exclaimed, 'You *missed*! How can you miss? Six more steps and you could have smacked her!'"

"Did she really miss?" Zuryzel shook her head in despair. "*I* could have hit Knife's heart at that distance."

"Then," Johajar continued, "she went on, still muttering about what a coward Knife was. I don't blame her, but Mother was appalled for some reason. I think she was so appalled she forgot the argument."

"Johajar," Zuryzel said quickly, "Lady Raven told me something." With that, she launched into a detailed explanation of the trek to meet Tiyuh, and how she had learned more from Lady Raven than she had from Tiyuh.

"So," Johajar interpreted, "she was called a coward. Father doesn't know, but Mother does."

"Mother must have been remembering how Lady Raven was accused of cowardice," Zuryzel surmised. "And the penalty."

"Lady Raven said it was harsh," Johajar continued, "but did she say what it was?"

"Ah … no." Zuryzel blinked in surprise. "I don't think so."

"Whatever it was," Johajar assumed, "Mother knows what it is, and she couldn't believe that Raven would use that same accusation on anyone. Do you suppose it is the death penalty?"

"I don't see it's important," Zuryzel shrugged.

"You'd know," Johajar agreed.

"Do you really think Fawn is a spy?" Zuryzel asked. "Those wounds are very real."

Johajar shrugged. "I haven't been doing much thinking. Only worrying. That's all I'm good for."

"That's not true!"

"Anyway," Johajar added, "if there already was someone contacting Hemlock and Knife *and* Ice, then they wouldn't need Fawn."

"But who contacted them?" Zuryzel asked.

Neither of the twins could answer.

"But your mind is at rest about Fawn?" asked Zuryzel.

Johajar shook his head. "Not really."

"Johajar," Zuryzel asked, trying to remain patient, "what could the foxes want her for if not a spy?"

Johajar was silent. Zuryzel thought she had won the argument. She stood up and walked a few paces when she heard her twin's voice.

"Sabotage?"

Zuryzel whirled around. "What do we have to sabotage here?" she asked, unable to keep a hint of contempt out of her voice.

"Not here," Johajar corrected. Zuryzel snorted and turned around again. She stopped walking when Johajar spoke again. "Where would we automatically send her? Someone who we had to keep alive because of her information?"

Zuryzel turned around again. "Somewhere safe." Then it hit her. She gasped.

"Pasadagavra!"

11

CHITE

In Pasadagavra, Feldspar woke early the day after the battle with the Darkwoods foxes. But with no knowledge of that event, he was feeling very peaceful. He was still having difficulty believing that there was a war on. The earth was good here in Pasadagavra, and the squirrels were friendly. He was beginning to enjoy the hours that Ol'ver spent alone with Ran'ta because it gave him the opportunity to wander the city alone, making friends with others.

He had even met Rhonndan and Rosemary yesterday. Rosemary had quite charmed him with her cute antics, and he had begun to admire Rhonndan for his friendship with Rosemary, even though he clearly knew that she was a fox. Both babes had dragged him over to see one of the smaller fountains not far from the carpenter's shop. Feldspar had been quite taken by the fountain.

In return, he had taken the two to the carpenter's shop. Both of them had picked out a trinket, Rhonndan a figurine of a maple tree by a pond and Rosemary a locket shaped like a nut. Feldspar had paid for them with the nuts he had collected. Both the babes had shown such good manners. They had politely thanked Feldspar for getting them the trinkets and then nicely said good-bye to him before going off to play with a few lost-looking squirrel babes from the Coast and Wind Tribes.

Feldspar smiled as he remembered it. He could scarcely think that Rosemary was a fox, despite her appearance. She looked, talked, even laughed like a squirrel.

Struggling to his foot paws, Feldspar realized that Ol'ver was still asleep. Feldspar smiled as he pushed his way through the branches of the willow. He was beginning to think that there was a whole lot more to Pasadagavra than what he had already seen.

He decided to follow Willow Brook to the lake. He really liked its shimmering waters and enjoyed listening to the laughing of the brooks that wound their way through the herb fields.

The lake was not really far away. In an hour's time he saw the dark, shining expanse of water and gloried in the beautiful sight before him—the sun not quite risen, the sky dawn gray, and the herbs swaying slightly, their colors darkened slightly.

Feldspar spotted Glor'a. The pretty field mouse was skipping pebbles across the smooth lake. He called out to her, and she greeted him smilingly.

"Good morning, Feldspar. It should be pretty nice today. Look, no red clouds."

Feldspar had to agree with her. The whole sky was gray, showing no sign whatsoever of clouds. The herbs were dancing slightly as early birds swooped here and there, searching for a few flying insects. The red kite that nested in a crook in the wall swooped low, plucking a fish out of the lake.

Glor'a went back to skipping rocks, counting the skips they made. Feldspar sat down and watched her in admiration. One of her rocks skipped eight times before it sank.

The red kite glided noiselessly up to stand in front of Feldspar. "Hello, good day," he greeted Feldspar. "You are new, are you not? What is your name?"

"I'm Feldspar. I just arrived three days ago. What are you called?"

The kite smiled a bird-like smile. "I am called Redstreak. Where do you come from?"

"I'm from the territory near Graystone," Feldspar replied.

Redstreak didn't ask about Graystone. Nor did he say that he had never heard of the place. He just looked into Feldspar's eyes, as if he could see right into his simple soul. "Do you miss your home?" he asked.

Feldspar didn't reply immediately. He hadn't thought much about Graystone. All while he had been traveling north, away from his home, he'd given little thought to the friends he had left behind. In his travels, he had met the river otter Doomspear nearly a whole two cycles ago. Then traveling even farther northward, one of his friends, Mudpaw, had disappeared. Still, he had forced himself to keep going. But now Redstreak's question brought the past into focus. He found that he really did miss his old home, but a part of the pain was gone.

He looked Redstreak in the golden eye. "Yes, I do," he replied softly.

"Do you, by chance, know the river otter Hannah?" Redstreak queried. "Hannah Pinefur?"

"Yes, I do," Feldspar replied, surprised. "She is one of my friends."

"What other friends do you have?"

"Well, there are Hannah, Chite, Swordpoint the warrior's son, Speareye, Opal—she came from up north; her family moved to escape the northern weather—Redfur, Lillia ..." His voice trailed off wistfully as he remembered his old friends.

Redstreak was smirking his birdlike smile. "Hmm," he mused. "I think you are about to get a very big surprise." He glanced over at the juniper bushes a little way around the lake. "Very, very soon."

"What do you mean?" Feldspar asked.

"Follow me and I show you," Redstreak shrugged. He raised his wings a little and flew lazily and low so Feldspar could keep up.

"I have been to Graystone sometimes," Redstreak said as he flew. "It is a marvelous place, but I have never landed there."

They traveled around the lake and Redstreak pointed out the shape of a mouse emerging from one of the juniper bushes. Feldspar blinked. No, it couldn't be ... Was it really? ... No ... *Yes!*

"See," Redstreak smiled, "I told you so." And he took flight.

The mouse looked up. A look of complete shock crossed his face. a look so familiar to Feldspar that he couldn't help but laugh a little.

The mouse set off at a run toward Feldspar, a broad smile twisting his features in two and his voice laughing merrily. When he reached Feldspar, he stopped laughing long enough to greet his friend.

"Feldspar, you old swashbuckler, how are you? Great Cerecinthia, you look well! Been in a lot of fights have you?"

Feldspar laughed along with his old friend. "Swashbuckler yourself, Chite. Or, should I call you Malachite?"

Chite pulled a face. "No, thanks. I still can't stand that name. Hey, how did you get up here?"

Feldspar shrugged. "Long story. How about you? I thought you were staying back at Graystone with Opal."

Chite shifted his foot paws. "Oh, I got sick and tired sitting around waiting for adventure to come to me at Graystone. There was no trouble whatsoever with the fox rogues down there. I decided to come up north and see if I could find you. Huh, I got lucky, didn't I? Opal would have liked to come too, of course. Thing is, though, she's had no trouble with adventure coming to her."

"What do you mean?" Feldspar queried. The Opal he remembered was a powerful warrior but sensible enough not to get into trouble too terribly often. Then a guess hit him. "What, has she been having *admirers*?"

Chite was grinning. "Not that kind of adventure. To begin with, she has something like a title now. She is officially called Opal Sling. Also, she's well on her way—hay-ha-ha-ha-ha." He burst into laughing. "You wouldn't believe it," he cackled, "but she's well on her way to becoming *leader* of Graystone. Ha-ha-ha-ha!"

Feldspar laughed with him. How his childhood friend could possibly become leader of the small settlement was totally beyond him. She must have somehow earned the respect of the others there. But how she had done that, he never could have guessed. Hotheaded, stubborn, and headstrong, she hardly had the best leadership qualities. Although, upon greater reflection, Feldspar admitted she did have a kind, gentle side. And, too, she was fiercely dedicated to her home. But how everyone else could have possibly seen the same thing in the headstrong warrior he could not comprehend.

"When did you get here?" Chite asked, changing the subject.

"Three days ago. When did you get here?"

"About two weeks ago. Have you seen the Fountain Room?"

"Yeah. That was one of the first things I saw. It's huge, isn't it?"

"Oh, yes. You seen the trebuchet?"

"The ... what?"

"I take it that you haven't. It's a weapon. Been over at the eastern side at all?"

"I wouldn't know."

"Well, I'll show you sometime today. It's huge! You wouldn't believe how big it is. If you think the fountain's big, then the trebuchet dwarfs it. I tell you, it's monstrous!"

"So how is everyone back home? Are they all faring well?" Feldspar couldn't restrain himself from asking.

"Oh, Redfur is doing okay. You couldn't imagine how good he is now with a bow and arrow. He hits a moving target almost every time. Lillia has gotten a bit snappish sometimes, but she's still the adorable maiden she always was ..."

"Oh, stop that!" Feldspar exclaimed.

"Okay, okay. Swordpoint was finally allowed to lead his own patrol, and he did a marvelous job. Speareye took Hannah for a mate."

"You're kidding!"

"No, I'm not. They're expecting a babe sometime in spring, I think. Maybe Opal will quit her talk about northern warriors when we get back down south. I mean, she likes it at Graystone. We collected at least four new hives of bees, and honey was flowing in like mad when I left. The river was bursting with trout. The foxes down there caused enough trouble to keep even me busy."

Anguish twisted his heart when he remembered his old friends. Then his gaze rested on Glor'a. For some reason that he didn't know, his pain eased a little. He remembered Glor'a's smiling brown eyes, so simple, so beautiful. He remembered her honest smile. And he thought of her kindness the day after he had arrived and how she had willingly and kindly showed him around. Maybe he should introduce Glor'a to Chite?

Chite began speaking again, jerking Feldspar out of his thoughts. "Do you know where we can find some breakfast? I've spent most of my time over at the east side; I just came over here last night. Do you know your way around?"

An idea struck Feldspar. "No I don't," he answered. "But I know someone who does. Wait here a moment."

He strode over toward where Glor'a was sitting. He had a feeling that she had been listening to him talking with Chite. She stood up as Feldspar approached her and showed him a smile full of gentle teasing.

"Feldspar," she murmured as he approached, "I think you *do* know where to find food. Why are you asking me?"

He matched her smile. "Well, mostly," he replied, his own voice light-hearted and gentle, "because I don't know if there is anywhere near where we can get salmon. You know, the way you described. I'd like to try it."

Glor'a laughed a little. "I know where to find it, but right now they won't have it out. They don't have it out until lunch. In the morning, they serve salmon baked in rosemary, sage, lemon juice, butter, and crushed almonds with sizzled potatoes covered in cheese, and cold goat's milk or cranberry and raspberry tea. Sometimes they even have cornbread with lots of butter. How does that sound?"

Feldspar nodded pleasurably. "That sounds good. Would you please show Chite, my friend, and me where that is?"

Glor'a nodded herself. "Sure."

"Thanks, Glor'a. This is a big favor," Feldspar replied. "But look, could you do me one more favor? When Chite asks how we met, tell him we met at the gates. Tell him that I asked you how to get to the, um, fountain."

Glor'a nodded again but didn't answer. Her eyes were locked with Feldspar's.

Finally, he forced himself to break the spell that seemed to hold his eyes with Glor'a's gaze. He didn't want to have Chite think he might like Glor'a, and he really didn't want to fall in love.

He led Glor'a over to where Chite was waiting and introduced them. Chite's eyes were curious, and he was smilingly pleasant with Glor'a. Feldspar noticed a twinge of resentment deep within himself as Glor'a smiled at Chite, but he pushed it away. After all, Glor'a was just being obliging. Being friendly was one of the things that he would expect Glor'a to do. And why should he care at all if Chite was flattering Glor'a slightly? Why would he care?

Because you care about her, a small voice said in his heart. But Feldspar pushed the thought away. He and Glor'a were friends, and that was all there was to it! He set off at a slow pace, matching his stride for Glor'a and Chite's.

Glor'a led they way around the lake a little until she came to a brook fringed with juniper. She ran lightly across some stepping-stones, her tunic rustling slightly. Then she paced to another brook and followed it off to a pile of rough, seaside rocks. A small opening sat in the middle of them, just over a rock ledge. Glor'a ran nimbly up the rough stairs to the ledge. Both mice followed her.

"Wait here," she whispered once all the mice were on the ledge. "Let me do the bargaining." With that, she disappeared into the cave.

She wasn't long in keeping and soon staggered out with a still-warm package and a flask. She shrugged apologetically at the two mice. "Sorry, they didn't have any goat's milk, though they did have lots of cranberry tea but without the raspberries. Sorry."

Feldspar took the heavy parcel from her, his strong paws holding it easily. "Well, at least they still had the salmon. And is that cornbread I smell?"

Glor'a smiled "Oh, yes. You should try it; it's really good. Some of it is studded with hazelnuts, but give me a slice of that; I should take some to old Onair. He really likes it, you know."

She bade Feldspar and Chite good-bye, taking with her a slice of the cornbread studded with hazelnuts.

Feldspar was sorry to see her go, but he was not downcast. Glor'a had not been kidding when she said that the salmon was good. Rich, moist, and firm, it flaked a little and tasted strongly of the wildness in which it had lived. The cornbread smeared with honey made a wonderfully messy accompaniment to the fish. The oozing honey and the butter soaking into the warm cornbread called for paw-licking finishes to the meal. And the cold and lulling cranberry tea put Feldspar completely at ease and unaware of Ol'ver walking up to him. Indeed, he did not know his friend was there until he hailed him.

"Ahoy, Feldspar, you were up early!"

Feldspar grinned as Ol'ver scurried over to him. "Ahoy, yourself. Hey, get over here. By the way, Ol'ver, this is Chite. Chite, this is Ol'ver, I met him on my way here. Chite is one of my old friends from Graystone."

Ol'ver was clearly hungry. He gazed longingly at the salmon that was left and smiled pitifully. "I don't suppose that there is the tiniest chance of that being for me. I really am hungry."

Feldspar smiled to himself. "Sure, take this. Huh, it's really good. That honey is the sweetest thing I've ever tasted!"

Ol'ver chewed slowly. When he swallowed, he asked, "I guess that you haven't been shown the sugar fields. Now, that I call sweet."

Neither Feldspar nor Chite had any idea as to what sugar was. Both of them knew only about crystallized honey as sweetening. Ol'ver looked astonished.

"You don't know what sugar is? It's wonderful, it's sweet, it's delicious, and it is one of the best things in the world! How *can* you not know about sugar? It makes a price crop!"

Chite sighed. "Well, if you know what it is, and if you know where to find it, show us!"

THE WALK

Zuryzel had not been wounded severely. Or at least, she had not been wounded to the degree that the Wraith Mice called "severe." Marruh, on the other paw, thought differently.

"Great Cerecinthia, hold still Zuryzel!" she exclaimed as Zuryzel squirmed beneath the healer's paw. "Let me get a bandage on this."

Zuryzel was quickly losing her patience. "Marruh," she muttered through clenched teeth, "I don't need a bandage! There are other beasts with worse wounds than I have. Oh let me go! Come on, it's just a few scratches!"

Marruh, though old, could hear perfectly. Nonetheless, she shook her head in a puzzled fashion. "What are you saying, Zuryzel?" she queried. "I am old, you know; you must speak up."

Zuryzel fumed. She knew perfectly well that Marruh was not hard of hearing. "You heard me perfectly! Don't pretend that you can't hear. Look, just let me go. There are others who have worse wounds than mine. For Cerecinthia's sake, it's just a few scratches!"

Marruh finished with Zuryzel. "There you go, princess," she murmured. "But how you could call those 'just scratches' is something I'll never understand."

Zuryzel's temper evaporated. She grinned mischievously at Marruh. "Well, to begin with, they weren't very deep. Also, I guess that being young does help …"

Marruh shooed Zuryzel out of the healing den.

The princess hastened out to the center of the camp where activity still buzzed. A patrol raced out of the camp, and fresh sentries relieved a few of their counterparts on duty. She took a deep breath and smiled for a moment as she smelled the fresh woodland airs. Then her smile disappeared as she spotted Asherad and Kiarna speaking to Sharmmuh and their patrol gathering up their armor. She watched apprehensively as Kiarna spoke to her troops in the Eastern Tongue. Zuryzel didn't hear a word of what she said. Asherad, on the other paw, sat down on a rock that served as a seat. He made eye contact with Zuryzel and nodded to a log opposite his rock.

Zuryzel didn't hesitate. She sat down a little stiffly and gazed into his dark gray face. His eyes were gentle, even regretful.

"We're leaving tomorrow, Zuryzel. I wish we weren't, but we can't stay here if the foxes are attacking. We nearly lost a few in that battle, and we can't afford to lose even one. A band of rogues threatens our kingdom, and there are no warriors in the settlement outside Miamur. We need to protect them—." Zuryzel held up a paw to tell her friend to stop. "I understand," she replied. "You don't need to explain to me."

Zuryzel had a feeling that she saw major relief behind Asherad's eyes. "Zuryzel, I-I would like to take a quick walk with you, you know, for old times' sake," he murmured.

Zuryzel willingly accepted the invitation. "Of course, Asherad. Where shall we go? Anywhere but the river, I hope?"

Asherad rolled his eyes but willingly obliged. The two young friends wandered out of the camp towards the hills that bordered the northern edge of the tribe's territory. Just as they were leaving, they passed Sibyna. Zuryzel thought that she heard the archer mutter under her breath, "For old times' sake, my bowstring!" The comment put Zuryzel on alert, and she became aware of a hostile sense in the air. Nervously, she turned her head a little and saw the source: Dejuday. He glared at Asherad with a look of complete dislike. That bothered Zuryzel. Why should he dislike Asherad? How could *anyone* dislike Asherad?

She shoved these thoughts out of her mind as she faced the open fields of the moor.

They wandered out through the forest until they reached the hills, carpeted with wildflowers of every color. The two young friends enjoyed themselves as they left their cares behind and they listened to the bees humming in the woodlands and birds singing above the trees. It was nothing short of paradise for Zuryzel.

Finally at a grassy knoll carpeted with wild violets and crocuses, the two young warriors sat down. They talked about old memories, savoring the recollections they had kept, some for nearly twelve cycles. Only when Zuryzel looked deeply into Asherad's eyes did she realize that she might never see her friend again.

A wave of longing to be young again, so young that she had no worry about being killed in battle or her friends ever leaving her and possibly never coming back, swept over Zuryzel like a great roller from the sea. She wanted Asherad and Kiarna, and even their older brother Galledor, to be with her in the upcoming war. She wanted to have her childhood friends, as well as her brothers, by her side forever.

But child no longer, Zuryzel was a grown princess of the Wraith Mice, and she had to endure the war alone, like any other Wraith Mouse leader. She wanted more than anything to be a good leader, yes, even more than having her friends by her side. Admittedly, she had almost as much ambition as her brother, Mokimshim. She wanted to be a Wraith Mouse queen, well honored by history for her justice, honesty, and devotion to those she ruled over. And more. She wanted to rule over Arashna, the Wraith Mouse capital, and she wanted to have the respect of all the Wraith Mice and the river otters that sometimes served as soldiers for the army. She wanted to be like her father, King Hokadra. In a word, Zuryzel wanted to be great.

But right now, none of that seemed to matter. All she could dwell on was the fact that she might never see Asherad or Kiarna—her two oldest friends—after tomorrow.

Neither Zuryzel nor Asherad had need of any words now; both of them seemed to guess what the other was thinking. Zuryzel could see grief, and even pain, in her friend's dark blue eyes, almost as if he feared leaving Zuryzel's side.

And a hint of something more Zuryzel saw, but what she could not quite explain.

The Trebuchet

Feldspar woke up early the following morning. He had loved the sugar fields he'd seen yesterday and had enjoyed the taste of the new sweetness, but he still preferred honey over sugar. Now, he wandered along toward the lake but then decided to go to the Water Garden on his way. He told himself that it was because he hadn't seen it in a while, but he knew in his innermost being he was hoping to see Glor'a there. He felt he had hardly seen her enough.

To his delight, he found Glor'a sitting beside one of the Spider Streams, smelling a hyacinth. She looked up as he sat down beside her and smiled happily, her eyes shining with joy. Happiness rising within him, Feldspar greeted her; then she did the same to him.

Glor'a asked, "Did Chite show you the trebuchet? I hear that it is a great war weapon, capable of destroying many at a time."

"No," Feldspar replied. "I didn't see it, though if you want to see it, I remember a passage going toward it. I think I could find it again."

Glor'a agreed willingly. "I'd like to do that. Let's stop by and get some breakfast on the way. Have you ever had a raspberry-and-maple tart?"

Feldspar shook his head. "Well, if you know where to get some, let's go. I think that the trebuchet is outdoors, and it looks as if it might rain a little later today."

Both young mice stood up and wandered toward the city gates. Glor'a stopped at a small table on which sat some tempting, sweet-looking pastries. She picked out a few, some of them sprinkled with crystallized rose petals, and also lifted up a beaker of cold drink. She smiled. "Tarts, along with lemon-and-mint tea, cool from the stream, I think they say."

Both mice munched away at the tarts as they walked up a narrow passage that Feldspar easily found. It ended at a solid oak door. Feldspar tapped on it.

The door opened, and a squirrel looked out. He smiled at the two mice. "Come to see the trebuchet, I take it?"

Glor'a obviously knew the squirrel. "That's right, Argoss," she replied cheerfully. "That is, if we're allowed."

Argoss smiled. "Of course, you are. It's cold out here, though."

Feldspar followed Glor'a out to the mountain terrace. However, he was not prepared for the size of the trebuchet. Like everything else in Pasadagavra, it was huge, and it looked powerful. Made of oaken wood, it had a huge pouch holding a boulder at one end of the arm. A pile of similar boulders was heaped nearby, well out of way of falling over the precipice that they were situated on. Feldspar shook his head in amazement at the whole contraption.

"How does it work?" he questioned the squirrel.

Argoss demonstrated how it worked on a smaller, paw-held model. He loaded a pebble, pulled back the arm, and pressed on a lever. The pebble zoomed over the edge of the precipice and off into space, where it fell, down, down, down, to the very floor of the field below, lost to sight. Glor'a's eyes widened.

"So," she mused, "if that were a real boulder, with the real trebuchet, then the boulder would probably crush everyone it hit. My goodness," she added with a shudder, "I should think that it will do a good job taking care of the foxes. Brr."

Argoss smiled. He put away his model and then checked the position of the sun, rising above the mountains just to their left. The snow on the peak glistened like a jewel, shimmering like water with the sun on it.

Feldspar shivered a little in the sharp cold. He glanced at Glor'a and asked, "Do you want to go in? It is cold out here."

Glor'a didn't object. They said good-bye to Argoss and the rest of the trebuchet crew and headed out the door.

Inside, Pasadagavra seemed subdued and the air stifling, more so than usual, after the cool mountain air. Feldspar wished that the wind could blow freely inside, other than what blew in from the often-open gates of the city and the fortress.

But he couldn't help but enjoy himself anyway. Glor'a was so pleasant that he felt that he could easily be content with just her to talk to all day. He scarcely saw Ol'ver straddling a rock and talking to Ran'ta. He was pretty sure that Glor'a didn't see them because she kept talking easily to Feldspar, her eyes bright and friendly instead of shaded with envy that her best friend was more or less ignoring Glor'a because she was in love. Or, did she see them and just not care?

They wandered down toward the fortress, calling hello to all the sentries they saw sitting at opened diamond windows, watching the field.

They were on the fourth level when a shout went up from one of the sentries.

"Wraith Mouse approaching!"

Both mice hastened down the last three layers. They arrived at the main gate just in time to here Jaccah shout an order.

"Open the postern!"

Two squirrels pulled open the small door, and the female Wraith Mouse Muryda hastened in. Feldspar recognized her as one of the patrol around Dombre, one of the fortresses that lay between Pasadagavra and Darkwoods. He remembered Ol'ver wanting to get to Pasadagavra fast, but he had insisted they make certain they were going the right way. Muryda was panting a little but did not look too tired. Indeed, she looked very pleased. She smiled in a friendly way as she spoke to Jaccah and King Fuddum. Her words were falling out rather fast.

"Well, I've got news this time. The word from the Bow Tribe and King Hokadra is that one of the Oracles, Blood, is dead from some illness. And his apprentice, Fawn— you know about the Blight, right? They discovered that Fawn doesn't have it any longer. They nearly killed her because of it. Princess Zuryzel helped Fawn to escape. She got Fawn out safely, but Fawn is no longer in fighting condition. They sent Fawn away somewhere, but I don't know where. She also brought word that the foxes have employed Warhawks, the leader of which is a female named Chiraage. Apparently, they're affected by the Blight, too. Also," here Muryda lowered her voice a little, "Fawn said that Oracle Hemlock has a spy somewhere in the main army. She doesn't know who, so she can't tell us whom to watch, but it's probably either a river otter or a Wraith Mouse. This spy seems to know the secrets of Mirquis and Dombre. King Hokadra hasn't indicated who he suspects, so far as I know."

Jaccah spoke a question that was nagging her mind. "When did you first have the indication that Fawn didn't have the Blight?"

"When two squirrels," explained Muryda, "Karrum and Biddah, were captured. Fawn let them go, and later, King Hokadra had Zuryzel go and help Fawn get out if she needed it. Well, she surely did."

Without warning, Muryda uttered a swift farewell and backed out the postern. Jaccah shook her head, annoyed by the swift departure. She didn't seem surprised, though. Feldspar couldn't help but wonder if runners and messengers commonly did that—tell and run. But he was still perplexed by one thing.

"Glor'a," he whispered, "What's the Blight?"

"It's an affliction that the Serpent sends to some of his followers," Glor'a replied. "It makes their eyes red, and it makes them cruel and evil to an unnatural extent."

Feldspar shuddered. Thank goodness, he thought, the Blight didn't possess his own fox friend, Redfur.

He was also glad that it had not taken Rosemary either.

14

OPAL

pal the Graystone mouse crouched down in the bracken, her fur and tunic melding perfectly. Behind her crouched her two friends, Lillia the mouse maiden and Redfur the fox. Redfur had been found and rescued as a lost babe, and he now was an excellent tracker.

Behind Opal, Lillia began to complain. "We've been out here for at least an hour and haven't seen anyone. The only sign we've seen of any living creature is our own tracks. What are we doing out here?"

"Shhh!" Opal hissed. "We don't know that the bird we saw went away. That bird was bigger than any I've ever seen before. We need to find it and make sure that it's not a threat!"

"Oh," Lillia muttered, "if you've never seen it before, and no one has seen it before, than it was probably lost and will be gone before you can say double jack!"

Opal flicked Lillia with her tail. "Quiet. If you must complain, then do it mentally."

"You're not leader of Graystone yet, Opal," Lillia challenged. "Don't tell me what to do."

Opal didn't turn her head. "One," she whispered, "I don't know what you mean by yet. Two, I am leader of this patrol."

Redfur sighed a little. "She is right, you know, Lillia."

"Three," Opal continued, "that bird might come from up north. If it does, it might have news of Chite, and maybe even Feldspar. Are you sure you want to miss the chance to hear about them?"

Lillia didn't answer.

"Right," Opal continued, keeping her voice low. "Let's try over by the pond, shall we?"

All three friends slunk through the bracken, keeping as low to the ground as possible. The pond was not far away, but they took it slow, making sure that they were not visible. When they reached the pond, all three of them were disappointed.

"Oh, that's just wonderful," Lillia grumbled. "We don't have a clue where this bird is—" A loud screech from a Warhawk drowned out the rest of her sentence.

Without thinking, all three of them dashed for the woods. They barely made it to the trees in time. The huge bird swooped down, ran into the trees, and nearly bowled them over. Shrieking in frustration, it flew up and tried to dive in between the trees, but the woods were too dense for its wingspan.

Opal loaded her sling with a pebble, and Redfur notched an arrow to his bow. They waited for the Warhawk to drop in closer before taking a shot. The pebble found its way to the bird's head, and the arrow hit just below its left eye.

The hits didn't affect the bird at all.

Opal quickly motioned with her paws for her companions to stay perfectly still. Without them moving, and with the dense foliage surrounding them, the warhawk quickly lost sight of its prey and flew off toward the north.

Opal blew a sigh of relief. "Well, that answers that," she whispered. "Those birds are a threat. Let's get back to Graystone."

Redfur and Lillia needed no second bidding. They willingly followed her through the forest. Before another hour had passed, all three came in sight of the gray walls of Graystone. They hastened to the open gate; all of them with paws shaking slightly, and welcomed the greetings shouted by the sentries, calling them in.

None of them needed so much as a first asking to enter the safety of the walls. The Warhawk showing no sign of injury when hit in the head by both a stone and an arrow had made them quite nervous.

The Mission and the Dream

Lady Raven was not the best of tree climbers, but she sat on a high branch with Sharmmuh and Queen Demeda, trying hard not to look down. She clung to a branch with one paw and her rapier with the other.

Biddah swung up to sit beside her leader as she made the report from the evening patrol. "Not a single Warhawk, fox, or rogue out there, ma'am. No sign that the foxes have come into our territory."

Sharmmuh nodded and dismissed Biddah with a flick of her bushy tail.

Biddah leapt down to where Karrum was sitting. He began talking to her, but Biddah only half heard him. Zuryzel had wandered back into camp with Asherad, and now she was talking to her father. Her face expressed both concern and surprise, and Biddah couldn't help but wonder what they were discussing. She pushed away the thought and turned her attention to Karrum.

"Zuryzel, I want you to go to Dombre and take command there. Tell Mokimshim, if you see him at Mirquis that he is to take command there. He must send someone else to report to me."

Zuryzel was a little surprised. "Me? Why are you sending me? I'm not very old."

There was no hesitation in Hokadra's eyes. "You are a very good leader, Zuryzel. You have excellent sense. You are respected by the others, you know."

Zuryzel was surprised. She opened her mouth to say something, but her father held up a paw to silence her. "Leave as soon as it's dark. Take Dikiner, Karena, Orgorad, and Shinar with you, and a few others that you decide. But leave Sibyna here. She should be here when the war reaches its height. She deserves no less."

Zuryzel dipped her head respectfully and called to the warriors that her father had named. After a brief hesitation, she called to a few others, including Dejuday and Colobi, most of whom were archers. She wanted to be able to defend Dombre, and it had few archers of its own. To her troop, she advised they gather weapons and provisions.

Then she went over to say good-bye to Asherad and Kiarna. She felt tears coming to her eyes as she grasped her friends' paws. Taking a deep breath, she murmured her farewell.

Kiarna's eyes were shining with unshed tears. "Good-bye, Zuryzel, Wraith Mouse princess. Bear King be with you against the foxes."

Asherad had taken a deep breath. His own eyes had tears in them, but his voice held steady and stubbornly determined. "Good-bye, Zuryzel. We'll see you again, after we settle with the rogues. So good-bye until then."

Zuryzel wished she could share her friend's hope. She smiled at the two through her tears, willing with all her heart that she would see them again. She nodded at them once, and then slipped over to her patrol. Zuryzel knew they were thinking of the Bow Tribe camp and the other fortresses around the world that had been lost and taken from them.

Zuryzel could scarcely think how she would cope if she never saw Biddah or Sibyna or her father and mother or her brother or Kiarna and Asherad again.

Suddenly, she thought of the Bear King. She had to trust him. He would help her get through this war. There was a weakness in the foxes, and sooner or later, it would be discovered. The Bear King would guide them to it.

Whatever that weakness, Zuryzel guessed that it had to do with the Serpent.

By dusk, Zuryzel had found her brother, Johajar. They shared a quick look and slipped out the camp the back way.

Queen Demeda was waiting for them. She sat on a log, savoring the night breezes and watching what she could of the sunset through the trees.

"Did you tell him?" Zuryzel asked.

Queen Demeda looked at her daughter. "Your father was worried by your theory, Zuryzel, but there's nothing we can do. I myself saw Fawn heading south."

"You really followed her?" Johajar asked.

"As long as it was night," Queen Demeda revealed. "She has a long way to go."

"Did you hear Sharmmuh missed?" Johajar grinned. "She was close enough to spit at Knife, and she missed!"

"They don't fight very often in this part of the world," Queen Demeda shrugged. "Hitting a stationary target is, after all, a lot easier than hitting something that is moving with remarkable speed."

"Great Bear King," Johajar scoffed, "they're right by the Darkwoods foxes. How can they *not* fight?"

"They didn't always used to be the Darkwoods foxes," Queen Demeda murmured sadly. "That was once a great field with an enormous mine underneath it. It was supposed to be the richest mine in the world, before it fell. They were good foxes, those who lived in that castle." She sighed heavily. "The Darkwoods foxes conquered them. But the foxes that lived here before protected the Bow Tribe from any trouble coming from the west."

"And from the east?" Johajar persisted. "There had to be rogues and that kind of riff-raff drifting in from the Unsettled Lands."

"There was Miamur," Zuryzel pointed out.

"Like they would do anything," Johajar protested.

"There was the Sling Tribe," Queen Demeda explained. "When I was young, just a little younger than you, they were the mightiest force on the earth. Their main city, Ezdrid, was populated by well over a million warriors and over ten million civilians. They had six other major cities and uncountable smaller villages. They were unstoppable." She smiled wryly. "Besides, there was worse riff-raff drifting in from the west."

"They protected the Bow Tribe?" Zuryzel asked skeptically. "The only Sling Tribe squirrels *I've* ever met are unfriendly, proud, uncharitable, and spiteful. They aren't friends of the Bow Tribe, are they?"

"They were friends of the foxes before now and they have no enmity for the Bow Tribe," Queen Demeda corrected. "Just the Stone Tribe. Besides, they were smart enough to know that if rogues and enemy armies were all around, they'd have a harder life." She paused. "Not *that* hard, but still, harder. Besides, why fight with someone you have no reason to fight with? With their armies and weapons, they were left alone by everyone around anyway."

"If they had such a magnificent army, why did they let the Darkwoods foxes take over?" Johajar asked sardonically.

"There was a pestilence," Queen Demeda explained sadly. "It wiped out four of their cities, all but three of their villages, and brought the population of Ezdrid down to less than a twentieth of what it had been. Then hordes of insects came and ate all their crops, so another city was wiped out from starvation, and Ezdrid's population was halved again."

"How did such a great sickness start?" Zuryzel gasped.

"They're not sure," Queen Demeda said sadly, "but they think it might have been in the water. There isn't all that much water in the Sling Tribe land, and it would have been easy for almost all of it to become contaminated. It might have been in mosquitoes, too, or even the insects that ate their crops." She shook her head irritably. "Around that time, of course, Scythe became ill. The Darkwoods foxes began to conquer westward, bringing that illness with them. It preceded the army and spread into Arashna."

"I don't remember that," Zuryzel protested.

"It was when you were infants," she explained, "and it was never as bad over in the west as it was in the east."

Zuryzel blinked. That meant two forces worked against the conquest of the Darkwoods foxes: the Sling Tribe and Scythe. Zuryzel was willing to bet that the Sling Tribe was seriously suffering from something now, or she knew they would destroy the Darkwoods foxes. If the pestilence and the famine had happened so long ago, why hadn't their populations since then increased greatly? She shook the offending thoughts away. In spite of her mother's partialness to the Sling Tribe, Zuryzel detested them and did not much care what happened to them. Well, she cared, but she had more important matters to worry about.

"Mother," Zuryzel asked, "did you know Father is sending me to Dombre?"

"Yes, I knew," Queen Demeda answered. She looked at Zuryzel and Johajar. "I also know Mokimshim will be in control at Mirquis." She sighed. "If all goes according to plan, he won't be there very long. You two," she continued, looking both her children in the eye, "have a long future ahead of you, but I fear for your brother. He is nothing like either of you. His future, I fear, will be … more tragic." She sighed again. They sat in silence for a moment.

"I have to go," Zuryzel whispered.

"Go well," Queen Demeda replied, trying to smile.

Zuryzel found her patrol talking nervously by the camp entrance. They stopped talking when she approached, looking almost skittish. Zuryzel nodded nervously before announcing, "Let's go." She glanced back as they left the border of the camp, knowing she'd never see the place again.

The patrol traveled all through the night, stopping to rest at a place known to the Wraith Mice as Many Caverns. A small garrison, headed by Arpaha, of only river otters—because they knew the land best—held the place.

Arpaha herself greeted Zuryzel and her patrol. "Welcome, with all courtesy. Come in, quickly. You look pretty tired."

Zuryzel was tired, but she tried not to show it. After all, she told herself, one could be a lot more tired.

Zuryzel followed Arpaha to the barracks in the back of the caves. To her surprise, she found the place quite comfortable, with a pleasant, secretive, moon-like smell and feel. A lone stalagmite near the center grew up almost to the ceiling, topped with a carved crescent moon. Outside, silver light from the moon reflected on the dancing waters from the waterfall and pool next to the caves, but no water dripped within.

Zuryzel fell down gratefully onto the soft mattress of one of the beds. Though she slept soundly, she didn't know what to make of her dream.

She saw an icicle hanging, waiting, on a winter's eve. Without warning, a flame leapt up from the icicle, small at first, but steadily growing. Then she saw three jewels, one diamond, one pearl, one topaz, glittering in candlelight but giving an odd, sinister feeling about them. Next Zuryzel saw a beautiful emerald. Surrounding the emerald were a crow, the icicle, a river, a stone, rapids, and a tree. Behind the emerald was the crescent moon. The emerald crushed a ruby, and the moon crushed the sun that was behind the ruby.

At this point, Zuryzel jerked awake. What a strange dream!

Reaching up, she brushed her paw around her neck. As she did so, she touched the key Herttua Crow had given her. She'd forgotten it entirely! Taking it, she examined it closely.

It was a raven, pure and simple, though finely detailed. There couldn't be a craftsman alive with that kind of carving skill. Tracing her paw around her neck again, she found an imprint on her fur where the bead had rubbed against her when she had slept.

Key? she thought. *Either Herttua Crow is deceiving me, or more likely, Lady Raven lied to Herttua Crow. This isn't a key. This is why I had the dream. This is magic of some sort. Something to do with the Bear King. It rubs against fur and sends dreams. Lady Raven knows this. I doubt Herttua Crow does. Or if she does, she does not understand. But why trust it to me?* She put it back around her neck and hid it beneath her tunic.

Out of the corner of her eye, she spotted what looked like a pair of smiling black eyes, full of pride, looking at her. Zuryzel blinked and the image vanished.

She shook herself and stood up. The moon was shining again, and it would be wisest to travel by night to Mirquis. The territories of the Sling and Prairie Tribes skirted the trail, and Zuryzel had no wish whatsoever to run into Wazzah, Warriorqueen of the Sling Tribe. She went to speak to the sentries guarding the caves.

She spotted a female river otter she knew named Goldenray. In hushed tones, they discussed the position.

"No beast around?"

"None save you and me."

"Was it quiet all night?"

"Yes, except for the two scouts returning. I heard their report; there's nothing to worry about along the way towards Mirquis or the Okirraray River."

Zuryzel nodded. "Thank you, Goldenray."

Swift and silent as a shadow, Zuryzel hurried back to the barracks. Dikiner and Karena were already awake, their eyes bright with energy, and Shinar was stirring. Zuryzel glanced about the cave and noticed with a flicker of unease that Orgorad wasn't there. She sought out Dikiner and held a whispered conference with him.

"Have you seen Orgorad? Did he wake up?"

"He went out late last afternoon. He said he was hungry. Why?"

Zuryzel frowned. "None of the sentries saw him go. But they should have seen him. Unless he didn't want to be seen."

Worry fell across Dikiner's eyes. "Why wouldn't he want to be seen, you might wonder. Well, there are two logical reasons. Either he was seeing some sort of maiden or friend that he doesn't want you to know about, or …"

Zuryzel finished the sentence. "He's the spy that Fawn heard about. Oh, I don't think I like this. Right," she decided, "I want you to watch him. Don't make a big deal out of it, but keep him in sight. I'm watching him a little myself, so I'll give you three nods when you can take your eyes off him. When I give you four nods, keep watching him."

Dikiner nodded promisingly and turned out of the barracks.

Zuryzel sighed, the exuberance she had felt earlier and her dream completely forgotten. She couldn't help but feel that it was a good thing that she had brought Orgorad along. She also felt that if there had to be a spy, she hoped that it would be Orgorad—she really didn't like him very much.

Pushing those thoughts to the back of her mind, she focused on the present demands. She needed to reach Mirquis and Mokimshim before dawn, and it was a good long way to Mirquis. And besides, she needed to make sure that they were not being followed. That would be a hard task. She knew these woods, but so did others.

She led the rest of her patrol to the edge of the glade that harbored the caves. Before too long, Dikiner arrived with Orgorad. Orgorad looked sleepy, but he kept up as Zuryzel began the night's marching with a quick pace.

As soon as they were deep in the woods, Zuryzel called Shinar to her.

"Shinar," Zuryzel whispered, "go to the back of the column. Keep your eyes peeled for any signs that we have a follower. If you see anything, have Karena tell me about it. If you see more than one follower, come up to me and tell me personally."

Shinar nodded twice before slipping off into the night. Zuryzel watched Shinar take up a position at the back of the line, her eyes constantly scanning the forest behind them.

Turning her eyes to the barely visible road ahead, Zuryzel could tell that no creature other than a Wraith Mouse and maybe a river otter or two had been this way for a long time. At the thought of river otters, Zuryzel remembered Danaray and her sister, Anamay. She hoped that they would find Herttua Crow. Many beasts really needed to know what was happening to her and her small band of archers. No one was really worried, though. All of Lady Raven's tribe were crack shots, but Herttua Crow's archers were the elite. They had special bows, with strings twined from finest tree bark strands, and they used poison arrows.

Ugh! Zuryzel never liked the thought of what one small nick could do even to a fully-grown beast if it came in contact with the tip of the archer's arrow. She had often felt rather cowed by the size of Herttua Crow's heavy longbow, capable of shooting farther than any bow on the earth. Her arrows, also especially long—nearly a third of Herttua Crow's own height—had the huge wing and tail feathers from a dead jay that had been found the day Herttua Crow was born. Each arrow was made out of oak and was so straight that they didn't look like real arrows.

As she marched through the woods, Zuryzel let her mind wander as she often did, drifting from the place where she was to the place where she wanted to be. She was thinking of Arashna, the beautiful castle that was the Wraith Mice capital, when a small white flake drifted past her eyes. She held up a paw and slowed her pace to a stop. The whole patrol stopped with her. They watched as more flakes fell to the ground. Zuryzel grimaced. *Snow.* That would make the whole journey longer and harder.

Zuryzel pushed aside the worries that clouded her mind. She dropped her paw, and the whole patrol continued onward, now with an increased air of urgency.

For hours, they hurried while the snow came down harder, sticking, then accumulating, and finally deepening on the ground. As they advanced, the trees began thinning out. And quite suddenly, the patrol stood on the top of a steep slope, overlooking a huge lake. In the middle of the lake stood a small island, just big enough to hold the castle Mirquis. The banner of the Wraith Mice, a black field with a crescent moon in the center, fluttered from every tower and turret in the castle. A drawbridge, roughly the size of the radius of the lake, was lowered. Zuryzel knew that it would be drawn in when the foxes threatened the castle.

Zuryzel led her patrol across the bridge. A few sentries hailed them, and her patrol began to disperse. Zuryzel saw Mokimshim standing nearby. He smiled at her and held out his paws. She hurried over to greet him, and he clasped her paws willingly, as he always did, clearly delighted to see his sister.

"Wonderful to see you again, Zuryzel. I hope that nothing, well, disastrous, has happened since I left?"

Zuryzel let go of her brother's paws. "Only a small skirmish. The vixen Knife, the Oracle, you know, led an attack. She tried seducing father into joining the foxes, but no luck, of course. Father told me to tell you that you need to send someone else along with your report."

"Zuryzel," Mokimshim asked eagerly, "have you heard about the forest shadows?"

"The *what*?"

"Well, I don't know exactly what they are, but those who have seen them call them forest shadows. They're a terror, apparently. We can't tell what creatures they are or what sort of place they come from or even how many there are. They move quickly, and a few *river otters* have completely disappeared. One of them we found with a spear wound. He was alive, but only just. He's still alive, though. Streamcourse came here a few days ago. She said that she thinks these 'shadows' are river otters, but she's not sure. She's talked about Mudriver and Nighthawk, two new rogues, and she thinks that they may be the ones."

Zuryzel shook her head. "Not Mudriver. I've met his two daughters, Danaray and Anamay. They were out looking for Herttua Crow Blue Arrows, but they haven't found her. You can't be new from the eastern plains and still hope to be wood experts. Besides, Miamur always speaks well of Mudriver. On the other paw, Nighthawk, I can see as the culprit. He is new here, but he knows woodland, from what Doomspear tells me."

At the mention of Doomspear's name, Mokimshim clapped a paw to his forehead. "Doomspear! We found a spear wound in that otter's body when we found him! It could be Doomspear. *Spear*, Zuryzel," he added when Zuryzel looked blank. "Doom*spear*."

Zuryzel shrugged. "Doomspear is just called that because he uses a huge and semi-poisoned spear. If the otter you found was barely alive, then he can't have had any poison. Any beast can use a spear. It could have been a fox, for all we know. Besides, Doomspear has risked *his* life who-knows-how-many times for us. Why would he want to kill us or our allies?"

Mokimshim nodded sheepishly, looking rather putout. "I guess you're right. It seems that Nighthawk is the most logical culprit. Well, you might as well get some sleep. You look worn out."

Zuryzel smiled and stalked away with a light foot. Fatigued, but not enough to go to sleep for a while, she intended to visit an old friend.

Wandering through to the hall near the soldiers' quarters; she kept her eyes open wide for a certain face. She continued in her meanderings, well out of the way, acting as if she was heading toward her room.

Finally, another pair of black eyes met her own. They smiled at her before looking away slightly. Zuryzel rolled her eyes to herself, and then she hastened along the passage to her rooms.

She stopped at the torch bracket outside her door. She knew her friend would come the other way and leave toward the torch. It would be impossible to see the bracket in the dark. She blew out the torch and slid the removable bracket out just a little from its holder. The princess took a step back and nodded in satisfaction. She had set all pieces in place and now only needed to wait. Opening her wooden door, she entered and sat down on the bed, impatient to see her friend falter into her traps again.

A tapping brought her gaze to the door. To her own surprise, she hesitated for a moment and then called, "Come in."

The beautiful ornate door opened to reveal Zuryzel's friend, Harclayang. "Hey," he greeted her. "It's not like you just to show up without sending any word. What's happening back at the squirrel's camp? Has it been invaded by the foxes?"

"Mm, mm," Zuryzel smiled. "Have you heard of Fawn?"

"Certainly."

"Well, when I went to get her out, I found out something rather startling. The foxes have recruited Chiraage and her Warhawks. Father wants me to take command at Dombre."

Harclayang smiled. "Might I come with you?"

Zuryzel shook her head, maybe a little too earnestly. "No. Mokimshim would have to give me permission first, and I don't think that he'd want to give you up."

Harclayang swelled slightly at the flattery. "You're probably right. Oh well, I just hope that I can see you again soon. I'll let you rest now."

He stood up and walked flamboyantly out of the room. Zuryzel stood up and closed the door behind him.

Zuryzel waited. She considered Harclayang her friend only in the broadest degree of that word. He flirted like no one's business, and he was the *worst* showoff in the world. Zuryzel like to set her traps to bring him back down to earth.

Suddenly, a loud clang sounded near her door, followed by a yelp of pain and another clang. It was an old trick. Harclayang had walked into the torch bracket, and the bracket had fallen on his paw. The bracket was at forehead level, but with Harclayang's springy, vain step, it would have been just at his nose.

The Sling Tribe Camp

anaray and Anamay had been trying to get back to their father's camp to report to him, but they had encountered a tad bit of trouble.

The Sling Tribe had left Ezdrid, and now at least three hundred of them huddled in a grove of aspen trees surrounding the two otters. Some of the soldiers bore wounds. That didn't surprise Danaray. The Sling Tribe was friend to no one anymore and, thus, drew more than its share of skirmishes and injuries. But she did wonder about their great distance from Ezdrid and close proximity to the border with the Stone Tribe, who they hated. She and her sister continued to listen in on the squirrels' discussions.

"What if we were to go to the ruins of Alkzor?" Deggum, Wazzah's younger brother, suggested.

Danaray ducked lower behind some tall grasses, watching just a little behind Wazzah on the edge of the grove. Anamay shivered behind her.

"Not to Alkzor," Wazzah replied. "We just came from a fight on our southern border. We can't have a fight on our western border too." Danaray couldn't see Wazzah's face.

"Perhaps if we were to go to the moors past the mountains?" Fraeggah, Wazzah's sister, suggested.

"No," Wazzah replied. "We are too many and would be easy prey for eagles in the mountains. Besides, I do not think that territory could support us as well as the Moor Tribe."

One of the younger squirrels was waiting on the edge of the grove. Danaray felt the hair on her neck stand up, and she fitted her knife into her paw, ready even though she knew none could see her tribe.

"We could always go to Pasadagavra," Deggum suggested dryly.

"Don't be ridiculous," Fraeggah scoffed. "We are enemies. They won't help us now."

"But Ezdrid has fallen!" Deggum insisted. "They must listen to that! And anyway, however they might like to be our enemy, they are in our debt because we kept Darkwoods away from Pasadagavra as a threat."

"They will not recognize that debt," Fraeggah argued.

"They are honor-bound to take in helpless creatures," Deggum reminded his sister.

"The Sling Tribe is not helpless!" Fraeggah snapped.

"Yes, Fraeggah," Wazzah murmured sadly, "we are." She smiled wryly. "Our enmity with the Stone Tribe could work in our favor. At least they would know—if they had any brains, that is—that we would not, could not, go to Pasadagavra unless we had no other choice. And we *are* good warriors, however depleted and starved we are now. They cannot ignore that."

"They could try, what with the Rangers heading towards Pasadagavra with the rest of the Wraith Mouse army," Fraeggah pointed out. "We could just go all the way west towards Eeried where there are no foxes."

"We are unfamiliar with the ways of survival in the wild," Wazzah reminded her sister, "and our young would not last with winter coming on. Pasadagavra is truly our only hope."

The young squirrel on the edge of the grove stood up, and her eyes fixed intently on the spot where Danaray was half-hidden by the grass. Danaray froze, watching the young squirrel.

"The foxes are close behind us," Wazzah was saying, oblivious to the two otters nearby and her sentry's discovery, "and winter is even closer. The day is wearing on. The only shelter happens to be the pines by the Onyx Watchtower. We must leave now, or we will spend the night on the open prairie."

That got Deggum and Fraeggah moving. The tribeprince and the tribeprincess began circulating around the tribe, gathering all toward the end of the grove.

Eyes still focused on Danaray's location, the young squirrel jumped and began to spin, but Danaray was faster. The knife whizzed into the squirrel's throat before she could make a noise. She fell silently.

Danaray and Anamay slid away after that without too much difficulty. Of course, they were skilled on this sort of terrain, but it was only a matter of seconds before the slain squirrel was noticed. Danaray and Anamay desperately wanted to keep their presence in Sling Tribe land hidden—with a bit of luck, it would look as if the foxes had thrown the knife—because the Sling Tribe was incredibly aggressive. Especially, as the overheard conversation had indicated, having been forced out of a city that had never before actually fallen, they would be extra jumpy.

It did not take long, as the otters had guessed, for the squirrel to be missed. Deggum noticed her first—long before Danaray and Anamay were far enough away. He shouted in dismay, causing the two sisters to freeze in their tracks. They spun around in terror to find several Sling Tribe warriors sprinting in their direction. The sisters gave up on camouflage and just flat out ran.

"The river!" Danaray gasped. "Get to the river in Stone Tribe territory!"

"That's too far away," Anamay retorted. "We have to lose them!"

"Head toward the river anyway," Danaray snapped. She and Anamay swiftly changed direction and headed west. The pines would be harder for them, but if the Sling Tribe really intended to go to Pasadagavra, they couldn't follow the sisters in the opposite direction to the river.

Danaray risked a backward glance. The squirrels were hurrying now, their tails streaming out behind them, but they were obviously undernourished. Danaray and Anamay had the sheer advantage of energy.

They passed a single formation of rock, and the Sling Tribe squirrels let them go past that. They ran still, until they were so far away from the squirrels that the gray-brown prairie had curved enough to hide their pursuers.

"That was too close," Danaray gasped. "How are we going to make it back to Father?"

"Head back and look for Herttua Crow, I guess," Anamay panted. Her brown eyes shone brightly.

"Back toward sea otter territory?" Danaray's reply was scathing. "Not a chance."

"What else can we do?" Anamay challenged.

"Report to King Hokadra," Danaray suggested.

"Dana, we don't have anything to report," Anamay persisted.

Danaray sighed. Her sister was right, but she was still unhappy to go into the land of the sea otters. Of course, she knew she'd give in eventually. "Let's just go take a look south and see if we can find any way to Father first," she declared firmly.

"But it's as Wazzah said," Anamay persisted. "Winter is coming. We need the rivers to move fast, and the rivers will be frozen!"

She doesn't want to let me tell Father about Mollusk, Danaray realized, *so she's trying to keep me away from him until I forget.*

"Winter is here, Anamay," Danaray reminded her sister. "The Sling Tribe judges winter by the first snowfall, and it wouldn't have snowed at Ezdrid or any other part of their territory yet."

"All the more reason to hurry our tails after Herttua Crow!" Anamay insisted.

"Still," said Danaray firmly, "we have to try to find Father. Once it snows, we'll go back after Herttua Crow; but for now, we stick to finding Father."

"And if we can't get after Herttua Crow after we find Father?" Anamay demanded.

"What's to stop us?" Dana asked.

"Anything!" Anamay was worked up. "Father may forbid us!"

"Ana," Danaray told her sister with a steely note in her voice, "I am not going to let you alone in sea otter territory, so forget that notion. We are going to find Father, and then we will go find Herttua Crow."

Anamay's defiance seemed to submit into sullenness. "Fine."

"You did promise me not to sneak off to find Mollusk," Danaray reminded her sister.

They looked for their father Mudriver but found no trace of his camp. Three days later, they reached the Okirraray River and plunged into its cool current to start towards the south to find Herttua Crow.

THE LITTLE VILLAGE

Biddah was lonely without Zuryzel. True, she still had Karrum, but she couldn't be with him every minute of the day. They had separate patrols and sentry duties, not to mention scouting missions. Sibyna felt a different loneliness, particularly at night when all her duties of the day were over and she had no one with her. Fortunately, she kept herself so busy in the daytime that she could not think of her mate and her friends. Biddah spent every possible moment with her, but she did not have much time. Herttua Crow was no longer at the camp, Zuryzel had gone to Dombre, and Kiarna had gone to Miamur. The camp seemed gloomy in the squirrel's eyes without her friends and, true, because they had received no word as to what the foxes were doing.

Feldspar wandered through the streets of Pasadagavra with Ol'ver and Chite. The air was thick with the scent of culled herbs. Several cooks had gathered as many fine-tasting spices as they could that morning for making more food. Much was needed to feed the occupants.

Sweet scents of honey and baked fish reached their noses as they rounded the corner into the Little Village. Several squirrel babes were playing a tag-like game as they scrambled over the jungle gym. Rosemary and Rhonndan were playing chase with a few of their newfound friends—the Prairie Tribe had arrived at Pasadagavra that day after a small raid on their village. At first, their babes had looked scared and bewildered. Now, those same little ones were laughing and screaming with delight as they chased Rhonndan and Rosemary all over the playground.

Feldspar's eyes sought out Jaccah. He had passed her several times but had never spoken to her. Now he watched her sitting comfortably and smiling happily on a carved wooden bench as she watched her son and his friend at play.

A young adult squirrel maiden flopped down next to Jaccah. She watched the baby fox racing along on the earth, easily outrunning the squirrel babes. Suddenly, the tiny vixen raced toward a maple tree. The squirrel next to Jaccah stiffened a little. Rosemary tried to climb up the maple like a squirrel, but her claws slipped. She came crashing down to earth, and the squirrel babes tagged her.

The squirrel next to Jaccah stood up, but Rhonndan got to Rosemary first. Jaccah pulled her companion back down to the bench. "Relax, Shjeddah!" she exclaimed. "Rosemary's just fine. Look!"

Rosemary was back on her paws, chasing her playmates around the playground once more.

Oracle Hemlock was furious. Now that Fawn had betrayed the Serpent, he needed another Oracle. But of course, he couldn't appoint one until he had found and killed Fawn. Knife was supposed to take care of that, but Knife had failed in her attack, and now there was precious little chance of ever getting at Fawn.

Fang and Knife entered his chambers. Both of them were worried about the position of Fawn's former clan. And both of them had suggestions to make.

Fang cleared his throat to get Hemlock's attention. "Hemlock, the fact is we need a fifth leader."

Hemlock did not reply.

Knife spoke up, a little nervously. "We need to appoint a fox to be leader of the clan without a leader. I would suggest Claw."

Again, no reply.

"Claw is a noble and loyal soldier," Fang urged. "He would make a good leader now and a good Oracle later."

Hemlock looked up. "You are right. Very well. Claw it is. Knife, can you instruct him as well as train your own apprentice?"

Knife blew a silent sigh of relief. "Yes, I can. Both seem easy to teach."

"For you," muttered Fang bitterly.

"All right. Fang," Hemlock continued, "go get Ice. Tell her to come up here double sharp."

Knife and Fang rolled their eyes at each other. Knife lowered her voice. "No need. Watch. I'll show you how she 'foresees' every meeting."

Knife reached into her pouch and picked out a small pebble. She hurled it through a gap in the curtain door. A small squeak issued from outside, easily identifiable as Ice's.

Fang shrugged a little. "If she didn't wear so many beads and jewelry, then we might not have found out."

More like, Knife reflected, *if we didn't do the same thing when we wanted to "foresee."*

Ice stalked into the room with as much dignity as she could. Her eyes did not flash annoyance, but her voice was a little less insubstantial than usual.

"Good afternoon."

Knife wiggled a rather cruel-looking claw at Ice. "Good afternoon, yourself, Ice. Having difficulty foreseeing, are you?" Knife was really enjoying herself. Ice was looking more disgruntled than ever.

"No, thank you, Knife," she replied coolly.

"All right, stop," Hemlock broke in. "We need to discuss something." He paused for a minute. "Do we attack the squirrels right away, or do we wait a cycle and carry out the original plan?"

Neither Knife nor Fang had any doubt.

"Follow the original plan!"

"The army is still tired, whether or not Fawn is a traitor."

"Knife is right. We'd stand a better chance attacking later."

"But make it look as if we'll attack soon. Get them on their guard."

"And when we don't attack, they'll let their guard slip."

"That's when we attack. I mean really attack."

"We're already working on taking out the prairie east of the trail. The west side of the trail has been completely abandoned."

Ice put in her bit. "Attack exactly one cycle from now. Attack on the first day of the third week of the second month with any spring."

Hemlock held up his paws. "All right. That's what we'll do, word for word."

None of the foxes noticed the invisible Johajar hurrying from the room. Nor could the guards see the Wraith Mouse scurrying toward the red main door.

18

DOMBRE

alf a cycle after her arrival at Dombre, Zuryzel woke up one morning feeling especially refreshed. She loved the wonderful fortress with its powerful walls and battlements and arrow slits and a layout that made a most effective defense. Three encircling layers composed the stronghold, each with a strong wall and a gate separating it from the other layers. The keep had fifteen different secret exits, of which only the king—and probably Mokimshim, too—knew all. If one was used, it would be blocked off afterward, leaving one of the many others for the next escape. At one time, the fortress had had seventeen secret tunnels. Only two had been used.

Zuryzel missed her friends, true, but she had plenty of new ones at Dombre and more than enough duties to fill her days. With all she had to do, she usually stayed up late at night and rose early in the morning.

She grinned to herself at the thought of one of her more enjoyable jobs, supervising the training of some of the young recruits from Arashna. It reminded her of her own training. Her father had instructed her personally. It made her proud to think of that. For Mokimshim and Johajar, King Hokadra had chosen great and distinguished warriors to train them. But he had personally trained his only daughter, Zuryzel. Now Zuryzel was one of the best warriors in all the land.

She had promised herself many times that she would one day train her own children, if she had any. But for now, she contented herself by occasionally teaching a few of the younger, less trained warriors.

She decided to go and look at the progress of a young warrior called Crispisin. Crispisin had just arrived from Arashna a few days before, and Zuryzel had taken a special liking to him. He was reserved, pleasant, and eager to learn. Zuryzel had considered training him herself on a regular basis.

But she could not quite do that. Her responsibilities to keep the fortress safe, for the time being, and the area free of river otter rogues took too much time to allow regular training of the novice. She had gone out on patrol far down south, almost within sight of Mirquis just a few days ago, with Shinar, Orgorad, and Karena, leaving Dikiner in charge of the fortress. She had seen for herself the forest shadows that Mokimshim had told her about. Shinar had seen them too, and she was convinced that they were river otters, but not Mudriver's band. They moved too expertly, too silently, too invisibly, for them to have come from the eastern plains. Besides, Shinar had grown up north, not far from Dobar, and Nighthawk had been a common nuisance up there for her and her band of rogues, whom she was destined to lead someday. Shinar insisted that she would recognize Nighthawk, even under the waters of a muddy pond. She was pretty sure that Nighthawk was the head of the forest shadows.

Zuryzel got out of her bed and put on her undergarment. It was all one piece and soft as a dove's wing. Over this she put on her light chainmail tunic made out of the finest, purest metal rings. Third came her cloth tunic, dark blue, like all the war tunics of the Wraith Mice, and because she was a princess, trimmed with purple around the hem and sleeves. Finally, she donned her favorite piece of clothing, her cloak. Black all over, it had a pattern of the moon's cycle around the edge and on the hood. A clasp of milky quartz edged with silver in the shape of a waxing quarter moon secured it at the neck. As it was the middle of winter, Zuryzel truly needed the extra layer of the cloak for the constant heavy rain as well as the snows that soon would come.

Zuryzel sloshed across the dripping wet courtyard to the training facilities and hung up her cloak as soon as she entered the room. It was large enough for several warriors to train their trainees at one time.

She spotted Crispisin immediately. He was trying to disarm Dikiner, and he was doing a pretty good job of it, despite his lack of experience. Dikiner was really struggling hard.

Crispisin raised his training sword, giving Dikiner a chance and then deftly brought his own weapon down and flicked the blade out of Crispisin's paws.

Crispisin looked put out, but he wasn't breathing nearly as heavily as Dikiner. Zuryzel could scarcely retain a laugh as she went over to join them.

She nodded encouragingly at Crispisin. "Well done! You're doing very well."

Crispisin's eyes glowed with pride. Zuryzel smiled. "Here, try it on me."

Crispisin's eyes glowed even brighter at the challenge. Raising his blunt blade, he faced Zuryzel. The Wraith Mouse princess selected a training blade from a nearby stack and faced her student.

"All right," she urged, "attack me."

Crispisin's blade moved skillfully through the air towards Zuryzel's blade. Zuryzel saw it coming and swiftly whirred her blade towards Crispisin's head, giving him instructions as she went.

"Raise your blade and parry. Now attack. Thrust. Parry. Duck. Swipe. Dodge. Thrust. Upward parry. Now clash. Good! Downward stroke. Now thrust. Now flick. Clash. Now move your blade in a zigzag pattern quickly!"

Crispisin swiftly zigzagged his blade, but not quickly enough. He looked rather downcast as his blade whizzed out of his paw. Zuryzel nodded encouragingly.

"You did well. A bit more practice and you'll be able to pull that off. It just takes practice."

Crispisin bowed. "Thank you, Princess."

Zuryzel nodded farewell to Dikiner and wandered over to assess the other trainees. They all showed encouraging progress, and a few, she noted, were doing exceptionally well.

After she had checked on the training, she strode out to check on the sentries. She emerged through the gate to the outer wall just as a surprised shout rang up from the wall.

Hurrying up the steps to the top of the wall, Zuryzel spotted Shinar at the head of her patrol. The patrol was made up entirely of river otters, for they would probably have had to swim the river. It certainly looked as if they had. They were dripping wet and staggering as if they barely had any strength left.

And trotting beside Shinar was the squirrel maiden Biddah.

She looked tired too. Zuryzel understood that completely—it was a good four days to the Bow Tribe from Dombre.

The patrol hastened across the drawbridge to the island. Shinar instantly led her patrol over to the barracks. Biddah looked puzzled and slightly nervous until she saw Zuryzel hurrying down to meet her.

Wraith Mouse and squirrel maiden clutched at the other's paws, both of them thoroughly overjoyed to see each other again. The squirrel looked as if she was holding a million things inside, bursting to tell her friend. Zuryzel smiled understandingly.

"Come to my chambers, Biddah. Tell me everything that's been happening."

Biddah followed Zuryzel through the fortress to the princess's chambers. Biddah looked slightly overawed at the sight of Zuryzel's well-furnished rooms. Seating herself down in a comfy chair, Biddah instantly began to tell Zuryzel all the news.

"Well, Johajar discovered that the foxes are going to attack in almost exactly a half cycle. Your father sent me along to tell you and Mokimshim about that. Sibyna's lonely without you and Karena. She told me to tell you that she misses you and that she hopes that life at Dombre is smooth. And, Karrum and I are to be wed!" she finished, her eyes glowing.

Zuryzel smiled, delighted for her friend. "That's wonderful news, Biddah. I'm sure that you'll be very happy. I'm sorry that I won't be around for when you are wed."

Biddah shrugged. "Just think of me; I'm fine with that."

Zuryzel smiled. "Will do. But, do me a favor and tell Sibyna the trees out here are falling over."

Biddah looked puzzled but nodded.

Zuryzel knew that only Sibyna would understand. It was their secret way of saying there was a hidden foe—Mokimshim's forest shadows.

After exchanging more news, Zuryzel offered to show Biddah around Dombre. They slipped silently out of the room and just caught Orgorad mumbling under his breath.

"Should definitely do something about that. It's just not right. Totally wrong to…"

"What did you say, Orgorad?" Zuryzel demanded quietly.

Orgorad did not hesitate. "I said Knife is so barbaric, what she did to Fawn, something *special* should be done about her." He met Zuryzel's eyes. Despite his sure tone, something behind them made him seem less than confident, almost *pleading*.

Zuryzel nodded. She turned to Biddah. "Well, you need to get to Pasadagavra before nightfall. Come on, get something to eat, and then you can set out." Then she began briskly walking off again

Biddah almost corrected Zuryzel, but Zuryzel's look, unseen by Orgorad, stopped her. The squirrel looked thoroughly puzzled at the knowing gleam in Zuryzel's eye. Zuryzel explained once a distance away from Orgorad.

"I never told him who clawed Fawn. I wonder how Orgorad found out."

Biddah looked worried, but she tried to look at all sides of things. "He could have asked Fawn. He did talk to her a little, you know."

"I know, but tell King Hokadra about that. And another thing: when you leave, take a route that swings toward Pasadagavra and then goes back down south to your camp."

Biddah nodded grimly. Without so much as eating anything, she was racing off toward Mirquis by sunhigh.

THE SLING TRIBE

Feldspar woke to almost complete darkness. Under the willow, he could clearly hear the brook babbling and birds singing their morning song. But very little light penetrated, giving him no clue as to the time.

Feldspar pushed himself out from under his blanket and emerged at the edge of the brook. It was clear that the only light came from torches staked along the bank and their reflection shimmering in the water. Normally the light slanted through the clear diamond roof.

Feldspar began wandering along the bank to see if he could figure out what time it was. Before too long, he spotted Glor'a hurrying towards him. She had on warm, waterproof boots and a very warm-looking tunic. Her eyes were dancing with pleasure at the sight of Feldspar.

"Good morning, Feldspar. Guess what?" she exclaimed. "It's snowing. It's already pretty deep. Do you want to see?"

Feldspar was only too ready. He hastened back to the willow and pulled on some warmer clothes. Then he followed Glor'a out to the main gate.

A large band of bundled-up young babes were racing out the postern when Glor'a and Feldspar arrived. Feldspar could just spot Rosemary and Rhonndan racing at the middle of the group, being herded out by Shjeddah, Rimmah, and a few others.

As soon as the babes were outside, they scattered everywhere, churning up snow and hurling it at each other and their chaperones.

Laughing, Feldspar and Glor'a hurried away off into the woods behind Pasadagavra. There the whole world was white and muffled, and the snow was clean and undisturbed. The two mice wandered for a while, thoroughly enjoying the peace and quiet. Glor'a ambled over to a snow-covered branch, and then, quite suddenly, whirled round and playfully hurled a snowball at Feldspar. Feldspar laughed happily and ducked behind another branch so that the snowball only grazed his ear. He hurled his own snowball at Glor'a.

She dodged it completely, racing off to one side of Feldspar. Then, quite suddenly, she slipped and disappeared from sight.

Feldspar hurried over to the place where she had disappeared. He barely kept himself from sliding down the snowy slope. Glor'a sat at the bottom of the slope, laughing, gasping for breath, and covered in snow. She called up to Feldspar.

"Try it. It feels really good."

She scrambled out of the way as Feldspar accidently slid down, the snow having given way under his weight.

Both mice sat laughing for a while, both of them elated. Then Glor'a stood up, tugged on a branch over Feldspar's head, and ran.

The snow that fell and coated him did not stop Feldspar. He raced after Glor'a to the field just outside Pasadagavra. Glor'a ran away from the fortress for a while but then slowed to a stop, staring ahead. Feldspar hurried up beside her.

The Sling Tribe was arduously trekking across the field, their young ones bundled on the backs of their parents, the lead tower-squirrel from the Onyx Watchtower leading them as though guiding them.

Both mice turned wordlessly and ran back to Pasadagavra, their paws sinking heavily into the snow. The raced straight to the squirrel chaperones.

"Shjeddah," Glor'a panted, "a tribe is coming. I saw them. I don't know who, but judging by the skinny tail of their leader, I think I can guess."

Shjeddah nodded and instantly called to the young ones. They followed her and Rimmah inside, puzzled. Feldspar and Glor'a followed them.

Ol'ver and Ran'ta were strolling along near the city gate. When they saw Feldspar and Glor'a, both of them broke down into laugher.

"Oh my, hee hee, you look like ghosts; you're all covered in snow!"

"I'll say you do, ha ha ha ha. What brought you back in so early?"

Glor'a replied in a single word. "Tribe."

Ol'ver shrugged. "Who? Don't tell me that it's the Sling Tribe. Oh, that would be funny."

"Well," Feldspar replied, "we think it is."

Ran'ta shook her head. "But that would be impossible. They *hate* the Stone Tribe."

Feldspar shrugged. "Well, do you want to find out?"

Ol'ver was about to make a comment when Chite wandered up. "Hey," he greeted them cheerfully. "Did you know that the Sling Tribe just arrived?"

Glor'a shot Ran'ta a look that clearly said, *I told you so*, and turned to Chite.

"Are they in yet?"

Chite shook his head. "No. They're still outside. From what I heard, King Fuddum and Jaccah are debating whether or not to let them in."

Glor'a shrugged. "That's hardly unexpected. The Stone Tribe and the Sling Tribe never were on the friendliest of terms."

Chite didn't look concerned. "Come on," he suggested. "I'd like to see how this turns out."

Ran'ta shivered. "No thanks. You go on—I won't say I'll catch up because I won't. I'd rather stay away."

Ol'ver glanced at Ran'ta. She gave him a small, almost inconspicuous nod, and he shrugged. "I'll go."

Glor'a's eyes were flickering from Ran'ta to Feldspar, as if she couldn't decide whom to go with. But her gaze rested on Ran'ta. "I'll stay here with Ran'ta."

Feldspar's fur prickled, and he wasn't sure what from. But he did know that he wished Glor'a were coming with him.

As Feldspar, Ol'ver, and Chite set out briskly for the main gate, Feldspar cast a small glance over his shoulder. Glor'a hardly seemed to hear Ran'ta talking to her. Her eyes met his and smiled in an encouraging way, as if saying, "Go on. I'll be right here when you get back." Feldspar smiled a little at her and turned to follow Ol'ver and Chite to the main gate.

Several squirrels were bustling about, seeming even more busy than usual, making sure that all their children were safe inside the Little Village, removing precious objects from obvious sight.

At the main gate, Jaccah stood beside her mate, Argoss, and slightly behind her father, Tribeking Fuddum. His voice was stern as he called out.

"Warriorqueen Wazzah, do you come to Pasadagavra in peace?"

Wazzah's voice was agitated but determined at the same time as she replied, "Yes, I and my tribe come here in peace, seeking refuge, not war. I swear it!"

Tribeking Fuddum glanced at his daughter and nodded. Jaccah hesitated for a while, but the sounds of the Sling Tribe's young ones crying from the cold wore on her heart. She called up to the gate-squirrels.

"Open the gate!"

The heavy gate opened to reveal a poor, thin, gaunt bunch of squirrels. Some of the babes looked barely alive from the cold. Feldspar saw Jaccah give Wazzah a cold look, but he also saw it soften with pity and sympathy at the sight of the babes. But soon her look turned to apprehension as the lead tower-squirrel hastened up to her. Feldspar could just make out what he said to Jaccah and Tribeking Fuddum.

"I couldn't risk bringing more squirrels as an escort. Sire, we need more Stone Tribe warriors out there. Verrah got lost wandering just yesterday, and we saw a runner from Dombre, saying that the foxes were planning to attack exactly a half cycle after tomorrow. We need more pairs of eyes out there. It's far too dangerous to send more who are unfamiliar with the territory."

Tribeking Fuddum looked uncertain for a moment. Then he rubbed his eyes wearily. "Jaccah, tell Shjeddah that she will join the watch guard at the Onyx Watchtower. You'll look after Rosemary in her absence, I trust." Jaccah nodded and wordlessly swept off.

A whispering grew amongst the squirrels watching the Sling Tribe. Feldspar heard the onlookers quietly criticizing the tribe.

"Why are they here?" one asked, just loud enough for Wazzah to hear. "Couldn't they defend their own territory?"

"Could they simply not withstand the cold?" sniggered another.

The speaker quailed under Deggum's savage glare.

Fuddum approached Wazzah. "I must ask why you need to seek shelter."

Wazzah looked at Fuddum. Her head was held proudly, and her jaw set. Feldspar felt a stab of grudging admiration at her stubborn pride.

Wazzah did not lower her head. She did not bend in embarrassment when she addressed the tribeking.

"The foxes overran my territory. There was a long battle at Ezdrid, the capital. Many now lie dead in her streets. The Darkwoods foxes now indulge themselves in our home." Her voice was filled with anger.

"You couldn't fight them in your own city!" one of the watchers laughed. "So much for the great Sling Tribe warriors!"

"You should have fought them," another shouted.

Wazzah's jaw set tighter. Her eyes smoldered with anger, but her voice was calm.

"We have fought them. For as long as I have been Warriorqueen, we have fought them. They torched half our territory, our farmlands. They fought with us on the southern border of Ezdrid. We have fought them since before they became the Darkwoods foxes. We have fought them before they even set eyes on that fortress. My tribe was picked off one by one. Warhawks attacked us even before that. We suffered more losses than there are squirrels in the Stone Tribe." Quiet, dignified rage radiated from the Warriorqueen, and no one answered her challenge.

Fuddum flinched a little from her stare, and Wazzah's eyes calmed. "I am a Warriorqueen. I look only to the future, not to the past. The foxes have become the enemy of both Sling Tribe and Stone Tribe; indeed, they are the enemy of the whole world."

As she turned away from Fuddum with a grateful nod, Feldspar saw a momentary look of helplessness and despair cross the proud Warriorqueen's face.

20

THE WIND

Hemlock wandered the foxes' castle late into the night. He was pretty certain that the whole fortress was asleep except for the guards. But he couldn't sleep for his nervousness. He felt as if something was about to happen and waited.

He was surprised when Fang and Claw hastened down the passage toward him. He gazed curiously at Fang. "What are you doing up so late Fang?"

Fang looked somewhat agitated. "Looking for Knife. Almost all of today she was in some state. She saw things everywhere, and she said some pretty strange things, too. It was as if she was speaking in riddles. But, well, you know how she can speak to the wind? Well, the wind is blowing hard now. I need to find her! I don't like the state she's been in one bit."

Worry struck Hemlock's cold heart. "All right. Let's find her."

Judging by the fact that the wind blew from the south, they searched the south passages. It did not take long to find Knife, but that didn't lessen Hemlock's unease. He had never seen Knife like this. She stood perfectly straight, a single silken shawl draped over her, fluttering in the heavy wind. Almost as if blown by the wind, her eyes were changing colors in a sickening way.

"Knife?" Hemlock queried uncertainly.

Knife didn't react.

Fang shrugged. "I don't think she can hear you. I've tried talking to her all day, but she seems oblivious. It's really weird."

Knife stood absolutely still. She said nothing for a while. Even the clinking and clanking accompanying Ice trying to sneak up in a mysterious way did not rouse her from her trance. She just stood, staring south, her eyes still dancing nauseatingly.

Then she spoke. Her voice had a strange, calm quiet to it, deprived of either good or evil. "The wind speaks truth. Remember these words."

Fang tipped his head to one side, his eyes glowing, as Knife continued.

"The moon is shining brighter than the brightest star, even more so than the sun. The one of pure might and evil will be slain, and without, the rest will scatter and be afraid of the daughter of the fleetest bird. The jay that died on the day of new life has given his flight to victory. The children of the mollusk and the south star will seek the truth. The stoneflower will rise and be victorious."

Now she paused. It seemed as if something very urgent was about to leave her lips. When she spoke again, her voice was barely above a whisper.

"The one who thought she was senseless will find the answer. She will hear much and make a decision. She will find who she is and be feared by the creatures who know no fear. Her kin who rejected her will accept her. She will prove herself worthy. She is a descendent of many great warriors, and she will rise to their standards. For cleverness is her strongest point."

She paused and her eyes closed. It looked as if she was asleep. Fang shrugged, totally bewildered.

"Like I said, she's different today. It's totally unreal. She's said some things that I guess are about us. For example, 'Darkest woods will burn, red gates hold, curses will be seen.' I suppose that we're the only ones who use curses."

Claw rolled his eyes. "Of course, Fang. But the rest of what she said is rather cryptic."

"You don't say, Claw," Hemlock snorted. "What in the name of the Blight is the 'daughter of the fleetest bird'? And that last bit. She spoke only of one creature, of that I'm sure. But how can you think you're stupid but really be clever at the same time? You'd be too idiotic to tell that you are clever!"

"It could mean Zuryzel."

Hemlock looked strangely at Ice. "What makes you think that?"

Ice shook her head. "Not the last bit. The bit about the moon. You never know, but it could be Zuryzel. Her name means 'moon' after all."

Claw rolled his eyes. "Now I know this has nothing to do with Zuryzel."

Ice's eyes gleamed, but not with malice. Was that *triumph* in their crimson depths?

Fang shrugged. "Knife is really good at solving riddles. We should ask her when she wakes up."

"You think she's really asleep, then?" asked Ice.

"Well, I wouldn't say she's anything else," replied Hemlock. "If she is, there's no word for it. Fang, shake her."

Fang nervously prodded Knife. Her eyes flew open. "What happened?" she whispered, her eyes back to the usual red.

"You fell asleep," replied Fang.

Knife looked so skeptical that even Hemlock gulped.

None of the foxes noticed Sibyna racing through the castle at top speed, her camouflage almost forgotten.

Biddah woke groggily to excited shouts. She must have slept a long time upon her return to the Bow Tribe camp, and now she realized that dawn had come and gone. Sibyna stood surrounded by many impatient creatures and looked quite overwhelmed.

King Hokadra hurried out of the bushes that held his bed. He held up his paws for silence. "Sibyna," he urged her sternly, making his way through the crowd to stand in front of her. "What happened?"

Sibyna looked thoroughly excited, now that the noise had died down. "Knife made a prophecy. She listened to the wind and said some very interesting things. I remember what she said."

Hokadra waved the crowd away. "Go on, off with you all. You must have something else to do. Sibyna, Queen Demeda, Johajar, Mokimshim, Lady Raven, Sharmmuh, come with me."

Sibyna followed eagerly. Raven's blue eyes shone with something—was it laughter?—and the merest of smiles played on her lips.

"Now Sibyna," said Hokadra sternly, "tell us everything."

Closing her eyes, straining her memory, she recited Knife's prophecy.

Perfect silence followed as each mentally pondered the puzzle. Sibyna noticed Lady Raven with a thoughtful and hopeful look on her face, as if she had thought of something but did not dare say it out loud. Biddah had a feeling that she knew what Lady Raven was thinking of. Her official title was Lady Raven the Swift. Daughter of the fleetest bird would probably be Herttua Crow Blue Arrows. On the other hand, Sibyna reflected, she could be thinking of something else. Lady Raven had one of the nimblest minds, and she could make some of the most interesting connections.

To her surprise, however, Sharmmuh was the first to speak up, in a very hesitant voice. "Well, I think I know about the stoneflower. You see, a rather rare name for a squirrel maiden is Zinta. Normally it's given only to a Tribeprincess or Tribequeen. The word means stoneflower; it grows in the mountains."

Johajar thought about this for a while. "In that case, it could be the name of one of the squirrels from the Mountain Tribe. What do you think, Sharmmuh?"

Sharmmuh nodded slowly. "I don't know much about the Mountain Tribe. For all I know, Zinta may be a very common name up there. Who can tell?"

"Sometimes you can have a very good idea," Raven murmured. Sibyna was now sure she knew something, but didn't speak about it. There was a kind of knowing in her eyes that said more than any words could.

Hokadra dismissed the meeting. As the others moved off, Sibyna lingered a little, because Hokadra had stopped Raven with a stern speaking of her name.

"What do you think about this?" Hokadra asked. Sibyna, already a few steps away, strained her ears.

"I think," she said quietly, "that the stoneflower isn't a fox. And if it is victorious, then the foxes aren't going to rule the world, at least not for forever."

Hokadra nodded. "What about the rest of it?"

Raven shrugged. "It is a prophecy. It could mean something any time, even at the end of the world. We can't assume that all the prophecies made by them refer to this war or right now." Her eyes glittered with bitterness. "Or maybe they are referring to something only *connected* with this war." She set her jaw harder. "You know what I speak of."

Hokadra nodded, his mind somewhere else, somewhere in the past. Sibyna had stopped dead, bent over her shoe, praying she wasn't noticed.

Hokadra looked at Raven again. "You said something was coming," he said, his voice earnest. "Something that will turn the world around."

"Not turn the world around," Raven corrected. "Turn it *back* around. Turn it the way it is *supposed* to be."

Hokadra looked almost hopeful as Raven glided out of the clearing. Sibyna hurried on, not wanting to be caught.

21
ANGER

Danaray and Anamay's fatigue showed in their gait. Constantly, they stumbled over tree roots, their paws still not used to dodging them with every step, having grown up on the eastern plains where there were very few trees.

To Danaray's eyes, Anamay looked particularly weary-looking. Her mind seemed elsewhere, and she seemed swamped in misery and despair. This made Danaray nervous, unsure of the source of her sister's sadness, but she tried to hide her concern.

"Ana," she finally said, "do you want to sleep for the night?"

Anamay just shrugged.

The response positively alarmed Danaray. She stopped. "All right," she urged gently. "What is it?"

When Anamay looked up, Danaray felt sick by the look of pure despair in her eyes. But Anamay began to speak in a slow, tired voice.

"It's Mollusk," she whispered. "I can't get him out of my head."

Danaray's temper rose, but she had enough restraint to hide it.

"Well," she muttered, not quite as gently as she had before, "why don't you try thinking of something else? Think of Father!"

Anamay's despair mingled with resentment in her eyes. "It's not as simple as that!" she whispered, a little louder than she had before. "I won't see him ever again, thanks to you! I keep wondering if he'll remember me or if he'll fall in love with some other maiden or if … But you wouldn't understand! You just have no idea what love means!"

That did it. Danaray's voice, when she found it, turned into a low, dangerous growl.

"Anamay, you have not even the sense that the Bear King gave to a hornbeam! To begin with, you fall in love with someone who is supposed to be your enemy, a sea otter. We both know they live selfish lives. Oh yes, I've heard the stories. The Wraith Mice protected them from that major band of rogues thirty cycles ago, and what do they do? They take over the fortress of Zurez! They were protected at Zurez by Streamcourse's band, and what did they do? They slaughtered half of her warriors! They care only for what is theirs, not even so much as thinking of the lives that are at stake, at Pasadagavra, at Mirquis, at Dombre, and in all of the tribe territories!

"They pretend to own the lands belonging to river otters, making many of them rogues, and then say that the river otters need to get a decent life when they took all hope of decent life from the river otters. They're selfish, Anamay! Well, normally I'd say, go ahead, keep thinking about Mollusk, and learn your lesson! But you know what? *I* keep thinking about the lives at risk! Tribes, kingdoms, yes, rogues too, they're all ready to give their lives to fight against the foxes, and yes, to keep them from attacking the sea otters, hoping that the current generation will turn out to be decent. But do the sea otters care? No! They couldn't care less how many lives are lost, or if the whole army left alive to fight the foxes is killed slowly and painfully, not to mention all the babes and infirm. Just so long as the foxes don't kill any of their own, then they don't care. They live selfishly, so much so that I would just love for Nighthawk and Shorefish to destroy them. I mean it! I have never hated any creature so much as a sea otter. And, *of course*, they call themselves followers of the Bear King, gracious, kind, selfless, better than the rogues that are constantly and 'purposelessly' attacking them. I'd prefer the rogues to them any day!"

Anamay looked frightened now. "Mollusk's different!" she insisted pleadingly.

"You're blind, Anamay," growled Danaray, her teeth bared in a snarl. "You're blind, and I hope you do end up as his mate. You'd get along perfectly with the sea otters. You're just as selfish as they are. Love Mollusk if you want; that's your business, and I won't interfere anymore—that sure didn't work. But you are so swamped in misery about your own heartache that you can't even think of the risk of thousands of lives. So many creatures are dying due to the foxes' greed and the sea otters' selfishness, and you don't even give a thought to that! You just moan about not being with a sea otter so much that you can't even think of the misery of others! Don't you remember what happened to Fawn? She was clawed by a fox, because she decided not to be so cruel anymore. Or what about Streamcourse? Hemlock killed her mate when she had only one child, who later disappeared when he went out to avenge his father.

"And I'll tell you one thing: if you have difficulty thinking of the hard times that others are going through, I want you to think of whom we are looking for and her mother. Lady Raven and Herttua Crow left their safe, comfortable home, the half of the earth that they love, to come and fight for creatures that they didn't even know. They could have stayed perfectly safe up north, without needing any creature to protect them, which is more than the sea otters could say, but they didn't! They came south to fight, knowing they could die and knowing their participation could even bring the destruction of the Rangers, all that to help others survive. And most important, every single one of the Rangers came willingly. They did not come grudgingly! It is a whole lot more than your sea otters could say. They just can't leave their life of happiness, even though thousands of others are suffering because of it! You're just like them, Anamay. All you can think about is one of them when thousands of others are suffering, and you don't even give a thought to that!"

Toward the end of the heated lecture, Danaray's voice had grown in volume until she was shouting. Anamay cowered, and her face was a mask of fear and uncertainty.

Danaray saw the effect of her words, but she held no guilt in having given vent to her fury.

Nothing short of hatred for her sister overwhelmed Danaray. She drew her knife, hurled it in Anamay's direction, and stormed off through the trees, hearing the knife whirl past her sister, who, by the sounds that reached Danaray's ears, was now sobbing. Cold contempt threatened to drown Danaray. Her sister was selfish and did not even care about the lives that were at stake, or even her own family and friends, the ones that she had grown up with all her life. She was *worse* than the sea otters!

Danaray began to run, her paws no longer stumbling over roots as she raced through the night. Just past a stream, she flung herself down and closed her eyes, tears coming nonstop and dripping into the rivulet, mingling with the fresh water and flowing away, away, away.

The rhythm of her weeping slowed her racing heart, and her weariness gently took over.

So soundly did she sleep that she never saw the two figures racing expertly through the night toward her sister.

22.

THE CAPTIVE

The next morning, Danaray woke, knowing she could not abandon her sister, despite her misguided thinking. She would come to understand eventually, Danaray believed. She easily found her way back to where she had left Anamay the night before. But she could find no trace of her. Anamay was gone. Vanished, as if into clean air. A mounting fear, a horror threatening to overwhelm Danaray, was tugging at her heart: had sea otters taken her sister?

Trying hard not to think *attacked* Anamay, she followed a likely trail from the area, indicated by the line of broken ferns, branches, and such. Danaray followed it until she lost it, still not being very good at forest tracking.

She had only one choice left: she would have to find Mollusk or Brine and talk to them. She still hated every single sea otter, but she needed to find her sister. Despair welled up inside of her when she realized that the last thing she had said to her sister, and possibly the last thing that she would ever say to her, was that she was selfish.

By sunhigh, Danaray had found the island where Anamay and Mollusk had met. She sat down on it, trying to hide herself until she saw Mollusk or Brine. Sitting in a patch of bracken, she watched and waited.

Anamay struggled against the powerful paws that gripped her. She kicked, bit, thwacked away with her tail, clawed desperately with her swimming claws, but to no avail. The two sea otters who had control of her were being rather savage. One called to the other.

"Oh, she's a feisty one, eh, Anemone?"

"Yes, she is, Kite. Crustacean will be pleased to see her!"

Anamay kept struggling until she kicked Kite painfully on the nose. He cried out in pain, and then Kite and Anemone dropped her. Then they bent down and hauled her by the foot paws.

Anamay cried out in pain as they wrenched her ankles, but Anemone and Kite, who was bleeding heavily from his nose, took no notice.

Her cry rose to a wail when Kite and Anemone dragged her painfully across some roots to the sea otters' camp. It was bare earth, surrounded by little houses of dried clay covered with reeds. A well sat in the middle. A few shouts rang out, and immediately the center of the camp was swarming with sea otters, some shouting jeers in Simalan.

"Silence! Silence!" A very old looking otter exited from the biggest of the huts. A respectful silence fell across the clearing, and the otters parted to let him pass.

He paced forward until he stood in front of Anemone, a maiden, Anamay realized with a start who blocked his view of the captive.

"What is going on, Anemone?"

Anemone replied without pride but with simple honesty in her voice and her words. "We found this river otter on our territory."

A grudging admiration for Anemone filled Anamay. She was nothing like Fraeggah or Deggum, who had swelled up so proudly when they had caught her. Her almost casual use of "we" showed her truthfulness and humility—she alone had not caught Anamay.

Suddenly Kite grabbed her from behind. He hauled her up onto her paws, muttering, "On your foot paws, mud dog."

Anamay's ankles gave way under her. With a cry of pain, she collapsed. Kite was about to haul her up again when the old otter ordered, "Leave her be!"

Anamay pulled herself up as high as she could, ready to bite if she should be touched again. But there was no need.

The old otter squatted down in front of Anamay. "What is wrong with your ankles, maiden?"

Anamay hoped her reply sounded fierce. "They are wrenched. Those two," and she gestured with her paw to Kite and Anemone, "dragged me by my foot paws."

The old otter frowned at Kite and Anemone. "Do not do that again," he ordered wearily. He turned back to Anamay and asked her, "What is your name?"

For a moment, Anamay considered giving her name in the common tongue. But she swiftly decided that that would be a bad idea. "Anamay," she replied.

"I see," replied the old otter. "Do you mean any harm to us?"

"No!" Anamay retorted indignantly. "I've never even heard of otters with white faces!" she lied, praying that the Bear King would forgive her.

An amused smile spread across the old otter's face. "We are sea otters," he explained.

Anamay frowned. "You're a long way from the sea." Now that she said it, she realized it was true; why didn't the sea otters live by the sea?

The old otter continued to smile, but he did not reply. Instead he turned to his clan. "Officially it is my decision, but I will ask you. Has any here any reason to keep this otter prisoner?"

There was a low murmuring. One voice that Anamay recognized with a jolt of horror belonged to Brine rang out clearly. "Prisoner, no. But her ankles are wrenched. We would be just as bad as some of the rogues out there if we let her go now, disabled."

The old otter stood up and turned to Brine. "So what do you suggest, Brine?"

Brine's reply had no hesitation. "Let her stay here until her ankle has healed. *Then* let her go."

Anemone raised her voice. "Crustacean, she is a river otter. How will she live here? *I'm* not looking after her."

"Then I will," retorted Brine.

Crustacean held up his paws. "Both of you are right. However, if Brine is willing, I will let her look after Anamay. Anamay, if that is all right with you?"

Anamay thought for about three seconds. Then she nodded.

🦫

Brine raced over to where she had met Anamay. Danaray saw her coming. She stood up and held up her paws to show that she was unarmed.

Brine swam the river without a single struggle. She did not even shake herself off when she loped up to where Danaray waited.

"Brine," Danaray whispered urgently, "do you know where Anamay is?"

Brine nodded regretfully. "Yes. Two otters, Anemone and Kite, captured her. Her paws were wrenched. Crustacean is keeping her but not as prisoner. As soon as her paws are healed, she will be set free. Do not worry, Danaray."

Danaray stared in astonishment. "How did you know who I am?"

Brine shrugged. "I saw you following Anamay that one day, and I asked Anamay who you were. She told me, and she told me that you might be here."

A creeping dread spread through Danaray. "Oh dear," she whispered. "The last thing I ever said to her was that I didn't like Mollusk and she was selfish because she kept thinking about Mollusk and not concentrating on her task while lives were at risk."

Brine clutched her paw sympathetically. "I'll tell her that I saw you and that you're sorry. Don't worry. I'll look after her."

Danaray nodded gratefully. "Thank you. I'd better go tell Father. Tell her that I'm going to tell Father *everything*."

Brine nodded. "Yes, and I'd better tell my own father. He'll need to know."

Danaray nodded and dove into the river without a sound. She let the murky, dark, cooling water encourage her, remembering that she could swim like an arrow from a bow in the river, even swimming upriver with ease. She swam east, always east, to where her father stayed and guarded the eastern lands.

INTERPRETATION

Fang lifted out a heavy parcel of paper and sneezed. "Oh, I know I put them here somewhere!" he exclaimed.

"Are these it, possibly?" Poison, Knife's apprentice, asked, holding up a stack of papers.

Fang nodded dumbly. Poison was irresistibly beautiful, and when she tried, she could put any male under her spell.

Ice quickly intervened. She took the papers from Poison and handed them to Fang. "Here, read them to me." She moved slightly, shielding Fang from Poison's stare.

Fang shook himself and read out a few of the lines Knife had said when she had been in a trance.

"The world is changing. It has already begun. The sun shines with pure radiance now, but it will darken later. One of three was born to lead. Watch for the one, for there will be no safety for us until it is dead."

Scorch, the apprentice to Fang, held up his paws. "Quiet. I can hear Knife and Claw."

He was right. Knife and Claw entered Hemlock's chamber. Knife glanced around, somewhat in surprise. "I heard that there was a meeting, but we didn't hear the bell. Why not?"

Poison shrugged. "It sounded. I don't know why you didn't hear it. *I* did."

Claw shrugged. "Well, we didn't—"

"*Obviously*, Claw," exclaimed Hemlock. "But never mind that. Fang, continue."

And he did. "The star will not rule the sky, but the sun and moon will rule. The world will never be the same."

Knife looked thoughtful. "Is that all?"

Fang nodded. "Yes. What do you think, Knife?"

Knife shrugged. "Well, I should have thought that it would be rather obvious, all that bit about 'one of three.'"

Scorch and Ice glanced at Knife blankly while the other foxes frowned at the parchment.

Fang nodded, however. "I think you're right. It *is* obvious."

The other foxes remained silent.

Knife stamped her paw impatiently. "For Blight's sake!" she exclaimed.

"Mokimshim, Zuryzel, and Johajar!" exclaimed Fang, sounding thoroughly exasperated. "The children of our main and old enemy! They are the ones who will take on the fight if something happens to Hokadra!"

Hemlock frowned. "What makes you say that?"

Knife and Fang spoke alternately.

"Well, there are three of them, to begin with—three heirs." Knife shrugged.

"One of them 'was born to lead'—meaning he or she might lead—and in these days, lead usually means head an army or kingdom." Fang seemed to read Knife's mind.

"That most likely means that they're royal in some way."

"And I would guess that 'born to lead' would be Zuryzel," Ice murmured.

Fang rolled his eyes. "As before mentioned, I now know this has nothing to do with Zuryzel. Most of Ice's ideas tend to be totally opposite."

Scorch shrugged. "Whatever. I didn't follow you. Please read on, maybe it will get clearer."

"I thought there was no more," Ice snapped.

"There is, but I didn't know—ouch!" Fang hissed as Hemlock cut his shoulder.

Poison sighed. The idea was that Knife would know very little of what she had said, but Scorch and Fang had messed it up.

Fang continued to read. "One was lost. She is returned. She is the daughter of many great ancestors. The bloods of the dangerous creatures flow in her. She is powerful, strong, and swift. One day, she will be identified by the speaker of these words.

"The two powerful and feared warriors will be respected and given the highest honor possible. In one, thrives the blood of many creatures, their lifeblood living again, ancestors who died but live again. The other will have that of paw's design. It is powerful, undefeatable, and strong enough to cleave stone in two."

Zuryzel was nearly overjoyed.

Dikiner had come back from a patrol the previous night with information of Knife's words, and Zuryzel was so hopeful that the prophecy really did mean her. However, she tempered her feelings, not daring to hope too much for the one thing that she really wanted.

Dikiner had waited until the two of them had been alone before telling Zuryzel of what Knife and Fang thought of Zuryzel.

"They admire you, Zuryzel," he had commented, a gleam of half-amusement, half-serious thought in his eyes. "They admire you in a grudging sort of way. They'll certainly be looking for you. In their eyes, they will have no peace until you are dead, or they are dead. Then again, if they die, they'll go to the Serpent's Land, and then of course, they won't have any peace period."

Zuryzel still swelled inwardly at the thought that, even if the prophecy didn't mean her, the foxes thought that it did. She had wanted to be distinguished by history, like one of the heroes of old. This was her chance! Like Zureza, the first ruler of the Wraith Mice. No real documents existed about the beginning of the earth. Only legends. Zuryzel dreamed of being in a legend like Zureza.

Zuryzel's thoughts trailed off. How could she even hope to compare to the old standards? she wondered. She had tasted the bitterness of leading, and she really didn't think that she would like to be a queen. Her ambition was abating. She knew now that there was scarcely any reward to leading like this. The tedium bored and oppressed her, as in constantly having to arrange patrols that mostly proved futile. But at least she had had help on that from Dikiner. With Zuryzel's permission, he had gotten Karena to watch Orgorad for him, and he had helped in so many other ways, more than Zuryzel could ever thank him for. She constantly turned to him for assistance, having him organize patrols here and there, help her with the sentries, and such. She was concerned that this meant that she was not a very good leader, but that seemed not so important now.

Most of all, Zuryzel wanted her father. She couldn't tell why, she just knew that she wanted him. He was quiet and serious, kind and helpful, friendly and cheerful, even during a dangerous time. She longed to have him with her, to help her with the command she was given, not to mention to fight by her side. She couldn't explain it, but she always felt safer when she thought of him.

She brushed her thoughts away like a cobweb on her shoulders and stood up. Putting on her warmest cloak, the one with the moon patterns, and slipping on her shoes, she strode over to the door. She had long since given up racing when no one saw her. It was just far too cramped in Dombre, and she was finding that she didn't enjoy running for its own sake as much. True, if ever she wandered out of the castle, she would lift her long, maiden's tunic and run with abandon across the open ground when no one saw her. But most of the time, she just liked to walk briskly.

Her first stop, like every morning, was the training facilities. She still liked to assess Crispisin. He was making excellent progress with his slashing and zigzagging sword movements, but he was still working on his duck-and-weave motions. With Dikiner's permission, she would teach him some of the best motions that she had learned. As Zuryzel was finding out, she took great pleasure in teaching another, especially such a naturally adept student as Crispisin.

Dikiner and Crispisin were over in their usual corner, but Zuryzel noticed that there were fewer trainers and trainees than usual. With a slight frown, she wandered up to Dikiner, standing politely off to the side so as not to interrupt the lesson.

Dikiner must have seen her out of the corner of his eye because he let Crispisin get him in a strike with the practice swords that ordinarily he would have easily blocked. He smiled at his bright pupil before hurrying up to Zuryzel.

"Did you want to speak to me, Zuryzel?"

Zuryzel nodded. "Where is everyone? Usually there are a lot more trainers and trainees in here. Where is everyone?" she repeated.

Dikiner shrugged. "Well, Shinar took hers out on patrol last night, and they haven't returned yet. Orgorad went on a different patrol, putting his student on sentry duty. Karena went with him, and she sent hers to the archery range with Colobi. Dejuday took his to the river to practice tracking. Everyone else is here."

Zuryzel nodded thoughtfully. She thanked Dikiner and requested to assess Crispisin, to which Dikiner gave his willing approval.

"All right, Crispisin," Zuryzel challenged, "try to disarm me!"

Before Zuryzel had time to raise her practice blade, Crispisin slashed downward. Zuryzel barely flicked her weapon out of the way in time. Then she thrust upward at Crispisin's blade and tried to flick it out of his paws. Crispisin brought his blade in and tried another attempt at Zuryzel. Then the two Wraith Mice were slashing, dodging, and attacking with a will. Zuryzel was finding it very hard even to approach Crispisin's blade with his swift responses and attacks.

She drew back, breathing heavily, but Crispisin scarcely panting. She shook her head in admiration and exclaimed, "Moon and clouds, Crispisin, you're fast!"

Crispisin's eyes glowed. Suddenly Zuryzel slashed with her blade, but Crispisin had not lost his guard. He drew his blade back and crashed it powerfully down on top of Zuryzel's. She barely held on.

She nodded approvingly. "Well done! I think that before too long, if it's okay with Dikiner, you could be doing more experiential practice. How about sentry duty tonight?" she suggested, with a glance at Dikiner.

Dikiner nodded, and Crispisin gave a cry of delight.

Zuryzel smiled and whispered to Dikiner, "You've been teaching him well."

Dikiner smiled, but shook his head. "*You* taught him half of what he knows. I can't take full credit."

Zuryzel shifted uncomfortably. "I'm sorry," she whispered. "I didn't mean to interfere."

Dikiner shrugged. "You didn't. You were just doing what you are supposed to do. It was hardly interfering, anyway. If you hadn't come up, I would have asked you to. You are an excellent leader." Here he paused. He looked long into Zuryzel's eyes. Then he spoke again. "I see something in you, Zuryzel. You are a born leader, and you will make a good one, one day. You care about the goings on in your domain, and you control them well. You have the blood of many great leaders in your veins. Not all things are passed down from parents to offspring, but I think that the Bear King gave you all the leading talent that he gave to the kings, queens, and warriors of the past."

His words stirred her own hopes of the same, and they rose within her. But she let them fall back down; she just didn't have the faith in herself that he had in her. "But I constantly need help," she replied humbly. "I'm incapable of leading by myself. I'm not able to do it without others doing it for me!"

Dikiner shrugged again. "Every leader needs help. Your father needs help from you sometimes! The point is not that you do everything by yourself—no one, not you, not even your father can do that; the point is that you know what to do, get whatever help you need, and make sure it gets done. You're still the one who makes the decisions. Besides, as my father told me, 'The only thing you'll successfully do alone is fail.'"

Zuryzel felt pride thrilling through her. She hoped that it did not show too readily. With a nod and a thankful murmur to Dikiner, she smiled and hurried off to check on the sentries.

FIGHT AND FLIGHT

Biddah stood her post nervously.

Exactly a cycle had passed since Ice had set the date for the foxes' attack, but even though the dawn was half over, there was no sign as yet of the foxes.

All waited with strained impatience. Biddah felt her paws shaking on her bow, and next to her, Karrum was biting his lip fearfully.

Sharmmuh swung up and glanced at them. Both of them shook their heads.

Sharmmuh shrugged, showing no trace of anxiety. "The patrol said that there is a heavy mist shrouding the moor. They may be lost."

Karrum sighed wearily. "Let's hope they are. I wish we knew that we could win this battle. But we all know that we're going to have to retreat to Mirquis, and then to Dombre, and probably even to Pasadagavra. Why don't we just go there immediately?"

Sharmmuh explained. "To slow the foxes down, mainly. We are trying to give time for other creatures to get to Pasadagavra, those who can't fight for themselves."

Karrum looked incredulous. "It was a cycle ago when we found out the exact date of the attack! Why didn't the others get there in time?"

Sharmmuh twitched. "We weren't able to get the news out immediately. Some may have only just heard of it. We don't know."

"Do you think that the foxes have changed their attack date?" Biddah suggested hopefully.

Sharmmuh was about to reply when Raven and Queen Demeda hurried up through the forest. Raven breathed out two words.

"They're coming."

There was no fear of any kind in Raven's eyes or expression. On the contrary, she looked eager, as if she wanted the battle to commence there and now.

It did not, however. Only silence escaped through the trees, even when Lady Raven positioned her remaining six-score warriors in the nearby shrubbery to attack the foxes from behind. Hokadra had cautioned her against the plan, but Raven was totally unconcerned.

"Even if the numbers of the foxes are so big that you couldn't get help to me," she had said, "I will easily be able to draw away. It is not as though we're fighting in a canyon."

Whiskers twitching, eyes intently scanning the scene before them, and lips tightly pursed, the expressions of the Rangers showed eager anticipation as they thought of the battle ahead. They were ready for anything—lightly but hardly skimpily armed, protected with a lightweight bark tunic soaked in special water to make it harder than any weapon, and especially equipped with drab brown cloaks that did not billow overmuch.

The faintest sound of drumming could be heard, echoing eerily in the still forest. Every single squirrel, Wraith Mouse, river otter, and Ranger was well hidden, each one's fur bristling from tension. A few dark, shadowy figures began racing through the trees, nearby and back again, and still no one else moved. The defenders remained completely silent.

And then the foxes became close enough for Biddah to hear the tramping of their feet. But still the defenders waited.

Biddah looked around the camp, moving her eyes but barely her head. The whole camp had completely stripped. Nothing remained—no beds, no piles of armor, no precious possessions of any kind, nor even any of Marah's healing supplies The foxes would never suspect that it had once been a tribe's home.

The drumming and the footsteps mingled now, and the shape of Hemlock in the lead of many soldiers emerged through the trees.

Still the hidden troops made no movement, watching as Hemlock advanced just a bit past them.

Then Hokadra raised his sword and waved it.

Finally, a shout went up from behind the column of foxes. Hemlock whirled around and found that many of his vanguard were dead. Before any arrow could be strung or a spear lifted or even a blade raised, he had leapt back to the rest of his warriors.

Biddah loaded her bow with an arrow, and at Tribequeen Sharmmuh's signal, began firing into the ranks of the foxes.

But there were so many foxes! They seemed to go on and on. Lady Raven raised her voice in a desperate war cry, and Biddah and Karrum raced through the branches to where the Rangers were suddenly surrounded. Ice had led another band of foxes behind Hemlock, with a huge gap in between. Lady Raven was surrounded, but not a single of her Rangers had been slain—in fact, very few of them had even been wounded, though they looked a little apprehensive at the sight of many more foxes arriving. Indeed, the wave led by Ice was twice as large as the already reduced wave led by Hemlock.

Karrum glanced at Biddah, as if to make sure that she was still unhurt, and commented calmly, "I bet that the double-wave idea was not Ice's!"

Biddah nodded and began firing into the front ranks of the foxes to ease the fighting load on Lady Raven.

Biddah's arrows lasted for at least two hours, though she had to reuse her arrows several times. Lady Raven was fighting her way through the last of Hemlock's wave without much difficulty. King Hokadra and Queen Demeda were being driven slowly back across the forest with their Wraith Mice, but the river otters were wrecking havoc, appearing here first, then almost immediately falling back, drawing the foxes into the thick nettle clumps that agonized most of them, and then attacking from behind the unsuspecting foxes. Only a command from King Hokadra brought them back to the ranks of the Wraith Mice. The squirrels were sitting in the trees above them, shielding them from archers, though none would ever have even hinted that Lady Raven needed help in any way, shape, or form. Nor did she.

By the time the sun had beat off the mist, the resisting army had been driven from the Bow Tribe's home.

At the edge of the camp, the archers and spear throwers hurled a horrific salvo of weaponry at the foxes, and then the whole army raced out from the trees.

The squirrels ran expertly along branches without making the trees rattle, as if they were not running at all. Their paws kept to the sturdier branches, leaping lightly from limb to limb. The river otters were natural woodland warriors, and they melted perfectly with the woods, while the Wraith Mice had only a little difficulty, it not being night. Lady Raven and the Rangers were clearly racing with them—Biddah saw them every now and then—but other than that, they were completely invisible, melding perfectly with the tree trunks and bracken, their paws scarcely even passing through the groundswell as they ran.

At the end of the woods, the warriors halted. Lady Raven shrugged as if the major battle was absolutely nothing to be scared of. (Indeed, Biddah had to agree with her when she looked at the Rangers—none of them had so much as a scratch, even though they'd borne the worst of the battle.)

"Well," Lady Raven commented, "I would suppose we could rest. It is definitely not as if the foxes are right behind us—or will be anytime soon; they are all covered in metal!"

Oracle Hemlock was in high good spirits. He had managed to conquer what no other fox had. He held up his paws and announced to the exhilarated troops that they could rest.

His eye fell on Fang. He alone did not look exhilarated, but instead he looked rather troubled. Frowning, Hemlock wandered over to him. "What are you worrying about now, Fang?"

Fang did not react to Hemlock's irate tone. "Only about eight, or at most ten, score were slain on our side and not a single one on their side except for two Wraith Mice and a river otter. We couldn't use our Warhawks, and that is one of the things that worry me. But besides that, the foes number at least six times the number of our slain. Most of them did not even get to slay any. I'm not forgetting that most of the dead are dead to that black mouse's rapier and her band. That does not make much sense if they were fighting to defeat us. They had to have another purpose in fighting—to delay us!"

At that moment, a fox raced, panting, up to Hemlock. "Knife wants you to come to the castle immediately."

Hemlock rolled his eyes. "She is a fool. I have just won a battle, and I plan to conduct another one soon. Why must she see me now?"

The fox shrugged. "She says that it is thoroughly urgent, and that you would regret it if you did not come."

Hemlock glanced at Fang, saying, "You and Ice share command here until I get back, but don't even think about going after the foes or going along with any of Ice's ideas." Then he followed the messenger back to the castle.

At the entrance to the corridor that led to his chambers, Knife was waiting for him. She looked bewildered, exasperated, and even a little fearful. "Poison had some sort of a vision," she explained. "I mean, she's had nightmares before, but now she is hysterical. I've never seen her like this before. She keeps going on about stuff that makes no sense; she's so incoherent. I haven't been able to get any sense out of her, nor has anyone. The only words I've been able to get out of her are 'claws' and 'teeth.'"

Hemlock snarled at her. "You summoned me because Poison had a nightmare?"

He instantly regretted his outburst as Knife raised her claws threateningly. Her voice was a dangerous growl. "It was anything but a nightmare. She has been sobbing since you left, when she awoke. That is almost a whole day now. I highly doubt that she would be this upset over just a nightmare!"

Hemlock did not reply to the challenge. "Where is she?"

Knife lowered her claws. She jerked her head and set off.

As they entered Poison's room, Hemlock had a feeling that Knife had good reason to summon him. He had never seen Poison like this, or, for that matter, any creature like this. She was curled up on her bed, gasping and sobbing, shaking all over. Every now and then she would cry something indistinguishable. She shied away from Knife as Knife approached her slowly.

"Poison," Knife murmured in a singsong voice, "what happened?"

She reached out a paw to stroke her apprentice, but at the sight of Knife's claws, Poison screamed. Knife instantly lowered her paw. She took a cup of liquid that another fox brought her, and without Poison seeing her claws, held the drink to Poison's lips. Poison drank almost greedily. Then she fell back.

"Now Poison," whispered Knife, "what happened? Where?"

Poison took a deep breath and began in a voice deprived of feeling: "There was a huge field. It was surrounded by woods on the one side and a chain of mountains on the other. One mountain was pink, and it looked hollow, too, because some of it was clear. Its peak had very little snow on it, and it was perfectly clear so I could see into the mountain. Many creatures were living there.

"From the edge of the woods, a cry—like a warhawk's—sounded out. For a moment, a glorious arrow that looked blue shot across the sky, and black feathers obscured my vision. Then I had a brief vision of Chiraage sinking into a black sea, and then I was back at the field. From the mountains raced squirrels, many, fresh, free, and swift, with a rolling line etched on their cheeks. They carried double-ended throwing spears. Then the creatures came. They were like nothing I've ever seen. There were some big, some small, some black, some tawny, and one of the biggest led. They had huge claws, ripping teeth, horrific speed ..."

The young vixen began to lash around again. Knife smacked her head with her paw, claws cutting a little fur, and Poison went limp.

Knife and Hemlock stared at each other in fear for a moment.

None of them noticed Lady Raven perched on the windowsill, her fear of heights completely forgotten. She slipped down the low-growing tree and raced with all her speed to the field where the others waited, her Ranger's skills so good that she could, if she wanted, sneak up unseen and slice through Ice's shawls. (*Why* did *she wear all that?*) *She* knew what the creatures were in Poison's dream, though there was no way she was going to tell anyone except Hetmuss Cinder what she had heard of them.

25.

THE SUCCESSOR

anaray had long since given up all hope. She was trudging wearily east, always east, without giving much of a thought to her own self, not caring if she ran into foes. She knew that she should be trying to track Herttua Crow Blue Arrows down, but she couldn't do that without Anamay. She needed her sister's better tracking skills to help her see the subtle markings on the ground, in disturbed stones, or in broken nearby leaves or branches to show her the way. Even on the open fields she had lived in all her life, Danaray sometimes lost the way. She had gone back to where she had found a small trail through the woods but had lost it immediately.

After five days of weary trekking, she breasted a rise and found herself looking down into the camp of her father, Mudriver.

She loped down into the camp and was almost instantly greeted by the many friends she had.

"Danaray!"

"You're back!"

"We sure missed you!"

"Where's Anamay?"

Danaray smiled, but she could not meet the gazes of any of the warriors she had trained and grown up with.

"Dana!" called a voice at the edge of the crowd. Danaray smiled truly at the sight of her father, Mudriver. His sleek brook-brown fur mirrored hers, as did his brown eyes. He hurried forward to clasp his daughter's paws. "Good to see you again. Well, did you find Herttua Crow? What about Anamay? Where is she?"

Danaray felt a pang in her heart. She could only mumble, "It's a long story."

Mudriver was anxious, Danaray could sense it, but he did not lose his friendly smile. "Come into my tent, Dana," he urged.

As Danaray followed him, she realized with a sickening feeling of dread that her father was very thin and weak. He seemed to stumble over everything. To Danaray's dismay, he was limping by the time they got to his tent.

He carefully seated himself in a chair, and Danaray realized that he did not have many more cycles to live. His frame, once sturdy and strong, now bent even when seated and looked small and thin.

Danaray stood respectfully, but—to her distress—her father motioned her to sit. This she did, but on the floor.

"Now, Dana," urged her father, "tell me everything that happened."

Danaray told him the whole story, beginning where Anamay had been captured. Her father frowned. "Why did you leave her?"

The tears that Danaray had been fighting for many days threatened to spill, but she held on to her self-control. "Father, she … she had been meeting a … sea otter. For a month. Sh-she was in love with him. She was moping about and constantly losing the trail, and I could never pick it up. I-I got fed up with it, and I shouted at her. I even lost my temper and threw my knife at her. I didn't hit—but, oh, for a moment, I just hated her!" She could no longer hold on to her control. Her tears fell from her eyes like raindrops from the clouds. She looked pleadingly up at her father. "Did I do the right thing? I mean, shouting at her?"

Her father did not look angry, only calm. "Yes, you did. She knows what she was doing was wrong, but she kept on doing it. Perhaps … perhaps she is happy where she is. The sea otters are not wholly bad, you know. Streamcourse told you one story; others may tell it differently. She does not know everything. Besides," he continued, almost warningly, "you have other endeavors to endure right now." He began to cough a little.

Danaray found a pitcher of water nearby and offered her father some. He willingly accepted. Then he continued his calm speaking, though his words did not soothe Danaray.

"My daughter, I have been fortunate to live as long as I have. My cycles are running to an end. I prayed to the Bear King that he would send you back soon to me, and not long after, you arrived. My daughter, you are to lead the warriors now. I have complete faith that your leadership will be a good one. You must promise me that you will not think only of your sister and will resist the foxes to the best of your ability."

"Promise?" whispered Danaray through her tears. "I swear it on my life. I will fight the foxes with all my strength, Father. I swear it on my life!"

Kermunda, the healer, had hurried into the tent with a bundle of herbs clamped in his paws before this. He stood back respectfully but keenly listened until Mudriver called him over.

"Kermunda, you must help Danaray with her leadership when she needs it. I trust you to help her always."

Kermunda nodded, looking slightly surprised. Danaray could scarcely prevent a sob from leaving her lips. But while she tried to prevent herself from crying, she was having difficulty speaking.

"Father ...," she whispered, unable to say more.

He raised his paw a little, and she clasped it. "My daughter," he whispered. "Danaray. Oh, Dana."

With that he breathed his last, and his paw went limp.

Danaray could no longer restrain herself. A strangled moan escaped her lips. Her tears fell thick and fast. She clung to her father's paw, for what reason she did not know. She was aware of Kermunda standing next to her, his head bowed, but that seemed insignificant. Her father was dead. The father she had loved for all her life was dead.

Kermunda tapped her shoulder. "Danaray, I'm sorry but you have to tell the others."

Danaray gasped with realization. "What will they think? He dies the day I come back ..."

Kermunda did not seem worried. "We all knew, unless the Bear King intervened, your father would likely not live past today. Everyone thought how lucky for you and your father that he lived long enough for both of you to see each other one last time. And because we had feared we would have to go looking for you, we welcome you with joy, Danaray." He sighed. "Don't worry," he added. "I'll help you. Your father ordered it. And besides, I would even if he didn't order it."

Danaray was surprised by his immediate loyalty to her. She straightened up, sniffed, let her father's paws rest on his chest, and followed Kermunda out of the tent.

Even the smallest of the otters would have guessed by Danaray's face that something terrible had happened. With eyes smudged from tears, she, nevertheless, held her head high with a look of powerful determination. She quickened her pace till she walked side by side with Kermunda, showing that she had as much authority in her tribe of warriors as a healer.

She stalked to the center of the tents, her head raised, constantly asking the Bear King for strength. The day had grown overcast, and rain was just beginning to patter on the harsh dried ground as Danaray stood tall on a huge boulder, as she had seen her father do, as she had done once when her father had told her to announce the news of the hares being defeated. Her father!

Her tribe gathered almost immediately when Danaray summoned them. They saw by her face that their leader was dead. But, still, Danaray had to announce it.

Her voice had a burr in it, but she spoke with control over her sadness and declared, "It grieves me to announce the death of my father, Mudriver. He died not long ago in his tent where he now rests."

The whole tribe, including Danaray, bowed their heads, and many tears flowed. But Danaray found it in herself to stem them, at least in front of her tribe.

She was just wondering if she should tell her tribe about Anamay being captured, when a voice called out from the back of the crowd, "You're our leader, now."

Danaray was startled almost out of grief for a moment. It wasn't uncommon for the leadership of her tribe to pass from parent to child, but the tribe could decide differently. Such open acknowledgement to Danaray before any kind of discussion had been held startled her, but apparently none of the others. She dipped her head to them.

"I will try to lead this tribe as well as my father did. I can never take his place, but I promise to do my best."

Murmurs of grim approval broke out in the crowd. Then, gradually, members of the tribe moved away to pay their last respects to Mudriver.

Danaray sat down on the rock as rain splattered onto it. She was not seen by any creature, and she relished the solace. She longed for her sister, but she could not have Anamay, and she realized with an almost heart-stopping pang that was all her fault. Sobs of despair now spilled forth, softly muffled by the pounding of the rain on the rock.

Anamay was not unhappy in the least. She had stayed at the sea otter's camp for a while now. She was still officially something like a prisoner, but she hardly felt it.

She spent most of her time in the woods by the stream with Brine. She was furious with Danaray for thinking that the sea otters were selfish, because that was the last word she would use to describe them, or at least, Brine and Mollusk and their father.

The rest of the sea otters, she really didn't know about. She could scarcely look at them and not wish for the time before she came west. She longed for her father and her sister when her patience was a lot less short and she scarcely ever got mad, except for something serious. Then again, Mollusk was serious.

Still, Anamay had absolutely nothing against Brine. Most of the things Danaray had said about the sea otters had happened before she was a warrior. And now, from what Anamay figured out, the sea otters didn't even know anything about the foxes. At least, Brine didn't. She would listen, wide eyed, to Anamay's stories before telling her some of the things that the sea otters had lived through.

"Not too many cycles ago," she had said one night, "there was a rogue here named Sky. She was not exactly a bad type, as far as rogues go, but she broke lots of promises. For example, when she promised truce, she would attack. It was very frightening. That's how my mother died, killed by Sky. Some other rogue finally killed her. I'm not sure of his name … Foamtail, or something like that …"

"Streamcourse?" Anamay had asked.

Brine had nodded. "That's right. The only thing I know about Stream-course is that he has a white tail—has since he was born."

Anamay nodded, both in agreement with Brine's statement and in thinking how she'd never felt comfortable with those stories Streamcourse had told everyone. From the beginning, her relationship with Mollusk had shown her a different side of the sea otters, the real one.

🦫

Anamay lived on in blissful happiness, her mind staying on her happy life. She understood the sea otters completely. They had no need to leave their homes. They didn't even *know* about the foxes. How could they ever take on the war as their war? But even thoughts of that war were fading from her mind.

Anamay had already forgotten about Herttua Crow Blue Arrows, Lady Raven the Swift, and the Rangers, who had sacrificed their comfort and happiness ranging the northlands to make themselves an enemy to creatures *they* had never heard of in places that they did not know about. Even the sea otters had heard of Pasadagavra. The Rangers had not been so privileged.

Thoughts of her family also were drifting away. She, of course, had no idea what her sister was going through or that her father had died. Anamay rarely thought of them. It never crossed Anamay's mind as to what Danaray would say if she saw her sister, happily mingling with the sea otters, oblivious to the battles others were fighting, lives they were sacrificing.

Anamay leaned back and smiled as Brine talked on.

ONWARD TO MIRQUIS

The small defense army halted at the edge of the caves. They had not been able to travel far due to the absence of trees. The squirrels moved more directly and thus faster along tree branches, and now without them, the warriors more warily on the ground. At the entrance of the caves, Arpaha greeted the party. Her warriors were assembled and ready to leave. King Hokadra nodded to Sibyna.

"Check and make sure that nothing remains that could give us away. This place must not be discovered. It must be ready to use again before too terribly long, and the foxes would only foul it up."

Sibyna nodded and slipped into the caves, greeted by the dim, dancing light within. Scouring the caves, she found only a silver candlestick and the carved crescent moon on top of the stalagmite.

She knew that her orders contradicted each other here. The moon might give away the fact that the Wraith Mice used this place. But then again, the moon *claimed* it for the Wraith Mice.

She closed her eyes and thought hard about what the most important problem was, and she decided to figure out a way to leave the moon in place yet not let it give away the cave as belonging to the Wraith Mice.

Stalking high-headed to the entrance to the caves, Sibyna turned to look back. To her delight, a huge thorn bush grew across the rock face. With only a little shoving, she could cover up the entrance to the caves completely. She took some of the exposed roots and dug them into the soil to help the plant to grow there perfectly, working the top of the disturbed ground to make it look untouched. The caves now looked like solid rock, giving no clue to the entrance.

With all her speed, she practically flew across the open trail to catch up with her comrades. She had barely left the caves when trouble struck.

It began to rain again. The rain actually made the Wraith Mice stand out more in such open terrain, especially in the daytime.

She put on an extra burst of speed and soon halved the distance between herself and the rest of the soldiers. She did not glance back—if someone was following, her looking back would do no good—and put all her energy into catching up with the others.

After about two hours, she reached the main body of soldiers. Her heart was beating unusually fast, but she still had enough strength to keep up with the swift march. Skirting the outside ranks, she soon leveled up with King Hokadra and spoke to him in urgent whisper.

"Well? No one would know it was there?"

"No. I even covered the edge with an old bush growing nearby. The foxes won't even be able to get near because of that bush. It is all sealed up.

The king nodded and dismissed her with a wave of his paw.

She fell back without getting in anyone's way and fell into step with Biddah. Having to keep silent on the march allowed her mind to wander freely, and it encountered the same old questions. But she had no immediate answers to questions anymore, at least not to ones of any significance. Concerns about the war, all of Knife's prophesies, everything fell back into mist, like a mountain on a foggy day. Sibyna wondered, with sadness, if she would live to see the day when she would find the answers.

But then again, she knew she could not read the future. Ever since the Rangers of the north had actually left their boundaries nearly four cycles ago, they had been friends with the Wraith Mice, going back and forth from their land to the lands below and now staying south to help wage war on the foxes. Sibyna could be certain of one thing: the line of Lady Raven would not die out. Most of one prophecy referred to Herttua Crow Blue Arrows, but more important, the rest of the prophecy, about the one who thought she was stupid, clearly referred to a Ranger as well—cleverness of the Rangers, and especially Lady Raven, was almost legendary.

Sibyna's mental wanderings took her to the many legends of the tribes. They all shared the same ones about the Bear King, and she had always found most of them easy to believe. They spoke of such utter nonsense that she knew no one other than the Bear King himself could ever have made the stories up.

The travels of her mind helped the time pass more quickly, and towards the end of the night, Mirquis and the lake it sat in came into view. A close look told Sibyna that arrangements at the fort lacked a thoroughness she would have found under Hokadra's command, but they were more than passable. Mokimshim had done a good job with his first command. The sentries were just being changed as the rest of the army arrived. Mokimshim personally greeted his father, mother, and brother, telling his father of events and discoveries at Mirquis.

"I thought about sending a runner up to tell Zuryzel that you arrived when the patrol spotted you, but I figured that I should wait until you actually set paw here. The situation here has gone pretty well—no major problems. We caught sight of a Warhawk once or twice, but it never came near enough for us even to shout at ... Should we send someone up to Zuryzel?" he suggested.

Hokadra nodded, and replied, "That's a good idea. We need to tell her to send someone up to Pasadagavra to warn them, too. Send ..."

His gaze drifted around and landed on Sibyna. He hesitated for a moment and then finished with, "Sibyna."

Sibyna nodded to show that she had heard and set off for the gateway. Hokadra called after her.

"Look out for rogues, and get to Dombre as quickly as you can! Stay there until Zuryzel sends you back."

Sibyna raised a paw to show that she had heard and took off out of the gate.

When a whole patrol was traveling, it took nearly two and a half days to reach Dombre from Mirquis. But Sibyna, a runner and one of the fastest Wraith Mice, raced through the scanty forest toward Dombre, covering the distance that would have taken six hours for a patrol in only one hour. She ran on, her paws practically flying, staying to the thickest of growth to avoid the rain. When night came, the rain ceased, and the moon came out. It shed its light in a powerful radiance, making shadows every few pawsteps. By the time the sun had passed its zenith the next day, Sibyna had come in sight of Dombre.

By this point, she was tired. She slowed her powerful run to a slow, even lope down an incline to the shores of the lake.

The wooden bridge had been raised, so Sibyna had to lift her tunic a little and struggle from sandbar to sandbar to get to the island. Actually, it was not very far. Once at the shore of the isle, she swiftly lowered her tunic and strode boldly to the half-open gates.

Not quite to her surprise, it was Shinar who greeted Sibyna, her eyes alight with young energy. "Welcome, Sibyna. Zuryzel will be glad to see you. Come with me, quickly, there is something you should see!"

She led Sibyna to the training facilities. Sibyna was absolutely astonished when she saw that Zuryzel was assessing Crispisin—and she was struggling to keep hold of her fake weapon. Next second, she had lost hold of her practice blade to a strong thrust from Crispisin.

Zuryzel retrieved her weapon and noticed that Shinar was standing in the doorway with Sibyna behind her. She turned to Crispisin, congratulated him, and hurried over to where Shinar and Sibyna waited.

"Whew," she gasped. "Crispisin is shaping up to be really good. Welcome, Sibyna. I sure have missed you. What news? Have the foxes attacked?"

Sibyna nodded. "I've got lots to tell you!"

Zuryzel gave her a quick nod and turned to Shinar. "Shinar, would you lead the moonrise patrol for me? Ask Dikiner if Crispisin could come—it's time he had his first patrol. Take Orgorad and Karena with you, too."

Shinar nodded and bounded away. Zuryzel smiled. "She'll make a wonderful leader one day—she's efficient, quick, and definitely respected enough. I trust her with most of the patrols when I need her ... So you said you have news to tell me. Come up to my chambers."

Sibyna just noticed Dikiner giving her a quick grin over Zuryzel's shoulder. She smiled back and followed the princess.

She couldn't help but notice how grown-up Zuryzel had become since she had last seen her. She held herself proudly—but not vainly—and radiated a quiet, in-command authority. Sibyna could scarcely believe that the Bear King had given her all the necessary leadership skills and none to her older brother, who would be king one day.

Once in Zuryzel's chambers, she did not sit down out of respect. It just did not seem right, for Zuryzel bore herself almost like a queen. Sibyna thought she saw a brief flicker of horror behind Zuryzel's black eyes at her remaining standing, and the princess motioned her to sit.

Sibyna obliged. With swift words, she described all that had taken place since Zuryzel had gone away.

"Your father said for me to stay here until you sent me back," she finished, looking rather tired to Zuryzel's eyes.

Zuryzel could understand that. She had run for almost four days straight without much of a rest at the halfway point of Mirquis and had traveled the fastest during the last half, the time when one would normally want a slower pace. Zuryzel stood up and motioned for Sibyna to rise as well. "Go, sleep," she urged her friend. "You look tired. And ... if you want to know, Orgorad should be back from patrol before too long. If you want, you can wait for him."

Sibyna nodded, looking gratified. She stood up and slipped from the room.

Zuryzel wished she could sleep, too. Training Crispisin was very tiring. Yet she was so far from sleep that she wondered if she could possibly stay awake the whole night and dwell on her worries.

Two Wraith Mice had been slain. That news was not too terribly worrying, though it was grievous. She had more concern about the Warhawks. She knew of none that had ever been slain. If a Warhawk died, it was from old age or at the claws and beak of another Warhawk. There was no way to slay a Warhawk.

There had to be, though. Somehow or other there had to be, just as there had to be a weakness in the foxes. True, the foes of the foxes had the Bear King on their side, but they had to have another weakness, one that even a creature that did not have the Bear King could use to defeat the foxes. There simply had to be, just as there had to be one with the Warhawks.

Zuryzel dismissed the problems when night fell and shrugged off her chain mail. She lay down to sleep as twilight's last hint of light faded to be replaced by the stars and moon.

Another dream-filled sleep took her to morning. It took a while to wake up, and when she finally did, the hint of dreams she didn't remember was tormenting her memory

She splashed her face, scrubbed it with a little of her soap, and bathed it off slowly. The water was not quite warm, but Zuryzel loved it like that—just enough coolness to wake her up. Without much further ado, she tugged on her chain mail tunic and her normal tunic over that, dressing in preparation for anything, not sure of what the day would bring. She could not assume that the foxes would simply be content with besieging Mirquis—they might try to come to Dombre to cut off any escape. If that were the case, Zuryzel needed to be ready at any time to defend Dombre.

But she had one thing to do first. Silently, she crept out and searched for Sibyna, easily finding her in the archery practice building, practicing with her bow. Zuryzel stayed hidden, not wanting to be seen by her friend. Then, not quite to her surprise, Orgorad entered with his apprentice, who was a little older than Crispisin. The apprentice began practicing on the target while Orgorad walked nervously over to Sibyna.

He began speaking to his mate in a low voice. Sibyna lowered her bow to reply to his words. And Zuryzel perked up her ears, the better to hear their barely audible exchange.

"Hey, Sibyna."

"Hello."

"When did you get here?"

"Last night."

"What … what's been going on, well, recently?"

"The foxes attacked us exactly when we were expecting it. The battle took almost all the morning."

Zuryzel slipped away. She had no need to hear more. All Sibyna's hopes had come true. Perhaps Orgorad had only been friends with Gavenya the whole time. Who knew? But Zuryzel knew one thing: the Bear King was kind to his creatures.

NIGHTHAWK AND SHOREFISH

Anamay found herself in trouble, her peaceful world shattered.

Nighthawk had attacked the sea otter camp. They showed no mercy to the sea otters, and the sea otters had not had any warning whatsoever. The babes were outside playing when the first javelin had hurtled from the underbrush, slaying Kite instantly. With a swift movement, Anemone nudged them all into a sturdy tent, and lifted the javelin from Kite's body. She hurled it back at the first river otter pushing her way through the foliage to the camp, but the river otter had simply stood back and let the spear fly harmlessly past her. Deftly, she thrust out her paw and caught the javelin by the handle, and twitched her tail.

It was dyed white.

Anamay understood instantly. *Shorefish!* That was the first hint she got as to who was attacking the camp. She still could not walk, so she almost crawled back over to Brine and Mollusk's home and wedged herself between a rock and the wall of the tent. She took up her knife, which she had placed there, and crouched down, putting her weight on her knees.

Brine was in close combat with a huge river otter, but she used his own weight against him, dodging him nimbly, until she thrust her javelin into his stomach.

Mollusk was battling with Shorefish. She was quicker than a flash of lightning, and she stabbed him in the shoulder with her javelin, barely missing his heart. He sliced out with his own spear and gave her a nasty cut across the shoulder.

But Shorefish was used to living a life of hardship, and the cut did not seem to bother her. She stabbed at Mollusk again, only to be distracted mid-stab by a glimpse of her father.

Nighthawk had fought his way through the teeming mass of warriors and rogues, past his daughter, and made his way to the tent where the babes were bundled. Anemone, remaining by the tent with the babes, was bravely holding off two rogues and did not see him coming. But he did not attack her; instead, he sheathed his own spear across his back and reached into the tent and yanked out one of the young ones who had hidden there.

As she had learned in such situations, Anamay did not stop to think. With as much strength as she possessed, she hurled her knife at the unprotected back of Nighthawk. Anemone turned just in time to see the knife whiz past her. The rogue leader led out a moan of pain and collapsed, dead, outside the tent. Anemone swiftly lifted up the babe he had taken out and bundled her back inside. Anamay hobbled painfully across the clearing and, with a glance at Anemone, sank down to the earth just inside the tent.

Anemone patted her shoulder and hurled herself off into the thick of the battle—except the thick had almost completely dissolved. Shorefish had realized that her father was dead, and she howled out to her rogues in a tongue that Anamay did not understand. Then they vanished before another spear could be thrown.

The sea otter tribe was very much the worse for wear. None had escaped without wounds, most pretty serious. Brine had a terrible slash on her back, and Mollusk was bleeding from the spear wound that had almost killed him. Anemone was by far the worst—she had several deep cuts along her back, and on one leg, almost all the fur had been ripped off. She did not let this hinder her, though. With amazing strength, she struggled over to where Anamay sat.

Anemone grinned ruefully at her when Anamay's eyes grew wide at the horrific leg injury. She stooped down and lifted Anamay. Anamay found herself able to walk a little with Anemone's help. Anemone sank slowly to the earth at the center of the clearing, where most of the sea otters had already gathered, and Anamay sank with her. In spite of her leg, Anemone stood up again and hurriedly limped over to where Crustacean stood. She spoke to him in a low urgent voice. Crustacean nodded once, and took his place at the front of his tent to address the clan. Anemone sat down beside Anamay again as Crustacean began to speak.

"I am proud to have a clan of such warriors. You fought well, every one of you. I know Shorefish will not dare return for some time. I would also like to thank Anamay"—his eyes gleamed kindly and thankfully at her—"for slaying Nighthawk as he was sneaking up on the tent with the young ones. If there are no objections, I would like to invite Anamay to join the clan, by way of thanks." He gazed around at his warriors, who shook their heads to indicate that they had no objections. Then he turned to Anamay.

Anamay felt joy welling up in her heart. When Crustacean turned to her, she took a deep breath and spoke up in a clear voice.

"I would be honored."

Crustacean nodded approvingly. "Then welcome to this clan."

The whole group, focused on the proceedings, failed to notice four, bright, brown eyes also watching the meeting, widened in horror. They also failed to hear a small conversation going on in the foliage around the clearing.

"Her sister won't be happy about that," murmured a deep male voice.

A female's voice, full of bitter knowledge, replied, "Did you seriously think that you needed to tell me that?"

"No," the first voice replied. "I was just thinking out loud."

"Well, in these parts, thinking out loud can be dangerous. Particularly with the numbers we've got."

"We'll be fine. They just fought another battle, and they don't have the strength to fight us. But still, I see what you mean."

"Let's make ourselves scarce and get the crews up north to Pasadaga-vra. There may be something we can do there."

With a flash of a spear tip and a swirl of gray tail-fur, the creatures left.

The same day, at late evening, a young sea otter named Pine witnessed a very strange scene. He had been sitting down by the river, and suddenly he was surrounded by strange voices, even though the only thing that moved was the river. But the surrounding foliage suddenly came alive with friendly whispers.

"Why, hello," commented the male voice that had "thought out loud" when watching the gathering at Crustacean's clan. "I certainly didn't expect to see you here. Aren't you supposed to be up north?"

A young maiden's voice replied. "Well, I was. But Arpaha said I should take my crew down south and search for Herttua Crow Blue Arrows. She went after the foxes, but now they need her up north."

"Well," replied the first female's voice, "we'll come with you. I would love to see Opal again. What about you?"

"Oh yes," replied another male. "She is very friendly. She was the one who looked after me when I was taken by those rogues."

"By the way," continued the first male's voice, "it might interest you to know Crustacean's band was attacked by Nighthawk today."

"Well," commented the new female's voice, "good for Nighthawk. Pity he is the way he is, you know. I'll say one thing for sure—we could do with Sky to help us now. She knows these lands like the back of her paw."

"I know, but you had better not say that right now, old pal. One of those whitefaces is looking at you with a spear in paw."

Pine was totally stung by the first maiden's reference to him as a "whiteface." He drew back his spear and hurled it; next minute, he had to duck as the spear turned apparently in midair and flew back at him. Now the creatures in the woods didn't bother keeping their voices down.

"Well done, that!"

"You certainly have a way with spears!"

"Well, I should certainly hope so!"

"Oh all right!" declared the first maiden, rather sternly. "We have someplace to be, so let's go!"

"Couldn't we go to see how Mudriver is first? We need to, you know. Danaray went after Herttua Crow Blue Arrows, and besides, we can always send Windride to Opal."

"Oh, that reminds me," whispered the first male suddenly. "The two of us spotted Shorefish and the rest of their band but no Nighthawk. Where was he? we wondered. Well, Anamay is with Crustacean's group—they must have taken her captive sometime before—and she killed Nighthawk, you see. So then Crustacean and his band took her into their clan, as a way of *thanks*, if you will. Well, someone is going to have to tell Mudriver, someone is going to have to find Windride and send him to Opal, and someone is going to have to get recent news to Shinar's clan. Who's for what?"

"I'll tell Shinar's clan the news!" offered the second maiden.

"I'll find Windride," suggested the first male.

"Good," agreed the first maiden. "I'll find Mudriver and tell him about Anamay. While you're at it, friend," she added, "tell Windride that if he sees Danaray to tell her about her sister, too. Right, let's split up. Remember, we can't be seen!"

To Pine's eyes, nothing moved in the forest. Yet he could feel a rough three hundred creatures slipping through the forest around him, and he scrambled down into the river and swam as fast as he could toward his own camp.

28.
SPY AND WITNESS

At the edge of the foxes' camp, a cloaked figure hurried through the mist toward Hemlock's tent. He stood apprehensively outside, well watched by four guards.

The curtain rustled, and Hemlock beckoned the figure in. He followed the fox nervously, his paws shaking under his cloak.

Hemlock bade him sit, and offered him wine.

"No," replied the figure in a small voice. "I am not thirsty."

Hemlock put away the wine and turned to his spy. "So, have you information for us, my friend?"

The hooded head bobbed up and down a few times. "Yes. The whole army is gathered in Mirquis. A runner was sent to Dombre, and I think another to Pasadagavra, but I'm not sure."

"Any more?"

"Not that I can give without betraying my blood. You know I cannot do that—I am still a Wraith Mouse!"

"I know. Tell me," Hemlock continued, a threatening sneer on his face. "Did you talk to *her* again?"

"Well, I had to give her a report on my patrol—"

"Not Zuryzel, fool. Sibyna!"

"Oh, um, well ... not, not really."

"But you did?"

"Well, yes."

Hemlock's gaze had no expression on it whatsoever.

"I couldn't help it!" whispered the figure desperately. "I love her! I'm sick of pretending I don't."

"Unless you want her to die slowly and painfully, you will keep acting your part."

"Yes, Oracle."

"Remind me," growled Hemlock, "why you agreed to spy for us."

"Because I think that Mokimshim would ruin the whole earth. He cannot be king; he simply cannot lead. But," the figure added, its nerves draining from its voice as it spoke, "I am still loyal to King Hokadra and to Zuryzel especially. Do not slay her, or I swear you will regret it! Sibyna as well."

"Tell me," snarled Hemlock, "what it is that creates such loyalty for Zuryzel in you?"

"Not loyalty, exactly," the figure muttered hastily. "She is young and weak, but I still believe that she can handle being a ruler. She is still young, but clearly destined for something. If you prevent her from growing to be as magnificent as her father, you *will* regret it."

"Go," snarled Hemlock. "And remember, I still hold power over Sibyna. Make one false slip, and she gets burned to death. Make two, and Zuryzel gets beaten to death with a poisonous whip! Go!"

The figure retreated hastily out into the night.

Morning of the next day saw Lady Raven and Orlysk Rainbow returning to Mirquis from their scouting trip. Neither of them looked weary so much as disturbed. Without even meeting the eyes of anyone else, they hurried for King Hokadra's chambers.

Biddah followed them. She climbed a stunted tree just outside the king's window to listen to their conversation.

"Well Raven? Did you find anything of the spy?"

Lady Raven sort of hesitated, before replying, "Well, kind of. We saw him—definitely a *him*—but we could not see who it was."

"Was he a Wraith Mouse?"

"Yes."

"Did you recognize the voice?"

Again, Lady Raven kind of hesitated. "No, not really," she replied finally. "I know I heard the voice somewhere, but where, I could not remember. Besides, the voi*ces* were too low to easily distinguish."

"What, voices?" asked Hokadra in alarm. "Raven, you seriously didn't—"

"Of course I did," snapped Lady Raven bad-temperedly. "How else was I going to find anything out?"

"You went straight into their camp? But you could have been seen, or gotten lost!"

"Yes, and if I didn't find out exactly who the spy is, and if I had a chance to, who knows how many lives would have been lost? Besides, saying that a Ranger has a chance of getting lost on such a short distance is about as far from the truth as you can get!"

Zuryzel was a bit apprehensive. Her father had sent no news since he had sent Sibyna. True, Zuryzel could send Muryda, who really was the fastest Wraith Mouse on the earth, to Mirquis, but common sense told her not to. No news is good news, she told herself. At least she had heard no word that Mirquis had fallen—yet.

She was hurrying to the archery targets when she passed Dikiner. He looked very tired. His paws were dragging a little and his head was hanging low. Quietly, she slipped up to him. "Are you all right?" she whispered.

Dikiner shrugged. "I was on sentry all day yesterday and on patrol last night. Patrol in the day and sentry at night isn't so bad, but never, *never* do patrol at night after sentry."

Zuryzel nodded. "Go get some rest. I'll handle sentry and patrols today. And in the future, don't give yourself so much to do."

Dikiner nodded and walked slowly over toward the barracks, stumbling from time to time.

Zuryzel searched for Shinar. She found her, of all places, on the wall. "Shinar," she whispered. "I thought you weren't doing sentry. I thought you said that a river otter isn't built for standing on wall tops."

Shinar shrugged. "I did, and I am not on sentry. I had nothing else to do, so I came up here. Actually, it's not so bad. Not too unlike standing on the lookouts outside my cave. Did you want me for something?"

"You up for patrol?"

Shinar sprang upright. "Always am, if it means I get a chance to swim. Where would you like me to go?"

"Try for the Keron River, where it swings around west. Go from there to the edge of Eagle Shadow Fields; make sure that there are no rogues around. From there, go north and sweep that area above the fortress, then go east. That should take you in a rough circle around the fortress and give you enough area to take on. Can you handle it?"

Shinar nodded vigorously. "Oh yes, I can. Father always made me go on much bigger patrols, so I sure can handle it. Should I take with me only otters?"

Zuryzel nodded. "If you like. Take who you will, but you shouldn't have to swim the river. I'll tell you what; take Crispisin, Dejuday, Orgorad, and Karena with you, and make the rest be otters. That way some can swim the river, if necessary, while those who can't swim can stay together on the bank."

Shinar nodded and bounded away down the wall stairs.

Well, thought Zuryzel, *even if I don't know how the others are doing, at least things are running smoothly here.*

She hastened down the steps herself and decided to go find Sibyna.

It did not take her long. Sibyna was in the archery range, practicing with her strong yew bow. She was just sighting down another arrow when Zuryzel walked up. Sibyna did not see her, instead focusing on the target—a piece of wood with a blue dot in the middle that was swaying slightly.

Sssssssssthuck! The arrow hit the very center of the blue dot. Sibyna was reaching for another arrow when she caught sight of Zuryzel. She carefully hung up her bow and hurried over to greet her friend.

Zuryzel smiled. "Nice shot. You're really good at that."

Sibyna shrugged modestly. "I just practice as much as I can. Did you want to see me for something?"

Zuryzel nodded. "Yes. Would you do me a favor and arrange the sentries today?"

Sibyna nodded. "Consider it done."

"Thank you. Tell me if any creatures other than those who've been here for more than a day are sighted. Shinar took out a patrol, so keep a look out for them, too."

Sibyna nodded again, patted her friend's paw, and hurried off.

Zuryzel followed her out of the archery range and hastened up to her room, actually two and a half rooms. She had a bedroom, a small room for keeping notes on the happenings of each day, and a small washroom. The furnishings much resembled the barracks. It had a simple bed with a plain blanket, a rather rough and splintery desk, lacking any ornamentation, and a washroom made out of stone. The only difference between this and the rooms in the barracks was that this was smaller but for the study—it could only fit one, at most, while the barracks rooms held two or three, depending. Zuryzel hastened into her washroom and scrubbed her paws, but with no soap—soap she could only use when she bathed her body. Then she hastened back outside to her bedchamber.

She sat down on the chair, her only piece of fine furniture. It had a soft cushion, and a back delicately carved to look like a crescent moon rising over the sea. She just thought for a while, but then she began to fall asleep though she wasn't tired.

Once again, she dreamed of the icicle that was burning, and still, her non-dreaming mind had no idea what it meant. The idea of Ice the Oracle passed over briefly, but then again, what could the flame mean?

Then, like always, the vision changed but this time to one she had never had before. She saw creatures in chains, working laboriously in a field thick with wheat. She saw a fox with a whip, and to her horror, she saw him strike a young Wraith Mouse maiden. What did that mean?

Then she saw something that made her blood run cold.

Behind him strode her brother, Mokimshim. But this was not the Mokimshim she knew. His head was tilted confidently and haughtily back, and he wore a golden crown on his head. He carried his sword, unsheathed, in one paw, and his eyes did not seem quite focused. Besides how he bore himself, something seemed odd about her brother.

"Mokimshim?" Zuryzel whispered uncertainly.

He turned to look at her. "There you are, Jewel."

Zuryzel woke with a start. *Jewel?* Had she been imagining things? Had that dream been one only from her imagination, or had she just seen what would happen when her brother became king? *Jewel?* Why would she need to conceal her name from her brother?

She simply had no answer to that question—yet. But Zuryzel could not shake off the feeling that her brother, if he did not turn completely evil, would at least go badly astray. He could not be the spy for the foxes—he hated with a passion—but Zuryzel would definitely need to keep a steady eye on him.

Hemlock fumed with fury.

Knife had sent him a message from the castle. Poison had had another dream about the strange creatures. She had woken up even more distressed than the last time. Apparently, Poison had also seen a glorious blue arrow that had been imbedded in Chiraage's wing, slaying her. This convinced Hemlock that these dreams were only nightmares. Whoever heard of a bird being slain by an arrow in its wing? And besides, whoever heard of a blue arrow?

He was stunned when, the next day, Knife herself arrived. She was looking so worried that Hemlock thought she had spoken to the wind again, except that there had been hardly any wind recently. Yet still, she looked worried.

"What," snarled Hemlock, with Ice right behind him in case Knife got angry, "are you doing so far from the castle? I told you to command that place! Are you incapable of even that?"

Knife's snarl overrode his. "I figured out some of that prophecy, but if you're not interested in hearing it, I'll go back!"

Hemlock lowered his claws. "Fang," he called, "come with Knife and me. Ice, you stay here and don't do anything until you hear word from me! Understand?"

Ice nodded dumbly as Fang hurried over to Hemlock and Knife. Hemlock turned his anger to Fang.

"Keep your claws on Knife's neck. If she tries anything, snap her neck!"

Fang nodded and took up his position behind Knife. The three foxes turned to walk to the castle with Knife secured like a prisoner. However, Hemlock had made one mistake. With Fang holding onto Knife's neck, his teeth bared at her head, they whispered to each other, Hemlock none the wiser.

"Did you really find out some of that prophecy?"

"Not really. Actually, I was trying to think of some way to get Hemlock where we can control him, so I figured out a possible explanation for part of it. But now that I think about it, I think I could be right, even though I'm lying!"

"Talk about crafty. So have you figured out how we're going to control him?"

"I thought you were going to do that."

"I did, but if you don't like it, well …"

"Let me hear it."

"We frighten him. He is cruel and powerful, like you and me. But unlike you and me, he is brave enough only when he has a bunch of soldiers at his back. All we have to do is scare him!"

"True, Fang, but you did not think of that yourself."

"Well, no. Other Oracles have done it before us. I read it in the records. There is nothing wrong with it, is there?"

"No, but put it this way. You are powerful and strong; you do the act ing—you are the might. I am clever and witty; I'll do the thinking—I am the brain. Nothing on you, of course, but, though your cleverness exceeds Hemlock's, it does not rival mine; at the same time, I do not rival your strength. We each have a part to do—what each does best."

"Right. We need superior thinking and superior strength. We need all the cleverness we can get, and we get more out of you. Me, I'm all the strength we can get."

"Correct, but don't even try flattering me. I'm not vain, you know."

"I'm not. I'm just agreeing with you."

"Good. Now, here's what we can begin with …"

And so it went on until they reached the woods of the foxes.

Anamay's world had repaired itself.

She still lived with the sea otters, and she relished that life as much as ever. Peace held sway over their little world, and she never heard any disturbing talk of the foxes there.

Well, almost none.

When Anamay had first met Anemone, she had thought that Anemone was just like every other sea otter. She soon found that she had misjudged her. Most sea otters were content with their way of life, and acted with prudence and calmness. Anemone was a different story completely. She acted more like a warrior with enough fiery, hot tempered attitude for an army of sea otter warriors. Once, when Anamay's ankles were still healing, she had heard Anemone arguing furiously with Crustacean.

"Then what do you call that attack?"

"Another rogue attack, Anemone. Nothing to worry about."

"How can you describe Kite's death 'nothing to worry about'?"

"It had nothing to do with the foxes, Anemone. Relax."

Now Anamay was listening more acutely.

"You're just saying what everyone wants to hear!"

"I'm saying what is true."

"No, you're not! You say that the foxes aren't our problem. But you can't ignore them forever, Crustacean. They will come here—and we will be defenseless and powerless to stop them. What will you do then?"

"You are talking nonsense, Anemone. Go, calm down. No, you are dismissed. That means you can argue no further."

Anamay took that as the cue to make herself scarce.

She hobbled over to where Brine and Mollusk were sitting and told them what she had heard. None of them seemed too shocked.

"You have to understand Anemone," Brine had explained. "Her mate disappeared earlier this cycle, leaving her alone with her son and expecting her daughter. She is a really good tracker, and this was during the time with Sky. Most creatures think that he was taken by Sky, but Anemone insists that he wasn't. She followed his tracks and found that some sort of a great fight had taken place—she said she saw blood and tracks that weren't river otters'. By the time any others could be sent out to try to track the prints— she had been ordered her to stay behind to take care of her son—it started to rain. The tracks were washed out."

Anamay noticed all the babes in the clan outside playing in the center of the clearing. She glanced at her sea otter friends. "Which one is her son?"

Mollusk indicated one playing toward the edge of the clearing, apparently hiding from his friends in a game of hide-and-seek. "That one. His name is Eagle. He's only about two cycles old."

Anamay stared at the babe. Something about him stirred her memory. Something about his very eyes told her she had seen him before, but where? Perhaps it was just playing around the camp. No, that couldn't be right. There was nothing in his features that suggested she had seen him before. It was just the look in his eyes. His bright, brown eyes, so gorgeous, dancing with hidden strength and skill, simply reminding Anamay of someone, but she couldn't think of whom.

Eagle's head turned. He stared straight into Anamay's eyes. They held such an intense pain—so great that not even her love for Mollusk could heal it—that her very heart seemed to shrink. She felt as if she was staring at someone she had known and loved all her life but would probably never see again. The look wounded her to the heart, more so because she could not remember anything about the creature that she thought she saw. Who was she thinking of?

She turned back to Mollusk. "From what my sister said, well, I would be surprised if it was foxes, but that doesn't mean it couldn't have been."

A look flashed between Mollusk and Brine. "Well," Brine said slowly, "put it this way. Northstar is the leader of that clan. She … came from somewhere up north and probably had a quarrel with every tribe that exists up north."

"I beg your pardon?" Anamay asked nervously.

Mollusk took a shot at explaining. "Every clan of the sea otters gathered here. We all came from different places. My father remembers having a makeshift camp a little north of Zurez. He says that before that, we lived on an island that was overrun by corsairs."

"Corsairs?"

Brine lowered her voice fearfully. "Not so loud. They're creatures that live on ships and range the seas. They … er … have no quarrel with killing … often. Father says they are the worst evil anywhere."

Anamay shuddered. "I've never heard talk about them on the plains where I grew up. Mostly we worry about a large mass of criminal rogues."

"What do they do?"

"Attack Miamur. They all committed some crime or other and banded up. Mostly we worry about them and—" she broke off.

Brine let out a snort of laughter. "Sea otters who can't leave their life of comfort?" she teased.

Anamay felt her face flush with embarrassment. "Well, my sister has a friend who was attacked—"

"You're thinking of Moonpath," Mollusk interrupted, a glint of fury in his eye. "The land here was never owned by anyone before us, nor was Northstar's. But Current—one of the other chiefs—conquered the land of *two* tribes before this. He … uh … killed the chief and his sons and tried to kill his daughter, Moonpath. She survived somehow."

"Current has the biggest clan," Brine continued, "and he is probably watched more. His clan *is* a lot like what I bet your sister thinks. I remember one incident when a small band—I never heard what they were—attacked him. Current left the boundaries of his clan's land—a deed he should not have done—and destroyed the rest of the attackers. When he reached where the mothers and children were sheltering …" She shook her head sadly.

"What did he do?" Anamay asked Mollusk nervously.

Mollusk looked away.

"Why didn't you do anything?" Anamay challenged quietly.

"What could we do?" Mollusk asked. "Crustacean wouldn't let any of his clan do anything. He … well … he agrees for the most part with Current."

"What happened to Anemone's mate might have been revenge for that tribe," Brine guessed.

Suddenly an idea came to her like a tidal wave. "Do you know where this happened?"

Mollusk nodded uneasily. "Yes, but that's in another sea otter clan's territory. Not that they aren't friendly to us," he explained hastily, "but we'd be in trouble if they found us there without first talking to their chief."

Anamay stared at Mollusk in puzzlement.

Brine hastily explained to the bemused river otter. "When sea otters from different clans want to be mates, the maiden leaves her home. If anything happens to her mate, she must stay with the clan she married into."

"Is there any chance we can slip over there unnoticed?"

"Not really. Patrols are frequent."

"Why don't we try? To possibly prove that the creatures who took her mate are not foxes from the five clans."

Brine and Mollusk glanced at each other, before nodding slightly. The three otters stood up silently and scurried toward the river border. The surface looked deceptively smooth and slow, but tossing a stick in it proved the current wild and fast. The two sea otters hesitated, but Anamay plunged in.

Her ankles did not slow her down at all, and she paddled strongly across, waiting on the opposite bank while the sea otters followed her.

At the other side of the river, they began to make their way very cautiously through the thick foliage. They encountered no living creatures until they arrived at the site where Anemone's mate had disappeared.

Even two cycles could not wash away all the evidence. No wind could penetrate the small area, and little grew on the bare and dry ground Anamay studied the place for a while before she murmured, "This is the place he was, all right. Now, as for who captured him …"

She crawled cautiously across the clearing before pausing to touch the earth on the farthest side. She carefully brushed earth from its place to reveal a print in the earth, clearly a fox's.

Brine and Mollusk's eyes widened. "How did you know that was there?"

Anamay turned to look at them. "I could see no obvious tracks, so I looked for signs of hidden ones. Those who try to hide tracks either brush them away or fill them in. But you cannot really brush away any prints without making it obvious that you have disturbed the ground. So it is common to fill them in. But even that a good tracker will note because the filled in soil will vary from what surrounds it. So the tracker must be able to tell various types of earth from others. The earth here is not, by any means, the same type as it is in the rest of the woods here; it's darker and softer, and it holds moisture more. Let me see if I can find any others."

She began searching the area for other prints, and soon she had found nearly a hundred. She began to murmur to herself.

"Fifty creatures to one. Not very fair. Here is Anemone's mate's prints—it looks as if he was unshod. Hmm, only fox tracks otherwise. Clever, clever these creatures!"

Brine looked stricken. "So, the foxes really did capture him!"

Anamay shook her head. "Not quite. It looks as if they did, but they didn't. See how far away the prints are from each other? Look at this pair—they're closer together than fox paws generally are. These too, and these—most of them are. There is a fox here and there, but probably nothing to worry about. I know some river otters worked on making shoes that would leave prints like those of other animals. Crazy, isn't it? But I wouldn't be surprised if he was captured by rogues—there could be rogue foxes too, you know … Oh hello, what's this?"

She had unearthed a stone. It was blood red and smooth and round, shaped like an oval, but flat. A hole had been drilled through the center, making the stone into a rough bead. The edge looked as if some creature had put some sort of gold substance—or something yellow—there, at any rate, but it was washing off.

Brine and Mollusk both looked at it and shrugged. "It looks like something Sky, or any other rogue might have. For some reason they love things that glitter."

Anamay nodded, but she did not quite believe that. She had seen this bead somewhere, probably when it was in better shape. She could not put a name to it, but she certainly had seen something like this, and not too terribly long ago.

However, she shrugged too. "You're probably right. It looks as if the foxes of the clans are totally innocent of the capture of Anemone's mate."

Mollusk sighed with relief. "Good. No need to tell any creature why we were here, or even give away the fact that we were here. This is my idea of good luck—we come to prove something we don't want to prove, and there's nothing to prove."

Anamay and Brine nodded their agreement. With a swish of their tails, all three otters vanished into the undergrowth. But Anamay looked back. She hadn't done any tracking, she reflected, since she had been captured. She loved the challenge of following tracks, especially in a faint trail; she had given all that up in joining Crustacean's clan, yet she didn't mind. Let Danaray be furious. She didn't know. She'd never even *seen* a sea otter before she followed Anamay when she went to meet with Mollusk. All she had was the word of other, vengeful otters. And she now knew how reliable they were. Like most river otters, Danaray just wanted a reason to fight. Anamay reflected with pride that she had such a characteristic and yet also had rebelled against her savage nature. Not everyone wanted to fight—she didn't, and as far as she could tell, most of the sea otters didn't want to fight either. She felt at home here, happy in this little world of peace. Bear King surely knew her being here wasn't much of a loss for her side that wanted to fight.

But for the first time during her stay at the sea otter camp, Anamay felt a pang of pain. She missed her sister, not Danaray who had no pity or feeling but hatred for the sea otters, but Dana, the sister who loved her with all her heart. She realized with a horrible shock that she hadn't seen her father for over a cycle and a half. Was he still alive? Had Danaray gone back to tell him what Anamay had done—had been doing? Was her father angry with her? Would he still want to accept her as his daughter?

He never could, Anamay realized. She had joined the sea otter clan, and she could not go back on her word. She had not considered what she would feel at her family's shock, thinking only that life with the sea otters offered happiness forever with Mollusk and maybe a family of her own. But along with that, it kept her wondering what her birth tribe—the otters, warriors, friends she had grown up with—must also feel. Were they hurt? Angry? Shocked? Appalled? Sad?

Anamay did not want them to be angry with her, but she would rather they feel angry than hurt or sad. She had betrayed them, she realized. They had trusted her with a single mission—to find Herttua Crow Blue Arrows and tell her that Streamcourse's band had gone after the foxes and that she might be needed up north—and Anamay had failed them. She had betrayed them by visiting Mollusk and again by joining his clan, though a little comfort found her when she remembered what Brine had said about Current and his tribe. Though she loved Mollusk, Anamay found herself understanding Sky, the rogue Brine had told her about. The land—Brine's land—had once belonged to river otters and was now held by the worst excuse for a clan there ever was. Current's clan.

The fathers of Doomspear and another otter maiden had owned other *land* there. Who was that other maiden?

To her dismay, Anamay did not remember her name. It was Star … Star … no, Moon … Moon …

And then like a comet, it came to Anamay.

Moonpath! The rogue who had been attacked by Current! Anamay felt a shudder. Moonpath, she knew, wore a veil. Anamay had always assumed it was for some reason of heraldry. But could it be to cover scars? Current had tried to kill her.

"Anamay," Mollusk whispered, as soon as the three otters were in their own territory, "do you think it is something to worry about?"

"What?" whispered Anamay.

"That stone. It looked as if you'd seen it before."

"Well, remember, I am a river otter," Anamay reminded him. "I probably saw it on one of my sister's friends' jewelry, or something like that."

Mollusk nodded thoughtfully.

"Hey, you two," called Brine, "I'm off to see if I can't collect something for supper. See you at the camp!"

Mollusk nodded. He matched Anamay step for step until they came to a huge fallen tree. He gently helped her onto it before sitting down beside her.

"Um, Anamay," he whispered. "Are you … are you happy with my clan?"

"Oh, yes," replied Anamay quietly. "I think it is the best place on the earth."

'I'm glad you think so," Mollusk replied.

He lowered his voice a little more, and whispered, "Would … would you be my mate?"

Anamay felt that she was swimming in joy. She had wanted to hear that for such a while. She blinked happily at Mollusk and whispered, "Yes, I will."

Mollusk's eyes brimmed with happy tears. He put his paws around Anamay's shoulders and pressed his cheek against hers. Anamay returned the simple, loving gesture.

However, the two otters were not entirely alone. Just below the log where they sat, a young male river otter with gentle gray eyes was crouching, his eyes wide with horror. Silent as the moon, he crept out from under the log and away into the forest, muttering to himself.

"Oh, Danaray is going to be mad; everyone will be mad. What are they going to do? Mudriver's daughter, the mate of a sea otter!"

29.
LADY RAVEN'S DIPLOMACY

Biddah felt her paws trembling on her bowstring.

Oh, curse the world of war! She had barely had ten days of peace at Mirquis when the foxes were sighted by a patrol. Every single creature that could fire an arrow or throw a spear was packed on the wall tops, and those who could only use swords and short-range weapons were grouped in the main hall.

Biddah caught Harclayang's eye a ways away. He was clinging onto a spear as if his life depended on it; he had become a little less flamboyant recently.

Then Biddah heard it—a pounding on the peaceful earth, that of many paws tramping the high road in perfect discipline and unison. On the crest of a hill that was not far from the lake, Biddah saw a creature stand tall and raise a powerful pike.

Ice.

And Poison and Scorch hurriedly backed her up. They carried a cutlass each, and Poison had a long scroll. The whole of the foxes soon crowded the hill. They were armed to the teeth in powerful armor. It surprised Biddah to hear Orlysk Rainbow giggling beside her. She glanced at her curiously.

"Rainbow?"

Orlysk Rainbow explained. "They're all covered in heavy metal. They can't be too fast—we'll have an easy time defeating them!"

Biddah nodded, but inwardly she felt that Orlysk Rainbow was underestimating her enemy. Biddah was terrified.

Ice took the scroll from Poison. She cuffed Poison's ear sternly and beckoned to Scorch. The two foxes strode confidently down the slope.

Ice did not really look different, aside from the fact that she had been stern with Poison. Other than that, she walked slowly down the slope with an arrogant tilt of her head and Scorch hurrying in her wake. She beckoned to a group of foxes that had been standing grouped around something.

It was a boat. A boat with smooth lines and a pointing prow. Arpaha gasped in surprise. "That's a river otter's boat—I'm sure of it!"

The boat was set in the lake. Ice and Scorch got in, followed by six other foxes who began rowing. Closer and closer they got, until they reached the confined shore of the island. One of the six raised a white banner as they all stood on the bank.

The second they were in firing range, Lady Raven put an arrow to her bow, followed by Sharmmuh. However, King Hokadra placed one paw on both arrows. Sharmmuh said nothing, merely lowering her bow with an incredulous glance at Hokadra, but Lady Raven glared at him.

"What?"

"Don't fire, Raven," murmured Hokadra. "I think they come to parley."

Lady Raven snorted. "They don't come to parley—they come to trick! They're not fools, Hokadra."

"You are probably right, Raven; but we are not going to descend to their level."

"*Descend to their level?!* Have you ever heard, 'All is fair in love and war?' Well, when you fight an enemy, you don't *descend to their level*; you use your brain, and you fight like a warrior, not a soldier. There *is* a difference you know. If you're going to fight the foxes, you have to fight better than they can, but you have to use all your wit, not discipline or rules of war!"

Hokadra did not reply. Ice had started to speak.

"King Hokadra, Oracle Hemlock wishes you to be wiped out, but I expect you know this. However, he has given me permission to deliver this message to you."

She paused.

Hokadra snorted. "Tell Knife—or was it Fang who thought that up?—that you're not getting around me."

Scorch waved his claws threateningly. "You dare doubt the word of an Oracle?"

Raven retaliated, trying hard to hide a grin. "I think a phrase closer to the mark would be, 'You dare *believe* the words of an Oracle.'"

Ice flicked Scorch with her claws, before reading out her scroll. "Oracle Hemlock, oldest Oracle of the fox clans, has written these words in his own paw, to the defenders of Mirquis. 'Hokadra, Tribequeen Sharmmuh, and Arpaha, with all due respect, do not fight this battle. You cannot win. I give you permission to leave this place and go east. You must scatter once there and never regroup. We know that your forces are divided, some here, and some at Dombre. Come out—you cannot win.'"

Twang.

Lady Raven loosed an arrow toward the opposite corner of the fortress. To the surprise of almost everyone—not, however, the Rangers—a young vixen cried out and grabbed her arm, pierced by Raven's arrow, dropping the bow fitted with an arrow with which she had been about to shoot Hokadra.

Raven wasted no time in raising her voice to Ice, her words echoing with a power that silenced even King Hokadra.

"You carry a banner of white, indicating—according to the rules of war, which I believe you verbally support—that fighting must cease while you parley. And yet, I see an archer aiming her arrow at the one up here with whom you speak. You understand now why I would not dare *believe* an Oracle."

Ice gave her a very ethereal glance while Scorch snarled, and both of them got back in the boat and were rowed to the other shore.

Hokadra glared at Raven, who completely ignored his gaze. Instead, she loaded another arrow to her bow.

To take her mind off of her worries, Biddah studied Lady Raven's bow. It was a good bow, supple but strong, made out of yew. The ash arrows, fitted with mallard wing feathers, had tips merely wood sharpened instead of with added steel at the end like Herttua Crow's arrows. And for the bowstring, shrub fibers had been twisted strongly together with an odd weaving sort of braid and rubbed with wax to keep the fibers together..

A wind began to blow, ruffling Biddah's fur. Lady Raven's head lifted, and she turned her eyes to the sky. Biddah watched her, puzzled. The wind was supposed to have no friends—and anyway, since when could Lady Raven speak to the wind? Surely Knife was the only creature alive anymore that could do that.

If only Herttua Crow were here now! Biddah thought. What would she do if she saw the teeming horde of foxes? Biddah closed her eyes momentarily, trying hard to picture the Ranger's face. It was not hard.

Biddah heard waves of jeers from the foxes below. The squirrel felt shaky, but in spite of herself, she smiled. If Herttua Crow were here, she would retort with some sort of smart play on words. She would begin fiddling with one of her arrows, probably imagining how and where she would soon be using them. And their threats? She would merely laugh at their talk about overrunning the fortress. Herttua Crow would not be afraid. She, the most powerful warrior in the world, would not back down to the foxes. Indeed, she would probably shout back at them, "Are these insults the best you can do? Some warriors you are. I'm inclined to believe that you're nothing but verbal popinjays. Perhaps you'd like an arrow for decoration?"

In the early afternoon light, Ol'ver finally woke up. He yawned and glanced at his companions. They were curled up next to him, their eyes closed and their breathing gentle. He stood up silently and began to creep toward the edge of their willow tree.

Whump!

Four strong paws bore him down to the ground. Gasping, he lay flat on his back, Feldspar and Chite kneeling on his paws.

He glared at them. "Oh, the nerve of you two! I though you were asleep."

Feldspar narrowed his eyes in mock ferocity. "You promised to go with us to the east side of Pasadagavra today. You're not creeping off with Ran'ta and getting distracted. Come on!"

The two mice got off their friend's paws. Ol'ver rolled over and sat for a moment. Then he stood up properly. "Well, let's go," he sighed.

The three friends scrambled out of the willow tree, all of them shaking with excitement. So far, they had seen most of the sights on the western side of Pasadagavra. Today, they would be going to the east side to stay there for a few days. That was where the wall carvings were—carvings that, in pictographs, told of Pasadagavra's history. It promised to be a thrilling experience for them. However, Feldspar had a more important reason for going—to keep Ol'ver away from Ran'ta for a while. Glor'a had become a bit fed up with never being able to see her friend, and Feldspar wanted to give her a few days with Ran'ta, where she could not get distracted. Chite had wanted to go because there were a few places on the east side that he wanted to show to his friends, and Ol'ver had agreed to go because his friends were going.

The mice hastened to one of the many stands that held food. They selected a few sacks full of dried salmon sprinkled with crushed thyme, picked up a few canteens of sweet lemon-flavored water, and then set off east.

They had not passed the main gate when an urgent cry came from the lookout. Heads from everywhere turned in the direction of the shout. Wazzah and Rimmah, the Coast Tribe squirrel, leapt up next to the lookout. Within seconds, Wazzah spotted what had horrified the sentry first. Her paw shot out.

"There!"

Rimmah's eyes widened. "That's Verrah! Oh, some creature, help her!"

Wazzah leapt from the ledge and practically flew past the other squirrels. Feldspar, Ol'ver, and Chile crowded onto the lookout ledge to see what the fuss was about.

Verrah was struggling along on all fours, hauling herself painfully but swiftly across the uneven field. Some of the most horrible wounds any of them had ever even seen covered her body, and she was in deadly danger. A band of five river otters were scrambling after her, their paws hitting the earth and rising again so fast that they were a blur. Feldspar had no way of knowing who was in the lead, but it seemed evil enough.

The three friends glanced at each other. Then they sped towards the main gate, a few levels down.

The postern was open. Several squirrels had raced through the open gateway, yet none of them could reach Verrah before the river otters did— except one. Wazzah had nearly reached Verrah. On the run, she unwound her sling from her paw and snatched up a small pebble to load it without stopping. She bent down and practically lifted Verrah from the earth, looping Verrah's paw about her shoulder, but she did not turn. Standing her ground, she raised her sling at the first rogue otter that was approaching them and whacked him soundly on the side of his head.

The three mice were too far away to hear the dying gurgle of the otter.

Then Wazzah turned and ran. She heaved her burden across the uneven clumps of grass until they were in the entryway of Pasadagavra. Gently lowering Verrah onto the smooth stone, she held Verrah's head in her paws, supporting it.

Tribeking Fuddum and Jaccah thrust their way through the crowd to Verrah's side. Jaccah gently stroked the squirrel warrior's brow until Verrah stirred. Her commanding voice softened with her calm and soothing question.

"Verrah, what did this to you?"

The squirrel shuddered all over. Then she began in a hoarse voice, "They attacked us. Warhawks. Warhawks swooped out of nowhere. One came when the others were outside. I heard their screams and went to see what was going on. Then suddenly, I felt myself lifted into the air, higher … higher … higher … and then … I could do nothing. Nothing. I felt so helpless, knowing … oh … so horrible … It let go and … I dropped … falling through nothing … nothing … and then … I hit the trees. I … I landed on the top of a huge oak, just outside the door to the tower. One carried Shjeddah off, and the other Warhawk grasped the other two squirrels. They weren't as lucky—one was dropped on top of the tower, impaled, and the other dropped just outside the tower and landed on a stone. I barely survived and crept away. But the Warhawk, it was huge! So huge!"

She gasped horribly and her body went limp.

Wazzah looked bitter, and Jaccah looked as if she was about to be sick. Feldspar understood how they felt. He and Chite had grown up in a land that knew nothing of war and strife and such unspeakable suffering. The biggest war that Feldspar had ever known was when a fox named Gorkave had set his heart on conquering Graystone but had later been slain by Opal. Feldspar had never known horrific birds that dropped creatures to kill them or such evil and determined fighters who could even think of bandying with such birds.

He turned and found himself looking into the brown eyes of Glor'a. Steely and almost threatening, they registered her anger as her paws clenched and unclenched. But her expression softened as her eyes met with Feldspar's. She sighed and whispered, "It's horrible, isn't it?"

Feldspar could only nod. Glor'a glanced from Feldspar to Verrah. Then she sighed again. "Feldspar, come with me. There is something I need to tell you that I should have told you long ago."

She turned to go along the passageway, Feldspar right behind her. She paused as they emerged from the fortress not far from Willow Brook. Then she turned to face Feldspar.

"Feldspar," she whispered, "I told you that my family sent me here because it is safe, right? Well, that's not true. When I was very young, my mother took a journey south of Diray. She ran into the Oracle Fang, vicious beast. She escaped him but not before he found out where she lived. It took them the better part of ten cycles to figure out where Diray was, but when they did, they came after my mother. The foxes threatened to attack and burn Diray and kill everyone inside it if they did not get her. But she had died several cycles before. Well, I looked like my mother, so they shoved me into the Oracle's paws in my mother's place. The cowards! Those at Diray are the worst sort of cowards there could be. Anyway, I was dragged along and put in the foxes' prison. I escaped about three cycles ago, helped by two river otters, Wave, the younger sister with the most brilliant blue eyes, and Rain, the elder brother."

Feldspar sighed sympathetically. "Are the foxes really that bad?"

Glor'a nodded gloomily. "They're worse."

Her eyes met with Feldspar's. The look in them made Feldspar feel uncomfortable. And the painful thing was he knew why.

He looked away.

"Was your home filled with cowards like that?" Glor'a whispered curiously, with a hint of resentment in her voice.

Feldspar shrugged. "Not cowards, exactly. Just not warriors. My friend Opal was the only one there who had seen anything like a real war. Her family moved down from the northern moors."

"Oh?"

"Yeah."

Glor'a did not look at him as she said, "I'm going to find Ran'ta."

Feldspar blinked. What had he said?

"Glor'a," he called.

She stopped. "Yes?" she inquired icily.

"What will you do after the war?"

Glor'a looked startled. "I-I don't know."

"You could come to Graystone," he offered.

Glor'a's eyes flashed nervously. "I'll think about it."

30. REBELS

Knife uncorked a bottle of wine and filled two beakers. She passed one across to Fang and sat down with the other.

Fang shook his head admiringly. "You can bring everyone under a sort of spell with fear better than Poison can with her beauty. You even have Hemlock supplying the wine!"

Knife nodded agreeably. "Now, 'tis time you and I think out our plan properly. The bit I think I figured out is 'the one who was rejected.' I think it means Fawn. You know, I think that there is someone out there, like Sage or Blood, who will tell her the truth about something. It makes sense—we rejected her! Now all we need to do is tell Hemlock what we suspect about Fawn …"

Her words trailed off into the air as the wind picked up. Silently she stood up and went to her window.

Fang watched in apprehension as Knife's eyes started to dance and change color.

Knife listened to the words the wind brought.

I say this for a friend. 'I am Lady Raven. I lead the Rangers at the northern half of the earth. Fear me and my kin, for one day, they will see your carcass fed to the tide of the sea.'

Knife gasped and her eyes turned back to their usual red. *The fool,* she said to herself, and dismissed the thought of the creature ever carrying out such a threat.

Turning back to Fang, she said,

"Well, Fang, the next thing we need to do—and this is going to be difficult— is ..."

Their earnest conversation filled the evil room. Both of them knew what they had to do to gain power.

Fang nodded and his features split into a fiendish grin. "I like it; it's strong, crafty, and just like you and me!"

Knife cautioned him, "True, but if it fails, you won't like it so much." Then her face gave way to an equally cruel, cold smile. "But still, with me to think it and you to do it, how could it fail?" Letting that last question sink in, her smile faltered, and she groaned. "Ice, that's how. I just thought. She won't hinder us on purpose, but she's too dumb to carry everything out properly. Scorch can't help her either, nor will Poison. Oh, not that Poison isn't clever, but she'll spend all her time flirting, the idiot! If Blood wanted to keep her out of mischief, he should have killed her instead of making her an Oracle apprentice! Ah well, one of us can take vacations to the front to see how they're doing their job, what do you think?"

Fang nodded without hesitation. "I'll do that!"

Knife shook her head. "No, you stay here. You've got enough brawn to control Hemlock, so you'd be better here alone with him than I would be. Besides, he suspects me, so he won't have me with him, but he trusts you."

Fang nodded. "I suppose you're right."

Danaray was in good humor for a change, not lonely and tired. She had told Kermunda about Anamay and found the loss easier to bear, especially since she was fighting rogues almost every day, not to mention battalions from the foxes' army. Easier to bear, that is, until one day.

A gray-eyed male river otter raced into the camp that day. Danaray knew him well—he was Rain, the son of Sky. Rain was panting hard as he ran toward the camp. Danaray went out to meet him.

"Danaray," he gasped. "I have news ... Anamay ..."

Danaray put a paw to her lips and beckoned him into her father's tent—her tent now.

He stood respectfully as Danaray sat down in her father's old chair. Then she nodded to him.

"I heard it all ... I was following Anamay, with Mollusk and Brine, you know them? Well, Brine went somewhere, I don't know where, and I hid under a huge log. I heard ..."

He broke off, his eyes wild, and stared into Danaray's eyes. "They'll be *mates* by now!"

The news did not surprise Danaray, but it did sicken her. "Oh, really?" she murmured, her voice a dangerous calm. "I see. Well, that means that Anamay is no longer part of this tribe, meaning, she is an enemy. If she is going to behave like this, then she is worse than the sea otters."

Rain sighed. "I think she will be punished pretty soundly later on. Those sea otters took the land that belonged to my grandfather. It fell to such a pitiful sort of clan. Anamay was born free of them—now she is enslaved to their 'not our war' business. I know Northstar—she constantly wishes that she was born a river otter. Anamay threw away her most priceless gift. Can't wait till she meets Northstar; then she'll get punished."

Danaray nodded

At that precise moment, Anamay could not have been troubled with anything.

She was going to Zurez! The legendary fortress of the sea otters, captured from the Wraith Mice. Right by the sea. The sea! Anamay had never been to the sea before, but she had heard all about it from Danaray. She could not wait to see it for herself.

The journey took Crustacean's clan about thirteen days. On the fifth night, they met up with another clan of sea otters. Crustacean smiled fondly at the new chief.

"Hello, Current. It is very good to see you again. I hope your clan is all in good order?"

Current's voice had an arrogant note in it. "Oh yes. You don't honestly think that anything *could* happen to any of us? Well, except for Northstar and her lot. Those troublemakers!"

Anemone said nothing but shot a hate-laden glance at the back of Current as she wrapped Eagle and her daughter, Saline, up in blankets she had warmed by the fire.

Anamay lay down beside Mollusk and tried to put Northstar out of her mind, but that proved impossible. "Mollusk," she whispered, "who is Northstar?'

Mollusk sighed resignedly. "Well, you're probably going to meet her so you might as well know. She is a cheiftainess of one of the sea otter clans. She's an old fool. She keeps talking about the foxes and about the territory we own belonging to river otters and saying that we should live by the sea all the time. Well, we don't so that the sea has a chance to replenish itself. Anemone admires her, but she is a fool. Don't listen to anything she says— she can act almost like a witch sometimes."

Anamay promised quietly, "I won't."

But she had cast her lot before she met the subject of the wager.

"Still, though," Mollusk added in an undertone, "I'd rather have her be my chief than Current. Current is just an arrogant idiot. And, to be honest, I doubt the sea needs a chance to replenish itself as long as we use its resources wisely."

RAINBOW'S OPINION

Zuryzel had passed a weary night on the battlements. Her scouts had seen traces of Shorefish – how was it she could travel so fast? – but no one had seen Nighthawk. The Wraith Mouse princess worried that Shorefish was planning something, and she knew there was evidence that Nighthawk was friendly with Hemlock.

Anyway, she was on her way to her chambers for a small, two hour rest, when Shinar found her with an annoyed look on her face. "Zuryzel, Lurena from Mirquis is here."

"Where?"

"She's getting a quick drink, and then she'll come—oh, here she is."

Lurena, one of the runners from Mirquis, raced up behind Shinar.

"Zuryzel," she gasped, "your father sent me to you. I have a message."

Zuryzel dismissed Shinar and beckoned to Lurena. "Come with me."

She led Lurena up to her chambers and nodded for Lurena to sit down in her chair. This Lurena did, panting a little.

"Now," murmured Zuryzel, "tell me the message."

"Well," Lurena panted, "he says to send someone up to Pasadagavra and stay there. He saw some Warhawks not far south of Mirquis yesterday. He wants to get word through to Pasadagavra before the passage is over-whelmed with Warhawks. Also," she added, "Orlysk Rainbow told me to give this to you. I can't read the Eastern Tongue, so I can't tell you what it's about."

Zuryzel unrolled the roll of parchment. She was surprised to see Orlysk Rainbow's paw-script, and not Lady Raven's scrawl.

Zuryzel,

Lady Raven and I saw the spy. We could not identify him, but it is a male. And this is important: whoever he was, he loves Sibyna. I don't need to tell you who I suspect now.

Do not breathe a word to Lady Raven; she told me to tell no one because she is not sure of what she heard. But I am.

Orlysk Rainbow

Zuryzel glanced at Lurena. Her paws trembled a little, but all she said was, "Have Sibyna and Muryda come here, and get something to eat."

Lurena nodded and scurried out of the room.

Only one name danced in Zuryzel's mind now. *Dikiner!*

🐁

Hemlock, Knife, and Fang sat in the courtyard eating a meal. Knife and Fang sat on either side of Hemlock, both of them winking slyly behind his back.

Chiraage flew up and alighted not too far from them, making Knife wince. However, she turned to face the Warhawk.

"What news do you bring us, friend?"

Chiraage folded her wings. "All is well."

Hemlock had a sudden idea. "Chiraage," he queried, "do you ever fly beyond the Salt Lake? I mean, normally?"

The Warhawk nodded empathetically. "Oh, yes, I fly to the top of the earth!"

Hemlock glanced hopefully into her red eyes. "Do you know of any creatures who can speak with the wind, like Knife?"

Behind his back, Knife glared at Fang, who nodded, winking at her. Knife rolled her eyes.

Chiraage nodded. "Yes, yes, yes! Two creatures there are, word reaches my ears! I was just learning to fly nearly a hundred of your generations ago—and, by my life, I am still young—but I lived during the time of Lady Panther the Berserker!"

Knife's curiosity was aroused. "Then Lady Panther was real?"

Chiraage nodded again. "Evilness, yes. And Lord Jet the Warrior, too. Well, you see, Lady Panther led the Rangers, who still live—but they are not as famous. She has two descendants left alive, Lady Raven the Swift and Herttua Crow Blue Arrows."

Fang glanced at her questioningly. "What happened with Lady Panther and all that?"

Chiraage shrugged her massive wings. "Lady Panther always went crazy in combat; whenever a battle came, no one could stop her. But she was killed by a particular fox, I'm not sure whom. Her son, Lord Jet the Warrior—I admit it, he frightened me, and I would probably be scared out of my wits if I saw him with any means of reaching me—could speak to the wind. You see, his mate was captured, but he did not know who had taken her. So he sat out on a hill one day and just whispered, 'Where is she? Where is she?' The wind answered him back, telling him all. Lord Jet befriended the wind, and I think the wind swore an oath of friendship with all his descendants. Still, that will do them no good. They are mice—and mice are weak. I've even slain one of them, you know. Why, he was not so very strong!"

Hetmuss Cinder glared at Chiraage through his fox disguise. "I know you did, slime scum! He happened to be my brother, and if you feared Jet, fear the Rangers of today!" He whispered so low even he could not hear himself.

Knife and Fang excused themselves. Fang looked disturbed, but Knife's face was the picture of fiendish delight.

"Oh, perfect, we can use Herttua Crow to help carry out our plan. Not that she'll do it willingly, but still, we can take care of phase one of our plan! But," she added, "what possessed you to tell Hemlock of what I heard?"

Fang shrugged. "Well, you said to intimidate him!"

Knife looked incredulous. "We got lucky that Chiraage's words only intimidated Hemlock more! What if Hemlock hadn't believed her? Or what if Chiraage had not had any news? That was too desperate a gamble for my liking, Fang. We need to be careful. Hemlock does not know any of what they said, does he?"

Fang shook his head. "No, I wouldn't gamble that much."

Anamay stared up at the fortress of Zurez with disappointment and sadness. Although made of blackest stone with carvings around the outside, it looked far from marvelous, hardly befitting royalty let alone inhabitants of any kind. Instead, it looked like a perfect display of ruined majesty. Anamay guessed that the carvings were originally silvery-white but had been painted over in crude, charcoal paint. Dull green covered the oak gate, as though it had seen only neglect for many cycles. It, too, had carvings, these of the moon, but they had been filled in with clay. The fortress walls gave little hint of its once sturdy battlements, now crumbling on all sides. And, saddest of all, in the middle of the wall over the main gate, stood a crescent moon. Like rest of the carvings, it also had traces of silvery-white, as though made out of silver, underneath drab, ugly brown paint. Mollusk noticed the look on Anamay's face. "The inside's not like this. You'll see. It's bright and merry."

Anamay realized that Mollusk was right. The gate was thrown open, and a middle-aged sea otter greeted Current and Crustacean.

"That's Palm," explained Mollusk in a whisper. "Chief of another clan, a bigger and more arrogant idiot than Current, if that's at all possible. Looks like Northstar isn't here yet. But she'll be here soon—her territory is farther east than ours, a bit south, too.

Inside, Zurez looked strange. Brightly colored tapestries of orange, red, and yellow on the walls everywhere did give a happier feeling to the fortress, but at the same time, they seemed to be hiding something—more carvings, if nothing else. Dozens of golden chandeliers hung from the halls, which were numerous. It looked like a cheery fair, but it did not feel right. The colors did not belong there, not in the place of the moon.

Mollusk patted her paw. "Why don't you look around and get acquainted with it? See you in the main hall in an hour?"

Anamay smiled. "Of course."

She set out to explore the curious fortress. Before long, she spotted Anemone with Eagle and Saline at her heels. Anemone was glancing to and fro, as though making double sure that they were alone. Anamay hid behind a stone column until Anemone went along down the corridor. Silent as light, Anamay followed her, not suspicious, but curious.

Anemone stopped dead at a pale yellow tapestry at the end of a corridor. "This is it," she whispered to Eagle and Saline. "This is where Zureza is laid to rest. Remember, this is our secret."

Anamay did not see what she did, but she heard Saline's voice, soft and sad. "It looks as if she's crying."

Anemone sounded captivated. "She probably is. The castle she loved, that was named after her, is desolate, covered in hideous tapestries that make this place look like the chambers of the sun, when it was made to look like the moon, the friend of all Wraith Mice. If I had a choice, I would hand Zurez back to her people and not have Zureza's grave defiled."

"Perhaps then, Zureza will smile," said Eagle.

"Come," replied Anemone briskly. "Let's go keep watch for Northstar."

As Anemone hurried past her with her two children, Anamay barely had time to pull to one side.

Then slowly and steadily, as though drawn on by a magic spell, she walked down the hallway. When she reached the faded tapestry, she drew it aside.

A most sorry sight met her eyes. A body weighted with woe and a face drawn in sadness looked down at her with a tear falling from one eye. The mournful, gray figure belonged better at a funeral than in a nook honoring the famous. Anamay could guess that the creature was Zureza, first warrior queen of the Wraith Mice, the namesake of Zurez. She stared at the creature, weeping over her fortress lying in decay and hideous coverings, and Anamay was caught up in all the grief and stillness of the soul—her heart seemed literally to stop beating.

A voice seemed to hail her from Zureza, but it danced in Anamay's own mind.

"Anamay, why? Why did you not heed what your sister said about the creatures that ruined my home? Why did you give up all the freedom you had, the joy of being a respectable creature to mingle with the worst sort of liars and selfish creatures? The Bear King has a plan for you, Anamay, and he will use your faults for your benefit. But tell me, why did you give yourself up and betray your kin? Why?"

Anamay felt tears coming to her eyes, and for the first time in ages, they were of grief. She could not hold onto her self-control and bowed her head and started babbling to Zureza. "I'm sorry, Zureza," she whispered. "I should have listened. I see now what they did to you and your home. I am sorry, Zureza. One day, I will try to help Zuryzel in some way, if it will make up for what I did. I am sorry. I did not want to believe Dana. I was wrong. I am sorry."

Anamay raised her bowed head. To her astonishment, the tear on Zureza's face had moved, and another two flowed slowly out of her eyes until they froze, one on either cheek. Anamay knew that they would move again one day.

"Anamay! Anamay!" Mollusk's voice echoed down the corridor. Anamay hastily hid Zureza's face with the tapestry and raced down the corridor to where three other corridors met.

Mollusk came racing out of one of them. "Hey," he panted, "d'you want to see Northstar arrive? She's coming!"

Anamay nodded wordlessly and hurried off after him. On their way to the southern side of the castle, the two otters passed a set of doors. Anamay knew there was something special about them because they were the only double doors in all of Zurez; the others were all single doors. She paused.

"Mollusk, where do these go to?"

Mollusk snorted. "Oh, its one of those stupid things Wraith Mice think up. They never open, like they're locked. But there is no key anywhere. I bet it goes to some white room or something like that."

Anamay hurried on after him, but not without a second look at the oaken doors. Then she rounded a corner and saw them no more, so she followed Mollusk to the wall.

Anemone stood with Palm, Current, Eagle, and Saline, scanning the forest that grew up outside of Zurez. She pointed. "There!"

Two figures vanished back into the trees. Palm snorted.

"Well," he grumbled to Current, "make way for the old fool, eh?"

"The only reason you call her old is because she is younger than you," Anemone retorted coolly.

"Maybe so," muttered Current, "but she is still an overdressed fool."

Anemone turned her head in a slow, incredulous, quarter-circle. *Really!* exclaimed Anemone. "Well, pray tell, Current, how many layers have you under that cloak? How many beads? And can one even count how many stones you have set in that thing you call a crown?"

"What, do you have a problem with a little ornamentation?" demanded Current.

"Only when you accuse others of overdressing!"

"There they are, Mother!" called Eagle, wisely breaking up the argument.

Anamay gazed out into the forest. A whole horde of sea otters was breaking through the cover of the trees. They carried food sacks and weapons. A few of the mothers carried babes on their backs.

They paused at the entrance gate, which was quickly thrown open, and then the whole clan walked nonchalantly inside.

Anamay spotted Northstar immediately. Her first thought was, *Old fool indeed!*

32

NORTHSTAR

Anamay had been prepared to hate Northstar, but she found nothing to support such a reaction. Instead, she instantly recognized an inner beauty in the sea otter. She was carrying a young otter on her back, and in one paw, she carried a powerful-looking spear. The expression on her face showed quite clearly that she felt the same way for Zurez as Anamay did.

She wore a brown, loose-fitting dress and, about her head, a woven hat with small shells tied onto it. Around her neck dangled a single, beautiful clamshell. And a huge, beautiful conch hung by a blue cord from her shoulder.

Northstar was clearly young, not much older than thirty cycles, but she seemed to radiate wisdom, understanding, and friendliness. Her eyes were dark and wild. Anamay had seen wild eyes like that, but they had always reminded her of the plains outside of Miamur. The sea otter's wild eyes reminded her of what she had heard of the sea—the roaring rollers, the gentle, muffling, small waves, and the ferocity of the storms.

Once again, Anamay was reminded painfully of someone, but she could not think whom.

Once inside the grounds, the otters put down their burdens. Crustacean, Palm, and Current hurried forward and greeted Northstar formally. Northstar dipped her head respectfully to each one but did not seem to try to flatter them. Anemone bounded down the wall steps to greet Northstar, Jay perched on her back and Eagle almost keeping up with her. She put Jay down, and her two offspring immediately scurried off to one of the older-looking babes from Northstar's clan.

Mollusk tapped Anamay's shoulder. "Come on," he murmured. "I'll show you our room."

He led Anamay to the northern wing of the castle. He pushed open a door.

Anamay could not remember the last time she had seen something like this. It had a soft bed with a bright red blanket on it. The only other furniture were a table with a lamp on it and a beautiful bench with a back, covered with yellow cloth, that was big enough for two. Curtains of bright yellow slightly covered a window that faced west. Through the open window, Anamay could hear the faintest steady rhythm, which she guessed was the surf. A huge ridge blocked it from view, however. A few lone seagulls called to each other in their strange language that Anamay could not understand.

She turned away from the window and smiled at Mollusk.

"It's wonderful," she whispered.

Suddenly there was a horrible screech. Mollusk's face twisted with fury as he hurried to the window

"Fools!" he exclaimed. "That bird wasn't anywhere near us!"

"What happened?" asked Anamay.

"One of those idiots from Palm's band just shot a seagull!" exclaimed Mollusk. "They say that the seagulls try to steal babes for food, but that's not true. A seagull saved my life once, when I was younger. Come on, let's see if we can help the poor bird."

Both otters dashed out of the castle for the ridge. Halfway up, they saw the downed seagull with Northstar kneeling by it with one of her warriors, who Anamay guessed was Ripple. Northstar looked up.

"Fools," she hissed venomously. "What did they think they were doing?"

Anamay tore a strip of cloth from her tunic, nodding her agreement—she'd always had a friendly spot for birds. She passed the cloth to Northstar, who bound it around the wing of the bird.

"There, friend," she whispered. "That should help."

The bird stood up, flapped his wing experimentally, screeched its wailing call, rested its good wing on Northstar, and took off, allowing the wind to take it back to its home.

Ripple shook his head in disgust. "What's the matter with Pine, the idiot! That bird was flying back to sea, not stealing anything!"

Mollusk nodded his fervent agreement. "No kidding! Poor bird. Where do you think he went?"

Northstar sighed resignedly. "Who knows? Maybe for his home, perhaps one of the islands in legend. We can not know what is in a sea bird's mind."

Anamay did not nod but asked, "Why did Pine shoot the bird?"

Northstar's eyes darkened till they looked like a storm at sea. "Because he is cruel and savage, that's why."

Mollusk's eyes darkened too. "Never a truer word was spoken, that's for sure."

Ripple glanced at the sun. "Great Cerecinthia, we need to get back!"

Northstar stood up and dusted herself off. "You're right. Let's go."

Ripple and Mollusk took the lead, both of them glowering after what had happened, muttering under their breath. Northstar fell into step with Anamay.

"So, Anamay," she whispered to the river otter. "I hear you are the daughter of Mudriver."

"It's true," Anamay whispered back.

"Do you know … do you know he is dead?" whispered the sea otter.

Anamay stared at Northstar in shock. "He is? How did you hear that?"

Northstar met Anamay's eyes evenly, and there was sympathy in them. "I have friends. Streamcourse, Rain, Doomspear, Moonpath. They tell me things happening far away."

"Have you met my sister?" Anamay could not restrain herself from asking. "Danaray?"

Northstar shook her head. "No, but I've heard only the highest praise of her. She sounds wonderful."

"She is," whispered Anamay, but she said nothing more. It hurt too much. For the first in a long time, she missed her sister—even to see Danaray mad at her would have been welcome because then she would have known that it was Danaray and that her sister cared for her and wanted the best for her and would try to understand, if she could.

Lost in thought, she, at first, missed seeing the blue eyes watching her. But when she happened to glance toward the woodlands, she made out the shape that only a skilled river otter tracker could.

Another otter, clearly not a sea otter, was watching them with the wounded gull. Anamay recognized the river otter immediately—she knew her well—Wave, Rain's younger sister. She had her paw resting on the gull's back.

Anamay did not give her away until she saw the otter motioning to Northstar. Anamay nudged Northstar and nodded in Wave's direction.

Northstar noticed Wave immediately, probably because she was waving. Northstar pointed to the eastern horizon, and then to the middle of the sky. Wave nodded once and vanished into the foliage while the gull took flight.

Northstar whispered to Anamay, "Wave brings me news from Pasadagavra, about once every fourteen days. But you see, we cannot meet in the open—I'd be considered a traitor."

Anamay nodded, knowing full and well what Northstar meant.

Opal, sitting sentry atop the walls of Graystone, gave a cry of delight. Windride the bald eagle soared majestically out of the sky and landed almost next to her. Her cry brought Lillia and Redfur. They, too, laughed with delight at the sight of Windride.

The eagle dipped his head to Opal. "Well, young friend, I bring news from up north."

Opal, Redfur, and Lillia held their breath.

"First off, of your friends, Feldspar and Chite. Well, I have not seen them, but my friend, Redstreak, has. They are at Pasadagavra."

Opal let out a low whistle.

Windride continued, "The foxes have burst their boundaries. They are now planning to conquer the earth."

"What? You mean the five clans led by Hemlock and 'Fraud'?"

"Ice had hardly any say in anything, so I wouldn't say that. But yes, those foxes. Apparently, Oracle Blood is dead, and his apprentice, Fawn, forsook the Blight."

Opal whistled again. "What do you know? So it is true that there will be good in every kingdom … Oh, speaking of which!"

"Well, as for my other news … Apparently, and this is urgent, Herttua Crow Blue Arrows is tracking a band of foxes, about a battalion, detached from the main army of foxes, heading this way."

Opal forgot how to whistle in her shock. "Why … Herttua Crow Blue Arrows … Why here? … What? … Why?"

Windride cuffed Opal lightly, nearly knocking her over. "All I'm supposed to tell you is that. If you see her, tell her from me that she must go north, and fast!"

Without a word, Windride took off, leaving Opal still openmouthed, Lillia and Redfur gazing curiously at her.

"Herttua Crow Blue Arrows?"

Opal shook herself. "I'll tell you later."

33.

SROZKA

The time had come to abandon Mirquis.

Biddah watched nervously from her position on the wall top. Soon, she knew, Orlysk Rainbow would slip up and "relieve" her of her sentry duty, that is, provide for her escape time. Already, the defenders were beginning to trickle through the secret passageway that King Hokadra had unearthed and were making their way slowly towards Dombre. Arpaha's band went first, in broad daylight, with a few squirrels and a few of the more senior Rangers, including Hetmuss Cinder, and a single Wraith Mouse per group, the ones who knew the way. Then followed the more experienced middle-aged Rangers, led by Mokimshim and a thoroughly disgruntled Lady Raven ("No, Hokadra, I'm supposed to command my Rangers, not run away! I'm a leader" … "Raven, go. Zuryzel would have assurance that everything is fine if you leave.") Next, most of the Bow Tribe, led by Sharmmuh and quite a few of the younger Wraith Mice, left, and finally, it would be Biddah's turn.

The night was deepest when Orlysk Rainbow tapped on Biddah's shoulder. "Go on," she whispered. "Queen Demeda wants you in the main hall."

Biddah rose shakily and followed a few of the dark shapes making their way down the wall stairs to the main hall. She caught up with Karrum, who gently squeezed her paw.

"Don't worry. We'll be all right. The Wraith Mice know what they're doing." But his paws clasped her tightly anyway, betraying his nerves. He spoke again, trying to sound braver. "Queen Demeda will be the best to get stuck following. I respect Sharmmuh, but can you imagine following her underground?"

Biddah could, and she did feel better when she thought of the Wraith Mouse queen.

Biddah was surprised by the state of the main hall—with no candles, dark and whisperingly quiet. Karrum and Biddah clasped paws so hard that they were beginning to loose circulation—and their nerves did not improve when Queen Demeda whispered right next to their ears, without them feeling her presence.

"Right," she whispered. "This way."

Following her voice, the squirrels found a small hole in the earth in the northeast corner. It was not very dry, but it was not as damp as a tunnel or cave normally is. Clinging to each others' paws, the squirrels stepped gingerly down into it until Karrum felt the back of another squirrel, who flinched.

"All right," whispered Queen Demeda. "Go very slowly forward and keep to the left. There is a small barrel of torches up ahead a bit. Can anyone grab one?"

"Here it is," called a Ranger from the front.

"Good. Now, pass it back to me. I've got some flint."

Biddah felt a wooden barrel pressed gently into her paws. She tentatively passed it to Queen Demeda, who opened it slowly. They heard the sound of stone striking steel, and a few sparks appeared, followed by a burst of light as Queen Demeda lit a torch.

"Here," called the Wraith Mouse queen. "Pass this along to the front."

Pressing a second torch into the first one, Queen Demeda soon had enough light to see by. She lit five torches total and ordered them to be held at regular intervals.

"All right," she said again. "Go forward, but not too slowly."

As the band of squirrels and a few Rangers progressed, Biddah heard hisses.

"Queen Demeda, who didst thou bring with thee?"

"Who is with thee?"

"Who art here?" Queen Demeda sounded shaky as she replied, "Fear not, friend Graeka. I bring only friends to your realm."

A strange, serpentine creature was slithering along the top of the passage, drawing level with Queen Demeda. "How goeth the war? Thy plan is put into action, yes?"

"Yes," replied Queen Demeda sadly. Then she called, "Halt!"

More of the creatures slid along the walls of the tunnel. One, very old looking, stopped just above Biddah. "What is thy name, young one?"

"My name is Biddah," replied the squirrel cautiously.

The giant creature rested its wet but not unpleasant tail on Biddah's shoulder, then on her face, feeling her features. "My name is Creeka. Thou art frightened of me, yes?"

Biddah realized with a jolt that Creeka, along with the rest of her kin, was blind.

"Thou needest not fear me, Biddah. I cannot harm thee. I am too old for that, yes. And besides, I am an earthworm. It is against my nature to harm one like thee, so young, and beautiful with enough of decent life before thee."

"I do not fear you, now," replied Biddah.

"Come," called Queen Demeda. "We must go with all speed. The woods are a fair distance, and we must reach them by moonset."

"I wish thee Godspeed, Queen Demeda," declared Graeka.

"Godspeed, Godspeed," chanted Creeka. Soon all the earthworms, scores and scores of them, picked up the chant, and the hisses followed the group of refugees through the tunnel. Biddah realized that the earthworms were following, and although she did not fear them, she felt tinges of unease run through her body and bristle her full tail.

The tunnel sloped upward into a smooth, sheer, stone cliff. For everyone that wanted to climb it, there was an earthworm to push the creature up it. A younger one lifted Biddah on its head, chatting away to her.

"Hello. My name is Srozka, granddaughter of Creeka. She liked thee, Biddah. Pray tell, art thou truly afraid of us?"

"No, not anymore," replied Biddah.

"Thou hast a fair voice. Dost thou like it here?"

"Well, I'm not too fond of the dark, but it seems warm."

"Dark? What is dark? Canst thou explain it?"

"Well … for a creature like me, we sense things by seeing in the light. When we have no light, we have dark, and in dark we cannot use the sense. But when it is light, we can use it. We distinguish shapes and creatures through light, as you do with feeling. Do you understand?"

"I understand a little, Biddah. Not much, though. I still do not understand 'light' and 'dark.'"

"Everything is dark for us here without the torches. I really can't understand how you find your way down here in such darkness," commented Biddah, impressed.

"So we knowest what we are."

Biddah had a sudden thought. "I bet Lady Raven enjoyed coming through here."

"Thou must mean the bad tempered mouse with the sharp stick."

Biddah could scarcely suppress a giggle. "Oh yes. She's not normally like that, though. She just didn't want to have to run instead of lead her Rangers through last."

"I see. Well, we are nearly at the top, Biddah."

Without warning, the open night burst on the squirrel. She stepped gingerly off Srozka's head and toppled onto the grass just thirty pawsteps away from the woods.

She turned to Srozka. "I hope I will see you again, Srozka."

The earthworm tapped Biddah's face in farewell. "Thou will, Biddah—whatever 'see' means." Biddah sensed a smile in the earthworm's voice. "I will wait for thee when thou must leave Dombre as well, to take you straight to Pasadagavra. The tunnel thou camest by was not one of the secrets of Mirquis; we dug it ourselves. So we have a tunnel straight to Pasadagavra to take thee there. Fare thee well!" She vanished into the hole with the rest of her kin.

"Come," Queen Demeda ordered, and she took the lead.

After an hour's marching through the dark woods and after many hisses that Biddah thought at first were the earthworms but proved to be the wind, Dombre came into sight.

The gates were shut, but a small band of sentries standing guard at the lake's shore greeted the party immediately. Biddah instantly recognized Dejuday, Colobi, and Dikiner, all of them looking very disgruntled.

Dikiner whistled twice, and a temporary drawbridge was lowered. The group struggled wearily across. Zuryzel, Sibyna, and Shinar greeted them, the latter two with mischievous grins on their faces.

"Well, Zuryzel," said Queen Demeda wanly, "how've things been going?"

"Nothing of significance to report, Mother," replied Zuryzel. "We ran into Shorefish's crew multiple times; every time they were handled. Never saw her, though. Yesterday they came so close we decided to dismantle the drawbridge. That's why we're using a new one, one that we can destroy fast. We also dumped some sand and rocks in the lake here and there, so it will be difficult to bring a boat through. I sent Muryda up to Pasadagavra with Sibyna, and, well, Sibyna came back, as you see. Muryda, apparently, went on to Pasadagavra. She wanted to warn me about the fact that no one was at the watchtower."

"Hmm," murmured Queen Demeda. "Thank you, Zuryzel. Oh, by the way, what sort of temper was Lady Raven in when she arrived here?"

Mokimshim appeared, grinning. "She was scared stiff and tired. Guiding her through that tunnel was about the most interesting time of my life. When she heard the hisses, she stopped dead still, and I swear—"

"Mokimshim, don't say that," Queen Demeda ordered.

"All right. I'm sure her fur went pale. And then when we got to the cliff and Snoka pushed her up ... Ha ha ha ha!"

Queen Demeda sighed. "She doesn't like the dark, then, either. Can't say I blame her."

"Me, neither," Karrum whispered to Biddah. "That certainly was the most interesting time of my life, too."

Biddah nodded. She glanced at Zuryzel, who met her gaze and smiled a little. Biddah nodded in return and whispered to Karrum, "Did you not like them?"

"It's not that," replied Karrum. "But they looked so much like what Sharmmuh says the Serpent looks like, and I can't think that that tunnel wasn't too different from the Serpent's Land."

Biddah had not thought of that. "You're right. Let's ask Zuryzel about them," she suggested.

Karrum nodded. Only a few steps brought the squirrels to Zuryzel's side. "Zuryzel," whispered Karrum, "Erm ... about Graeka and the earthworms ..."

"Yes?" urged the Wraith Mouse princess. "What about Graeka?"

"Well," continued Biddah, "has he ever struck you as ... as similar to the Serpent?"

"No," replied Zuryzel firmly. "Not one little bit. There is a story about them from before the time of Zureza. They lived in harmony with the Serpent and his legions—grass snakes, corral snakes, anacondas, pythons, and I could go on—under the rule of the Bear King. But then, the Serpent rebelled against him, and so did his legions. Only the earthworms, which are simple and kind, unlike the snakes, stuck to the Bear King. Wait—and there was some sort of snake that stuck to him too ... cobra! But they live in the east. Anyway, even if the story were not true, Graeka is too kind, too simple, to remind me of the Serpent. Besides," she added with a touch of humor, "the Serpent is too crafty to be blind."

Biddah was impressed by Zuryzel's view and complete trust in Graeka, but she tried not to let it show.

Yawning, Feldspar woke a few days later. Verrah's disastrous arrival had delayed their trip to the east side of Pasadagavra for some time. Feldspar had not seen Glor'a in all that time, but he was not really worried—Ol'ver had not seen Ran'ta either.

Beside him, Chite and Ol'ver were sound asleep, still, both curled up tightly. Feldspar sighed, and wandered out from beneath their willow.

He dangled his footpaws in the stream for a while, the cool but not cold water waking him up even more. He detected the faint smell of freshly culled herbs and the faintest hint of baking fish. *Yum!!* He loved that baked fish almost as much as he liked Glor'a.

The willow rustled behind him, and Chite, still half-asleep, emerged. He collapsed down beside the rivulet and gulped some water.

"You ready to go east today, Chite?" grinned Feldspar.

Chite leapt up, his weariness forgotten. "You bet! Let's wake Ol'ver!"

He bolted back under the willows before Feldspar could say another word. Feldspar grimaced, knowing only too well Chite's method of waking someone up.

He happily recalled one time, when he was only six cycles old. He, Chite, and Opal had slipped out in broad daylight and into the woods outside Graystone. They had found a warm bed under a fallen rowan and had slept until dawn, when Chite had woken up. He had snatched up Opal's paw and twisted it behind her back, and then leapt on her back, keeping clear of her paw. Opal had woken up with a shriek, her mouth right next to Feldspar's ear. Feldspar had jerked awake to see Opal hurl herself on Chite's back, knocking her head fiercely against his. He remembered leaping up to pull them apart only to see them snatched away by one of the elders at Graystone. He had taken them all back to Graystone, laughing the whole time.

Feldspar heard Ol'ver's anguished shout, so similar to Opal's shriek that he knew what had happened. Next he heard Chite's shout of pain, just like eleven cycles ago. Then, Ol'ver and Chite stumbled out from underneath the willow, arguing furiously.

"What was that for?"

"Well, you were sleeping away like a hog, sleepy-paw!"

"And you couldn't just shake me, cruel-tail!"

"Really, Chite!" exclaimed Feldspar. "You didn't learn your lesson after waking Opal up?"

Chite fiddled with his belt and muttered, "Ready to go?"

"Let's get our packs, first."

Feldspar ducked back beneath the willow. He lifted his roll of spare tunic and blankets, as well as Opal's canteen, onto his shoulder, and they set off east at an easy wander.

Feldspar was half hoping they would pass Glor'a and Ran'ta, although he also was half hoping they would not. They had planned this expedition for some time, and Feldspar did not want Ol'ver distracted by Ran'ta.

But just as they were passing the city gates, Feldspar spotted both mouse maidens. His eyes and Glor'a's met for a while, but she looked away frostily. Feldspar suspected that she had been upset when he told her of Opal.

However, he sped up his pace, so that instead of walking behind Ol'ver, he was right up with him, blocking both Ran'ta and Glor'a from view, and Ol'ver continued on the way, none the wiser.

Feldspar was totally lost east of the city gates, so all of their journey was a wonder to him. Chite took the lead, skipping a little, eager to show his friends the part of Pasadagavra he knew very well.

"See over there?" he asked, pointing up a twisting pathway. "That's the weaving place. And over there," he pointed to their right, "is where they keep the silkworms."

"We can skip those things," Ol'ver stated shortly, shuddering at the thought of the wriggly worms.

34. Night

As Feldspar, Chite, and Ol'ver continued walking east and as the sun began to decline beyond the monolithic city, they had the first impression that the war was coming to Pasadagavra.

A few squirrel warriors rushed by with an unusual urgency, and Feldspar began to feel a little nervous. Perhaps the foxes were already here.

He pointed them out to Ol'ver and Chite. Chite looked nervous, too, and suggested, "Let's go to the walls and see if we can find out anything. They usually don't have warriors here!"

Chite needed a little time to remember the way to the walls, and then they hurried there without any setbacks. Sure enough, so many warriors lined the wall that Feldspar could not see between their scanty armor—or could he?

Yes he could! But no view of the field filled the gaps. Instead, his fur began to crawl when he realized that foxes covered the field below—at least ten score times another ten score. In the lead stood a very beat-up looking fox, wielding a scimitar.

Feldspar had to gather every ounce of self-control to keep from shaking in fright. "Let's go back to the west side and save our vacation for another day!"

Ol'ver and Chite nodded fervent agreement, and the three friends made themselves scarce.

"Still," said Chite. "Let's not go west just yet."

That same day, not half an hour later, Zuryzel and her patrol ran straight into trouble on the Eagle Shadow Fields.

The princess's patrol consisted of herself, Dikiner, Shinar, Orlysk Rainbow, Colobi, and Crispisin. (She would not have brought Dikiner along if she did not think she would need his sharp eyes and ready mind—he had been working harder than usual lately.) They were several miles from both Dombre and the completion of their patrol when Colobi trotted up to Zuryzel's side.

"Zuryzel," she whispered, "I think it's going to rain."

At the same moment Zuryzel looked at the gathering storm clouds, Shinar whispered, "Zuryzel, don't look now, but we're being followed. Shorefish and her band are right behind us."

"Well," muttered Dikiner, "that rules out going back to Dombre."

"I don't suppose it would be a good idea to get to the river, either," added Shinar.

"Probably the best we could do, though," pointed out Zuryzel. "The nearest river is the Dellon. I know Shorefish is a river otter, but the Dellon is really wild. I can't imagine her wanting to go near there."

"There's a cave in the bank not far north," added Colobi. "Let's make for that. It's easy to hide and fight there."

"Good idea, Colobi," agreed Zuryzel. "Well, let's go. Shinar, tell the others to keep their eyes peeled."

Shinar practically vanished just at the moment that it started to rain.

Zuryzel felt as if the world couldn't get worse: an enemy river otter, as cunning as they came, following them, no protective shelter, and now pouring rain. The magic of the Wraith Mice was strong, but Wraith Mice were very visible when rain came—their magic was rendered powerless. Besides, they were all tired by now, and probably didn't have much strength for magic. And what about Shinar and Orlysk Rainbow?

Sliding through the now muddy ground, they moved toward the closest grove of trees where they stood a better chance in fighting the otters. The patrol kept a sharp lookout, determined not to let the rogues get the advantage. Zuryzel placed her dark paw on the hilt of her sword, remembering how her last encounter with Shorefish had destroyed her former weapon but now feeling the strength of this new blade run through her.

The first arrow struck, but it came not from Shorefish.

Orlysk Rainbow had, with lightning speed, tugged her bow from her shoulder, sheathed her knife, snatched an arrow, and let fly. An otter with a spear in his paw, which Zuryzel guessed was aimed at her, went down. Orlysk Rainbow's arrow had, however, gone right through him, and wounded another.

Shinar leapt up and came down painfully on a spearhead that had been thrown at her. Dikiner barely managed to pull Colobi out from a spear's path, gasping as it pierced his shoulder. Crispisin ducked a stone from a sling, and hurled the spear that Dikiner had pulled from himself.

"To the river!" Zuryzel shouted, switching to Simalan so Shorefish wouldn't understand.

Zuryzel barely had time to note that she had not seen Shorefish herself in any skirmishes before they were off.

Zuryzel gasped as an arrow thudded into her left paw, but regardless, she tugged a staggering Shinar with her. Orlysk Rainbow let off an arrow as she was moving; dodging all missiles sent her way. The grove of trees was not far off when Shinar stumbled and leapt upright with a shriek.

She had nearly fallen into a deep, covered pit.

"Keep your eyes open for covered pits!" shouted Zuryzel, fighting to make herself heard.

They encountered no more pits on the way to the trees, so Zuryzel hoped that the rogues had not thought they would try to come this way.

One bold sword bearer caught up with the patrol. He lifted his blade, about to kill Shinar, who could not really fight back. In a flash, Zuryzel drew her sword. In another flash, the otter lay dead at her footpaws.

"Come on," hissed the Wraith Mouse.

Into the groves, through them, and past them on the banks of the Dellon River, the small patrol sprinted. Shinar had barely been able to keep up, but she had proved her worth.

"The cave is this way," said Zuryzel.

The storm showed no sign of letting up, so they made their way upstream, until Shinar said, "No need for that now, Zuryzel."

From the surrounding bushes, smiling faces and lithe brown bodies were emerging. Zuryzel lifted her blade but relaxed it when she recognized the river otter crew.

Orionyap the river otter saluted Zuryzel with his saber. "Good noontide to thee, princess," he grinned. "What's all the rush?"

Zuryzel matched his grin. She had met Orionyap only a few times, but she knew him well. "Shorefish," she explained. "We were out scouting, and we're trying to get back to Dombre without running into her again."

Orionyap twirled sword deftly. "Well, you might as well get to Dombre some other way. I'll take some of my crew and make certain she stays away. By the way, don't go too far north—the band of foxes from the hares' fortress just reached Pasada-Pasadagavra," he finished, carefully sounding out the name of the fortress.

Zuryzel nodded. "Right. Thank you."

Saluting her one more time, Orionyap called out orders to his crew in Simalan.

Zuryzel wasted no time. She turned her patrol east toward Dombre, and they set off at a swift trot, about all that Shinar could manage.

"That's about all of them now," murmured Dikiner, half to himself.

"All what?" queried Zuryzel.

"All the river otter crews," explained Dikiner. "All the ones I know of are fighting the war, for or against the foxes."

"Well, you don't know all of them," commented Shinar, "if that's what you think."

"What are you talking about, Shinar?" murmured Zuryzel.

"Kiskap," whispered Shinar admiringly.

"Who's Kiskap?" asked Dikiner.

Shinar looked at Dikiner incredulously.

"Kiskap, leader of the Hoeylahk Tribe!" she exclaimed in almost a worshipful whisper. "You know, the tribe of otters up north, who live by the sea, speak with their own language, have ships and seagoing canoes, on the northwestern coast, parallel with the Ranger's dominion?"

"Not really. I've never been further west than the Dellon River," shrugged Dikiner. "I think I've heard a whisper about them here and there, mainly about their war cry. Aren't they a legend?"

"No," murmured Zuryzel with a frown. "I don't think so."

"That's exactly who I mean!" muttered Shinar.

"Well, mother told me about them," explained Zuryzel, "from the time she was held captive on the slave ship. Apparently they're half river otter, half sea otter, but they all look like sea otters. I think most of them were held captive on one ship that had raided their home coast. Mother even met one. I think Mother said her name was Star."

"Star?" Shinar echoed blankly. "I thought they had their own language."

Zuryzel shrugged. "Perhaps. Perhaps Star was only her name in the common tongue."

Dikiner shrugged as Dombre wove into view through the rain. "Perhaps."

Zuryzel didn't know why, but a desire to find out as much about the Hoeylahk Tribe as she could suddenly possessed her.

"Bear King," she whispered, "who are the Hoeylahk Tribe?"

And to her great surprise, a voice answered from within her.

"You can find that out, Zuryzel. You have the wit, skill, and knowledge to figure it out. I will not tell you. This is for you to do."

Yes, she thought, this she could do. She decided to ask her mother first.

35

THE BATTERING RAM

t was the middle of the night at Dombre. Zuryzel knocked tentatively at her mother's door. After a brief moment, she heard a faint, "Come in."

Queen Demeda looked tired and sad, but her eyes shone brightly. "Zuryzel!" she smiled. "What can I do for you?" she nodded for Zuryzel to sit on a stool.

Zuryzel obeyed, keeping her bright, dark eyes on her mother. "Mother, I wanted to ask you about … about the Hoeylahk."

Queen Demeda tipped her head to one side, puzzled. "Why?"

Zuryzel shrugged. "Just curious."

Queen Demeda rubbed her eyes wearily. "Well, I suppose the best place to start would be when the corsairs took me captive. I was chained in front of my friend and at the same oar as an otter. At first I thought she was a sea otter, like the ones who took over Zurez. But she was not—I can't remember her name, but I think it was Star. Well, they were three-creature oars, so I had a job pulling it with her—she was, you understand, very young. It makes me feel old, to think about it. Then this one day, well …" She closed her eyes dreamily before continuing. "Five more prisoners arrived."

Zuryzel was listening intently. She had never heard this part of the story before.

"They put up such a fight. We all thought that they were otters. Otters are renowned for being terrifying beasts. Imagine our surprise to find that they were nothing but five young mice! They looked as if they were about eleven cycles old—younger than Star—but they were lean, strong, and vicious. One of them was a tawny maiden with black eyes. Another was a maiden the color of the damp earth up by Dobar with green eyes. Two males were gray, one with black eyes, one with gray. And the last one was a black maiden with pale blue eyes."

Queen Demeda's eyes glittered as Zuryzel's mouth fell open. The princess could manage only two words. "Lady Raven?"

"Well, she wasn't 'lady' then," said Queen Demeda. "She was just Raven, the courageous, eleven-cycle-old daughter of Lord Condor of the Rangers. The tawny maiden was named Sparrow, the other maiden was named Fern, and the two males were Shale and Hetmuss Cinder. You know Hetmuss Cinder."

Zuryzel registered all the names as Queen Demeda continued.

"The crew feared them, even in chains. Then one night, when Fern was supposed to be interrogated, she managed to get out of her captor's hold and snatched up one of her arrows."

Queen Demeda shuddered more than Zuryzel had ever seen anyone shudder. "I can tell you, Zuryzel, I am more afraid of those arrows than of the whole army of foxes. Their poison can't kill you. But it gives you so much pain that you wish it would. It keeps you alive until you can't stand any more torture. Ooooh, Zuryzel, she whirled that arrow around and got poison into three of the strongest, cruelest of the foxes on that ship. And they screamed and screamed for hours! The other foxes would have drowned her had not the Hoeylahk Tribe had the Bear King's help to arrive just on time. Lord Condor and the Rangers were with them in a black ship called *Deathwind*. Slaughter raged unchecked but in total silence. That's all I know of the Hoeylahk Tribe—that I owe my freedom to them and Lord Condor, Lady Raven's father."

Zuryzel sat mulling the whole story over and over in her mind. So Lady Raven had been captured by corsairs! That was much more interesting than the Hoeylahk Tribe.

A tap sounded on the door. "Come in," Queen Demeda called.

Orlysk Rainbow entered. Her blue eyes looked as if they were laughing. "You'll never guess," she giggled. "The foxes have arrived. They have some huge, half-rotted hornbeam that takes nearly four score of them to carry. Ha ha! They're trying to get it across the lake! What good will that do them, I ask you!"

Zuryzel knew the answer before Orlysk Rainbow finished. She leapt up and exclaimed, "Battering ram!"

Orlysk Rainbow looked blank. Zuryzel remembered that she had not seen a fortress before she came south, so she knew nothing about besieging them.

"They're going to knock the gates down!" Zuryzel explained.

Orlysk Rainbow showed disgust with the explanation, clearly considering the foxes stupid. "Why don't they just use a boulder?" she queried. "All they'd have to do is build a ramp and find the right sized rock. It would be much faster—just one good shove!"

"Well, don't tell them," advised Queen Demeda. She too had risen to her paws. "Come on. Let's go pay the wall a visit!"

The three warriors hurried through the passages of Dombre to the walls. Queen Demeda hurried to stand between Hokadra and Lady Raven. Zuryzel stood quietly next to Sibyna and Biddah. Biddah's paws trembled, but she took a firmer grip on her bowstring and they stopped. Sibyna had gripped a duck-feathered arrow in one paw, and her bow in another. Zuryzel rested her left paw on her sword hilt. She smiled. Any right-pawed fox would have a surprise in fighting her—she was left-pawed!

Not too far away, Lady Raven had her bow ready with an arrow fitted with starling feathers, and beside her, Harclayang, Zuryzel's admirer, stood gripping his spear. Zuryzel had noticed that his paw step had less buoyancy of late than it used to. Zuryzel liked the change. Harclayang met Zuryzel's eye from across where he stood on the curving battlements and gave her an encouraging nod. Zuryzel was grateful for his encouragement.

Scorch stood on the bank, waving his scimitar. Ice was giving orders to others not too far away. And Poison sat perfectly still in front of about four score other foxes, balancing carefully on the huge hornbeam log floating in the lake, being paddled by the soldiers on board toward the island Dombre stood on.

Zuryzel bristled. She was taken aback by the speed that the log was advancing across the lake. Poison sat perfectly still, as did the others, and Zuryzel knew if only one of the many foxes lost balance, the log would capsize. No twang pierced the air as an arrow sped from its bow to one of the foxes directly behind Poison. The vixen screamed and fell, and instantly the whole of the log's occupants gave loud cries and fell into the black waters.

Only Poison survived the fall. The other foxes either knocked their heads on the log and drowned or else thrashed so wildly about that they pulled each other down to their deaths. But the vixen fell onto a mound of debris on the bottom of the lake and stood upon it, dripping wet and shivering helplessly, a most undignified position for a vainly beautiful Oracle's apprentice.

Zuryzel did not need to turn to know that Lady Raven was the reason the log flipped, but she looked anyway. A puff of ash had settled on the Ranger's face, and Zuryzel understood: she had coated her bowstring with a thin layer of ash, which, though it slowed the arrow, made the attack silent, destroying any warning in its flight. King Hokadra glanced around to see who had fired the arrow, staring accusingly at Raven, but Lady Raven had swiftly taken another one identical to the first and drew back her bowstring.

Zuryzel sighed. Yes, "swift" fitted Lady Raven well.

Poison was making her way back towards the shore, still dripping wet, by finding the sandbars that peppered the lake.

Zuryzel shook her head. She whispered to Biddah, "I think we'll do our best to stand out the siege as if we want to defend Dombre!"

Biddah nodded her agreement, but her eyes suddenly widened as she stared past the foxes' army. Zuryzel looked too—and her mouth went dry.

Smoke was billowing like an evil cloud of foreboding. Zuryzel understood and felt sick: the foxes were burning the great deciduous forests that had grown there for uncounted cycles. Soon it would be nothing but a barren wasteland. Zuryzel felt sick with horror. Even if the foxes were defeated, how could the creatures that had lived there before the war survive?

Feldspar shivered as he woke up.

There were no peaceful streams or moss-covered banks in the east of Pasadagavra. He had had to content himself by sleeping in small beds laid out for those such as him—in the lower branches of oaks. He did not like waking up in the branches.

He dropped gingerly to the earth and over to the small pump. He washed himself quickly and then shook out his blanket. Last night he had trouble getting to sleep. The creatures at Pasadagavra had seen the billowing smoke, and Feldspar had seen many tear-stained faces last night.

"Kreeeeeeeeeee!"

Feldspar jumped with surprise. Glancing around, he saw the source of the shriek.

Redswift, one of the red kites that lived at Pasadagavra had alighted practically right next to him. She fixed her fierce golden eye on him.

"Kraaaaa! Who are you, mouse?"

Feldspar was startled by her blunt manner, but he replied, "My name is Feldspar. I'm from Graystone."

Redswift nodded thoughtfully. "I see. I am due to set out south today, to those sorts of settlements. Would you like me to take a message to anyone you see down there?"

Feldspar knew better than to ask why Redswift was going south when there were Warhawks around. So he simply said, "My friends, Opal, Redfur, Lillia, and Swordpoint ... could you tell them that I miss them, that I'll be down sometime after the war, and that I ran into Chite and he hasn't changed?"

Redswift nodded. "I'll be there in two weeks. I'll see them then."

Feldspar stared in amazement. "But it took me over three cycles to get this far north!"

Redswift preened a golden bar on her wing, which Feldspar knew birds of prey took as a sign of swiftness. "Kraaaahaaaaa! I'm not called Redswift for nothing!" Then she took off with a powerful but graceful brush of wings.

"AAAAAAAHH!"

Ol'ver had rolled right out of his bed, and now he lay winded on the earth.

Feldspar grinned and scrambled over to him. "Are you all right, Ol'ver? That was some way to wake up!"

For answer, Ol'ver struggled to his feet and pulled the tail of the apparently sleeping Chite.

"YOOOOOWWW!" cried Chite, as he slid along the branch and slammed into the trunk of the tree, face first, and then tumbled off onto the roots. "Ol'ver, what was that for?"

Ol'ver was fuming.

"For knocking me out of my bed, you southern-lily!"

"Oi!" protested Chite. "I did not touch you, and I am not a southern lily!"

"Yes, you are! Is there no other way you can wake sleeping mice up? The only way you seem to know is pain!"

"All right, all right!" laughed Feldspar. "Enough of this! Let's head west today. I miss the Willow Brook."

Chite and Ol'ver glared at each other a moment longer before Chite turned and stormed off to the nearest well. Ol'ver shook his head pityingly.

"Stomping and storming all over, what a dunderhead!" He glanced at Feldspar. "Feldspar, those rogues you talk about down south ... what are they like? Are they like the foxes here?"

Feldspar shook his head. "They're worse."

Now it was Ol'ver's turn to shake his head. "No they're not, Feldspar. I've seen the way you look at the foxes here. You're impressed by the number and discipline. But the fact is they're just some rabble that is cruel and heartless like winter. Tell me, would the rogues down south leave you alone if you wounded them so much they could not fight back?"

Feldspar nodded.

Ol'ver sighed. "The foxes up here would not. If you let them live, they do more evil. Even if they're helpless at your paws and cry for mercy, you have to kill them. If you don't, they'll just take more lives."

Feldspar mulled over what Ol'ver had said, but he made no reply.

36

TIME

Zuryzel had just come in from sentry duty, exhausted, and lay down on her bed almost immediately. Responding to the volley after volley of arrows and spears had drained her physically, as well as mentally and emotionally. Perhaps that explained why she had such a strange dream.

There was swirling blackness. Yet the swirl seemed to have a pattern. Then a voice spoke from it, and Zuryzel saw the faintest outline of some creature that looked old and wise.

"Time?" she whispered incredulously. "*Time?*"

"Zuryzel," spoke Time in a beautiful voice. Zuryzel would have fainted had she not been dreaming. "I have long wanted to greet you—and to show you something."

Zuryzel stared in astonishment.

"There are many great things going on in this earth, and I will show you the ones you need to see. This is the first one."

Zuryzel felt as if she was whirring through space. She could not tell how long the sensation lasted. It could have taken a moment, or it could have taken a lifetime.

Then, quite suddenly, she was standing outside the foxes' castle. Something was not quite right about the creatures assembled there, and it took her a moment to realize what it was. Knife and Fang looked younger, and Scythe … Scythe was there, her head held arrogantly at an angle, her red eyes glinting. Zuryzel wondered if, at some time in her long life, Scythe had been a respectable creature, like Fawn, but had simply been led astray.

And there was some younger vixen there, with a startlingly beautiful face. She stood behind a handsome, slightly gone-to-seed, blood-red male. Zuryzel had never really seen him before, but she identified him immediately.

"Oracle Blood," she whispered.

She had been prepared to hate Oracle Blood, but now she could not. He had an old and wise look about him, yet he also had a glint in his eyes. Zuryzel guessed that, when he was young, he had been the most handsome of all the foxes. His eyes had such a faint red color that Zuryzel knew that their true color was light blue, not unlike the sea just before dawn.

As she looked around more, she felt a lump of cold hatred growing in her mind and her fur beginning to bristle. Standing not far away, conversing with an, at least, five cycles younger Oracle Hemlock, was Current the sea otter. He, in particular, the Wraith Mice hated for his hypocrisy. Zuryzel, however, had enough sense to listen to what the Oracle and the sea otter said.

"Are you absolutely positive this is what your creatures want?" asked Hemlock in an almost friendly tone.

"Oh yes," replied Current eagerly. "They sent me as the messenger. They said it would be my first task as chief. The other clans agree with us as well."

"Well," said Hemlock, "that sounds reasonable. However, we will require something from you first. What would you offer?"

"Fighting for you is out of the question, I'm afraid," stated Current, "but how about we bring you all the prisoners we can lay our paws on—with the exception, of course, of Sky. She should die at our paws."

"Of course," smiled Hemlock. Zuryzel was shocked that Current failed to see the threat in Hemlock's eyes and the keen glimmer in Knife's. They were all too visible for her.

"Very well, tell your creatures we accept," decided Hemlock. "And farewell, my friend."

Current disappeared through the forest, and Hemlock, Scythe, and Fang into the castle, Scythe exchanging an almost inconspicuous look with Oracle Blood. Only Blood and the other vixen remained.

Oracle Blood laid his head in his paws. Zuryzel could guess that this youngster, however evil, respected her elders—or Blood, at least. When he raised his head, he called to her, "Come here, child."

She obeyed and let Blood hold her paws. "I don't like this one bit, Sage. I don't trust those sea otters."

Sage!

"But you yourself said that otters are more trustworthy than foxes," objected Sage with respect deep in her voice.

"I said *river otters* are more trustworthy. But Sage, the sea otters are turncoats and liars. Hypocrites, too. One can't trust them, and one can't trust Hemlock, Knife, and Fang. That's not a good combination."

"But you said there are some respectable sea otters," Sage pointed out, respect still deep in her voice. "Perhaps this whole thing will prove of use because of them?"

"Good point," smiled Blood approvingly. Zuryzel saw the look of elation in Sage's face; she guessed that Blood scarcely ever gave compliments. "But still, much bloodshed will come from this even before this will benefit anyone. An alliance between otters and foxes can only go wrong. I don't know why Hemlock wanted one. If I'd had my way, there would be no alliance."

Sage nodded understandingly. "I see. For example, Current looks to me as if he cannot even capture a babe. So, he will get killed for his non-compliance. Then, the other sea otters will want vengeance. Right?"

Blood smiled fondly at Sage, and his smile was not unlike a grandfather's for his grandchild. "You need not always ask me, Sage. I see I'm not the only one who has brains. You're quite right, though I didn't think of that until you said it. Which reminds me, I have something for you."

His cloak swirled as he took a long package, wrapped up in bark of oak, which Zuryzel knew was a very rare gift in itself. Sage opened it up reverently and took out two things: a shortspear identical to the one Oracle Blood had made for Fawn, and a necklace, also identical to Fawn's. The necklace had stone beads on it, blood red and tinged with gold.

Sage put the necklace on and lifted the spear. She closed her eyes for a moment, and she looked so pretty that it took Zuryzel's breath away.

Oracle Blood smiled appreciatively. "You look like the princesses in those stories. Now, let's go find something to eat, shall we?"

Sage smiled, and she looked even more beautiful.

Then the whirring sensation began again, and once more, Zuryzel was faced with the swirling mists of Time, and once again, Time spoke to her.

"This vision is one of many I will show you, Zuryzel. But for now, I have only one humble present to give you."

Time approached Zuryzel. The Wraith Mouse shook with awe as Time's huge paw pressed a small object into her own. Zuryzel felt no fur on the creature's paw, only scales, like those on a bird's leg, and three claws that felt gentle to the touch. When Time spoke, Zuryzel felt a wisp of warmth touch her fur that gave her the feeling that her heart, until then lying down, sleeping, had suddenly awakened.

"We will meet in our dreams again, Zuryzel. The Bear King has granted it so. Wake now, and use discretion when you speak of our meetings."

Zuryzel woke with a feeling that she was still young, and would be forever. Then she felt something in her paw. She looked at it, a bead, but more wonderful than any she had ever felt, seen, or dreamed of. As it rested in her hand, a little warmth issued from it, like the warmth that had touched her fur when Time had spoken. Turquoise and edged with silver, it had a silver full moon on one side with a few ridges. Like a moon's soul. Zuryzel smiled. Then, it hit her.

Like the raven bead.

She reached under her garment and drew out the bead that Herttua Crow had given her. It shimmered palely, and as Zuryzel stared at it, she thought it moved its wings and flew. But a moment later, it was still there. Great Cerecinthia—Lady Raven had a connection with Time too.

Tap, tap, tap.

Zuryzel jumped in surprise. She hastily tugged on her tunic and rushed to the door, and opened it.

It was Johajar, and he looked a tad bit worried. "Zuryzel," he whispered, "have you seen Mokimshim?"

Zuryzel frowned. "No, why?"

Johajar gestured toward the window, where a little light was drifting through. "It's past dawn, and Mokimshim should be on sentry. But Colobi told me that she hadn't seen him for some time."

"Right," murmured Zuryzel. "Did Mother or Father order him to do sentry?"

Johajar shook his head. "No, he volunteered."

"Then let's find him," decided Zuryzel. "Hold on a moment."

She hastened into her study, found her chain mail, and tugged it on. Then she hurried out of her study and joined Johajar in the corridor.

"If I'm going out early in the morning, I may as well look like a warrior princess."

Johajar nodded worriedly. "I wish Mokimshim was as reliable as you are," he said abruptly but quietly. "Then I wouldn't have to worry about him so much."

Zuryzel was burning with pride at her brother's comment, but she hid it. "Mokimshim isn't a bad leader," she retorted fairly.

"Yes, he is," replied Johajar, in the same undertone. "He doesn't have a clue how to lead even a small patrol. Oh, he's got the brains, but he can't use them. He's always unsure where to go, and forever asking for help. He can't lead like you can," he added admiringly.

Zuryzel knew better than to let her brother's admiration flatter her. She replied firmly, "Mokimshim is getting better at it every day. He'll just have to learn. Don't say anything about this again."

Johajar smiled. "I wish I had your common sense."

The twins searched the castle and ran almost straight into Dikiner. "Hey, Zuryzel, could I have a word?" he asked, looking nervous.

"In a bit, Dikiner," replied Zuryzel. "Have you seen Mokimshim?"

Dikiner glanced at Johajar and replied, "Last I saw him he was heading toward the walls."

Johajar blew a sigh of exasperation and hurried off to the walls.

Zuryzel frowned at Dikiner. "Where is Mokimshim *really*, Dikiner?"

Dikiner looked anxious. "Well, that's what I wanted to talk to you about. Oh, it's nothing serious," he said hastily, noticing the look on Zuryzel's face, "but it's, well, Karena. He's been fawning all over her for days, but she can't get rid of him. She's tried, though. Would you ... would you please have a word with him?"

Zuryzel remembered all too well how fiercely protective of his sister Dikiner was and how he had always wanted the best for her. She was not surprised that Mokimshim never leaving Karena alone put him off. "Yes, I will."

Dikiner nodded gratefully. "Thank you, Zuryzel. He's in the archery range."

Zuryzel nodded and hurried off in that direction.

Dikiner had spoken truly. Mokimshim stood right behind Karena, admiring her archery skills. Karena kept an eye on Orgorad, practicing with Sibyna, Zuryzel could see, but she looked frustrated that she could not shake off Mokimshim.

Zuryzel hurried over and tapped her brother's shoulder gently. "Could I talk to you for a second?" she asked. Mokimshim nodded, and hurried after her as she left the archery range.

"Listen," whispered Zuryzel, "you were supposed to be on sentry almost an hour ago. Don't worry now; Johajar's doing it for you. Why don't you lead the next patrol, though, so you have an excuse for not doing sentry? Go talk to Shinar; she's in charge of patrols. And another thing—leave Karena alone for a bit. She didn't look all that happy with you there distracting her form her archery."

Mokimshim nodded sheepishly. "I guess you're right."

Zuryzel smiled at her brother. "You're impossible, Mokimshim. Well, I'd better be off. I need to have a word with Dejuday."

Mokimshim grinned, gave his sister a playful shove, and hurried away.

Zuryzel hurried to her own chambers but was stopped by a voice that she knew too well in an apparently deserted corridor.

"Zuryzel?"

Zuryzel smiled and turned to face Harclayang. His smile was more than friendly, and he looked delighted to see Zuryzel again.

"Hello," sighed Zuryzel. "Long time, no see."

Harclayang hurried up to her and squeezed her paws. "I've missed you," he murmured.

Zuryzel was glad to see Harclayang again, but right now she wanted to be alone. Besides, it was harder to pull off tricks in Dombre than it was in Mirquis. So she merely smiled and replied, "I've missed you, too. Did Mokimshim handle Mirquis well?"

Harclayang shook his head. "Oh, yes, considering who we're talking about."

"Don't say that."

Harclayang sighed. "You're right; I shouldn't. But he never seemed to know what to do! Oh, he's a good creature. But he doesn't seem to be able to lead. Not like you can," he added. "You look tired, Zuryzel."

Zuryzel realized she was from rushing all over Dombre in chain mail. She shrugged. "I didn't sleep well."

Harclayang touched her paw kindly. "Go sleep now. I'll see you later, perhaps?"

Zuryzel nodded. "Perhaps," she replied. She wandered off to her quarters again.

She removed her chain mail so she was clad only in a tunic, and sat down gratefully on her bed. No sooner had she seated herself, however, than another tapping on her door interrupted her rest.

She stood up wearily and opened the door. She was surprised to see Sibyna.

Sibyna looked worried but determined. "Zuryzel," she began, "could I talk to you for a second?"

Zuryzel wondered what could worry her so as she let Sibyna in.

Sibyna stood, but Zuryzel motioned her to sit. She did not like the way that her closest friends now treated her with this form of respect—why couldn't they just treat her as they always had?

Sibyna began fidgeting nervously, but she began fearfully, "Zuryzel, please don't be angry, but I … I … I … I saw you with Harclayang, and I want to tell you … please don't be angry."

Zuryzel was too tired to be angry about anything, even the foxes. "I'm not," she replied.

Sibyna seemed to be stronger now. "Look, I don't mean to interfere; I just want to tell you you're young. Your parents say you are old enough to fall in love, old enough to have a mate, but still, you're not using judgment. You don't love Harclayang—the way you were so quick to get away from him! I just wanted to give you advice. Be mild toward him and any other creature that starts acting like him to you. He clearly likes you, but use your judgment.

"I don't like him," Zuryzel assured her. "I just like to pull tricks on him."

Sibyna didn't look amused. "I … don't tell anyone I said this, but I don't want you to go through what I'm going through."

Sibyna's eyes filled with pain, and Zuryzel understood why her friend felt so insistent on giving this advice.

Sibyna continued.

"Besides, you'd be better off with someone you could get along with for a long time. Someone who really loves you." The pain left her eyes, and mischief replaced it.

Zuryzel frowned. "Who do you mean?"

Sibyna's eyes glowed knowingly. "Think on it for a bit," she grinned. "You'd be amazed."

With that, she stood and left the room.

Zuryzel was so bewildered. She thought and thought about whom Sibyna could mean, but she had no ideas. She closed her eyes. Face after face entered her imagination, but she did not think these were the ones Sibyna had spoken of. Then she tired of thinking too much and just relaxed, wondering if she could finally have some uninterrupted rest. And into her mind came a pale gray face and a pair of blue eyes.

Why was she thinking of Asherad?

37

THE LATE WIND AND THE SUMMONS

Knife paced her room anxiously, Fang watching her.

"Knife," he muttered after a while, "sit down. You're wearing me out."

Knife sat down in a chair for a moment and then stood up abruptly and hurried to the window.

A huge wind current blew this way every year before summer. But the first day of summer had nearly arrived, and still no such movement stirred in the air. Knife had waited and waited for it, and was becoming quite impatient with its delay.

Now, finally, the first hint of a breeze began. Knife stood gnawing anxiously on her lip as the wind picked up. Then she stood perfectly still, and her eyes began turning color. Fang watched her.

Something did not seem to be quite right. Knife was standing mostly still, as she always did, yet her expression, rather than trance-like, gleamed in purest triumph. Suddenly a cold, soulless smile that chilled even Fang spread across her face. Her teeth bared, and her tongue wavered about them as if she could taste blood. Then, just as abruptly, it all changed to a look of shock. Her paws began to tremble, and her eyes returned to their usual red. She looked shocked beyond her wildest imaginations.

"What?" asked Fang.

"It didn't tell me anything!" Knife exclaimed. "I heard the wind whispering, and then it seemed to growl in my ear, and it said, 'I will tell you nothing.' Just like that! This has never happened to me before in my life."

"That's just great," grumbled Fang. "No wind, no messengers, no nothing, unless you count the news that they didn't make it into Dombre because of one archer! What are we going to do about all this?"

"Only one solution," sighed Knife, sounding resigned. "Claw."

"*Claw?* What good would Claw do, may I ask?" exploded Fang.

"Well, he has brains to begin with," said Knife loudly.

"But he's a coward!" protested Fang.

"Well, if you have a better idea, let me hear it!" shrieked Knife, having lost her temper.

Fang subsided. "All right," he growled. "But the fact is Poison is out there. Claw isn't the ugliest of foxes, you know, and if Poison wants control—"

"Ice is there, too," Knife reminded him. "She might not be a genius, but she has enough sense when it comes to dealing with Poison."

"All right," repeated Fang. "Let's send him out there."

Knife stretched. "You know, I'm suddenly tired. I think I'll get some sleep."

Fang yawned. "Me, too."

The second he had gone, however, Knife went straight to a black stone desk. She opened a cupboard and took out an ancient scroll. The evil vixen unrolled it, revealing hieroglyphics. Knife had no great skill at languages or writing—and she dared not show this to Fang who had a talent for writing—but she had enough brains to guess certain parts. Some of it, Scythe, the fox who had mentored Knife had translated, and (to Knife's wonder) Ice had deciphered others. It seemed to be a collection of prophecies, but only one was completely translated. It read:

One day the late wind will speak silently.

Huh, thought Knife. *That's today. I wonder if the wind will be silent forever or if it will speak to me again.*

Knife read some more, all the while thinking hard.

Time to take matters into my paws, she decided. *We need help other than the Warhawks. They won't get us very far in Pasadagavra.*

She had brains enough to know what to do.

She took out a parchment and a quill. The feather was that of a young sparrow that had found its way into the vixen's arrow's path. She wrote out a quick, simple, short message in the common tongue, Ordian, the only language she could write in. After much crossing out, burning of rough drafts, and ruining several quills, her note read:

Captain Demmons,

I heard that your ship, Waveslayer, ran afoul of some reef. I am Knife the Oracle, and I would be more than pleasured to offer you the promise of timber of hornbeam to build another ship in exchange for service of your crew, and any you can raise, in our army as we attack the fortress of Pasadagavra. I can also assure you of plunder and slaves, of which there is much in the city. Send a reply if you reject; meet me at the castle of Dombre if you accept. This messenger I give you my permission to deal with as you see fit.

She reread it a few times. Yes, that would work. It held the promise of both a new ship and plunder for a corsair, and a slaver at that. This would work.

She hurried along the castle, thankful that it was the dead of night, to Fang's room. Once there, she rapped sharply on the door.

Fang looked distinctly groggy as he answered. "What do you want," he grumbled. "I thought you wanted to sleep."

Knife put a claw to her lips and nodded past Fang into his room.

Fang shook his head, but he took the hint and backed away from the door to let Knife enter.

"Do you mind telling me what this is all about?" he snarled wearily.

Knife unrolled her message for him to see. He took a single glance at it, and then stuffed his paw into his mouth.

"*Cary lemons?* What does *that* mean?"

"*What?*" asked Knife.

"You need to work on your spelling," Fang chortled. "You missed the curve in *Waveslayer* and the line in hornbeam. That's not all, either."

"Look," snapped Knife impatiently. "Just fix the spelling and translate it into Simalan. You can do that, can't you?"

"Of course," grinned Fang, looking insane with his red eyes. "But who are you going to trust to deliver it? *I'm* not going, and you can't order me. Besides, are you sure you want to do this?" he added, his amusement vanishing instantly. "Corsairs are vile creatures, and Demmons is by far and away one of the worst. They're very crafty and dangerous. Wouldn't it be better if we found reinforcements from somewhere on land?"

Knife waved a paw dismissively. "We have over ten times the number in a corsair crew. No fear."

"Yes," agreed Fang, "but you added 'any you can raise.' *That's* more than a crew of corsairs."

Knife shrugged. "How many corsairs can there be in the world?"

Outside Fang's window, the voice of the second maiden, the one who had greeted those who had witnessed Anamay's acceptance into Crustacean's tribe, hissed from a stunted vine. "More than you can handle, fox. Huh, I'd better either get that messenger or get the word to Pasadagavra. I'll go with getting the word to Pasadagavra. That way, if I can't find the messenger before it's too late, who cares? I'll tell Streamcourse, she can tell Lukkal, and Lukkal can get word to Arpaha. Then I'll go after the messenger with the crew."

Silently she climbed down to earth. The clouds, which always shrouded the castle of the foxes these days, thinned out a little, and the moon shone through to reflect sadly on Mirquis and Dombre but also to light the way for the indistinguishable figure hurrying to the woods.

Then all was plunged into darkness again as the wind picked up.

Opal, Redfur, Lillia, and their friend Swordpoint, the mouse warrior's son, crouched in the undergrowth, nearly five day's tracking nor'west of Graystone. Within three hours, they would come within contact of Kwang-ha`el, according to Swordpoint (Opal was sure it was much closer). Kwang-ha`el was the river otter city, and the southernmost city in the world. It was made out of stone, not just wood like Graystone. Then they could see Speareye and Hannah, and hopefully have some news from Pasadagavra, or any place Feldspar and Chite might be. Opal was beginning to get anxious; there had been no shortage of news from Chite, but Feldspar had sent no word whatsoever, and considering the state he'd been in when he had left Graystone … well … Opal was beginning to worry about her friend's life. And then, nearly two cycles ago, Chite had stopped sending news altogether. Opal clung to the hope that they had made it to Pasadagavra and simply had not been able to send messages about themselves. Northern-born warrior though she was, Opal did not dare think about the alternative.

"Pst, Opal," hissed Swordpoint. "I think someone's coming."

Opal, too, realized that she could make out the faint sound of paw steps over the Bakkarra River's roaring. The creature, whoever it was, was carrying something heavy and squelching in the mud of the early summer.

"Follow it," whispered Opal.

Even Lillia did not make a noise as the group trailed the shadowy creature, taking them closer to the Bakkarra.

Opal crept into view of the river. Next second, paws unceremoniously tugged her into the river.

"Oi!" she exclaimed as she floundered in the wallowing current to laughter of those on the bank. She lashed out, catching her attacker on the shoulder.

"Oh, for Cerecinthia's sake, Opal, not everyone you meet is an enemy!"

Opal's paws found ground, and she sprinted doggedly through the still-strong flow onto solid ground.

Redfur reached out a strong paw and helped her ashore. Then he threw an affectionate paw about her shoulders and shouted above the roar to Opal's attacker.

"Come on, Hannah, not everyone is a river otter, either."

Opal liked Redfur enough, but even though he was a fox and she a mouse and only slightly smaller, she could not accept even the hint of a friendly insult: she was a warrior, not a helpless maiden!

She shook herself vigorously, drenching Redfur as much as if he, too, had taken a dive in the river. He quickly let Opal go and rubbed water from his eyes. "Hey," he protested. "Hannah, you need to cut back on your jokes."

Hannah the river otter sat down on a rock on the bank, dripping wet. "Really, Redfur, you haven't changed. You're still impudent and disrespectful. Mm, mm!"

"Don't even start playing the prissy, well-brought-up, flirty, prim maiden, Hannah," snapped Opal angrily.

"Sorry, Opal," sighed Hannah.

Swordpoint sighed wearily. "Hannah, what are you doing so far from Kwang-ha`el?"

Hannah shook her head in despair. "Really, Swordpoint, you need to work on either remembering the way to Kwang-ha`el or honing your sense of direction. Kwang-ha`el is only a little ways *this way*."

"Told you, Swordpoint."

"And you might want to hurry along; there's someone you might be interested in seeing," Hannah continued, a note of excitement in her voice. "Come on, come on. We do need to hurry!"

The five friends followed the river to Kwang-ha`el, going slowly for Lillia's benefit. As they traveled, Opal thought back to her childhood and the memory, alone, of Kwang-ha`el overawed her. She remembered when she was little and lived in the north, not too far south of the Rangers' border. Her family had been of high standing, and she had received any training, lessons, or free time she desired, because of her family's rank, yes, but also because those three mattered above all else in her society. She had learned

Eeriedan, the Northern Tongue, Simalan, the Western Tongue, Ordian, the Common Tongue, Miamuran, the Eastern Tongue, and Huridan, the Southern Tongue, and others. She was proud of being born in the north, in the country of Eeried, the Land of the Warriors.

On one of the turrets over the main gate perched Redswift. She raised her head nobly and called out her war cry.

"Kreeeeeeeeeeeeeeekendeeen!"

Opal's eyes lit up. "Is that a red kite?" she whispered excitedly to Hannah.

"Mm, hmm. Her name is Redswift, and she has news of Pasadagavra—and Chite and Feldspar."

Opal blew out a sigh of relief. "Bear King be praised."

"Aye, and according to her, Feldspar is in a good state, too," Hannah added.

"Bet they found some pretty maidens up north," muttered Redfur with a snicker.

"Don't even start going on about that, Redfur," murmured Lillia in a concerned tone.

Opal rolled her eyes in disgust. "Stop being soppy, the lot of you," she snapped impatiently.

Redswift took off from the turret, soared up so high that she almost disappeared, and then dove beautifully from the sky to land right in front of them, out of earshot of Kwang-ha`el.

"Kreee! Do you come from Graystone?"

Opal nodded. She adopted her northern manner, keeping her language in Ordian but speaking with authority and a warrior's fearlessness. "Yes. My name is Opal. You have news of our friends?"

Redswift's golden eye turned to face Opal, who did not flinch. "Kraa! Warrior. I have news of Feldspar and Chite. They made it to Pasadagavra, which is by now surrounded with twice the number as when I left. They will come south sometime after the war."

Opal shook her head in disbelief. "After the war? *After* the war? Who knows when the war will end?"

"Yeah," Lillia added sadly.

Redswift shrugged. "Well, travel is almost impossible since the foxes are on the move. Would you like me to take a message up to your friends?"

"Yes," replied Lillia instantly. "Tell Chite he's dead meat for running off."

Redfur and Opal exchanged amused looks.

"Tell them that we all miss them," added Hannah.

"Tell them that we saw a Warhawk," added Redfur.

"Tell them we're keeping our eyes peeled for Herttua Crow Blue Arrows," added Lillia.

"And tell them that rogues haven't attacked for ages," added Swordpoint.

"And tell them that we found a bunch of ancient writings in Kwang-ha`el and that they're written in the ancient otter hieroglyphics!" added Hannah.

When no more pleas came, Redswift raised a talon to one eye. Then off she flew into the sky, vanishing from view.

"Come on," urged Hannah. "Come see Speareye. By the way, I think Rain is here."

DEMMONS

Zuryzel gazed about her on the walls of Dombre.

The fortress was meant to be evacuated immediately. However, King Hokadra had chosen to stand and fight for a while. Dombre was, after all, built better for fighting than Mirquis had been. Besides, they could outlast a siege without any trouble—Graeka's earthworms had dug many tunnels away from the original one, so it would be easier to bring in food and even send out a few patrols. But the question remained: how was Pasadagavra holding out? True, with its own farms and forests and waters, no enemy could ever lay siege to it, and it would be difficult to get into it, to say the least, but it was still surrounded. Even the greatest fortress could be conquered.

Zuryzel released that concern and let others in. She liked being on sentry because it gave her time to think what she had been shoving to the back of her mind all day. She had, for example, dismissed Dikiner from her list of suspects for the spy. Orlysk Rainbow had looked at her with a disbelieving expression when Zuryzel had suggested him, and Zuryzel valued Orlysk Rainbow's opinion.

"Zuryzel, don't be daft. How on earth would he manage to get to Hemlock's camp and back without your noticing?" she had argued. "You depended a lot on him. I'm not saying that's a bad thing!" she said quickly. "But how would he manage to get away?"

"Who do you think it is, then?" Zuryzel had wondered.

"I have no clue—I know I said I did, but I don't—but, Zuryzel, who-ever the one, the creature isn't doing this of his or her own free will. The spy mumbled something about Mokimshim not being able to lead—"

"How many times must creatures comment on that?" Zuryzel inter-rupted impatiently. "He's not going to get any better this way!"

"That's not the point," hissed Orlysk Rainbow.

"Then what is the point, Orlysk Rainbow?" demanded Sibyna, who had heard from Zuryzel most of what Orlysk Rainbow and Lady Raven had heard.

"The *point* is that the spy said he or she is helping the foxes only because Mokimshim cannot be king. Even then, the creature sounded intimidated. Hemlock said that if the spy disobeyed him, you would get burned to death."

Sibyna had shuddered. "Glad I'm not you," she commented.

Zuryzel merely shrugged. "I'd love to see them try."

A whisper interrupted their discussion. "Zuryzel!"

Dikiner and Shinar waited respectfully at the doorway. Briefly wondering how she could have ever thought Dikiner was the spy, Zuryzel beckoned them over.

"They're trying again," whispered Shinar. "Over there, see?"

Zuryzel did see. A huge boat with a hornbeam log trailing behind was silently approaching the island Dombre stood on. Zuryzel noted how cleverly Knife had staffed the boat in preparation for the attack. Because several motions in sword fighting were similar to those in rowing a boat, she had chosen sword bearers to row, which they did with apparent ease. The boat was making good progress.

Shinar twitched her tail impatiently. "Zuryzel, can I go do something about it?" she pleaded.

When it came to the foxes, Zuryzel wasn't sure she trusted Shinar to act with prudence. Otters were known for being rash, especially in danger-ous situations.

"What are you going to do, Shinar?" asked Zuryzel sternly under her breath

"Just knock the spigots out," replied Shinar. "It's simple enough. Don't worry; I won't let myself be seen," she added.

Zuryzel hesitated and then nodded.

Wisely—or luckily—Shinar did not bother going down into the gate, which was convenient because opening the gates would probably have given away the fact that the foxes had been spotted. Instead, she climbed up onto the battlements and dove soundlessly into the lake.

Dikiner stared wide-eyed. "Good thing we didn't put any sand or rocks that close to the island."

"No kidding," agreed Zuryzel. "I wish she wouldn't do that. How's she going to get back in?"

"Oh, she'll probably go in through a secret passageway or something after she's done a bit of spying on the camp," Dikiner shrugged.

"Well, if worst comes to worst, we'll have to haul her up over the wall."

"True, Zuryzel," Dikiner shrugged. "I'd better get some rope."

"Don't let anyone see you," Zuryzel advised. Dikiner nodded.

It seemed to take an eternity for Shinar to get back although she easily did the job she'd set out to do. Zuryzel could tell, because suddenly cries flew out from the boat and it began to go down, dragging the log with it. But where Shinar was, Zuryzel had no clue. She seemed to have vanished, as though she were a watery Wraith Mouse in the dark. Zuryzel was still scanning the lake as Dikiner hurried up, struggling a bit under the rope's weight. As he and Zuryzel let it down, they continued scanning the night for Shinar.

Far from being back soon, dawn was nearly about to spread its gray light over the earth when they heard Shinar calling quietly, "Haul me up!"

After Shinar's daring and successful feat, Zuryzel did not expect to see the river otter in such a condition. Rather than triumphant at her victory or at least smiling in delight, after coming over the wall, she collapsed to the ground, gnawing her lip, anxious and afraid.

"What?" asked Zuryzel.

"Bad news," murmured Shinar grimly. "Knife the Oracle and Claw the whatever have arrived at the front. But you'll never guess who else has either."

"Hemlock?" asked Dikiner, looking puzzled.

"No," replied Shinar. "It's worse."

🐭

Knife and Claw had spent many tiresome days and cold nights trekking through the former forest, now burnt wasteland. She had not expected Captain Demmons to arrive quite so soon, but he had—and with a vast army at his back.

As Knife had hoped, he did, indeed, recruit other corsairs. But she had not anticipated the vast number Demmons could summon. She realized what a fool she had been not to think that the most feared and respected corsair would summon more than one extra crew. The army at his back numbered at least eight hundred—more than twice the number of the foxes' army, including the castle guard, training soldiers, and the band attacking Graystone, wherever they were now. And looking closer, Knife saw that these foxes and ferrets were anything but primitive; they were equipped with a heavy sword or dagger apiece, and nearly four hundred of them had crossbows.

Captain Demmons made a fearful sight with steely eyes, a well-muscled body, and a bushy red tail bigger than any Knife had ever seen. His ratty and torn tunic and vest gave testament to his many battles—and the fact he cared little about impressing with something as unimportant as his garb.

If Knife eventually wanted to take total control of this army, fighting would get her nowhere; she had to rely on her own skill with luring and treachery. So, she put on a brazen face and met the terrifying corsair captain.

"Captain Demmons?" she inquired politely.

Demmons's voice had the burr of a creature that followed the sea. "Well, mate, you can see for yerself how big the army I brought is. Aye, yeh'll be wantin' us to help you attack that fortress place with yer?"

"That would be correct," replied Knife.

"An' I got the word off you that they'll be plenty o' booty for me 'n' my crew?"

"Indeed there will," replied Knife again.

"Well, if we're to be on the same side," continued Demmons, "we may 's well trust each other. So here, I found these in a pool nearby. I thought they might have been belongin' t' one o' the Oracles." He held out a lot of blue, white, and gray silks to Knife.

Knife was taken aback. "But … where exactly did you find these?"

"By a pool a little west o' here," explained Demmons. "But could we discuss this later? My crew's just tramped nonstop here from the sea. We're tired."

"Of course," replied Knife. "Poison," she called.

Poison trotted up obediently.

"Take these fighters and find them sleeping arrangements," Knife instructed the beautiful vixen. "And," she added under her breath, "no flirting. Find them arrangements and get back to the shore." She dug a claw into Poison's shoulder for effect.

The vixen winced, nodded, and hurried off, beckoning to the corsairs. She winced again as the entire horde followed her and called to some other vixens to help her with finding sleeping quarters for the corsairs.

"Captain Demmons," whispered Knife urgently. "When dawn breaks, would you show me where you found the silks?"

"Sure, though what good'll it do?" replied the vicious captain. Knife inwardly flinched from his belligerent tone.

🐁

"Corsairs?" Dikiner hissed, staring wide-eyed at Shinar.

"Demmons?" exclaimed Zuryzel in a whisper.

"That's right," replied Shinar gravely.

"And you said there were twice as many of them as there were of the original foxes?" Dikiner hissed incredulously. "What a horde!"

"And there's another thing, too," Shinar added. "Ice has gone missing! I heard Poison and Scorch talking about it. They couldn't find her anywhere. Then Demmons shows up with a bundle of silks from a pool just west of here."

"He killed Ice, do you think?" suggested Dikiner.

"No, none of the silks had blood on them. They were all there, all of them looked as if they had just been wet, but how they ended up in a pool, I'll never know."

"Do you think that Ice slipped in and drowned?" Zuryzel suggested.

"No," sighed Shinar. "That pool isn't very deep—at least, not the one I think Demmons was talking about."

"Well, the question is, do we tell King Hokadra about this or not?"

Zuryzel glanced over across the lake. "No need to get in trouble, which we will if King Hokadra discovers Shinar was fooling around outside the walls. They'll find out before too long. A horde like that is difficult to miss."

🐁

As dawn seeped into the woods, Demmons led Knife to where he had found the silks.

"Well," Knife commented looking at the pool.

Small and barely waist-high, the pool clearly did not contain a body. But it did have a blue-white dye floating in swirls on the surface. And on the banks some of the jewelry Ice had worn lay about—bracelets, earrings, and necklaces. None of them, Knife noted, were ripped or even dirty; someone had carefully removed them and laid them down. Looking around even harder, Knife saw no tunic and realized that, wherever she was, Ice still likely had that.

But this is so odd, thought Knife. *It looks as if she left willingly and without harm. But where did she go? And* why *did she go?*

A closer inspection showed Knife that no pawprints, or any signs, for that matter, to suggest that Ice had left the pool; nonetheless, she was not in the pool.

She took off her silks and jewels, washed away all the dye from her fur, got out of the pool, and wiped out her tracks, Knife thought. *Yes, over here, this branch was freshly cut. I wonder where she's going. The castle? But then why would she wash out her fur? Did she run away? That would make sense. She washed out her fur so she wouldn't be recognized. Or did she run away? Maybe she went out to search for Fawn! Yes, that must be it. She's thinking of claiming glory for herself. Well, I'll deal with her when she comes back. What color is her pelt? It's rusty red, that's right!*

Knife nodded to Captain Demmons. "Thank you, Captain."

Feldspar wandered the banks of the lake alone. He needed some time to himself, to think. And he hoped to see Glor'a.

He was nearly halfway around the lake when he spotted her sitting near the shore, wearing a tunic of turquoise with green trim. She glanced in his direction and looked deliberately back across the lake.

He almost ran to her but slowed his pace as he neared her. She did not stir.

He sat down beside her. Still, she did not stir. In silence, he sat beside her, the look on her face impossible to read.

"Glor'a?" he called quietly.

"Mm hmm?" she replied rather stiffly.

Her coldness hurt Feldspar, but he tried hard to ignore it. "What is it?" he whispered.

"What do you think?" she retorted rather impatiently.

"Why are you angry at me?" he whispered.

"Why shouldn't I be?" she hissed.

Feldspar remembered what he had said to her last time they had spoken. It took him about a second to guess what was ailing her.

"Glor'a, you don't really think I love Opal, do you?" he whispered, a note of pleading in both his voice and heart. "She is just a friend. But Glor'a … Glor'a, I love *you!*"

For the first time, Glor'a looked at him. And she smiled. Her smile shone brighter than the sun and the moon put together, and her brown eyes dazzled with a sparklingly clear light. Feldspar threw his paws about her and held her like that for a while.

"I love you too, Feldspar," she sighed happily.

Feldspar pressed his cheek against hers. Every particle of him, including his rational mind, wanted to stay like this forever, holding Glor'a, resting his mind from the horde of foxes outside the gates, simply holding and never letting her go.

But life intruded. They were sitting on the very edge of the lake, and soon a bunch of otter babes began frisking playfully around, sending splashes onto the pair. They stood up, shaking themselves, laughing at the young otters. Then they wandered away from the lake toward the herb fields.

A stand had been set up not too far away. As they got in reach of the smell, Glor'a gasped in delight.

"Salmon," she exclaimed quietly. "With cornbread and maybe even raspberry and cranberry cordial, honeyed and everything. Oooooh!"

Feldspar relished the smell, and they both hurried up to the stand.

There was no one there, so the two mice helped themselves. They took small wooden plates and loaded them with salmon and corn and filled two cups with the cordial. Then they sat down on a soft knoll to enjoy the little feast.

"If only the world were like this all the time!" Glor'a commented wistfully.

"Mm hmm," Feldspar replied without hesitation.

"Feldspar, when you went to the east side, what did you see?" Glor'a queried, tipping her head to one side.

"Well, apart from Chite and Ol'ver waking each other up by means of knocking the other out of the oak trees ..."

Glor'a laughed.

"We saw these carvings telling about the history of the place, including the myth that the lions built it."

"I don't think it's a myth," said Glor'a fairly. "I believe it. Squirrels could never have built these walls."

"I think you're right," Feldspar agreed. "Glor'a, the one thing it didn't explain is this: squirrel groups are known as tribes, but other creatures live in tribes, too. How do you tell by name if the tribe is a squirrel tribe?"

"Well," Glor'a mused, "I'm not exactly sure, but I think that only squirrel tribes in this part of the earth have fixed names; for example, Coast Tribe, Stone Tribe, Sling Tribe, Moor Tribe. They've been called that since the time of Zureza. But tribes of other creatures—such as river otter tribes—take the name of their leader—like, um, Doomspear's tribe. So when the leader changes, usually dies, so does the tribe's name."

"Hmm."

"What else did you see?"

"Well, we saw the weaving looms, huge, of course, like everything here. I'd guess they reached about half as high as this chamber."

"Wow."

"I bought something from them for you, but I don't have it with me."

"Oh, thank you."

"We did see the oak forest. Pretty amazing. Some great mind had the trees planted in special designs. I've never seen anything like it."

"How so?"

"Well, they look like different shapes from the top. There was a star, a moon, a sun, a spear, an owl, and a squirrel. Can you imagine planting oaks to look like a squirrel? A huge curving ladder sort of thing arched around the top of the chamber so you could climb up and see the shapes better. You really need to look at them from above to see the shapes. Or so we heard. So Ol'ver and I both dared Chite to climb it. He made it to the top, but he had to come back face down. Chite didn't know how to make a turn in the air, so he just took a deep breath and did what he had to do. This huge net hung underneath the ladder, and if you slipped, you landed in that. Chite almost slipped six times, and he really did one time, and then he went flying down into the net like a … a … oh, I'm not sure what."

Glor'a laughed merrily. "Wish I could have been there."

"Me, too," Feldspar murmured.

A small chickadee fluttered nearby, landing not far away. In the lake, a tiny fish jumped and sent small ripples to the shore. A subtle mixture of herb scents permeated the air. And Glor'a sat right beside him.

For a moment, Feldspar forgot the war. He forgot what he'd heard about the foxes and Warhawks and rogues. He forgot the dangers and miseries others had gone through. He remembered only that he had never had such a perfect day.

He had Glor'a with him.

For now, life was good.

INTO THE TUNNEL

old night swirled around Zuryzel as she waited irritably next to her mother, on guard. But this wasn't ordinary sentry duty. Her father was certain a big attack was coming this night, and every single fighter was put on guard. Zuryzel was standing by a small door that led out to one of the sandbars that peppered Dombre's lake. Queen Demeda was just as restless as Zuryzel, and she did not tell her daughter to stand still. Zuryzel was pacing anxiously, muttering to herself.

"I wish they'd just come," she muttered.

Queen Demeda shook her head. "So do I, but when they do come, we have every advantage. Remember that."

Zuryzel shrugged. "I thought we weren't supposed to defend this place."

Queen Demeda rolled her eyes. "True, but I think we got in too far to back out now."

Zuryzel stopped pacing and looked at her mother. "Has Biddah gone through the tunnel?" she asked fearfully.

"Along with most of the squirrels," a voice reassured them from the darkness.

🐀

The tunnel had a huge, yawning entrance with a rope dangling into it. Biddah lifted her own ration pack, ignoring its weight, and followed Karrum to the hole. The squirrels made the climb with ease. Biddah felt the subterranean cold that she had not felt for so long. It chilled through her fur to her very bones, and she wrapped her cloak around her more tightly, pressing herself against Karrum. She did not want the babe she carried to be cold.

Much bigger than the last tunnel, this one could hold a score and a half abreast. But no one seemed keen to touch the walls, so they proceeded single file. Clearly more than a tunnel, the cave was made entirely of limestone, and the floor was quite rough. Nonetheless, it looked safe.

"What about the air?" whispered Karrum fearfully.

"Fret thou not about the air," hissed a voice, and Biddah jumped in surprise. "Vents in these caves," it continued, "givest plenty of air but are far away where they reach the earth."

She relaxed when she saw the creature by the faint light. "Srozka," she sighed. "You frightened me out of my mind!"

"I apologize, Biddah," hissed the earthworm. "Follow me. Thou hast a long way to go; this cave is not very direct. Follow me, friends. Pray, wouldst ye come meet some of my friends?"

The squirrels obliged. Two other young female earthworms hissed their way over.

"These are Syra and Layda. Meet Karrum and Biddah," Srozka introduced them.

The earthworms touched their tails to the squirrels' foreheads. "Welcome, friends," Syra hissed. She had a strange, mysterious sort of voice that Biddah liked.

"Indeed, welcome," agreed Layda. She had a warm, gentle, kind sort of hiss. It warmed Biddah right through.

"We best hurry," hissed Srozka. "Let us go."

Biddah found their company quite pleasurable. They told stories the squirrels had never heard before—funny ones, serious ones, exciting ones. Every creature that heard them laughed, gasped, and sighed with the squirrel couple.

Different sections of the squirrel army from Dombre moved at different speeds, changing pace to suit themselves. The going was mostly slow, but Biddah found it endurable.

For hours and hours, they moved on. Then Syra hissed, "We're nearing the first chamber. That's where ye will be sleeping; 'tis time ye had some sleep. We've set up a bed for ye there."

The chamber was magnificent. Torches had been placed at frequent intervals, and a small fire glowed in the very center next to an underground lake. Biddah drank gratefully, and the water was not so bad. She filled a cup with the ice-cold water and mixed it with some raspberry leaf powder. Tasting it, she nodded in satisfaction.

"Try some," she urged Karrum.

He did.

"Mm, this is better than any raspberry tea I've ever had. Delicious! What other flavors do you have, Biddah?"

"Well," smiled the squirrel wife, "I have sage, mint, almond flower, rosehip, thyme, and some of that delicious peppermint type with some honey. Let's see if any of these pastries are warm."

"Biddah, Karrum," hissed Srozka, "I've a bed set up for ye. Follow ye me."

Up on a small rock ledge, Srozka pulled away a few rocks with her tail. "Here," she called.

A small chamber was imprinted in the earth. It had a rock slab covered in moss, a stone that resembled a table, and a dip in the rock, which was lined with tiny roots.

"Ye can bring fire and put it in the small pit," said Srozka, jerking her tail towards it. "I'll leave ye now, unless ye want something of me?"

"Go ahead," smiled Karrum.

Srozka left and slithered over to a hole in the chamber, where her kin were going. Karrum leapt wordlessly down. He had a small clay bowl in his paws, and on the way, he snatched up a flat, large rock. Taking the rock, he hurried over to the fire and scooped up some embers. Carefully, he carried this back to the small chamber.

"Now, we'll have warm pastries for dinner," Biddah smiled.

She left the pastries on the rim of the dip and poured some of the raspberry tea into a cup for Karrum. She put that on the rim as well, adding a little honey to sweeten it. Then she lifted out a slice of nutbread and split it into two pieces. Out of her pack, she pulled two wooden plates and placed the nutbread and a few acorns on each one. Then she took off the pastries and tea and laid them on the "table."

Karrum had spread his blanket and Biddah's across the stone slab. Then he hung both their packs up on rock protrusions. When Biddah called him, he sat on the floor across from her, the small stone making a perfect table for the two of them. They ate in silence, feeling oppressed by the dark and cold despite the efforts of the earthworms. Then they climbed onto the makeshift bed.

Biddah missed the trees dearly, but she vowed to herself to be brave and not let the dark scare her.

Many hours later, Biddah wakened in the cave. The small fire Karrum had made to warm their dinner had died, and Karrum had vanished. She heard a few creatures scraping coals together to refill their own small fires, and soon Karrum swung up, the clay bowl in his paw.

"Here," he said landing next to the dip and emptying the contents into it. Then he lifted down his pack and took out a small, sturdy branch, which he placed in the fire. Confident the fire would continue to burn steadily for sometime, he bounded over to their bed.

Meanwhile, Biddah had struggled to her paws and hurried over to her own pack. She lifted out some slices of cornbread studded with almonds and hazelnuts, placed them by the fire, and dribbled some honey on them. Taking out her only flask of cordial, she warmed it up for a bit and then poured it out into cups. Finally, she placed the cornbread on the plates and called to her mate.

Karrum had been busily packing away the blankets and the food Biddah had not used. He saved Biddah's blanket, though, placing it gently around the fire to warm. Then he downed his breakfast in a few gulps.

"Queen Sharmmuh said we could leave whenever we want," he told Biddah. "Let's go soon. But come here first …"

He wrapped the fire-warmed blanket around Biddah's body, twisting and twining it until it worked like a cloak. The effect was instantaneous. Biddah felt much warmer now, and she put on her cloak and lifted her pack onto her shoulder.

The two squirrels leapt lightly down from the ledge and walked cautiously off down the trail hewn into the earth.

The walk was warmer for Biddah, now that she had her blanket, and Karrum didn't seem to be shivering. Biddah had completely lost track of day or night, and so had Karrum. However, he was very optimistic.

"After all, this may be not very straight, but Pasadagavra is only three days fully away from Dombre. This can at most be five days long, and even then it would have to be really not straight. But we can squeeze our paws and keep on going. With the Bear King on our side, we might be able to make good time. I'd guess that this tunnel, or cave, or whatever it is, is at least four days long, but not too much more—"

"Eighteen days," hissed a familiar hiss.

"Syra?" asked Biddah uncertainly.

"Yes," hissed the mystical voice. "And it is eighteen days long. Nine of them are traveling upward. This is a cave, by the way, a lava cave. And it is perfectly straight to Pasadagavra, but it slopes downward."

"You were following us?" asked Biddah in surprise.

"Yes, I was. It is in mine nature, I suppose. I was named after a great sea serpent, which, it is said, will guard the earth when the seas rise and every creature will be in Cerecinthia or the Serpent's Land. She and her brother will remain in the icy seas, even after time himself hath gone home to Cerecinthia, forever, that they may guard the way between the Serpent's Land and Cerecinthia."

Biddah was shocked by the myth, yet with Syra's voice, she could not help but believe it.

40

THE BATTLE BEGINS

Lady Raven approached Zuryzel and Queen Demeda from the night. "I saw her down myself," she continued. "She looked scared of dark, but—"

"Not as scared as you, Raven," Queen Demeda teased.

Raven drew herself up indignantly. "I beg your pardon!" she snapped. Zuryzel knew it was a game by the way Raven's eyes gleamed. The same eyes turned gently on Zuryzel. "You scared, Zuryzel?" she asked gently.

Zuryzel shook her head defensively. "No, not really. I just wish they'd move their tails and come."

"So do we all," Raven sympathized unexpectedly. "But they think they have nothing to lose by waiting."

"What are they waiting for?" Zuryzel asked.

"Can you work it out?" Queen Demeda urged her.

Zuryzel paused. She thought. And she thought harder. "Mmm ... dawn?"

"Why dawn?" Raven pressed.

"Because it would still be dark," Zuryzel guessed, "but it wouldn't be night, so Wraith Mice couldn't vanish? But they'd still have cover to cross the lake, and by the time they reach here, it could be sunrise, so they'd have light."

"Good," Raven nodded. "That is probably exactly what they're waiting for."

Zuryzel sighed. She returned to pacing. Raven and Queen Demeda began a discussion about some battle or other that happened before Zuryzel was born. She ignored them.

The moon rose to its peak. The night seemed to get colder, but no wind stirred, just a pressing coldness. Zuryzel wanted something—anything—to take her mind from the coming battle.

"Mother?" she asked.

"Yes?" Queen Demeda asked, both her and Raven breaking off their discussion.

"Why haven't we simply gone straight to Pasadagavra when they didn't come right away?"

Queen Demeda's eyes were bright in the darkness. "Because we are stalling the foxes in order to allow others to gather at Pasadagavra. The more warriors there, the easier it will be to fight the foxes when they break through."

"Do you think they could possibly break into Pasadagavra?"

Queen Demeda shrugged. "I don't know. They have a great army, but that won't do them any good against stone. More than anything, they need cleverness, but I don't think they have enough."

Zuryzel glanced at Lady Raven, who looked steadily back. "You know the history, Zuryzel," she pointed out. "You know a little of the structural defenses. You could probably guess better than I could—I don't fight in fortresses."

Zuryzel was about to make a guess when she heard something. She tensed. She looked at Raven.

"You have more brains than Knife," Raven said. "Waiting for dawn would have been smart, but I do not think she has done that."

Zuryzel and her mother slipped into the night, and Raven glided off, not unlike when she had vanished in front of Zuryzel. But she returned a moment later, looking relaxed. "No worries," she whispered. "They're not coming yet."

"What did I hear?" Zuryzel asked, slipping back.

"Your brother in his armor," Raven chuckled.

"Lady Raven?" Zuryzel murmured.

"Hmm?"

"Do you fight often?"

Raven shrugged. "There's a battle most every day in the northlands," she explained. "Savages from the north that want to conquer the green, fair lands. Corsairs that have their eyes on treasure from the rich cities. Sometimes rulers from the east who simply want more land. We fight them all. Every day. It is our nature to fight, just as it was in Lady Panther the Berserker's. Yet we are cautious, more so than she. We are warriors." Her last sentence summed it up brilliantly. But she looked a tad worried as she continued. "Only eight remain up in Oria now, scattered over the land. I imagine they are a little hard-pressed."

"Do you really believe we'll get through this?" Zuryzel persisted.

Raven paused. She looked at Zuryzel; she shifted, but said nothing, not for a while, a few minutes that seemed to stretch into cycles. Finally she spoke.

"I do not doubt that the Rangers could defeat them—in our home where we know each blade of grass that grows, where we use the harshness to our advantage. Here, you know your lands where you have fought for so long. The corsairs struggle on this terrain, their paws tangling easily in thorns. And the foxes do not have a powerful enough leader. But … I don't know. As Tribequeen Sharmmuh so intellectually pointed out, you do not fight as often as the foxes do. None of you has ever faced such an enormous horde. Yet, have faith in your people. The Bear King is on our side; I know it."

She spoke calmly and with control, yet Zuryzel could detect a note of fear. Small, but there nonetheless.

It had nothing to do with the battle. Something else was bothering the lady of the Rangers. Some hidden secret, buried deeply, was rubbing the Ranger like a burr. Fear did not exactly describe it. More a nagging worry, it was beginning to plague Zuryzel as well.

Another noise sounded off the shore and almost made Zuryzel jump, her nerves on edge with the endless waiting. She was fighting for control, trying not to be so scared, but she could barely keep from melting into the night.

Raven glided off to the shore, and Queen Demeda leaned down and whispered into her daughter's ear. "When the battle starts, I want you to run. Get out of Dombre. Go west, to the coast. Get Ailur the mercenary and beg her to help us if you have to."

"Ailur!" Zuryzel protested. "Why Ailur?"

"She has been my friend as long as Lady Raven has been," Queen Demeda whispered. "I trust her, and she has friends in all places. If you follow the Eupharra River to the coast and then head south, she'll probably be in the first city you come to. Be careful. Remember what is at stake."

"Why me?" Zuryzel asked.

"I can't ask your brothers to go," Queen Demeda replied. "Mokimshim doesn't have your wisdom, and Johajar does not have your patience. And neither has your restraint." From her neck she took a necklace that she had always worn, as a sign of her rank in the Wraith Mice, and put it on her daughter's neck. "Now she'll know I sent you," Queen Demeda finished.

"But … you? Why doesn't my father give me his crest? Ailur will trust that more."

"Your father does not know I am sending you," Queen Demeda replied, looking at the ground, "but it is my right. Wait until the battle starts so you can slip away."

At that moment, Raven came back. She shook her head, and both the Wraith Mice relaxed.

"I hate this," Zuryzel muttered.

Raven's eyes gleamed kindly. "You get used to it."

Zuryzel wanted, longed for, something—anything—to pass the time. But a song would be only foolish, and a story might be hard to tell.

"I just wish that there was some way I could know these corsairs aren't as bad as they are supposed to be," Queen Demeda murmured. "They can't be as bad as our old captors, can they?" she added to Raven.

Raven drew her rapier and twirled it deftly. "I doubt it. But they have something to be said for them. Besides, there aren't nearly enough to be such a huge problem that you're in danger of losing. Their allegiance to the Darkwoods foxes makes them dangerous. That, and the fact that they know how to fight in ways land-dwelling creatures cannot begin to imagine … and their lack of honor. Yet it will destroy them in the end." Her blue eyes glimmered in the night.

There was a soft note on the wind, and Queen Demeda stiffened. "The east wall. They're on the east wall!"

Zuryzel knew what to do. She slipped into the room where most of the soldiers had been waiting, in a shelter attached to the wall. She pulled open the door—and nearly ran into Dejuday.

"They here?" Dejuday asked nervously.

Zuryzel only nodded. Dejuday looked sick with fear, but he called back to the rest of the soldiers. The sound of paws grabbing weapons and muffled arguments filled Zuryzel's ears, and she beckoned to Dejuday. He was the only one ready.

"Dejuday, listen." In a hushed voice, she gave Dejuday a quick summary of her mother's order.

Dejuday looked bewildered, but he nodded. "I see. Ailur will help us."

"Can you tell Biddah for me?" Zuryzel pressed.

Dejuday nodded. "Of course."

The two of them scurried back to where Raven and Queen Demeda waited. Raven was staring out of a gap in the postern. "They're here, too," she whispered. "Those soldiers had better hurry."

"They're coming," Dejuday promised. His voice was soft, but his eyes were bright, and Zuryzel realized he was trying to hide fear.

Queen Demeda was half leaning against the wall, and Raven was holding the door shut, though the foxes weren't attacking it. Zuryzel nearly tripped she was so nervous, but Dejuday caught her. Neither Queen Demeda nor Raven noticed. Zuryzel, still shaking, did not try to shake Dejuday's supporting paw off.

"I wish they'd just attack instead of waiting out there," she murmured. "I hate waiting."

"For someone with your patience, I am unsurprised," Dejuday teased quietly. He let go of her paw. "What can they gain by waiting there?"

"They're listening for us," Zuryzel realized. "I'm going to tell the soldiers to be quiet."

"I'll come with you," Dejuday offered. "No one should be alone just now."

No kidding, Zuryzel thought. The idea of being alone just now terrified her.

They quietly made their way back toward the shelter. The first soldier they found was Dikiner. He was calm as ever, and he looked questioningly at Dejuday as Dejuday motioned for him to be quiet.

"They don't know we're out," Zuryzel explained in less than a whisper. Dikiner nodded.

Only a few paces behind him was Shinar. She was trembling and nearly screamed with fright when she saw Zuryzel appearing out of nowhere.

"Quiet," Zuryzel whispered. "They don't know we're out."

Shinar nodded, but she looked scared.

The others were taking a long time, so Zuryzel found herself alone with Dejuday. He had calmed down, but Zuryzel was shaky, and not because of the foxes. Dejuday looked at her, leaning against the wall. "You're nervous?"

"About going to the coast," Zuryzel confessed. "I don't want to deal with lots and lots more corsairs, without even anyone to help me."

Dejuday's eyes were kind. "I'd go with you, but I doubt King Hokadra would be pleased if he found out."

"He doesn't know I'm going."

Dejuday nodded. "I got that part. You'll be in a sight of trouble when you get back, that's for sure."

"That's really helpful," said Zuryzel sarcastically.

Dejuday's voice softened. "I'm sorry," he apologized. "I'm just nervous. I mean," he added, sounding embarrassed, "it wouldn't be the same without Princess Zuryzel."

Zuryzel felt her fur grow hot in spite of the chill of the night. Before she could ask what he meant, Sibyna and Orgorad jogged up.

"What's going on?" Orgorad asked, looking questioning.

"They don't know we know they're out," Dejuday explained, sounding a little more abrupt than he normally did.

Orgorad nodded. "We'll be quiet."

"Do you want me to tell the others?" Sibyna offered.

Dejuday shrugged. "If you want."

"In that case, I'll just get my tail to the wall." Sibyna and her mate vanished into the night.

Silence hung between Zuryzel and Dejuday for a few moments. "Dejuday?" Zuryzel asked.

"Hmm?"

"Why did you become a scout? I mean ..." Zuryzel broke off, feeling her fur flush.

"Since I have no stealth or agility?" Dejuday grinned.

"That's not precisely what I meant."

"Sibyna said our father wanted me to be a scout, and she wanted it also," Dejuday shrugged. "I wasn't pleased at the prospect, but she is older than I am, so I had to listen to her."

"What did you want to be?" Zuryzel pressed.

"I wanted to be a palace guard at Arashna," Dejuday murmured with a faint trace of wistfulness. "Sibyna threw a fit when I told her that," he added, grinning. "She made some unsavory remarks about palace guards."

"They aren't that bad!" Zuryzel exclaimed quietly.

"That's what I told her," Dejuday agreed. He sighed heavily.

Dejuday had lapsed into silence, and Zuryzel could hear sounds of conflict coming from the east wall when the majority of the soldiers marched out into the night. Zuryzel stood in their way, motioning for them to be quiet. The order was passed along to the soldiers in the back, and Zuryzel led the way to the wall. She had lost sight of Dejuday in the crush. But she knew that he was there. She could almost feel him.

There were no foxes inside Dombre on the west wall, but Zuryzel could see fire not too far away, and the sounds of conflict were loud. She itched to get into the battle, but she forced herself to stay still, pressed against the wall. She glanced beside her and realized that Crispisin, the novice from the training bouts, was standing beside her.

"Don't worry," she encouraged. "You'll be all right."

Crispisin smiled shakily. "This is my first real battle."

"You were in plenty of skirmishes," Zuryzel encouraged.

"A skirmish isn't a battle."

"By that judgment," Zuryzel soothed, "this is my first real battle, too."

Crispisin's eyes grew wide. "But you're so good with that blade!"

"So are you," Zuryzel pointed out. "Just remember what Dikiner taught you, and you'll be fine."

Crispisin nodded, looking both eager and terrified.

Dejuday appeared on the other side of Zuryzel, making her jump. Dejuday grinned at her surprise. "That's what happened in the Darkwoods right after Scythe died, remember?" He kept his voice so low that Zuryzel could barely hear.

"I remember," Zuryzel agreed. After a brief pause, she added, "I wish she was still alive. None of this might have happened if she had outlived Hemlock."

Dejuday nodded. "She was wise, if not good. She knew power did not exist in conquering."

"She also knew that jealousy and greed are dangerous," Zuryzel mused. "Pity none of them listened to her."

"That's funny," Dejuday grinned. "She might have been evil, but she was so right."

"I don't think she was 'evil,' exactly, though," Zuryzel mused. "Maybe just pressured."

"Yes," Dejuday agreed. "Old and pressured."

Silence hung in the air between the two of them. Zuryzel knew that the battle would start soon. Her stomach rolled in fear, but Dejuday seemed totally calm. There was even a smile on his face.

"What are you grinning about?" Zuryzel asked curiously.

"Scythe would have been pressured to fight," Dejuday chuckled, "but in front of all Darkwoods, she declared otherwise, utterly alone. If she could do that, we could fight them with friends."

Zuryzel smiled too as the foxes began to pound on the postern gate. Three Wraith Mice were holding it shut. "And we have the Bear King!"

"You know, Scythe trained all five of them," said Dejuday, speaking in a slightly louder voice.

"All who?" Zuryzel felt like this conversation had just gone up a strange pathway.

"Blood, Hemlock, Fang, Knife, and Ice; all of them. She even trained others and outlived them. She trained so many, and even then ..."

Zuryzel thought that was irrelevant, but it was interesting. She pushed it to the back of her mind and watched as Queen Demeda motioned the three door-holders away. They slipped back, pressed against the wall. Something pounded against the gate, and the timbers split.

A fox—an older one, but not an Oracle—led the way in. He was a Darkwoods fox, but behind him were battalions of corsairs.

Why do I get all the corsairs? Zuryzel thought irritably.

The foxes made their way in, not noticing the defenders. Queen Demeda's plan was to split the main body from their captain. She let a few dozen pass through the gate before motioning to one of the Wraith Mice at the end. With a wild slash, he attacked the captain. The rest of the defenders came to life, driving at the invading foxes.

Dejuday and Zuryzel stuck to the wall side, an easy way for Zuryzel to slip away. They did not try to hamper the foxes from getting in because Zuryzel had to have an open way to sneak out. The Wraith Mice were doing okay, but the passage was narrow. Most of the invaders seemed to be trying to creep around the north walls toward the east wall. Zuryzel guessed they thought there was some secret way to escape toward Pasadagavra from the north wall.

Dejuday reached out with his blade and tripped one of the charging corsairs. He blundered into one of his companions, who fell under the pressure. In a few seconds the corsairs were jammed against each other, without room to swing their weapons. The Wraith Mice had stayed to the side, so they simply attacked those on the side. Zuryzel smiled at Dejuday. "Good move."

"Time to go," Dejuday advised.

They began to fight their way past the corsairs out into the open. In the confusion, they passed largely unnoticed. Those who did notice were slain by either Dejuday's or Zuryzel's sword before they could open their mouths.

Then it all went wrong.

Zuryzel felt some kind of snare wrap around her paws, and she was yanked to the ground. The wind was driven from her so completely she couldn't call to Dejuday for help.

Three corsairs stood over her. "Princess Zuryzel," one sneered.

Zuryzel lashed out with her sword, catching one on his paw. He yelped and jumped away. She tried to rise, but the corsairs were faster. One of them kicked her in the shoulder, knocking her back down. She tried to get up again, but he thrust his foot on her shoulder, pinning her down. She lashed at him with her sword, but his friend kicked her paw and stamped on it. She let out a faint cry of pain. Her tormentors laughed.

"See 'ow loud she screams now," the first one taunted.

Dejuday … Zuryzel thought desperately.

Suddenly, the fox that had taunted her let out a shriek of agony. Blood flowed from his back onto the ground like a red waterfall. The other one toppled backwards, dead. Dejuday lashed at the first one again, slicing him across his front with a deep slash. The corsair was in such pain that he collapsed and wailed in agony. Dejuday left him there.

"You owe me," he said, offering his paw to the princess.

Zuryzel gripped her sword in one paw and took Dejuday's paw with the other. Dejuday pulled her gently up, dragging her back around the fortress. They reached a corner, and flitting around it, they were totally out of sight of the corsairs.

"I got you out of Darkwoods three times. You still owe me."

"You left me in there once and I saved you from two corsairs," Dejuday retorted. "We're even."

He turned and guided her toward the shallows that led across the lake, still holding her paw as though afraid she would fall into more snares.

Zuryzel made a mental note to speak to her father about getting Dejuday a position as a guard in Arashna when she got back.

41

UNFORESEEN ENEMY

Mokimshim and Johajar were in trouble. At least, they were by Johajar's standards. Mokimshim wasn't worried because he knew what he was doing. He thought.

"You definitely had better know what we're doing," Johajar shouted over the noise of battle as three foxes rushed the two brothers. They were right in front of the doors—the closed doors—of the main hall at Dombre. Naturally, Johajar didn't trust his brother's plan. It was supposed to help the rest of the army get away, but Johajar wasn't so sure how it would. Mokimshim hadn't given him enough details to be totally sure of the plan.

"Don't worry," Mokimshim retorted, not for the first time, and six or seven Darkwoods foxes barreled around the corner. He was unafraid—the foxes didn't know he and his brother were there.

"Where's Zuryzel?" Johajar snapped as he slashed out and slew two. "Why can't she be here?"

"I haven't seen her anywhere," Mokimshim explained. "I think she already went through the—"

"Shut up!" Johajar shouted. "That's why we're here!"

"Oh, right!" Mokimshim exclaimed mockingly. "Hiding the—"

"Shut up!"

"*Wormhole!*"

Behind the doors there was a *thump* of a bar being lowered. Johajar had a moment of panic. "They're barricading the doors!"

"I know," Mokimshim replied, still calm.

"Your plan was to get us killed!" Johajar shouted in fury.

"No," Mokimshim retorted. Several more foxes barreled around the corner. The main army was getting closer. "The slithery ones have opened another pathway. And for the record, this isn't my plan."

"No wonder," Johajar retorted. "You couldn't convince the slitheries to do anything! Mother came up with this plan didn't she?"

"Yes," Mokimshim said through gritted teeth. The brothers were fighting with everything they had against their unprepared enemies, but they were being overrun.

"Well, I'm saying when we get out," Johajar snapped.

"Oh no, you're not," Mokimshim argued. "You don't even know the plan, and I'm the oldest."

"Don't start ordering me around," Johajar shouted angrily as he slew the last fox around them. "*I'm* the one who father always commended for battle planning, remember?"

"Vividly!" Mokimshim shouted. He whirled on his brother and Johajar actually had to raise his blade to deflect his brother's. He quickly disengaged the blade and smacked Mokimshim's face with the hilt. Johajar had used all his strength, and that was no small amount.

"If you want to be a battle planner, start studying the old battles," Johajar growled. "But for now, fight the *foxes* for the kingdom. If we can't work together, we'll both die."

Mokimshim nodded, his paw held over his bleeding nose. "I get your point."

Johajar's eyes were brilliant with rage. "Then I'm saying when we go."

Mokimshim nodded, his nose dripping blood. Johajar dragged a cloth used to polish swords out of his pocket and handed it to his brother. "Use this."

Mokimshim took the rag quickly. Behind the door there came the thump of another bar, slightly muffled. "They're almost done—"

Another band of adventurous foxes spotted the brothers. Mokimshim tossed away the rag.

"Let's lose them," Johajar said.

Instantly they both took off at a run toward one of the smaller alleys that had many branches. Both of them turned onto the smallest branch and then onto an even smaller one. They were slowly making their way to the one postern that the foxes had not used.

They had reached the darkest part of the alleyway, far from the postern, when Mokimshim whirled on his brother again. This time Johajar didn't see it coming and was knocked backwards by the hilt. He grunted in pain as his back hit the floor. The shock numbed his paw, and his sword skittered over the ground out of reach. Mokimshim stood over him, prodding his neck with the sword.

"I could kill you now," Mokimshim hissed, "and no one would ever know. I could come up with any story."

"But you won't."

"Oh? And why not?"

"The Bear King knows," Johajar retorted, totally unafraid to his brother's eyes. "If you killed me, it would be murder. A murderer could never become king—that is the law, part of the Wraith Mouse's magic. Zuryzel would be the queen then."

Mokimshim didn't move for a few heartbeats, heartbeats that stretched on like cycles to Johajar. He had known all day that today could well be his dying day, but it had never occurred to him that the sword that took his life could be his brother's. Mentally, he was begging the Bear King for strength. For he was afraid, though he didn't show it.

Then Mokimshim withdrew the sword from Johajar's neck. He extended a paw to help his brother up. Johajar did not accept, but he struggled to his paws.

"Forgive me," Mokimshim apologized. "I was angry, and I have worked very hard at studying old battles. I am proud of my work." Johajar detected a note of arrogance in his brother's voice. But he did not trust the arrogance. In his eyes, it was all an act.

"Then I apologize," Johajar acknowledged. "But your attack on me would have been murder."

Johajar left his words hanging, and a flicker of fear flitted over Mokimshim's face. That, Johajar reflected with satisfaction, was his one leading talent—he could make a speech that would curl the fur. Confidently, he addressed his brother.

"Let's get out of here. Where is this tunnel?"

🐁

Zuryzel and Dejuday made the gray plain of burned up trees just as the sun sent a small streak of light across the lake of Dombre. Zuryzel could not prevent tears coming to her eyes when she saw the number of foxes infesting her beloved fortress.

"Scum," Dejuday muttered. "One day, they'll pay for the loss of Dombre and the creatures that lie dead. One day ..." His voice trailed off. "Are you all right?" he asked the princess.

Zuryzel was clutching her wounded paw. "One of those foxes kicked my paw," she explained.

Dejuday winced sympathetically. "Do you think it's broken?"

Zuryzel shook her head. "No, but it really hurts."

Dejuday ripped some cloth from his sleeve. Carefully, he wrapped it tightly around Zuryzel's paw. The pressure helped the throbbing pain.

"Thank you," she said. And she wasn't only referring to the bandage.

Dejuday nodded respectfully. "I'll make up some story for your father," he assured her. "When will you be back?"

"I don't know," Zuryzel whispered, stunned by the realization. She always kept careful track of her time. "I guess … it depends if I get a boat."

"Should you really go alone?" Dejuday blurted out. "I mean, you're good with a blade, but corsairs are dangerous. We haven't even fought them before today! Is it … is it really safe?"

"I don't think I'll be all alone," Zuryzel pointed out gently. "Ailur is a friend of my mother's, and she'll help me. I may run into Arpaha, or maybe Doomspear. You never know. And besides, I have the Bear King."

Dejuday nodded. "I know."

Zuryzel narrowed her eyes in surprise as the truth hit her. "You *want* to come?"

"Well," Dejuday confessed, "the corsairs are strange. I would like to know more about them. And, anyway," he added when Zuryzel gave him a skeptical look, "I would like to see Arashna again."

"I'm not going toward Arashna," Zuryzel said. A wave of homesickness swept over her.

"Well, I don't want to go so much now," Dejuday grinned. "Go on; you haven't got so much time. See you again, when all this is over."

That was Dejuday. Always positive.

Right.

"You be careful!" Zuryzel called as she turned and set off across the barren gray lands.

She half-ran for a while, not turning back, until she reached a slope. At the top, she turned to look back.

There was Dombre and the lake and a dark mass that could be the Darkwoods army. Closer, though getting smaller and smaller, was a running mouse. Zuryzel smiled. Dejuday would get safely through the tunnel; he would not get captured again.

With renewed determination, she turned back toward her course—to the west where a few stars still shone in the disappearing darkness.

As she walked, Zuryzel began to memorize their pattern. One particularly bright star was shining just over on the horizon, a little to the northwest. Zuryzel set course for that star and soon saw the valley of the foaming river.

She began to walk alongside it and found she was headed straight for the star she had seen. She paused and turned back. Behind her, another bright star hung over, directly east of her. She guessed that Pasadagavra would be somewhere around that star. She memorized the constellation it was in and then turned back to the westerly star. The mercenaries she would bring back navigated by the stars, and they would know how to find Pasadagavra.

She began to hum an old song that her mother had taught her. It seemed to lift her spirits, and her steps became quicker until she was almost running, heading for hope—the hope that came from a place near her home.

🐭

Mokimshim and Johajar had barely made their way out of the fortress in time. There were no foxes behind them, but they weren't taking chances. Mokimshim was in the lead, because he knew where the tunnel was, and Johajar had the best hearing, so he could listen for pursuit.

"Here!" Mokimshim knelt over a large hole in the ground. It was large enough for one creature to get through. Mokimshim tossed his weapons down the hole, and slid himself down. "Come on!" he called to his brother.

Johajar hesitated. "What about Raven and Mother?"

"They're already down," Mokimshim called. "I can hear—"

The Wraith Mouse and the Ranger burst out of the trees. Johajar would have made some sarcastic remark to his brother, had Mokimshim been in a better mood.

"You made it." Queen Demeda sounded relieved. "I wasn't so sure we'd get away from the back gate."

"There weren't *that* many foxes back there, Queen Demeda," Raven chided.

"We'll see how long the door holds," Johajar shrugged. He jumped down after Mokimshim into the tunnel, followed by his mother and finally Lady Raven.

"That was a cunning assault," Raven murmured thoughtfully as she shoved a bunch of dirt to cover up the hole. "I wonder who came up with it?"

"Who cares?" Mokimshim snapped.

Lady Raven did not reply.

SPIES AND MORE SPIES

Knife's spy stood in the main hall at Dombre. He had slipped up from a tunnel that led off of the cave and now stood perfectly still, waiting for Knife.

Without wasting any time, she sprinted up to the hall from the cellars with surprising speed for her many cycles. She stopped, panting, just in front of the spy.

But before she could say anything, the figure spoke up, in a much more confident voice than usual.

"So, Ice vanished, has she? I thought she was supposed to be under your influence so entirely!" There was a mocking tone to the spy's voice.

"Ice is dead," Knife said coldly, not wishing to reveal the truth.

"Oh, sure, sly brush. One of the scouts saw Demmons taking you to that pool. Oh, and by the by," he added, sounding serious, "what possessed you to summon Demmons like that? He'll send you to the Serpent's Land so fast that you'll beat Hemlock there!"

"He will not," said Knife smoothly. "I have the upper paw—I have knowledge of the land."

"Yes, and he has the knowledge of weapons, something you seem to have overlooked! You don't."

The breath caught in Knife's throat—she *had* overlooked her lack of weapon skills. Her spy continued.

"Demmons is one of the best sword fighters in the world. You're no match for him—none of the land dwellers is. I doubt even Zuryzel could match him in sword mastery."

"Oh, is that so?" Knife snarled.

"Incidentally, which captains do you have here?"

Knife began automatically. "Demmons, Snillouf, Fotirra, Redseg, Jironi, Emmed, Riorat, Horeb, Uddio, and Epoi, and about forty others," she reeled off, stopping herself from listing all of them.

"That was a stupid thing to do, Knife," snapped the spy. "Jironi, Horeb, and Uddio? As well as Demmons? You idiot, the Rangers are going to be after you and all the others! And that's generally not something you would want, either. The Rangers are merciless, and have you heard of their arrows? Tell me, do you want that to happen to you?"

"You're talking nonsense. Go!"

The spy hurried out into the night.

Knife realized with a shock that she had gotten no information out of the spy, but her spy had wormed important information out of her.

She cursed silently and hurried out of the fortress.

🐀

A black shadow moved silently from shrub to shrub in the woodland. A dark green cloak and stiff brown tunic provided good cover during the day, but the darkness of night gave the best.

A stream barred her way, and Lady Raven stood carefully on the bank. Her shadowy travel was painstaking, but it would be worth it. She had slipped out of the tunnel before Queen Demeda had covered it—with any luck at all, Mokimshim and Johajar wouldn't notice her absence—and had seen and followed another dark shape. She knew immediately that it was Knife's spy. She had arrived at the same conclusion as Zuryzel and her twin, but not through mere guesswork. Let Hemlock place a spy among the infantry, and she retaliated. Only, she had placed her spy long, long ago. The first thing she had ever learned was that a good counterstrike, no matter what type, took lots of time and preparation.

The stream bank rustled and a fiery colored vixen slipped from a hiding place beneath some bushes. She was dripping wet and thoroughly bedraggled, wearing nothing but a very small tunic. But her icy blue eyes were the same as always.

"Your plan worked, Lady Raven," she observed.

"So it did, Ice. So it did." Lady Raven's dawn blue eyes glinted. "But I told you to remain with the others."

"Knife got suspicious when I ordered the main entryway clear every time someone had to be rescued from the cells," Ice explained. "She got even *more* suspicious when I cut down on patrols in the woods so Hetmuss Cinder and Johajar and whoever else could sneak in undetected."

"Knife's spy and Hemlock's spy are different, yes?" Lady Raven asked.

"Different as night and day," Ice confirmed. "And I recently found out that Fang has one also, *and* Hemlock has more than one."

"That's at least four."

"Probably closer to eight," Ice grunted. "Hemlock can threaten anyone, Fang can buy anyone, and Knife can convince anyone to spy. But I do know that one of Hemlock's spies only does it because he wants Mokimshim dead, and one of them is female."

"Do you know how many are Wraith Mice or otherwise?"

"Don't I wish. I think they're all Wraith Mice."

Raven sighed irritably. "Go figure."

"Hemlock and Fang plan to kill theirs," Ice added, "to keep them quiet. I don't know about Knife." She paused. "What do you suppose Hokadra will do? When he finds them?"

Raven shook her head helplessly. "I don't think he *will* find them. I don't think *I* can find them. They all suspected Fawn, of course."

Ice rolled her eyes. "That's just stupid. Why would Hemlock risk an Oracle just to spy when no one would trust her anyway? Hemlock isn't that stupid."

Raven blinked. "Congratulations on getting her out so cleanly, by the way," she said.

Ice wasn't sure if there was a sarcastic edge to Raven's tone or not. "I knew Zuryzel was in there, so I knew she could get Fawn away from Knife," Ice explained nervously. "Knife would've heard about Fawn's rescue of Karrum and Biddah, so I figured I only had to give her a reason before she attacked Fawn. Then Zuryzel could get her away. No one would suspect me, and I could stay."

Raven nodded. "I know. But you left now?"

"With Demmons coming, I was worried Knife might recollect old secrets," Ice shuddered. "Besides, Jironi and Fotirra made it."

Raven nodded. "Go keep an eye on the sea otters," she told Ice. "And look out for Herttua Crow."

Ice nodded obediently. "You have a plan?"

"Maybe." Raven's reply was not reassuring. She gave Ice a penetrating look. "See if you recognize Northstar."

Ice cringed inwardly. She had known Lady Raven for a long time, and Lady Raven *always* had a plan. But she just nodded again. "I will."

Raven tensed, exactly as she had when she had taken Zuryzel out to meet Tiyuh. "Get down," she hissed.

She and Ice dropped down into the bushes at the edge of the stream bank. A cold wind brushed through the plants, seeming to carry a shadow along on its eddy.

"Knife's spy?" she breathed to Ice.

Ice nodded silently.

"I think I'll follow him."

"Be careful."

The cold wind began to drift off in another direction. Silent as time, Raven followed, keeping low to the ground and slithering not unlike a worm.

The shadow went further along upstream, a fact which puzzled Raven. There weren't any tunnels going this way. Was he planning to desert? Soon, the shadow reached a point in the stream with banks rising high on either side. But instead of going up on the higher ground, he kept in the stream.

Raven remained above, looking down the steep side to where he stood, squinting and successfully ignoring her fear of heights.

Here the shadow stopped, looking around until he seemed to decide there was no one around. Raven smirked to herself. Spying on the spy!

Then the shadow became solid, the unmistakable shape of a mouse. Raven cursed inwardly for the top of the bank was too high up for her to make any distinctions.

The Wraith Mouse pulled at one small rock on the steep side of the bank, and to Raven's surprise, an entire platform of them moved. *A trapdoor!* she thought. The entrance revealed was large enough for several creatures to fit through. The Wraith Mouse went in and closed the door after him.

Regardless of noise, Raven slid down the bank side, very nearly falling into the stream. She grabbed the rock and very slowly opened the door. It didn't creak at all, but a mere trace of cool air told her the Wraith Mice was hurrying. But most astonishing, the tunnel went upward.

Raven shut the door silently and just as quietly slithered up the passageway at top speed. The cold air was getting colder; she was getting closer.

She heard a babble of subdued voices just up ahead, and by now the air was freezing, but Raven could not see the shadow. As the passage leveled out, Raven stood up. Ahead of her was a rock face with a wide crack at the edge. There was another rock just beyond that crack. Raven guessed that the tunnel had an exit, which was half-blocked by a stalagmite. She poked her head nervously around the stalagmite and then drew back sharply and cursed.

Blast! The spy had blended back into the main army, just up ahead past the stalagmite.

Raven looked back at the winding tunnel with an angry hiss. The tunnel the army was following must have been an underground river at one time that emptied out into the stream. How the spy had discovered it was anyone's guess...

"*Dralgdi!*" Raven cursed in her own tongue. "Call yourself a tracker? You couldn't track a squirrel in a desert!"

Blinking, she regained her composure. She peeked cautiously past the stalagmite, waiting for some squirrels to come along. They couldn't see well in the dark, and she could slide out without them noticing. But all the squirrels must have gone on, and Raven had to content herself with Shinar the river otter.

She timed it perfectly. She stepped out just as Shinar was passing. The otter blinked as Raven flicked a pebble with her paw. "Hello, Lady Raven," said Shinar respectfully. "I didn't see you."

Raven shrugged. "Have you seen Queen Demeda?"

"She's up a ways," Shinar gestured.

Raven nodded and picked up her pace. She kept her eyes skinned for her friend, not forgetting to look casual. She kept close to the walls—no one was looking toward the walls, and she wanted to watch without being seen—and kept looking for the one she had followed. Spy or no, she had yet to determine. She didn't fully trust Ice and hadn't been entirely truthful with her – but then, she *rarely* was. The Ranger lady was a good—for want of a better word—liar.

Raven knew who one of the spies was (and the Ranger lady actually *had* told Hokadra and Queen Demeda truthfully about her) and had put a plan into action through her a while ago. Because Hokadra was carefully controlling the amount of information that spy was getting, she had no need to worry about that particular one. The real problem concerned those not yet identified, mostly Knife's spy.

She felt a draft of cold air—but with a different feel to it than the spy's—and Queen Demeda appeared beside her friend. Raven didn't flinch. In a whisper, she related to Queen Demeda what had happened at the creek.

Queen Demeda nodded. "It figures. But why send Ice down to spy on the sea otters? Is that part of your plan?"

"No." Raven's voice was flat. "But Crow should be around there soon, so I wanted to have someone contact her."

"That's it?"

Raven nodded.

"*Do* you have a plan?" Queen Demeda asked.

"Maybe." Raven shook her head wearily. "Don't you have any ideas?"

"Several, Raven," Queen Demeda smirked. "Never doubt a queen of the Wraith Mice. Part of it has to do with that hoax you pulled after your mission in Hemlock's camp."

"I think I did pretty well," Raven argued.

"I didn't say you did badly," Queen Demeda corrected. "I said I have a plan that could work because of your fancy twist."

Raven frowned at her. "You're not telling me everything?"

"Is that a reproach from you?" Queen Demeda teased.

Raven winced.

"But you're right, as head of Hokadra's intelligence, there are things I have not told you," Queen Demeda advised.

🐀

Dejuday had waited outside the lake for hours until it was dark enough for him to vanish. Moving quickly and silently, he blended into the night. He had not heard the spy, but he had seen a flicker in the main hall and had seen Knife leave. Now that she was gone, he pushed aside a chill of fear as he slid aside a stone in the very base of the floor. After dropping himself into the tunnel, he pulled the stone back across. He knew no one would see it was moved.

He ran along the tunnel as fast as he could, ignoring the chill. Terrible a scout though he was, he had stamina. He was exhausted, his eyes were bloodshot with lack of sleep, and he continually stumbled because of the absence of light, but he kept going.

It took him a long time to catch up with the army, but when he did, he blended in. In the dim light, no one noticed his weariness or his haggardness.

The first creature that saw him was Sibyna. "Dejuday," she whispered, "have you seen Zuryzel?"

Dejuday shook his head, though it stung to lie. "Why?"

"No one's seen her," Sibyna whispered fearfully. "I hope she's okay."

Dejuday put on a worried face—it was not hard—and shrugged at the same time. "Wherever she is, I'm sure she'll be all right."

Sibyna seemed consoled. Dejuday turned his face away, not wanting his sister to see his guilt.

He closed his eyes and remembered the determination and fear mingled on the princess's face. He knew he had to lie, and he found that difficult to put up with because he had always prided himself on his honesty. But he would do it for the princess. Dejuday saw more in the princess than in anyone else he had ever known. She would one day make a queen worthy of the Bear King. That he believed.

THE GUIDING STAR

A s the sun was rising the second time since Zuryzel had been out on the gray plain—the Ashlands, she thought of them as—the river gurgled along happily, and the faintest sound of a bird woke the princess. She had to smile. Despite the harshness of the terrain, there was still life, still a few trees that had escaped death. Zuryzel walked all day following the sun, or her star.

Hope. That was what she would bring back. The foxes would be destroyed. Their castle, however good in the past, would be torn down. It had become nothing but evil and destroyed nobility.

Hope. It lay in the very creatures that had just destroyed all hope. But if Ailur was as trustworthy as Demeda believed, then there was nothing to fear. No price to pay for this chance, no treachery to fear. Corsairs were mighty.

But hope lay chiefly with the princess of the moon.

Zuryzel.